In the second book of the
# INN BOONSBORO TRILOGY
#1 *New York Times* bestselling author Nora Roberts...

"...writes a great story with likeable characters
so warm and real—nobody does it better."
—*New York Journal of Books*

"...opens *her* heart and invites the die-hard
romantics to stick around and snuggle
with this poignant tale about trust,
commitment, and optimism."
—*USA Today*

#1 *New York Times* bestselling author Nora Roberts introduces you to the Montgomery brothers—Beckett, Ryder, and Owen—as they bring an intimate bed-and-breakfast to life in their hometown.

Owen is the organizer of the Montgomery clan, running the family's construction business with an iron fist—and an even less flexible spreadsheet. And though his brothers bust on his compulsive list-making, the Inn BoonsBoro is about to open right on schedule. The only thing Owen didn't plan for was Avery MacTavish . . .

Avery's popular pizza place is right across the street from the inn, giving her a firsthand look at its amazing renovation—and a newfound appreciation for Owen. Since he was her first boyfriend when they were kids, Owen has never been far from Avery's thoughts. But the attraction she's feeling for him now is far from innocent.

As Avery and Owen cautiously take their relationship to another level, the opening of the inn gives the whole town of Boonsboro a reason to celebrate. But Owen's hard work has only begun. Getting Avery to let down her guard is going to take longer than he expected—and so will getting her to realize that her first boyfriend is going to be her last . . .

TURN THE PAGE FOR A COMPLETE LIST OF TITLES
BY NORA ROBERTS AND J. D. ROBB FROM
THE BERKLEY PUBLISHING GROUP . . .

## *Nora Roberts*

# Series

# eBooks by Nora Roberts

*Nora Roberts & J. D. Robb*

REMEMBER WHEN

*J. D. Robb*

NAKED IN DEATH
GLORY IN DEATH
IMMORTAL IN DEATH
RAPTURE IN DEATH
CEREMONY IN DEATH
VENGEANCE IN DEATH
HOLIDAY IN DEATH
CONSPIRACY IN DEATH
LOYALTY IN DEATH
WITNESS IN DEATH
JUDGMENT IN DEATH
BETRAYAL IN DEATH
SEDUCTION IN DEATH
REUNION IN DEATH
PURITY IN DEATH
PORTRAIT IN DEATH
IMITATION IN DEATH
DIVIDED IN DEATH
VISIONS IN DEATH
SURVIVOR IN DEATH
ORIGIN IN DEATH
MEMORY IN DEATH
BORN IN DEATH
INNOCENT IN DEATH
CREATION IN DEATH
STRANGERS IN DEATH
SALVATION IN DEATH
PROMISES IN DEATH
KINDRED IN DEATH
FANTASY IN DEATH
INDULGENCE IN DEATH
TREACHERY IN DEATH
NEW YORK TO DALLAS
CELEBRITY IN DEATH
DELUSION IN DEATH
CALCULATED IN DEATH
THANKLESS IN DEATH
CONCEALED IN DEATH

## Anthologies

FROM THE HEART
A LITTLE MAGIC
A LITTLE FATE

MOON SHADOWS
*(with Jill Gregory, Ruth Ryan Langan, and Marianne Willman)*

### The Once Upon Series
*(with Jill Gregory, Ruth Ryan Langan, and Marianne Willman)*

ONCE UPON A CASTLE          ONCE UPON A ROSE
ONCE UPON A STAR            ONCE UPON A KISS
ONCE UPON A DREAM           ONCE UPON A MIDNIGHT

SILENT NIGHT
*(with Susan Plunkett, Dee Holmes, and Claire Cross)*

OUT OF THIS WORLD
*(with Laurell K. Hamilton, Susan Krinard, and Maggie Shayne)*

BUMP IN THE NIGHT
*(with Mary Blayney, Ruth Ryan Langan, and Mary Kay McComas)*

DEAD OF NIGHT
*(with Mary Blayney, Ruth Ryan Langan, and Mary Kay McComas)*

THREE IN DEATH

SUITE 606
*(with Mary Blayney, Ruth Ryan Langan, and Mary Kay McComas)*

IN DEATH

THE LOST
*(with Patricia Gaffney, Mary Blayney, and Ruth Ryan Langan)*

THE OTHER SIDE
*(with Mary Blayney, Patricia Gaffney, Ruth Ryan Langan, and Mary Kay McComas)*

TIME OF DEATH

THE UNQUIET
*(with Mary Blayney, Patricia Gaffney, Ruth Ryan Langan, and Mary Kay McComas)*

MIRROR, MIRROR
*(with Mary Blayney, Elaine Fox, Mary Kay McComas, and R.C. Ryan)*

### Also available . . .

THE OFFICIAL NORA ROBERTS COMPANION
*(edited by Denise Little and Laura Hayden)*

# THE LAST BOYFRIEND

## NORA ROBERTS

JOVE BOOKS, NEW YORK

**THE BERKLEY PUBLISHING GROUP**
Published by the Penguin Group
Penguin Group (USA) LLC
375 Hudson Street, New York, New York 10014

USA • Canada • UK • Ireland • Australia • New Zealand • India • South Africa • China

penguin.com

A Penguin Random House Company

THE LAST BOYFRIEND

A Jove Book / published by arrangement with the author

Jove Books are published by The Berkley Publishing Group.
JOVE® is a registered trademark of Penguin Group (USA) LLC.
The "J" design is a trademark of Penguin Group (USA) LLC.
The NR® logo is a registered trademark of Penguin Group (USA) LLC.

For information, address: The Berkley Publishing Group,
a division of Penguin Group (USA) LLC,
375 Hudson Street, New York, New York 10014.

ISBN: 978-0-515-15148-0

PUBLISHING HISTORY
Berkley Books trade paperback edition / May 2012
Jove mass-market edition / June 2014

PRINTED IN THE UNITED STATES OF AMERICA

10  9  8  7  6  5  4  3  2  1

Cover photograph by Claudio Marinesco.
Cover design by Rita Frangie.
Sketch of inn by Nancy E. Rairden.
Text design by Kristin del Rosario.

This is a work of fiction. Names, characters, places, and incidents either are the product
of the author's imagination or are used fictitiously, and any resemblance to actual persons,
living or dead, business establishments, events, or locales is entirely coincidental.

*To Dan and Charlotte.*
*For the trust that let you reach for one another.*
*For the generosity and inclusiveness of that embrace.*
*For the humor that brings light to your lives.*
*And for the love, so rich and bright, binding it all together.*

Love sought is good,
but given unsought is better.

—SHAKESPEARE


The heart has its reasons
which reason cannot know.

—PASCAL

# CHAPTER ONE

A FAT WINTER MOON POURED LIGHT OVER THE OLD stone and brick of the inn on The Square. In its beams, the new porches and pickets glowed, and the bright-penny copper of the roof glinted. The old and new merged there—the past and the now—in a strong and happy marriage.

Its windows stayed dark on this December night, prizing its secrets in shadows. But in a matter of weeks they would shine like others along Boonsboro's Main Street.

As he sat in his truck at the light on The Square, Owen Montgomery looked up Main at the shops and apartments draped in their holiday cheer. Lights winked and danced. To his right, a pretty tree graced the big front window of the second-floor apartment. Their future innkeeper's temporary residence reflected her style. Precise elegance.

Next Christmas, he thought, they'd have Inn BoonsBoro covered with white lights and greenery. And Hope Beaumont would center her pretty little tree in the window of the innkeeper's apartment on the third floor.

He glanced to his left where Avery MacTavish, owner of

Vesta Pizzeria and Family Restaurant, had the restaurant's front porch decked out in lights.

Her apartment above—formerly his brother Beckett's—also showed a tree in the window. Otherwise the windows were as dark as the inn's. She'd be working tonight, he thought, noting the movement in the restaurant. He shifted, but couldn't see her behind the work counter.

When the light changed, he turned right onto St. Paul Street, then left into the parking lot behind the inn. Then sat in his truck a moment, considering. He could walk over to Vesta, he thought, have a slice and a beer, hang out until closing. Afterward he could do his walk-through of the inn.

He didn't actually need to walk through, he reminded himself. But he hadn't been on-site all day, as he'd been busy with other meetings, other details on other Montgomery Family Contractors' business. He didn't want to wait until morning to see what his brothers and the crew had accomplished that day.

Besides, Vesta looked busy, and had barely thirty minutes till closing. Not that Avery would kick him out at closing—probably. More than likely, she'd sit down and have a beer with him.

Tempting, he thought, but he really should do that quick walk-through and get home. He needed to be on-site, with his tools, by seven.

He climbed out of the truck and into the frigid air, already pulling out his keys. Tall like his brothers, with a build leaning toward rangy, he hunched in his jacket as he walked around the stone courtyard wall toward the doors of The Lobby.

His keys were color-coded, something his brothers called anal, and he deemed efficient. In seconds he was out of the cold and into the building.

He hit the lights, then just stood there, grinning like a moron.

The decorative tile rug highlighted the span of the floor and added another note of charm to the softly painted walls with their custom, creamy wainscoting. Beckett had been right on target about leaving the side wall exposed brick. And their mother had been dead-on about the chandelier.

Not fancy, not traditional, but somehow organic with its bronzy branches and narrow, flowing globes centered over that tile rug. He glanced right, noted The Lobby restrooms with their fancy tiles and green-veined stone sinks had been painted.

He pulled out his notebook, jotted down the need for a few touch-ups before he walked through the stone arch to the left.

More exposed brick—yeah, Beckett had a knack. The laundry room shelves showed ruthless organization—that would be Hope's hand; her iron will had booted his brother Ryder out of his on-site office so she could start organizing.

He paused at what would be Hope's office, saw his brother's mark there: the sawhorses and a sheet of plywood forming his rough desk, the fat white binder—the job bible—some tools, cans of paint.

Wouldn't be much longer, Owen calculated, before Hope kicked Ryder out again.

He continued on, stopped to bask at the open kitchen.

They'd installed the lights. The big iron fixture over the island, the smaller versions at each window. Warm wood cabinets, creamy accent pieces, smooth granite paid complement to gleaming stainless steel appliances.

He opened the fridge, started to reach for a beer. He'd be driving shortly, he reminded himself, and took a can of Pepsi instead before he made a note to call about installation of the blinds and window treatments.

They were nearly ready for them.

He moved on to Reception, took another scan, grinned again.

The mantel Ryder had created out of a thick old plank of barn wood suited the old brick and the deep open fireplace. At the moment, tarps, more paint cans, more tools crowded the space. He made a few more notes, wandering back, moving through the first arch, then paused on his way across The Lobby to what would be The Lounge, when he heard footsteps on the second floor.

He walked through the next arch leading down the short hallway toward the stairs. He saw Luther had been hard at work on the iron rails, and ran a hand over it as he started the climb.

"Okay, pretty damn gorgeous. Ry? You up here?"

A door shut smartly, made him jump a little. His quiet blue eyes narrowed as he finished the climb. His brothers weren't against screwing with him, and damned if he'd give either of them an excuse to snicker.

"Ooooh," he said in mock fear. "It must be the ghost. I'm *so* scared!"

He made the turn toward the front of the building, saw that the door to Elizabeth and Darcy was indeed closed, unlike that of Titania and Oberon across from it.

Very funny, he thought sourly.

He crept toward the door, intending to shove it open, jump in, and possibly give whichever one of his brothers was playing games a jolt. He closed his hand on the curved handle, pulled it down smoothly, pushed.

The door didn't budge.

"Cut it out, asshole." But he laughed a little in spite of himself. At least until the door flew open, and both porch doors did the same.

He smelled honeysuckle, sweet as summer, on the rush of icy air.

"Well, Jesus."

He'd mostly accepted they had a ghost, mostly believed it. After all, there'd been incidents, and Beckett was adamant. Adamant enough he'd named her Elizabeth in honor of the room she preferred.

But this was Owen's first personal, up-close, and unarguable experience.

He stood, slack-jawed, as the bathroom door slammed, then flew open, then slammed again.

"Okay. Wow, okay. Um, sorry to intrude. I was just—" The door slammed in his face—or would have if he hadn't jumped back in time to avoid the bust to his nose.

"Hey, come on. You've got to know me by now. I'm here almost every day. Owen, Beck's brother. I, ah, come in peace and all that."

The bathroom door slammed again, and the sound made

him wince. "Easy on the material, okay? What's the problem? I was just . . . Oh. I get it."

Clearing his throat, he pulled off his wool cap, raked his hands through his thick, bark brown hair. "Listen, I wasn't calling you an asshole. I thought it was Ry. You know my other brother. Ryder? He can be an asshole, you have to admit. And I'm standing in the hallway explaining myself to a ghost."

The door opened a crack. Cautiously, Owen eased it open. "I'm just going to close the porch doors. We really have to keep them closed."

He could admit, to himself, the sound of his own voice echoing in the empty room gave him the jitters, but he shoved the cap into his coat pocket as he moved to the far door, shut it, locked it. But when he got to the second door, he saw the lights shining in Avery's apartment over the restaurant.

He saw her, or a flash of her, move by the window.

The rush of air stilled; the scent of honeysuckle sweetened.

"I've smelled you before," he murmured, still looking out at Avery's windows. "Beckett says you warned him the night that fucker—sorry for the language—Sam Freemont went after Clare. So thanks for that. They're getting married—Beck and Clare. You probably know that. He's been stuck on her most of his life."

He shut the door now, turned around. "So thanks again."

The bathroom door stood open now, so he caught his own reflection in the mirror with its curvy iron frame over the vanity.

He had to admit, he looked a little wild-eyed, and the hair sticking up in tufts from the rake of his fingers added to the spooked image.

Automatically, he shoved his fingers through again to try to calm it down.

"I'm just going through the place, making notes. We're down to punch-out work essentially. Not in here, though. This is done. I think the crew wanted to finish this room up. Some of them get a little spooked. No offense. So . . . I'm going to finish up and go. See you—or not see you, but . . ."

Whatever, he decided, and backed out of the room.

He spent more than thirty minutes, moving from room to room, floor to floor, adding to his notes. A few times, the scent of honeysuckle returned, or a door opened.

Her presence—and he couldn't deny it—seemed benign enough now. But he couldn't deny the faint sense of relief either as he locked up for the night.

❧

FROST CRUNCHED LIGHTLY under Owen's boots as he juggled coffee and donuts. A half hour before sunrise, he let himself back into the inn, headed straight to the kitchen to set down the box of donuts, the tray of take-out coffee, and his brief-case. To brighten the mood, and because it was there, he moved to Reception, switched on the gas logs. Pleased by the heat and light, he stripped off his gloves, folded them into the pockets of his jacket.

Back in the kitchen, he opened his briefcase, took out his clipboard, and began to review—again—the agenda for the day. The phone on his belt beeped, signaling the time for the morning meeting.

He'd finished half a glazed donut by the time he heard Ryder's truck pull in.

His brother wore a Montgomery Family Contractors cap, a thick, scarred work jacket, and his need-more-coffee scowl. Dumbass, Ryder's dog, padded in, sniffed the air, then looked longingly at the second half of Owen's donut.

Ryder grunted, reached for a cup.

"That's Beck's," Owen told him with barely a glance. "As is clear by the *B* I wrote on the side."

Ryder grunted again, took the cup marked *R*. After one long gulp he eyed the donuts, opted for a jelly-filled.

At the thump of D.A.'s tail, Ryder tossed him a chunk.

"Beck's late," Owen commented.

"You're the one who decided we needed to meet up before dawn." Ryder took a huge bite of donut, washed it down with coffee. He hadn't shaved, so a dark stubble covered the hard planes of his face. But his gold-flecked green eyes lost some of their sleepy scowl thanks to the caffeine and sugar.

"Too many interruptions once the crew's here. I looked around some on my way home last night. You had a good day."

"Damn straight. We'll finish punch-out on the third floor this morning. Some trim and crown molding, some lights and those damn heated towel racks still to go in a couple rooms on two. Luther's moving on the rails and banisters."

"So I saw. I've got some notes."

"Yeah, yeah."

"I'll have more, I expect, when I finish going over two, and head up to three."

"Why wait?" Ryder grabbed a second donut, started out. He tossed another chunk without bothering to glance at the dog, who trotted with him.

Dumbass fielded it with Golden Gloves precision.

"Beckett's not here."

"Dude's got a woman," Ryder pointed out, "and three kids. School morning. He'll be here when he is, and can catch up."

"There's some paint needs touching up down here," Owen began.

"I got eyes, too."

"I'm going to have them come in, install the blinds throughout. If three gets punched out today, I can have them start on the window treatments by early next week."

"The men cleaned up, but it's construction clean. It needs a real cleaning, a polish. You need to get the innkeeper on that."

"I'll be talking to Hope this morning. I'm going to talk County into letting us start load-in."

Ryder slanted a look at his brother. "We've got another two weeks, easy, and that's not counting the holidays."

But Owen, as usual, had a plan. "We can get three done, Ry, start working our way down. You think Mom and Carolee—not to mention Hope—aren't going to be running around buying more stuff once we get things in place?"

"I do figure it. We don't need them underfoot any more than they already are."

They heard a door open from below as they rounded up to the third floor.

"On three," Owen called down. "Coffee's in the kitchen."

"Thank you, Jesus."

"Jesus didn't buy the coffee." Owen brushed his fingers over the oil-rubbed bronzed oval plaque engraved *Innkeeper*. "Classy touch."

"The place is full of them." Ryder gulped more coffee as they stepped inside.

"It looks good." Owen nodded as he toured through, into and out of the little kitchen, the bath, circling the two bedrooms. "It's a nice, comfortable space. Pretty and efficient, like our innkeeper."

"She's damn near as pain-in-the-ass fussy as you are."

"Remember who keeps you in donuts, bro."

At the word *donuts*, D.A. wagged his entire body. "You're done, pal," Ryder told him, and with a doggie sigh, D.A. sprawled on the floor.

Owen glanced over as Beckett came up the steps.

He'd shaved, Owen noted, and looked bright-eyed. Maybe a little wild-eyed, as he imagined most men did with three kids under the age of ten and the school-morning chaos that created.

He remembered his own school mornings well enough, and wondered how his parents had resisted doing major drugs.

"One of the dogs puked in Murphy's bed," Beckett announced. "I don't want to talk about it."

"Works for me. Owen's talking about window treatments and loading in."

Beckett paused as he gave Dumbass a quick head rub. "We've still got trim to run, painting, punch-out."

"Not up here." Owen crossed to the first of their two suites, The Penthouse. "We could outfit this suite. Hope could move her stuff in across the hall. How about Westley and Buttercup?"

"It's done. We hung the bathroom mirror and lights yesterday."

"Then I'll tell Hope to break out the mop, get this level

shined up." Though he trusted Ryder, he'd check the room himself. "She's got the list of what goes where, so she can run down to Bast, tell them what to deliver up here."

He made notes on his clipboard—shipment of towels and linens, purchase of lightbulbs and so on. Behind his back Beckett and Ryder exchanged looks.

"I guess we're loading in."

"I don't know who 'we' is," Ryder corrected. "It's not me or the crew. We've got to finish the damn place."

"Don't bitch at me." Beckett held up his hands. "I've got to make the changes to the bakery project next door if we're going to shift the crew from here to there without much of a lag."

"I could use a lag," Ryder muttered but headed down behind Owen.

Owen paused at Elizabeth and Darcy, gave the propped-open door a study. "Beckett, you might want to talk to your pal, Lizzy. Make sure she keeps this door open, and the terrace doors shut."

"It is open. They are shut."

"Now they are. She got a little peeved last night."

Intrigued, Beckett lifted his brows. "Is that so?"

"I guess I had my personal close encounter. I did a walk-through last night, heard somebody up here. I figured it for one of you, messing with me. She thought I called her an asshole, and let me know she didn't care for it."

Beckett's grin spread wide and quick. "She's got a temper."

"Tell me. We made up, I think. But in case she holds a grudge."

"We're done in here, too," Ryder told him. "And in T&O. We've got to run the crown molding and baseboard in N&N, and there's some touch-up in E&R, and the bathroom ceiling light in there. It came in, finally, yesterday. J&R in the back's full of boxes. Lamps, lamps, more lamps, shelves, and God knows. But it's punched out.

"I've got a list, too." Ryder tapped his head while the dog walked over to sit at his side. "I just don't have to write every freaking thing down in ten places."

"Robe hooks, towel racks, TP dispensers," Owen began. "On the slate for today."

"Mirrors, flat screens, switch plates and outlet covers, door bumpers."

"On the slate, Owen."

"You've got the list of what goes where?"

"Nobody likes a nag, Sally."

"Exit signs need to go up." Owen continued working down his list as he walked to The Dining Room. "Wall sconces in here. The boxes we built for the fire extinguishers need to be painted and installed."

"Once you shut up, I can get started."

"Brochures, website, advertising, finalizing room rates, packages, room folders."

"Not my job."

"Exactly. Count your frigging blessings. How much longer for the revised plans on the bakery project?" Owen asked Beckett.

"I'll have them to the permit office tomorrow morning."

"Good deal." He took out his phone, switched it to calendar. "Let's nail it down. I'm going to tell Hope to open reservations for January fifteenth. We can have the grand-opening deal on the thirteenth, give us a day for putting it all back together. Then we're up."

"That's less than a month," Ryder complained.

"You know and Beck knows and I know there's less than two weeks' work left here. You'll be done before Christmas. If we start the load-in this week, we'll be done by the first, and there's no reason we won't get the Use and Occupancy right after the holidays. That gives two weeks to fiddle and fuss, work out any kinks, with Hope living here."

"I'm with Owen on this. We're sliding downhill now, Ry."

Stuffing his hands in his pockets, Ryder shrugged. "It's weird, maybe, just weird thinking about actually being done."

"Cheer up," Owen told him. "A place like this? We're never going to be done."

On his nod, Ryder heard the back door open, shut, the sound of heavy boots on tile. "We've got crew. Get your tools."

∽

OWEN KEPT BUSY, and happy, running crown molding. He didn't mind the regular interruptions to answer a call, return a text, read an email. His phone served as a tool to him as much as his nail gun. The building buzzed with activity, echoed with voices and Ryder's job radio. It smelled of paint and fresh-cut wood, strong coffee. The combination said Montgomery Family Contractors to him, and never failed to remind him of his father.

Everything he'd learned about carpentry and the building trade he'd learned from his dad. Now, stepping off the ladder to study the work, he knew his father would be proud.

They'd taken the old building with its sagging porches and broken windows, its scarred walls and broken floors and had transformed it into a jewel on the town square.

Beckett's vision, he thought, their mother's imagination and canny eye, Ryder's sweat and skill, and his own focus on detail, combined with a solid crew, had transformed what had been an idea batted around the kitchen table into reality.

He set down his nail gun, rolled his shoulder as he turned around the room.

Yeah, his mother's canny eye, he thought again. He could admit he'd balked at her scheme of pale aqua walls and chocolate brown ceiling—until he'd seen it finished. *Glamour* was the word of the day for Nick and Nora, and it reached its pinnacle in the bath. That same color scheme, including a wall of blue glass tiles, contrasting with brown on brown, all sparkling under crystal lights. Chandelier in the john, he thought, with a shake of his head. It sure as hell worked.

Nothing ordinary or hotel-like about it, he mused—not when Justine Montgomery took charge. He thought this room with its Deco flair might be his favorite.

His phone alarm told him it was time to start making some calls of his own.

He went out, then headed toward the back door for the porch as Luther worked on the rails leading down. Gritting his teeth, he jogged through the cold and bitter wind across the covered porch, down to ground level, then ducked in through Reception.

"Fucking A it's cold." The radio blasted; nail guns thumped. And no way, he decided, would he try to do business with all this noise. He grabbed his jacket, his briefcase.

He ducked into The Lounge, where Beckett sat on the floor running trim.

"I'm heading over to Vesta."

"It's shy of ten. They're not open."

"Exactly."

Outside, Owen hunched against the cold at the light, cursed the fact that traffic, such as it was, paced and spaced itself so he couldn't make the dash across Main. He waited it out, his breath blowing icy clouds until the walk light flashed. He jogged diagonally, ignored the Closed sign on the glass front door of the restaurant, and pounded.

He saw lights on, but no movement. Once again he took out his phone, punched Avery's number from memory.

"Damn it, Owen, now I've got dough on my phone."

"So you are in there. Open up before I get frostbite."

"Damn it," she repeated, then cut him off. But seconds later he saw her, white bib apron over jeans and a black sweater with sleeves shoved to her elbows. Her hair—what the hell color was it now? It struck him as very close to the bright new-penny copper of the inn's roof.

She'd started changing it a few months back, going with most everything but her natural Scot warrior-queen red. She'd hacked it short, too, he recalled, though it had grown long enough again for her to yank it back in a tiny stub when she worked.

Her eyes, as bright a blue as her hair was copper, glared at him as she turned the locks.

"What do you want?" she demanded. "I'm in the middle of prep."

"I just want the room and the quiet. You won't even know I'm here." He sidled in, just in case she tried to shut the door on him. "I can't talk on the phone with all the noise across the street and I have to make some calls."

She narrowed those blue eyes at his briefcase.

So he tried a winning smile. "Okay, maybe I have a little paperwork. I'll sit at the counter. I'll be very, very quiet."

"Oh, all right. But don't bother me."

"Um, just before you go back? You wouldn't happen to have any coffee?"

"No, I wouldn't happen to have. I'm prepping dough, which is now on my new phone. I worked closing last night, and Franny called in sick at eight this morning. She sounded like somebody ran her larynx through a meat grinder. I had two waitstaff out with the same thing last night, which means I'll probably be on from now to closing. Dave can't work tonight because he's getting a root canal at four, and I've got a bus tour coming in at twelve thirty."

Because she'd snapped the words out in little whiplashes, Owen just nodded. "Okay."

"Just . . ." She gestured toward the long counter. "Do whatever."

She rushed back to the kitchen on bright green Nikes.

He'd have offered to help, but he could tell she wasn't in the mood. He knew her moods—he'd known her forever—and recognized harried, impatient, and stressed.

She'd roll with it, he thought. She always did. The sassy little redhead from his childhood, the former Boonsboro High cheerleader—cocaptain with Beckett's Clare—had become a hardworking restaurateur. Who made exceptional pizza.

She'd left a light, lemony scent behind her, along with a frisson of energy. He heard the faint thump and rattle of her work as he took a stool at the counter. He found it soothing and somewhat rhythmic.

He opened his briefcase, took out his iPad, his clipboard, unclipped his phone from his belt.

He made his calls, sent emails, texts, reworked his calendar, calculated.

He steeped himself in the details, surfacing when a coffee mug slid under his nose.

He looked up into Avery's pretty face.

"Thanks. You didn't have to bother. I won't be long."

"Owen, you've already been here forty minutes."

"Really? Lost track. You want me to go?"

"Doesn't matter." Though she pressed a fist into the small of her back, she spoke easily now. "I've got it under control."

He caught another scent, and glancing to the big stove, saw she'd put her sauces on.

The red hair, milk-white skin, and dash of freckles might declare her Scot heritage, but her marinara was as gloriously Italian as an Armani suit.

He'd often wondered where she'd gotten the knack, and the drive, but both seemed as innate a part of her as her big, bold blue eyes.

Crouching, she opened the cooler under the counter for tubs, and began filling the topping containers.

"Sorry about Franny."

"Me, too. She's really sick. And Dave's miserable. He's only coming in for a couple hours this afternoon because I'm so shorthanded. I hate asking him."

He studied her face as she worked. Now that he really looked, he noted the pale purple shadows under her eyes.

"You look tired."

She shot him a disgusted look over the tub of black olives. "Thanks. That's what every girl loves to hear." Then she shrugged. "I am tired. I thought I'd sleep in this morning. Franny would open, I'd come in about eleven thirty. Not much of a commute since I moved right upstairs. So I watched some Jimmy Fallon, finished a book I've been trying to squeeze out time to read all week. I didn't go down until nearly two. Then Franny calls at eight. Six hours isn't bad, unless you worked a double and you're going to work another."

"Bright side? Business is good."

"I'll think about bright side after the bus tour. Anyway, enough. How's it going at the inn?"

"So good we're going to start loading in the third floor tomorrow."

"Loading in what?"

"Furniture, Avery."

She set down the tub, goggled at him. "Seriously? *Seriously?*"

"The inspector's going to take a look this afternoon, give us the go or no. I'm saying go because there's no reason for no. I just talked to Hope. She's going to start cleaning up there. My mother and my aunt are coming in—maybe are in already, since it's going on eleven now—to pitch in."

"I wanted to do that. I can't."

"Don't worry about that. We've got plenty of hands."

"I wanted mine to be two of them. Maybe tomorrow, depending on sickness and root canals. Jeez, Owen, this is major." She did a little heel-toe dance on her green high-tops. "And you wait almost an hour to spill it?"

"You were too busy bitching at me."

"If you'd spilled, I'd've been too excited to bitch. Your own fault."

She smiled at him, pretty Avery MacTavish with the tired eyes.

"Why don't you sit down for a few minutes?"

"I've got to keep moving today, like a shark." She snapped the lid on the tub, replaced it, then went over to check her sauces.

He watched her work. She always seemed to be doing half a dozen things at once, like a constant juggling act with balls hanging in the air, others bouncing madly until she managed to grab and toss them again.

It amazed his organized mind.

"I'd better get back. Thanks for the coffee."

"No problem. If any of the crew's thinking about lunch here today, tell them to wait until one thirty. The rush'll be over."

"Okay." He gathered his things, then paused at the door. "Avery? What color is that? The hair."

"This? Copper Penny."

He grinned, shook his head. "I knew it. See you later."

# CHAPTER TWO

O WEN STRAPPED HIS TOOL BELT ON, CHECKED HIS
punch-out list against Ryder's.

"The third floor's full of women," Ryder told him, with
an edge of bitterness.

"Are they naked?"

"Mom's one of them."

"Okay, scratch the naked."

"Mom, Carolee, the innkeeper. Clare might still be up
there. Dude, they're a swarm. One of them keeps buzzing
down here, asking questions." Ryder grabbed his Gatorade
off the kitchen island where he'd spread out plans and lists
since Hope had booted him out of her projected office space.
"Since you're the one who opened the gates there, you're
the one who's going to answer all the damn questions. And
where the hell were you?"

"I left word. I went over to Avery's so I could make some
calls. Inspector's going to take a look at the third floor to
clear the load-in there. He'll check out the rest while he's
here. Furniture for up there's set, and they'll start hauling it

in, setting it up in the morning. Window-blind install's set. They'll start upstairs this afternoon. You want the rest?"

"You're giving me a headache."

"That's why I make the calls. I can start running trim on two."

"Third floor." Ryder drilled a finger into Owen's chest. "Women. All yours, brother."

"Fine, fine."

He wanted to work, to slide into the rhythm of nail guns, hammers, drills. Men. But he went back outside, cursed the cold as he rounded back and jogged up the stairs.

And entered the world of women.

He smelled perfume and lotion and lemon-scented cleanser. And heard women's voices over the din echoing up from below. He found his mother on her hands and knees, scrubbing the floor of the shower stall in The Penthouse.

She'd bundled her dark hair up, shoved up the sleeves of a baggy gray sweatshirt. Her jeans-clad butt swayed side-to-side to whatever played on her headphones.

Owen walked around the glass, hunkered down. She didn't jolt; he'd always believed her claim of having eyes in the back of her head. Justine just lifted her head, smiled at him as she sat back on her heels and took off the headset.

She said, "Hot damn."

"You ready for this, Mom?"

"I've been ready. We'll get her shined up, though I'd forgotten just how grimy construction dirt is. We split up. Carolee's back in Westley and Buttercup, and Hope's dealing with her apartment. Clare's going to give us some time this afternoon."

"I was just over at Vesta. Avery's got a bus tour coming in, and Franny's out sick. She wanted to be in on this." Owen studied the bucket of soapy water. "God knows why."

"It's satisfying work, in its way. Look at this place, Owen." Shoving a couple of loose pins back in her hair, she glanced around. "Look at what you and your brothers did here."

"What we and our mom did," he corrected, and made her smile again.

"You're so damn right about that. Since you're here, take the shelves out of that box. One's going right up there, the other right over there."

She pointed.

"There're shelves in here?"

"There will be when you put them up. Then you might get one of the crew to give you a hand, hang the mirror in the bedroom. When you're ready I'll show you how I want it."

"Wait, let me write this down."

"Just do the little shelves, and I'll walk you through the rest."

He got to use his tools after all. Maybe not the way he preferred—with a list, items in prioritized order waiting to be checked off—but he used his tools.

When he'd installed the decorative shelves, he drafted one of the crew to help him carry in the big wall mirror with its ornate gilded frame.

Justine stood, hands on hips, adjusting its position with "a little to the left, a little higher—no, lower." Owen marked, measured, drilled while she went back to her scrubbing.

"It's up," he called out.

"Hold on a sec."

He heard the whoosh of water as she emptied her bucket. When she stepped out again, she once more fisted her hands on her hips. "I love it!"

Walking to him, she stood so the mirror reflected both of them. With a grin, she put her arm around his waist. "It's perfect. Thanks, Owen. Go on over and get Hope, would you? She knows what needs to go up downstairs. I've got another acre of tile to clean."

"I can hire a cleaning service."

She shook her head. "This stage is for family."

He supposed that made Hope Beaumont family. She and his mother had hit it off, Owen thought as he crossed the hall. Right from the first beat.

The former beauty queen stood on a step stool in the apartment kitchen polishing the cabinet doors. She'd tied a bandana around her dark hair, had a rag hanging out of the back pocket of jeans flecked with white paint and nearly worn through on the right knee.

She glanced around at him, blew out a breath that fluttered her spiky bangs. "It didn't look as dirty as it was."

"Construction dirt gets into everything." He wondered if he should tell her she'd be sucking and mopping it up for days. Maybe weeks.

She'd find out for herself, he decided.

"Making progress," he said instead.

"We really are." She sat on the stool a moment, took a bottle of water from the countertop, and twisted off the top. "Are we really going to have furniture up here tomorrow?"

"It's looking good for it."

She sipped, smiled.

She had a smoky voice that suited the sultry looks, all big dark eyes, full, shapely mouth.

It didn't hurt, he supposed, to have a looker as innkeeper, but more to the point, much more important to him, her level of organization and efficiency marched along with his own.

"If you've got a minute, Mom said there were some things you wanted put up on the second floor."

"And the first if we can squeeze it in. The more shipping boxes we empty, the easier it'll be to clean, and the smoother the load-in should go."

"That's a good point." The woman, he thought, spoke his language. "I'm your man. Anything you need done in here?"

"I've got some shelves I need to hang."

Oh well, he thought. It was the Day of the Shelves. "I'll hang them for you."

"I'd appreciate it. They're over at the other apartment. I can get them later."

"I can send somebody over for them."

"Sure, if you can spare someone. But we can deal with what's on-site first. I've got everything Justine wants hung back in J&R."

His language, he thought again.

"Want a coat?" he asked as she got off the stool.

"I'll be fine. It's a quick trip." But she pulled the sleeves of her sweatshirt down to her wrists. "I talked to Avery this morning," she continued as they walked toward the back of the building. "She's frazzled with so many of her crew out. I'd hoped to go over, give her a hand tonight, but it looks like we're going to be in here most of the evening."

When they went out, she slapped a hand on her bandana before the wind whipped it off. "As cold as it is, I'll bet she's slammed with deliveries tonight. Who wants to go out in this?"

She nipped into Jane and Rochester, rubbed her hands together. "So we can hit W&B first. Or since we're right here, we could work back to front on the second floor. Starting here, with the bathroom shelves and mirror." She tapped the carefully labeled boxes. "Bathroom mirror."

She ran through the items for each room, working down to the first floor.

"That ought to keep me busy. Let's save steps, start where we are."

"Good. Why don't I show you where everything goes, then get out of your way. You can send someone up for me if you have any questions." Taking a folding knife out of her pocket, she slit open a resealed shipping box.

"I like a woman who carries her own knife."

"I've filled out my tools since I moved here. I nearly bought my own nail gun, then realized I'd gone too far." She took out two curved copper shelves. "So I compensated with more office supplies. What is it about new file folders and color-coordinated Post-its?"

"Preaching to the choir."

They chatted amiably as she directed the height, the space, as he measured, leveled, and drilled.

"It's perfect. Look how the antique gold of the mirror frame plays off the tiles, and the copper of the tub, the shelves. Wait until Justine sees this." Turning a circle, she aimed for the bedroom again. "I can't wait to dress this room. All the rooms. With the fireplace and that amazing bed going in here, I think it's going to be one of our most popular."

She pulled a notebook out of her pocket, checked off items, made notes.

He grinned when she tucked it away again. "It's nice to have somebody on my team for a change."

"Writing things down saves time in the long run."

"Again, preaching to the choir."

Together they gathered boxes, carried them to the porch door and through.

Hope started into Eve and Roarke, and nearly walked straight into Ryder.

"Mom wants the ceiling light up. Where the hell is it?"

"I'm carrying it," Owen told him.

"Then you install it."

"That's the plan. Hope's got some things over at her apartment for her place upstairs. Why don't you go over and get them?"

"I can get them later," Hope began.

"What are they? Where are they?"

"Shelves, wall shelves. Bath and living room. They're in marked boxes in my storeroom. In the second bedroom," she amended. "I'm using it as a storeroom."

"I'll take care of it."

"You need the key," she said when he started to walk away. She reached into her front pocket, offered it.

He stuffed it in his own pocket. "Have you got those door rack hook things in those boxes?"

"Some of them," Owen answered.

"Get them up, for God's sake. I don't want to hear about them anymore. Where's the one for the ADA room?"

Because her arms were starting to ache, Hope set down her boxes. "In Jane and Rochester, on the wall facing St. Paul, in a box clearly marked 'M&P, clothes bar.' If you're getting that, you might want to take down the two boxes in the same area, marked 'M&P bathroom wall shelves.' But don't put them up unless either I'm there, or your mother. And we want a small corner shelf beside the sink in M&P."

She took out her notebook, flipped pages. "These are the dimensions, the basic concept."

Ryder narrowed his eyes at it, then at her. "Why?"

"Because due to the ADA codes, the layout of the room, we don't really have a surface for something as basic as a toothbrush. Now we will."

"Give me the damn paper."

Hope tore it off. "I'm sure Owen or Beckett or one of the crew could take care of it if you're too busy."

He just stuffed the paper into his pocket and walked away.

"Are you sure he's your brother?" Hope muttered.

"Pretty sure. He's a little stressed with punching out here so we can make the deadline, riding the work on Beck's house, getting the demo finished next door for the bakery."

"It's a lot," Hope conceded. "Why aren't you stressed? You've got the same meal on your plate."

"Different categories, I guess. I don't have to boss. I get to negotiate." He set the shipping box on the floor of the bathroom.

Considering, Hope unboxed the little glass shelf. "Just a small thing, the kind of detail no one will really notice."

"Unless it wasn't there."

"Like a place for your toothbrush." She smiled, then tapped the wall. "Right here. If you don't need me, I'll go back up until you do."

Hope slipped into Westley and Buttercup on her way, found Carolee busily mopping the bedroom floor.

"Carolee, the bathroom looks great. It sparkles."

Justine's sister, her cheeks pink with effort, pushed at her blond hair. "I swear I haven't cleaned that hard in *years*. But it's worth it. I keep thinking, I'm going to work here! I'm going to come into this room all the time. You need me for anything? Boss?"

Hope laughed. "You're outpacing me. I stopped to get Owen going on the shelves and so on. I'm just going to see how Justine's doing, then I'll be in my apartment. My *innkeeper's* apartment. Oh, I nearly forgot. If you've got any time over the next couple days, I want to go over the reservation program with you one more time. Because we're going to start taking reservations."

"Oh boy." Carolee waved her hands in the air in triumph. "Oh boy, oh boy."

She felt the same way, Hope thought as she hustled back inside. She hadn't been so excited over a job since she'd first started at the Wickham Hotel in Georgetown. Not a good comparison, she reminded herself, considering how that had turned out.

And yet the debacle with Jonathan Wickham, and her decision to resign as manager, had opened the door for her to Inn BoonsBoro.

A beautiful building, beautifully appointed in a charming town with her two closest friends nearby. No, she'd never been quite this excited over a job.

She peeked into The Penthouse, saw Justine sitting on the wide windowsill of the parlor, looking out at Main Street.

"Taking a break," Justine told her. "That bathroom is *huge*—and I've got no one to blame but myself for that."

"I'll finish it up."

"It's done, but I think we'll give it one more going-over before the grand-opening party. I was just sitting here thinking how this place looked when I first dragged the boys in to look it over. My God. And I'm thinking, too, how pleased and proud Tommy would be. And how he's probably a little pissed off he didn't get to hammer in a few nails."

"He taught his sons how to hammer them, so he's had as much a part in creating this as they have."

Justine's eyes softened. "That's a good thing to say. Just the right thing." She held out a hand, giving Hope's a tug when they joined. "I wish it would snow. I want to see how it looks in the snow, then in the spring and the summer, on into the fall. I want to see it shine here, in every season."

"I'll keep it beautiful for you."

"I know you will. You'll be happy here, Hope. I want you

to be happy here, to have everyone who comes to stay happy here."

"I'm already happy here."

◦つ

HAPPIER THAN SHE'D been in a long time, Hope thought as she went back to polishing her kitchen cabinets. She had an opportunity to do good work for good people.

She tipped her head as she studied the cabinets. And to reward herself, she'd pop over to the gift store before closing and buy those gorgeous bowls she'd had her eye on. A little personal housewarming gift.

Ryder carted in boxes. "What is it with women and shelves?" he demanded. "How many linear feet of flat surface does one person need?"

"That would depend," she said coolly, "on how many things that person chooses to display."

"Dust catchers."

"Dust catchers to some, mementos and personal style to others."

"Where the hell do you want your flat surfaces for your mementos and personal style? I haven't got all day."

"Just leave them. I'll deal with them later."

"Fine."

He set them on the floor, turned.

His mother stood in the doorway, arms folded, giving him a look that still made his shoulders hunch and his balls shrink up a little.

"I apologize for my son, Hope. He's obviously misplaced his manners inside his crappy mood."

"It's nothing. Ryder's busy. Everyone's busy today."

"Busy doesn't serve as an excuse for rude. Does it, Ryder?"

"No, ma'am. I'd be happy to hang your shelves," he said to Hope, "if you'll show me where you want them."

"That's better." Justine gave him one last hard look before she went back across the hall.

"Well?" Ryder demanded. "Where am I putting them?"

"The suggestion I have at the moment wouldn't be the walls."

His grin came fast and bright, surprising her. "Since I don't have any mementos I'd like to stick up my ass, how about a second choice?"

"Just leave them there, and you?" She pointed toward the door.

Gauging her, he hooked his thumbs in his tool belt. "I'm not afraid of you, but I'm afraid of her. I don't hang these, she'll make me pay for it. So I'm not leaving until you pick your spots."

"They're already marked."

"What's marked?"

"I measured the shelves, I measured the space. I marked the areas." She gestured to the space between her front windows, then toward the bathroom. "I think you can take it from there."

Tossing down her polishing rag, she sailed out. She'd help Owen until his bad-tempered brother finished.

❧

AVERY KEPT UP with the progress across Main by texts, and a quick drop-in from Clare. With the bus tour finished and the rush quieted, she took a short break in the back dining room to scarf down some pasta.

For now, the video machines stayed silent. She calculated another hour or two before kids slid in after school to set them beeping and banging.

The quarters added up, she reminded herself.

"I really wanted to get over, just for a minute, to see." She gulped down Gatorade. Energy, she thought. She needed all she could get to finish it out till closing. "Hope sent me some pictures over the phone."

"I couldn't give them any real time either. The bus tour swarmed us, too. God bless them, every one." Clare smiled, picked at her own salad. "Beckett told me the inspector gave the thumbs-up on the load-in. All of it."

"All of it?"

"It's nothing but details now, and he'll be back, but he said they could start bringing everything in. Hope can't move in, of course, but we can really start setting things up."

Sulking, Avery stabbed at pasta. "I'm not going to be left out of this!"

"Avery, it'll take days. Weeks, really."

"I want to play now." Then she blew out a breath. "Okay, not now because my feet are already killing me. But tomorrow. Maybe." She stuffed in more pasta. "Look at you. You look so happy."

"I'm happier every day. Yoda threw up in Murphy's bed this morning."

"That's reason to celebrate, all right."

"Definitely not, but Murphy came running for Beckett. It was wonderful."

"Yeah, I'd be happy not to be on dog-puke detail."

"It's a factor." Clare's eyes danced. "But what really makes me happy is how the boys love Beckett, how they trust him. How he's part of us now. I'm getting married, Avery. I'm so lucky to love and marry two incredible men in one lifetime."

"I think you got my share. You should really give me Beck."

"Nope, I'm keeping him." Her sunny ponytail danced when she shook her head. "Pick one of the others."

"Maybe I should get both of them. I could use two sets of hands tonight. And I still have Christmas shopping. Why do I always think I'll have more time?"

"Because you always manage to find a way to make the time. Have you said anything to the Montgomerys about the space across the street?"

"Not yet. Still mulling. You didn't tell Beckett?"

"I said I wouldn't. But it's hard. I'm getting used to telling him everything."

"Love, love, sappy love." Avery sighed, wiggled her tired toes. "At times like this it seems like a crazy idea anyway. But . . ."

"You could do it, and do it right."

"You're just saying that because I could." Avery laughed,

and some of the fatigue fell away from her face. "And you love me. I've got to get back to work. Are you going over to the inn?"

"Laurie and Charlene have the store covered. I thought I'd give them an hour or so. Then I have to pick up the boys."

"Send me more pictures."

"I will." Clare rose, pulled a wool cap over her sleek blond hair, shrugged a coat over her willowy frame. "Get some sleep, sweetie."

"Won't be a problem. The minute we're closed I'm going upstairs and falling flat on my face for eight straight. See you tomorrow. I've got it," Avery said when Clare reached for the dishes. "I'm heading back to the kitchen anyway."

She waved Clare off, rolled her aching shoulders, then went back to work.

By seven she was in the zone, sliding pizzas into the oven and out again, boxing them for delivery, passing them to waitstaff for table service.

Her place buzzed with activity—and that was a good thing, she reminded herself. She dished up pasta, plated burgers and fries, glanced at the boy who sat at the counter playing the Megatouch as if it comprised his world.

She hustled back to the closed kitchen for more supplies just as Owen walked in.

He took one look around, frowned when he didn't see her behind the counter.

"Where's Avery?" he asked a waitress.

"She's around. The high school chorus decided to come in for pizza after practice. We're slammed. She must be in the back."

"Okay." He didn't think about it, just went over to the cash register, grabbed one of the order pads, and headed for the back dining room.

When he came out, she stood at the counter, cheeks flushed from the heat, ladling sauce on dough. "Orders from the back," he told her, slapping the slips in place. "I'll get the drinks."

She spread mozzarella, added toppings, watched him.

You could count on Owen, she thought, through the paper thin to the brick thick, you could count on him.

For the next three hours she did whatever came next.
Baked spaghetti, Warrior's pizza, eggplant parm, calzone,
gyro. By ten it was like being in a trance, cashing out, cleaning counters, shutting down the ovens.

"Get a beer," she told Owen. "You earned it."

"Why don't you sit down?"

"I will, when we finish closing."

When the last of her crew left, when she'd locked the
door, she turned. A glass of red sat on the counter beside a
slice of pepperoni pizza. Owen sat on a stool, with a glass
and slice of his own.

God, yes, you could always count on Owen.

"Now sit down," he ordered.

"Now I will. Thanks. Really, Owen, thanks."

"It's kind of fun, when you don't have to do it every day."

"It's kind of fun even then, mostly." She sat, took her first
sip of wine. "Oh man, that's good." She bit into the pizza.
"So's that."

"Nobody makes better."

"You'd think I'd get tired of pizza, but it's still my favorite
thing." Floating on exhaustion, she sighed her way through
another bite. "Clare said you're clear to load in. How'd the
cleaning brigade do?"

"Good, really good. Still some to go, but we're heading
down to the wire."

"I'd walk over if I could walk that far."

"It'll be there tomorrow."

"Everybody who came in here today, tonight, from town
or nearby talked about it. You must be so proud. I know how
I felt when I was on the wire here, hanging the art, unpacking kitchen equipment. Proud and excited and a little scared.
Here's my place. I'm really doing it. I still feel that way
sometimes. Not tonight," she said with a weak laugh. "But
sometimes."

"You've got a lot to be proud of here. It's a good place."

"I know a lot of people thought your mom was crazy
renting the space to me. How was I going to run a restaurant?"

He shook his head, thought her skin was pale enough to

pass his hand through. The absence of her usual crackling energy made her fatigue seem only more extreme.

He'd talk her through the slice of pizza, he decided, so she had some food in her. Then he'd get her upstairs so she could get some sleep.

"I never thought she was crazy. You can do anything you set your mind to. You always could."

"I couldn't be a rock star. I'd set my mind on that."

He remembered her blasting away on a guitar. More enthusiasm than skill, as he recalled. "What were you, fourteen?"

"Fifteen. I thought my dad was going to faint when I dyed my hair black and got those tattoos."

"It's a good thing they were fake ones."

She smiled, sipped more wine. "Not all of them."

"Oh yeah? Where— Hold that thought," he said when his phone rang. "What's up, Ry?"

He slid off the stool, listening, answering, looking out the glass door at the lights beaming on the inn.

When he clipped the phone to his belt again, turned, he saw Avery sound asleep, her head pillowed on the arms she'd laid on the counter.

She'd managed about half the slice of pizza, about half the wine, he noted. He cleaned off the counter, shut down the lights in the closed kitchen, walked back to shut off all but the security lights throughout.

Then he considered her.

He could carry her upstairs—she didn't weigh much— but he wasn't sure how he could carry her and lock up at the same time. Take her up, he thought, come back and lock up.

But when he started to lift her, she jerked up and nearly bashed his face with her shoulder. "What? What is it?"

"Bedtime. Come on, I'll get you upstairs."

"Did I lock up?"

"Front's locked. I'll get the back."

"I'm okay. I've got it."

When she pulled the keys out, he took them. But carrying her now just seemed weird. Instead, he put an arm around her waist, let her sleepwalk beside him.

"I just closed my eyes for a minute."

"You should keep doing that, for the next eight or nine hours." He supported her at his side, locked the door behind them. "Heading up," he said and pulled her up the stairs to her apartment.

"I'm a little foggy. Thanks for all and whatever."

"You're welcome for all and whatever."

He unlocked her apartment door, tried not to wince when he saw she'd yet to completely unpack from the move—fully a month before. He set her keys on the table by the door. "You need to lock up behind me."

"'Kay." She gave him a smile as she stood swaying with fatigue. "You're so sweet, Owen. I'd pick you."

"For what?"

"My share. 'Night."

"Okay. Lock the door, Avery."

He stood outside, waiting until he heard the lock click in place.

Her share of what? he wondered, then shook his head and went down the stairs to the back lot and his truck.

He glanced up at her windows as he got in. He could still smell the lemon she used on her hair, her hands.

He smelled it all the way home.

# CHAPTER THREE

✳

THE MINUTE SHE COULD BREAK AWAY FROM THE restaurant, Avery bundled into her coat, yanked a ski cap over her hair, and dashed across the street.

She spotted the furniture truck in the parking lot and quickened her steps as much in excitement as to get out of the cold. She walked into a buzz of activity—guys on ladders touching up paint, the thwack of nail guns from The Lounge and The Dining Room, the whirl of a drill.

She headed through the front arch, then went *ooooh* when she got to the railing leading up the stairs. Ryder poked his head out of the front door of The Dining Room.

"Do me a favor. Don't go up that way. Luther's working on the rails."

"They're so beautiful," she murmured, trailing a hand over the dark bronze curve.

"Yeah, they are. He's spread out on the stairs up there, and he's too polite to tell you to go around the other way. I'm not."

"No problem." She eased toward The Dining Room door, looked up. "God, it's gorgeous. Look at those lights."

"Bitching heavy." But he looked up as well at the big acorn globes with their oak leaf branches. "They look good."

"They look amazing. And the sconces, too. I can't poke my nose in for a few days, and look what happens. I don't have much time, but I want to see everything. Is Hope around?"

"Probably up on three, fussing with furniture."

"Furniture!" With a whoop, Avery ran back toward The Lobby and out.

Breath puffing in clouds, she ran up two flights of stairs. She opened the door of Westley and Buttercup, stood for a moment just grinning at the simmering fireplace in the wall, the dark slats of window blinds. She wanted to explore, to look at every detail, but she wanted people more.

She rushed down to the porch door, hurried through, following voices to The Penthouse.

Her mouth dropped open.

Justine and Hope angled two occasional chairs covered in silky fabric. The blues and golds in the pattern picked up the rich dark gold of the elaborate sofa where Carolee fussed with throw pillows.

"I think we should . . . Avery." Justine straightened. "Walk through to the window. I want to check the traffic flow."

"I'm rooted to the spot. My God, Justine. It's gorgeous."

"But does it work? I don't want guests bumping into chairs or having to wind and scoot. Pretend you just checked in, and now you want to walk through, look out the window on St. Paul."

"Okay." She held up her hands, closed her eyes a moment. "Well, Alphonse, I suppose this will do for the night."

"Alphonse?" Hope commented.

"My lover. We're just in from Paris." She strolled across the room, put a snooty look on her face as she glanced out the window. The look broke into a grin as she turned back, danced in place. "It's spectacular. And no bumping or winding. Are you actually going to let people sit on this furniture?"

"That's what it's for."

Avery ran her fingers over the rolled arm of the sofa. "You know, they're going to do more than sit. Just saying."

"Some things I don't need to think about. I want a little lamp for this chest. Something slim with a sparkly shade."

"I saw one at Bast," Hope told her. "I think it would work."

"Make a note, okay? One of us will run down, grab some accent pieces, and try them out."

"It's stunning," Avery said. "Just as it is."

"You ain't seen nothing yet." Hope winked at her. "Bring Alphonse into the bedroom."

"His favorite place. The man's a machine."

She followed Hope back, would have detoured into the bath, but Hope grabbed her arm. "This first." And Hope beamed like a new mother at Avery's gasp.

"The bed! I saw the cut sheet, but that's nothing compared to the real thing."

"I love the carving." Hope trailed her fingers over one of the tall posts. "And with the bedding, it really looks plush. I swear Carolee fussed with the duvet and shams, the bedroll for an hour."

"I love it—the oatmeal of the shams against the white bedding, and the throw."

"Cashmere. Just a nice touch."

"I'll say. The tables, the lamps. And this dresser!"

"The subtle gold sheen really works in here. I want to finish the whole space up by tonight. The journal, the books, the DVD, all the little details. We need photos for the website."

"I love the plush little stools and pillows at the foot of the bed. Everything in here says luxury. Even Alphonse would be impressed."

"And God knows he's not easy to impress. The Bast crew just left. They're bringing in Westley and Buttercup next. It's a job and a half getting these pieces up the stairs."

"I'm glad it's not mine. I can't stay long now, but Dave's back this afternoon, so I'm not working tonight. I can help."

"You're hired. I thought I'd bring a few of my things over,

things I don't absolutely need for now. We have to start on
the art, too, and I've got my eye on a few pieces from Gifts."

"It's really happening."

"I need your menu for the room folders."

"I'll get them for you." She wandered out, into the bath.
"You put stuff out! Soap dishes, the shampoo and stuff. The
little dishes."

"Photographs, or that's my excuse. We really wanted to
see it dressed. I'm going to put out the towels, hang the
robes. Ryder's going to take the photos. Apparently he's
good at it."

"He is," Avery confirmed. "I've still got a shot he took
of me and Owen when we were teenagers. It's nice, fun. Do
you know he came over and waited and bussed tables last
night?"

"Ryder?"

"No. Owen. Then he had to all but carry me upstairs.
Two doubles, a bus tour, a spur-of-the-moment high school
chorus party, a temporary glitch with the computer, and so
on. I was like a zombie by closing."

"He's a sweetheart."

"Yeah, most of the time."

"So's Beckett. What happened to Ryder?"

Avery laughed, circling a finger around the rim of one
of the oval vessel sinks. "Oh, he's got some sweet in there.
You just have to dig it out."

"I think it'd require explosives. But he does good work.
We can dress the place, but it wouldn't hold up without the
frame. And he's hell on details. So I respect that. Anyway,
I've got to get back to it."

"Me, too. I should be able to knock off about four, five
latest. I'll pitch in."

"Rumor is we should be able to start loading in The
Library sometime today. At least the shelves. And possibly
Elizabeth and Darcy."

"I'll be here. Hope!" After a quick bounce, Avery tossed
her arms around Hope, bounced again. "I'm so happy for
you. I'll see you later."

Avery hurried out, trotted down the steps just as Owen

came through the gate between the proposed bakery and the inn courtyard.

"Hey," she called out.

"Hey, yourself." Clipboard in hand, he crossed to her. "You look better."

"Than what?"

"The walking dead."

She punched him lightly in the stomach. "I'd put something behind that but I owe you. I forgot to ask how you made out in tips."

"Not bad. Pulled in about twenty-five." Instinctively he reached out to button her coat. "Just tell me Franny and Dave are back."

"Dave, yes, or he will be right about now. Franny, no. She's better, but I want her to take another day. I just had my eyes dazzled by The Penthouse. Jesus, Owen, it rocks."

"I haven't gotten up there." He glanced up. "What's in?"

"All of it. Parlor, bedroom. They're bringing in W&B now, or soon. I'm coming over later, getting in on the action. Are you going to be around?"

"It's looking like one or all of us will be around pretty much round the clock until it's done."

"Then I'll see you." But she backed up with him when the furniture truck turned in. "Oh, I want to stay. Damn needing to make a living wage."

"You can't stand here in the cold anyway." He took her hands, rubbed them. "Where are your gloves?"

"In my pocket."

"I think they work better if you wear them."

"Maybe, but then I wouldn't get a hand rub." Boosting onto her toes, she gave him a loud kiss on the cheek. "Gotta go, be back later," she said and zipped away at a lope.

She moved fast, he thought. Then again, she always had. He'd always wondered why she hadn't run track instead of cheering. When he'd asked, as he recalled, she'd rolled her eyes at him. Cuter uniforms.

He had to admit she'd looked damn cute in her cheerleading gear.

He wondered if she still had it.

He wondered if he should be thinking about Avery in her cheerleader uniform.

Then he wondered why the hell he was standing out in the cold wondering about anything.

He went inside, and work took over.

❦

THE HOURS FLEW and by the time the crew knocked off, Owen was ready for a beer.

But his mother wasn't.

Instead of hoisting a cold one, he hoisted boxes full of books up the steps of the inn.

Justine stood at the top of the steps, a rag in one of the hands fisted on her hips. "Take those right into The Library. The girls are in there, polishing up the bookshelves. Carolee and I are back in Nick and Nora."

"Yes'm." Puffing some, he trudged up, Ryder behind him with another load, Beckett bringing up the rear.

"Lot of damn books," Ryder muttered when his mother was out of earshot.

"Lot of damn shelves to fill," Owen commented.

The Library smelled of polish and perfume. Avery stood on a step stool at the far end, shining up the top shelves of one of the bookcases that flanked the hearth and mantel.

He and his brothers had built all of it in the family shop.

He remembered the work that had gone into it, the cutting, the sanding, the gluing, the staining. A lot of effort, he thought now, and a lot of satisfaction.

More satisfaction now seeing that wood gleam under the polishing rags.

"Looking fine, ladies," Beckett said as he set down his load. He wrapped his arms around Clare, pulled her back against him to nuzzle her neck. "Hi, there."

"Which one are you?" She turned her head, laughed. "Oh yeah. Mine."

"No making out till we're finished." Ryder jerked a thumb back toward the doorway. "We've got another load."

"There are two boxes in J&R." Crouched, Hope polished

the doors below the shelves. "They're marked 'Library Shelves.'"

"I'm done with my section." Avery hopped off the stool. "I'll get one of them. Give me a hand?" she asked Owen.

"Sure."

When they reached the room, Avery noted that the stacks of boxes had diminished, and it looked as though they'd been reorganized.

"You're cutting it down. Did you restack what's left?"

"It's easier to find things that way."

"You should come organize my apartment. Maybe then I'd find the purple scarf I bought at Gifts last month."

"It might help if you unpacked first."

"I mostly have."

He reserved comment. "Library's over here."

He moved around stacks to a corner by the bath.

"What are you going to do with your time when this place is finished?" she asked him.

"You mean other than working on the bakery building, Beck's house, maintaining the rentals, starting the kitchen rehab for Lynn Barney?"

"Lynn Barney's redoing her kitchen? I didn't know that."

"You don't know everything."

"I know most things. People talk over pizza and pasta." She reached down for a box marked "Library Shelves" in Hope's clear, bold print.

"That's too heavy. Take this one."

"What about the space under Hope's apartment? Her temporary apartment."

"We'll figure it out. One step at a time."

"Sometimes I like taking lots of steps at a time."

"That's how you trip." He shifted his box, propped open the door with his hip.

"But you get where you're going faster."

"Not if you trip." He shut the door behind them.

"I've got good balance. It's a great space," she added as he went through the same procedure with the porch door.

"Bakery and Beck first. The building's not going anywhere."

She wanted to argue. Why have an empty space on Main if you could fill it? But she tracked her eyes toward Nick and Nora and Justine's voice. Probably better to go straight to the top on this one, she decided.

In The Library she sorted through boxes with Hope and Clare, arranging books and trinkets on the shelves. Romances, mysteries, local history, classics. A collection of old bottles, an old model car that had been Owen's father's— iron candle stands made by her father.

"I thought we had tons," Hope commented. "I wondered if we had too much. But we need more."

"I've got some things at the bookstore, and there's always something at Gifts."

"We're going to put the tray with a whiskey decanter and glasses there, on that bottom shelf." Standing back, Hope surveyed. "But yes, a few more little things. We're good on books. You did a great job on them, Clare."

"It was a fun assignment for me."

"You know what it needs?" Avery leaned against the far wall. "We should have the crew out on the front porch, take a picture. Frame it, set it in here. The Inn BoonsBoro crew."

"Perfect. Fabulous idea. And when we get the furniture, the art." Hope glanced around. "The desk there in front of the window with a laptop for guests. The big leather guest book. The amazing leather sofa, the chairs, the lamps."

"I'll get Justine and Carolee," Clare began, "see what they think."

But as she started out, war whoops echoed up the stairs. "Sounds like my boys have invaded. I told Alva Ridenour I'd come get them, bring them in for pizza. Looks like she decided to bring them to me."

What sounded like a herd of stampeding buffalo thundered up the stairs. The women walked out in time to see Clare's three sons charge down the hall.

"Mom! Mrs. Ridenour said she and her husband wanted pizza, too. We got to come see the hotel." Harry, her eldest, flung himself at her for a hug, then started to race by.

"Hold it, hold it." Clare grabbed his hand, managed to wrap an arm around her middle child as Liam hugged her legs. After giving Harry's hand a squeeze, she hefted Murphy, her youngest, onto her hip.

"Hi!" Murphy gave his mother a wet kiss. "We did homework and had a snack and played Bendominoes and fed Ben and Yoda and Mr. Ridenour said we can each have *two* dollars to play Megatouch 'cause we behaved."

"That's good to hear."

"We wanna see the hotel." Liam tipped his head up. "So does Mrs. Ridenour and Mr. Ridenour. Can we go, Mom? Can we go see?"

"No running, no touching." She tousled Liam's already tousled golden brown waves.

"I thought I heard the troops."

"Gran!" As one, the boys surged forward to surround Justine. She hunkered down, gathered them in, and beamed up at Clare.

"I'm Gran." She gave each boy a mmm-sounding kiss on the cheeks. "That's the best ever."

"Can we see your hotel, Gran?" Murphy used his angel smile and big brown eyes. "Please? We won't touch anything."

"You bet."

"How about we start at the top?" Beckett rounded the stairs, took Clare's hand. "Ry's down showing off The Dining Room to the Ridenours. They'll head up in a minute."

"Will you come, Gran?" Harry tugged Justine's hand. "We want you to come with us."

"Couldn't keep me away."

"Beckett says we get to stay here when it's all finished." Liam grabbed Justine's other hand as Murphy held up his arms to Beckett. "And we can sleep in one of the big beds. Are you going to stay, too?"

"That's the plan. First night, we're all going to stay."

As they headed to the third floor, Avery leaned into Owen. "Isn't that the nicest picture? Isn't that really, really beautiful? Clare and the boys, Clare and Beckett, Clare and Beckett and the boys. Your mom with all of them." She sniffled a little, laid a hand on her heart. "It gets me."

"Takes the pressure off me and Ry. I'm joking," he said

when she narrowed her damp eyes. "Mom's crazy about those kids."

"Lucky kids. They have three grandmothers now."

"My dad would've loved them."

"I know." With a tug on her heart, she rubbed his back. "He was always great with kids. I remember those cookouts at your place, how he'd run around with us. I was nuts about him. Anytime he came over to hang out with my dad, he was always, 'Hey there, Red, what's the word?'"

She let out a sigh. "Looks like I'm sentimental tonight. Come on, take a look at what we've done in The Library."

"Dad thought of you like one of his."

"Oh, Owen."

"He did. Your dad was like his brother, so you were one of us. He always told me to keep an eye out for you."

"He did not."

"Yeah, he did." He gave her stubby, coppery ponytail a gentle yank before he stepped into The Library. "Wow. Nice job—and quick work."

"It was all organized," she said, and laughed. "As you well know. It needs some filling in, and I had this idea about taking a photo of the crew on the front porch. We could frame it, put it here. It's part of the history of the place now."

"You're right. We'll set it up."

"I can take it—especially if I can talk Ryder into letting me use his camera. Let me know when everybody can do it, and I'll be here. Where's Hope?" she wondered.

"She went into Nick and Nora with Carolee, probably finishing up in there."

"She'll never finish unless somebody makes her. Go make her." She gave Owen a nudge. "Tell her she should come over for dinner, and Carolee, too. You and Ry are probably ready for a beer and some food."

"I've been ready."

"Go get her going then. She'll listen to you. I'd better run over and warn my crew we're having a party of many coming in. I'll see if I can take over the back room for you."

"Us. You've got to eat."

Amused, she angled her head. "Keeping your eye out for me?"

"I'm an obedient son."

"When it suits you. See you over there."

They separated, but as she passed Elizabeth and Darcy, Avery heard voices. Assuming part of the tour had stopped at that point, she eased open the door.

There was Murphy in the empty room, standing by the open door of the porch, chattering away. To no one.

"Murph?"

"Hi!"

"Hi. Baby, it's cold out. You can't open the doors."

"I didn't. I didn't touch anything. She likes to go out so she can see."

Cautious, Avery crossed to the door, hunched against the cold as she looked up and down the porch. "Who likes to go out?"

"The lady. She says I can call her Lizzy like Beckett does."

"Oh." Avery felt a chill now that had nothing to do with the open door. "Oh boy. Um . . . is she here now?"

"Right out there, by the rail." He pointed. "She said not to come out, 'cause my mom would worry."

"She's got that right."

"She's waiting."

"She is? For what?"

"For Billy. Are we gonna get pizza now?"

"Ah . . . yeah, in a minute." Avery jumped like a rabbit when the door opened from the hall. Then she laughed, weakly, when Owen stared at her. "We're just . . . I don't know. Murphy, I hear your mom and Beck upstairs. You go on up, okay? And promise me you'll stay right with them."

"Okay. I just wanted to see Lizzy. She likes to have somebody to talk to. Bye!"

"Holy shit," Avery said when he scrambled out. "I heard people—and I mean people talking, so I opened the door. All I saw was Murphy, and the open door. But he said the lady—Lizzy—is standing out there by the rail. He sees her, and he talks to her. I heard *voices*, Owen, not just a voice. And—"

"Slow down, take a breath."

He came in, shut the porch door.

"But she's out there. Shouldn't you wait until she comes back in?"

"I think she can handle it."

"And maybe she is back in." Wide-eyed, Avery leaned back on the door. "That was so . . . so *cool*! Murphy Brewster, Ghost Whisperer. He said she's waiting for somebody named Billy. I have *got* to stay in this room. Maybe I'd have a close encounter—except that's aliens, isn't it? Wow."

This time Owen set his hands on her shoulders. She revved like an engine. "Now take another breath."

"I'm okay. It's exciting, and a little unnerving—but in a really cool way. Why are you so calm?"

"You sucked in all the excitement. Waiting for Billy?"

"That's what Murphy said, and he seems to have a direct line. Maybe Billy's her husband, or lover."

"Husbands are generally lovers."

"You know what I mean. And she's been waiting for him here all these years. Just waiting for her Billy. It's so romantic."

"Sounds tragic to me."

"No, well, yes, but romantic, too. A love that's eternal, that lasts—because they rarely do in reality, right?"

"I don't know about that," he began, but she was still bubbling over.

"It holds her here because this love is *powerful*. It's magic. It's what matters most. It's—"

The door at her back pushed open, knocking her forward and straight into Owen. His arms came tight around to balance her as she tipped back her head, looked up into his eyes. "Everything," she finished.

He didn't speak. They stood there, bodies pressed with the open door at her back, and the sound of running and laughter streaming down the hall outside the room.

He thought, what the hell? What the hell?

Then his mouth was on hers, and her fingers dived into his hair.

Hot and bright—it's how he thought of her, how the kiss struck him now. Hot and bright, full of light and energy. Of Avery.

Everything went frantic, breathless, with a sharp, grinding need in his center, a heated rush under his skin. He lost track of everything else, everything beyond the taste and movement of her, the demands of her mouth, the scent of lemons and of honeysuckle.

She balanced on her toes, clamped against him like a vise while the thrill and wonder ran a river through her. She let it rage, a fast, tumultuous ride that swept her toward the unknown even as it trapped her in the moment.

He broke away first, stared down at her like a man coming out of a trance. "What was that? What *was* that?"

"I don't know." And wasn't sure she cared, not when his arms tightened around her again. She held that shimmering instant, leaned in.

Someone banged on the door.

"Owen? Avery?" Beckett called out. "What's going on? Unlock the damn door."

"Hold on." Carefully, Owen released Avery. "Hold on," he repeated, to her this time. Catching his breath, he crossed to the door. It opened smoothly.

"What the hell?" Beckett demanded, then tracked his gaze to the open porch door. "Oh."

"It's nothing. It's okay. I'll take care of it."

"Murphy said you and Avery were in here." Beckett glanced over his shoulder to make sure the kids weren't close by. "Are you all right?"

"Yeah. All good. We're, ah, going for pizza."

"Right. Make sure that door's shut."

"I've got it." Quietly, Avery shut the porch door, turned the latch.

"Good enough. I'll see you at Vesta."

Beckett gave them both one last look before he walked away.

Staring at Avery, Owen stood where he was, one hand on the knob of the open door.

"I guess that was weird," she began. "Was that weird?"

"I don't know."

"I guess . . . all that talk about romance and love . . . It just triggered whatever."

"Yeah. Probably. Okay."

She took a long breath, crossed to him. "I don't want it to be weird."

"Okay."

"We should probably get out of here. This room, I mean."

"Okay."

"I'm going over to give Dave a hand."

"Okay."

She punched him in the chest. "Is that all you can say? Okay, okay, okay?"

"Right now it seems safest."

"Safest, my ass." She let out a long breath again. "It's not going to be weird, and don't say okay."

She sailed away, and down the stairs.

"Okay," he said under his breath.

He closed the door. When he stepped away, he thought he heard the whisper of female laughter behind it.

"Yeah, some joke," he muttered. Stuffing his hands in his pockets, he scowled his way downstairs.

## CHAPTER FOUR

✂

T HE COLD GRIPPED WINTER IN A BREATHLESS, FRIGID
   stranglehold. Under the harsh blue skies, every breath
of air blew bitter. Another hard frost slicked The Courtyard
pavers as Owen trooped up the outside stairs with Beckett
and Ryder.

"I don't want to hear about any changes, flourishes, or
what-ifs," Ryder muttered.

"Let's just take a look at this." Beckett led the way into
Jane and Rochester.

"Hell of a lot of boxes yet." Ryder stuffed his hands in
his pockets. "Looks like Mom bought enough lamps to light
half the town."

"We might as well take down what we can for N&N when
we go back." Owen gestured to the appropriate area. "What's
the problem in here, Beck?"

"I don't know if there is one, but it's about the only private spot in the building right now, and we've been surrounded since last night—plus you took off from Avery's
before I could corner you. Now, what the hell happened with
Elizabeth?"

"For Christ's sake." Ryder pulled off his cap, dragged his fingers through his dense dark brown hair. "You brought us up here to talk ghosts?"

"Murphy was in that room," Beckett reminded him. "Alone, hall door shut, porch door open. He just turned goddamn six. Clare's not so freaked by Lizzy anymore. If it hadn't been for Lizzy writing in the steam on the bathroom mirror down there—however she managed to pull that off— to warn us, we might not have gotten there in time when Freemont went after Clare. Still, Murphy's just a little boy."

"Okay." Ryder stuck his cap back on. "Okay, you're right about that. But this whole ghost thing's irritating."

"Park benches are irritating to you in some moods."

"Depends on whether or not I want to sit down."

Beckett just shook his head. "We got most of it out of Murphy. The kid's got no off button. He decided to go pay her a visit, and went on in. He told her about school, about the pups. She asked after his family."

"So Murph the Smurf had a social conversation with a ghost," Ryder commented. "He needs his own TV show. Murph, Host for Ghosts."

"Funny," Beckett said dryly. "She went outside, but told him not to come out, that his mother wouldn't like it. She'd worry. And she told him she liked to stand out there. How she was waiting for Billy. Now that the inn was being fixed, and there were lights and people, she thought he'd be able to find her easier."

"Billy who?" Ryder asked.

"Exactly. Murphy didn't get that part."

"Why are you looking at me?" Owen demanded. "I wasn't in on any of that. When I went in, Avery was already there, and she had Murphy. We sent him up to Clare so she wouldn't worry."

"Yeah, then he chatted away about Lizzy, about you and Avery being in there. And I couldn't get the door open. It wouldn't budge."

"So, she was playing games." Owen shrugged, trying for casual, ending with a jerk. "It's not the first time."

"Won't be the last," Ryder muttered.

"No, not the first or the last," Beckett agreed. "But when you opened the door from the inside, you looked like somebody'd knocked you stupid with a blunt object. I want to know what happened between the time you sent Murphy out and when you opened up."

"Nothing. Especially."

"Bullshit." Ryder let out a snort. "You can't lie worth dick. And if it was nothing especially, why were you all broody over at Vesta? Like a hen on a nest of cracked eggs, then you made noises about paperwork and took off." Grinning now, Ryder nodded at Beckett. "It was something especially."

"Cough it up, Owen," Beckett told him.

"Fine. Fine. Avery filled me in on what Murphy told her. She's all excited and dreamy. The ghost deal, the waiting for Billy thing. Like it's a made-for-TV movie. Romantic, love beyond the grave, all that stuff. You know how Avery can get on a theme."

"Not really." Ryder shrugged. "I've never had a romantic, love-beyond-the-grave conversation with Avery. You?" he asked Beckett.

"Not as I recall. Then again, Owen was her first boyfriend."

"Cut it out." Caught between embarrassment and annoyance, Owen shuffled his feet. "She was like five, maybe six. Like Murphy's age. Jesus."

"She said she was going to marry you," Beckett reminded him, snorting along with Ryder now. "And you'd have three dogs, two cats, and five babies. Or maybe it was three babies and five dogs."

"You got her a ring, bro."

Trapped, Owen bared his teeth at Ryder. "Out of a frigging gum ball machine. Just playing around. I was a kid, too, for Christ's sake."

"Kissed her, right on the mouth," Beckett remembered.

"It just happened! That honeysuckle-smelling, short-tempered ghost of yours shoved the porch door back open when Avery was leaning against it. The next thing I know she's wrapped around me, and . . ."

Brows lifted, Beckett angled his head as he studied Owen's face. "I was talking about when she was five."

"Oh."

"But bring us up to date," Ryder insisted. "You laid one on the Little Red Machine?"

"It just happened," he insisted. "The door knocked her into me."

"Yeah, anytime a woman trips, I'm all over them."

"Suck me," Owen said to Ryder.

"Must've been a hell of a just-happened lip-lock," Beckett speculated. "Considering how you looked when you unlocked the door."

"I didn't *unlock* the door because it wasn't *locked*. She did it."

"Red?"

"No, not Avery. Elizabeth. Then she laughed."

"Avery?"

"No!" Close to tearing out his hair, Owen paced between stacks of boxes. "Elizabeth. After Avery got pissed and left, I heard her laughing."

"Avery got pissed because you kissed her?" Beckett asked.

"No. Maybe. How the hell do I know what pisses a woman off?" Frustration rippled over him in waves. "Nobody knows because it can be any damn thing. It's an unsolved mystery. And the next day, that any damn thing is fine, and it's some other damn thing. No man knows," Owen said darkly.

"He ain't wrong," Ryder commented. "So. Back up." Ryder hooked his thumbs in his pockets. "Did she kiss you back? Men know that one, pal."

"Yeah, she kissed me back."

"Like reflex, or bring it on?"

"She was in it," Owen muttered. "It wasn't some friendly peck."

"Tongues?"

"Jesus, Ry."

"You're not the only one who appreciates details." Ryder nodded at Beckett. "Definitely tongues involved."

"I said she was in it, didn't I? Then Beck's banging on the door, and it's all surreal. She didn't want it to be weird, you know? So I said okay. She said she was going to go give Dave a hand, and I said okay."

"You're a moron." In pity, Ryder shook his head. "You're supposed to be the smart one. You're the smart one, Beckett's the nice one, I'm the good-looking one. And you're a moron. You just fucked the curve, dude."

"Why? Why am I a moron?"

Beckett raised his hand. "I got this. You kiss a woman till your eyes roll back in your head, and if your information is correct, she's just as in it as you. Then all you can say when she's obviously probing for what it meant is 'okay'? You're a moron."

"She didn't want it to be weird. I was trying not to make it weird."

"You get a shove from a dead woman and end up tangling tongues with an old girlfriend *and* the ghost blocks the exit? That's fucking weird," Ryder concluded.

"She's not an old girlfriend. She was five!"

Companionably now, Ryder laid a hand on Owen's shoulder. "Women never forget. You don't want it to be weirder than it is now, you have to talk to her about it. You poor bastard."

"Avery was right," Beckett speculated. "Lizzy's a romantic. The first time I kissed Clare was in this building—and after, I figured Lizzy maneuvered it. At least some of it."

"Then you talk to her," Owen insisted. "Tell her to back off."

"Kissing Red must've killed off some of your brain cells," Ryder decided. "You can tell a woman what to do—if you play it right—and maybe, *maybe* half the time she'd do it, or something close to it. That's a live woman. A dead one? I figure that's closer to zero."

"Crap."

"Better talk to Avery," Beckett advised. "And do it soon, do it right."

"Crap."

"So, now that we've had our heart-to-heart, ladies, let's get the hell back to work." Ryder walked to the door, opened it. "We've got an inn to finish."

❧

HE COULDN'T AVOID her—not that he wanted to. Exactly. But he couldn't, not between punch-out, load-in, cleaning, food breaks. In the normal course of things, he saw Avery at least once a week. Since work began on the inn, it was pretty much daily. And now with that work coming down the stretch, they tended to cross paths multiple times a day.

But—because he *wasn't* a moron—none of those times included the sort of privacy he knew the conversation they needed to have required.

Even if he could find a spot where a half a dozen people weren't moving through, by, or around, he got interrupted every ten minutes.

So he did what he decided was the next best thing. He acted as if nothing had happened. He talked to her, carted boxes for her, ordered food from her, just like normal over the next couple of days.

Since she behaved exactly the same way, he figured: problem solved.

For his last chore of the day—hopefully of the week, he thought—he carried a box of lightbulbs into Nick and Nora. He intended to work his way through the finished rooms, assembling lamps, screwing in the correct bulbs.

He hesitated only a moment when he saw Avery hanging glass drops on a floor lamp.

She glanced his way. "Some assembly required," she said.

"Looks good."

"I'm hanging these my way. I like it better than the way they have it in the diagram. Justine said she did, too."

"Works for me." He noted that the stacked glass ball lamps beside the panel bed had already been assembled.

"I'm Lamp Girl this evening," she told him.

He started to make a joke about being Lightbulb Boy, but thought better of it.

Damn it. It *was* weird.

"I'm the man with the bulbs, so let there be light." He took a bulb out of the box. "Listen, Avery—"

"Look!" Hope dashed in, still wearing her coat and scarf. "Isn't this fabulous?"

She carried a Deco-style statue of a man and woman.

"It's great! It's Nick and Nora Charles." Avery shifted to admire it.

"The amazing people at Bast gave it to us."

"Aww. Now I love it even more."

"It's just perfect!" After a moment's scan, Hope set it on the corner of the carved heater cover Owen had built. "Just perfect. I love that floor lamp. A little glimmer, a lot of glamour and style. Oh, when you're done there, Avery, maybe you can give us an opinion out in J&R. Owen, we're trying to decide on your grandmother's crocheted pieces, the ones your mother had matted and framed. They're so beautiful. She was an artist."

"If she'd had enough thread, she could've crocheted the Taj Mahal."

"I believe it. We've narrowed it down to two spots. We need another eye, Avery."

"You can have mine. That's the last drop. Thank God." She stepped back, nodded. "Excellent."

"Come on down then. We have to decide, then that's it for tonight."

"Good, because I need to run over, take care of a couple of things."

"After you do, come to my place," Hope told her. "Clare's parents have the kids tonight, and Beckett's got a dinner meeting with a client. We'll have some wine, and I'll cook something."

"I'm in. Two minutes here."

As Hope went out, Avery crouched to gather up the packaging from the lamp. "They're even prettier lit," she commented when Owen tested the lamps.

"Yeah. So, Avery . . . are we okay?"

After a humming beat of silence, she flicked him a glance. "There's that word again."

"Come on, Avery."

Still crouched, she gave him a long, steady stare from under her arched eyebrows. "I'm okay. Are you okay?"

"Yeah, it's just—"

"Sounds like we're okay. It wasn't my first kiss, Owen."

"No, but—"

"Not even my first with you."

He shifted the box of bulbs to his other hip. "That was—"

"So, no problem here."

"No problem," he agreed, but thought it felt like one. "I'll get that stuff. We've got a load to take out anyway."

"Good enough." She started out. "Oh, if you have time, maybe you can hang the mirror, that starburst deal there. Hope marked the spot on the wall."

"Sure."

"Have a good weekend if I don't see you."

"Yeah, you, too."

He frowned at the cardboard, frowned at the mirror, frowned at the empty doorway.

"Shit," he muttered, and went out for his drill.

∽✿∾

"ARE WE OKAY?" Avery gestured with her wineglass. "Jerk."

In Hope's living room, curled on the sofa, Clare smiled at her friend. "He just doesn't know how to handle it."

Far from ready to cut him a break, Avery huffed. "He didn't have any problem handling *me* the other night."

"Beckett got awkward and a little jerky with me after we almost kissed the first time. Maybe it's a Montgomery brothers trait."

"Once you had, he wasn't awkward."

"True." Clare's smile warmed. "Very true. Still, given your history—"

"History-smistory."

"What history?" Hope carried a tray of fruit and cheese out of her little kitchen. "I haven't had the opportunity to get all the details on this. Ghostly nudges, hot kiss, lame Owen aftermath."

"That sums it."

"History? Is this more than knowing each other forever? Clare and Beckett knew each other for years before they got together."

"I was with Clint," Clare reminded her. "We were a couple from the start, so I didn't have any history other than casual friendship with Beckett."

"And you had more with Owen?" Hope probed. "What have I missed?"

"They were engaged." Grinning now, Clare toasted Avery.

"What?" Hope's dark chocolate eyes rounded with shock. "When? Why didn't I know this? This is *huge*."

"We were kids. I think I was five—almost six. Our fathers were tight, so we had a lot of activities together. I had a crush on him."

"So she proposed to him—or more she announced they were going to get married when they grew up."

"Aw, that's so cute."

Softening a little, Avery shrugged. "It was probably a major embarrassment for him. I guess he was about eight. But he was nice about it. Patient," she remembered, softening a bit more. "I crushed on him for a couple of years."

"That's a long time at that age," Hope pointed out.

"I tend to dig in. Then he started hanging out with Kirby Anderson." The softening process halted as her eyes went flinty. "That ten-year-old slut. Owen Montgomery broke my heart with that boyfriend-stealing bimbo."

"I should point out, for Hope, that Kirby Anderson is now married, the mother of two, and an environmental activist living in Arlington, Virginia."

"She grew out of it." Avery shrugged. "But there could still be slutitude in there, dormant. Anyway, after that I was off boys until I hit puberty."

"But you forgave Owen," Hope prompted.

"Sure. I refused to pine. Besides, a girl's first boyfriend isn't going to be her last, right?" After gesturing, she cut a slice of Gouda and nipped into it. "Especially when he's an ass."

"Don't be too hard on him." Clare reached over, patted

Avery's hand. "He's probably flustered, not sure how to act. You know you mean a lot to him. To all of them."

"Yeah, yeah." But she sighed. "It was a damn fine kiss. He's learned a lot since eight—or I've learned. We both have. I wouldn't mind kissing him again."

"Really?" Hope drew out the word as she sampled an apple slice.

"Sure. What am I, stupid? He's a damn fine kisser—as I now know. And he's really pretty."

"Would you sleep with him?" Hope wondered.

"Hmm." Considering, Avery reached forward, snagged a tart, green grape. "We're both currently unattached, both adults. Maybe. Yeah, maybe, as long as we went into it clear-eyed. You can trust Owen. That's a big one, knowing you're with somebody you can trust." She bit into the grape, grinned. "And who's really pretty."

"Listening to all this, I'm glad I'm out of the arena." Content, Hope slid down in the chair with her wine.

"You won't stay out." Avery shook her head. "You're gorgeous, smart, interesting—and human."

"I'm not interested in dating right now. Not just because of Jonathan. In fact, now that I think about it, not at all because of that *dick*. Right now, all I want is to focus on the inn, on being the world's best innkeeper, and keeping that beautiful place perfect. Men, dating, sex? Just not currently on the radar."

"Careful," Clare warned. "Best-laid plans."

"But I excel at planning."

⁊⧵

OWEN DIDN'T SLEEP well, which he considered a pisser. He *always* slept well. He thought of it as a skill, like carpentry or adding up columns of numbers in his head.

But instead of dropping off after a full day of work, a sweaty hour-long workout, a relaxing soak in his hot tub, he'd slept in fits and starts.

He'd promised himself no work over the weekend, but when a man climbed out of bed before sunrise, what the hell was he supposed to do with himself all day?

His house was in order. It generally was, but with the push on the inn over the last couple of weeks, he'd barely done more than sleep there. Even he couldn't find anything to fuss over.

He and Beckett had designed the house, a couple of stones' throws from his mother's, from Ryder's, from the home Beckett was finally finishing. He liked being close to family, and still solitary and private on his wooded lot.

The space suited him and his efficient nature with its open kitchen and dining room serving as great room and entertainment area when he had anybody over. To the left, the laundry and utility room served the added purpose of mudroom.

He believed in multitasking, even for houses.

Now, wearing only loose flannel pants, he stood at the atrium doors leading out to his wide, paved patio, drinking coffee ground and brewed in the sleek and efficient machine he'd treated himself to on his last birthday.

Ryder called it Hilda, claiming anything that shiny and complicated had to be female.

Generally that first good, strong cup of coffee pleased him, perked him up for the day ahead. But right at the moment it did nothing to cut through his irritability.

She was the one being weird, he told himself—as he had countless times during the restless night. She'd said she didn't want things to be weird, then *she* acted weird. Trying to make him feel guilty, he decided, when he didn't have anything to feel guilty about.

It was all just stupid, and he needed to forget it. Because he damn well wasn't losing another night's sleep over it.

He thought about breakfast, but didn't feel like cooking. Not that he minded cooking, particularly a weekend breakfast where he could load up on bacon and eggs, sit at his counter, and play with his iPad.

He didn't feel like using his iPad either, and that was just wrong. He always felt like using his iPad.

So he'd work after all. He'd put some time in at the shop on the mantel for Beckett's bedroom fireplace. Maybe even get it finished so Beckett could just seal the chestnut.

No point in hanging out at home all day if he couldn't enjoy the loafing. Plus, his mother habitually rose early, he thought as he headed up the central stairs he and his brothers had built. She'd cook him some breakfast—and maybe he could pump her a little—subtly—about Avery.

Not that he'd tell his mother the full shot—it was too . . . okay, weird. But he knew no one who had better insight on people than Justine Montgomery.

He turned into his bedroom, switched on the little gas log fireplace built into the mocha-colored wall, and carried his coffee into the bath. Once he'd showered and shaved, he dressed in work clothes and steel-toed boots.

He made the bed—smoothing the sheets, drawing the white duvet up, stacking the pillows in their dark brown cases.

He took his phone off the charger, hooked it on his belt, took his pocketknife, loose change, wallet out of the tray on his dresser. Got a fresh bandana out of the dresser drawer.

He stood a moment, frowning at nothing. Too quiet, he realized. His house and grounds were exactly the way he liked them, work was plentiful, and satisfying. But it was just too quiet.

Time for a dog, he told himself. Time to seriously think about getting a dog. Maybe a Lab-mix like his mother's—or a faithful mutt like Ryder's.

He'd promised himself a dog, but with the time and demands of the inn project, he'd postponed the idea.

Better to wait till spring, he considered as he started downstairs. Easier to house-train a puppy in warmer weather. Or maybe he'd rescue an older dog—if he could get half as lucky as Ry had with Dumbass.

He pulled his shop coat out of the closet, pulled on a ski cap, gloves, plucked his keys out of the dish by the door.

A guy needed a dog, he thought. That was what was missing in his life. A good dog.

Maybe he'd swing by the animal shelter after he'd had breakfast with his mother, after he put in some shop time.

Nodding in satisfaction, he climbed into his truck. Sounded like a plan—and he liked a good plan.

He pulled out, drove past the little barn he'd built to house the jeep and plow he used on the property, down to the main road. He made the turn, turned again into his mother's lane to her house on the slope.

The dogs bounded across the drive—Cus (short for Atticus) with one of his many mangled balls clamped in his mouth, and his eyes wild with joy. His brother Finch gave Cus a body block that had both dogs rolling and wrestling.

Yeah, Owen thought with a grin, he definitely needed a dog.

He wound the drive, puzzled for a moment when he saw Willy B's truck parked beside his mother's car.

Early for a visit, Owen thought, even for Avery's father. Then again, Willy B dropped by often, Owen knew, and now that he was one of the featured artists at his mother's gift shop, he likely dropped by more with some new piece or design.

Stroke of luck, Owen decided as he parked. He might be able to finesse some insight or info out of Willy B on Avery—subtle, subtle.

He stopped long enough to snatch up the ball Cus had dropped pleadingly at his feet. He winged it, long and hard for the dogs to chase while he hurried up to the back door.

He heard the music when he was still ten feet away, and shook his head. Typical for his mom—who'd never yelled at any of her sons to turn that damn music down.

She'd always blasted her own.

He shoved open the door, caught the scent of bacon, of coffee. Grinning, he thought: just in time.

Then his eyes all but popped out of his head.

Bacon sizzled on the stove. His mother stood in front of the griddle.

So did Willy B, all six feet four inches of him wearing nothing but white boxers, with his hands on Owen's mother's ass, and his mouth locked on hers.

## CHAPTER FIVE

HE MUST HAVE MADE SOME SOUND THAT CUT through the blast of music and the jaw-dropping embrace. Maybe he screamed. He hoped he hadn't screamed, at least not outside of his head.

But his mother—an open robe over short red pajama pants and a thin (way too thin) white tank—stepped back. Her eyes met Owen's, blinked once.

Then she laughed.

She laughed.

Willy B had the grace to blush as red as his tumbled hair and trim beard.

"What?" Owen managed, shocked to the bone. "What—you— *What?*"

"I'm fixing us some breakfast," Justine said easily, and with that laugh still fluttering on the edges. "I guess I need to break some more eggs."

"You— But— What? Mom."

"Try to make a complete sentence, Owen. Have some coffee." She reached for a mug.

"Ah . . . I should . . ." Still bright red, Willy B shuffled his enormous feet. "Put some pants on."

"Yes!" Owen felt his hands flapping in the air, but just couldn't stop them. "That. Pants. You. Please God."

Rumbling in his throat, Willy B scooted off like a bear toward his cave.

*"Mom."*

"That's my name." All cheer, Justine beamed smiles. "Sit down, honey. Drink your coffee."

"What—"

Justine picked up tongs to take the bacon out to drain. "Finish it this time. I'll get you started. What . . . ?"

"What—" He had to swallow the tight, prickly ball in his throat. It didn't go down well. "What are you doing? Here. With him. Naked."

Eyebrows hiked, Justine looked down at herself. "I'm not naked."

"Almost."

Obviously fighting another smile, Justine closed her robe, belted it. "Better?"

"Yes. No. I don't know. My head. Did my head explode?" He patted his hands over it.

Without missing a beat, Justine took eggs and milk from the big refrigerator. "I was going to scramble eggs, but under the circumstances, we'll have French toast. You're partial to French toast. You haven't had breakfast, have you?"

"No. Mom, I don't understand this."

"What part of this don't you understand, baby?"

"Any of it. All of it."

"All right, let me explain. When people grow up, they often want to be close to each other. It's best if they really like and respect each other. An important part of that closeness includes sex, which means—"

"Mom." Heat crept up his neck, but he wasn't sure what emotion kindled it. "Cut it out."

"So you do understand that part. Willy B and I really like and respect each other, and sometimes we have sex."

"Don't, don't, don't say Willy B and sex, with you, in the same sentence."

"Then I can't explain, can I? Suck it up, Owen," she advised, and offered him a slice of bacon.

"But . . ." He took the bacon. He couldn't defog his brain to speak coherently.

"I loved your father. So, so much. I was eighteen when I first saw him—my very first day on the job for Wilson Contractors. There he was, standing on that ladder, torn jeans, big boots, tool belt, no shirt. And oh my God." She laid a hand on her heart. "I couldn't see straight the rest of the day. Tom Montgomery. My Tommy."

She got out a bowl, began to mix the eggs and milk with a fork. "I couldn't even pretend to be coy when he asked me out. I never went out with anyone else from that first date. Never wanted anyone else. I never loved anyone like I did your daddy."

"I know, Mom."

"We had a good life. He was such a good man. Smart, strong, funny. Such a good man, such a good father. We built the business together because we wanted our own. And this house, this family—it's all got Tommy all over it. All of you have him in you, some of it in the way you are, some in the way you look. You got his mouth, Beckett his eyes, Ryder his hands. And more. I treasure that."

"I'm sorry." Watching her, hearing her, he felt his heart drop into his guts. "I'm sorry. Don't cry."

"They aren't sad tears. They're grateful ones." She added sugar, a dash of vanilla, generous shakes of cinnamon. "We had a wonderful, interesting, busy life together, and he died. You don't know—I never let you know—how mad I was at him for dying on me. So mad, for weeks, months. I don't know how long. He wasn't supposed to die on me. We were supposed to be together, forever, and then he was gone. He's gone, Owen, and I'll miss him as long as I live."

"Me, too."

She reached across the counter, laid a hand over Owen's, then turned, got a loaf of bread.

"Willy B loved Tommy. They were as close as you boys are to each other."

"I know that. I know that, Mom."

"We needed each other when Tommy died. We needed somebody else who'd loved him, who could tell stories about him. Somebody to lean on, to cry on, to laugh with. And that's what we did, *all* we did, for a long time. Then a couple years ago, we . . . let's just say I started fixing him breakfast now and again."

"A couple . . . years."

"Maybe I should've told you." She shrugged as she dunked bread in the milk and eggs. "Maybe I wasn't sure I wanted to talk about my sex life with my grown sons. And the fact is, Willy B's shy."

"Are you . . . in love with him?"

"I love him, of course I do. I have for years, just like Tommy loved him. He's a good man, you know that. He's a good father—and he had to raise Avery alone when her mother took off the way she did. He's got kindness layered all the way through him. In love?" Coated bread sizzled on the griddle. "We enjoy each other, Owen. Like being together when we have time. We each have our own place, our own lives, our own family. We're happy the way things are, and that's enough for anyone.

"Now, can I tell him to come on down, have some breakfast?"

"Yeah, sure. Maybe I should go."

"You sit right there. I made enough egg batter for a damn army." She stepped out of the kitchen, set her hands on her hips and called out. "Willy B, you've got your pants on by now, so come on down here and have your breakfast."

Stepping back, she flipped another line of bread, plated bacon and French toast, slid plates over the counter.

By the time Willy B shuffled in, she'd put another line of bread on the griddle. "Sit down and eat," she ordered. "Don't let it get cold."

"It looks real good, Justine." Rumbling in his throat, Willy B sat on the stool beside Owen.

Out of the corner of her eye, Justine gave Owen *the look*.

"Um, so . . . how's it going, Willy B?"

"Oh, you know."

"Yeah." With no real choice, Owen dumped syrup on his toast.

"Ah . . . the inn's coming along real nice," Willy B ventured. "It sure makes a picture on The Square. Your dad, he'd be real proud and pleased."

"He would." Owen sighed. "The women have put some of your fancy work around. It looks good in there."

"Don't that beat all?"

At the stove, Justine flipped more bread, and smiled as the two men stumbled their way through breakfast conversation.

He got through it. He still wasn't sure what to think about it, but he got through breakfast with his mother's . . . with Willy B. The dogs trooped out to the shop with him, with Cus, always hopeful, carrying one of his balls.

Owen flipped on the lights, the shop radio, boosted the heat up. And after thirty minutes of fumbling, gave it up. His brain just refused to engage, and he wouldn't risk his hand at the fancy work.

He turned down the heat, turned off the radio, the lights. The dogs dutifully followed him out. To please Cus, he gave the ball a solid kick before climbing back into his truck.

Straight, sweaty carpentry, he decided, and headed over to Beckett's property. He had enough brain in him to do some framing in on the extra rooms they'd added on for Clare's boys.

He spotted his brothers' trucks as he drove back, and couldn't decide if it relieved or unnerved him.

What did he say? Did he say anything?

Of course he did. He had to tell them—plus it meant he wouldn't be flustered and weirded-out alone.

He heard the music from hammer and saw, and Beckett's iPod as he got his tool belt out of the truck.

The place was coming along, Owen thought, especially considering work on it was squeezed in and juggled around the inn project. They had the addition to the original, unfinished structure under roof—thank God, considering the weather. Windows looked good, he decided, and would offer a nice view. The decks and patios for outdoor living would have to wait till spring, but if they could knock the rest out by April, Beckett and his new family could move in right after the wedding.

He went in through what would be the kitchen door, did a short walk-through before climbing the temporary stairs to the second floor.

Freaking huge, he thought, but supposed that made sense for a family of five. The generous master suite included a full-size fireplace the boys had told Beckett their mom had always wanted. Another full bath linked two more bedrooms. Another bathroom, another two bedrooms spread out on the second level, he recalled.

As he headed toward the noise, D.A. wandered over to greet him. The dog sat, eyes trained on Owen's face. He thumped his tail.

"I got nothing." Owen spread his empty hands before giving D.A. a rub. He avoided saying the words *food* or *eat* so D.A. didn't get any false hope.

He walked into one of the bedrooms, where Beckett ran the saw and Ryder framed in a closet.

"You don't call, you don't write," Owen said over the din.

With a grin, Beckett straightened, pulled off his safety glasses. "Ry just showed up. I should've known you wouldn't be far behind. Appreciate it."

"No donuts?" Ryder asked, and D.A. thumped his tail.

"Not on me."

"Clare's opening the store this morning, then picking up the kids from her parents' about noon—running some errands. She can pick up some subs or whatever. They're coming here to help anyway."

"Pity him."

Beckett gave Ryder a shrug. "Dad gave us plenty of on-the-job training when we were their age."

"I didn't know enough to pity him at the time. And speaking of time, you could've saved a lot of it by cutting back on the bedrooms. What do you need five for anyway? Unless Clare won't sleep with you."

"One for each kid," Owen said, "master suite, guest room."

"Pull-out down in the family room would take care of anybody who stayed over. Or same deal in the office."

"Actually, we're going to need five. We're going to have another kid."

Owen paused in the act of pulling off his coat. "Clare's pregnant?"

"Not yet. We're waiting until after we actually get married, but then it's full steam ahead."

"You don't make a kid with steam," Ryder pointed out, then lowered his hammer. "Four kids? Seriously?"

"It's just one more than three."

Owen shook his head. "I think, when it comes to kids, the number increases exponentially. But what the hell. You guys are great with three, you should be great with four."

"Mom'll go nuts at the idea of another grandkid." Ryder pulled out some framing nails.

"Ah, speaking of Mom. I figured to do some shop work, so I stopped by the house this morning."

"To mooch breakfast," Ryder concluded.

"It was a factor. So anyway, Willy B was there."

"Another breakfast moocher." Pulling down his goggles, Beckett reached for the saw.

"Don't turn that on yet." A man could lose a finger, Owen thought.

With a frown, Beckett pulled his glasses off again. "Is there a problem with Mom?"

"No. I don't know. No. It's not a problem for her, anyway."

"Who's got a problem?" Ryder demanded.

"Just let me finish, damn it. I went in the kitchen, and Mom was already cooking breakfast, and Willy B was there. In nothing but his boxers, and they're . . . you know."

Now Ryder set his hammer aside. "They're what? Exactly?"

"They're . . ." Owen made a circle with his arms. "Except Willy B's hands are on Mom's ass, and she's wearing a robe, but it's open, and there's not all that much she's wearing under it. And I don't want to talk about that part."

"He had his hands on her?" Ryder said softly. "Okay. He's big, but he's old. I can take him."

"Hold on." Beckett shot out a hand, shoved Ryder back. "Are you saying Mom and Willy B are . . ."

"That's what I'm saying. And they have been for a couple years now."

"Fuck," Ryder muttered.

"Don't say *fuck* when he's telling us about Mom and Willy B. I don't want that verb and those names together in my head." Beckett walked over, picked up the liter of Coke he'd brought along, gulped straight from the bottle. "Everybody take a breath, okay. You're saying Mom and Willy B are . . . involved."

"She says they're . . . involved now and then. She laid it out for me when he went up to put some pants on. They've been friends forever. They both loved Dad. You know he loved Dad, that's no bullshit."

"Yeah, yeah."

"Ry," Beckett murmured.

"Okay, shit. Okay, yeah they were tight. It's not bullshit. But if this is all good for Mom, why are they sneaking around?"

"It's more being discreet, I think, at least that's how it struck me once she'd laid it out. She talked to me about how she felt when Dad died, and she cried."

"Shit." Ryder paced to the window, stared out.

"She and Willy B care about each other, we know that. They leaned on each other when Dad died, we know that, too. I guess, after a while . . ."

"They started leaning on each other naked."

"Goddamn it, Ry." Beckett pressed his fingers to his eyes. "Stop putting those pictures in my head."

"They're in mine, so they might as well be in yours, too. It still feels like I should go punch him—at least one good punch. On principle."

"She wouldn't like it." Owen shrugged. "And he's still Willy B, so you know he'd let you punch him if you needed to do it."

"Goddamn it, he would, too. It's no good that way. I've got to think about this." Jaw tight, Ryder picked up his hammer, set a framing nail, and whaled on it.

"I guess we all do." Beckett put his safety glasses on, turned on the saw.

Nodding, Owen strapped on his tool belt.

It was better to work, he decided, better to push through the strange day with the smell of sawdust and the sounds of nails hammered into wood.

By the time Clare and the kids arrived with provisions, they'd finished framing in on the second floor, and had started on the main level.

"You work so fast!" Clare wandered what would be her office—her own home office!—off the kitchen.

"We got a system." Beckett draped an arm over her shoulders as the boys stomped around the subflooring.

"It works. Well, we're here to help, if we can. And as payment I've got beef stew in the Crock-Pot. A manly meal for manly men."

"I'm in," Owen told her.

"I hate to miss it, but I've got a date." Ryder tossed a hunk of his sub in the air. Dumbass caught the high fly like a veteran center fielder.

"Can you teach Ben and Yoda to do that?" Liam demanded. "Stuff just bounces off their face mostly."

"D.A. here, he was born knowing how to field food, but yeah, we could teach them."

"Not in the house," Clare said absently as she pored over the blueprints.

Ryder just grinned at the boy, broke off another small hunk. "Go ahead, practice with D.A."

"D.A. stands for Dumbass," Murphy announced, "but we're not supposed to say *ass*. It a bad word."

"Depends, doesn't it?"

"On how?"

"Well." Considering, Ryder took a pencil out of his tool belt, drew on the subflooring. "What's that?"

"It's a donkey. You draw good."

"Nah, it's a jackass."

"Mom! Ryder drawed a jackass on the floor!"

"Drew," Clare corrected, and sent Ryder a sighing look.

"I like to draw. Can I draw on the floor?"

Ryder handed over the pencil. "Have at it, midget."

Happily, Murphy sat on the floor and drew a box with a triangle on top. "This is gonna be our house when we get married."

Liam trooped over to Owen. "I need more for D.A. to catch."

Owen obliged him with a chunk of sub.

"You're gonna be our uncle."

"That's what I hear."

"So you have to buy us Christmas presents."

"I guess I do."

"I got a list."

"A man after my own heart. Where is it?"

"On the frigerator at home. It's only ten more days till Christmas."

"Then I better get on it."

Liam looked across the room where Beckett was teaching Harry how to hammer in a stud. "I wanna hammer, too."

"Then you better help me finish framing in the pantry."

"What's the pantry?"

"It's where your mom's going to keep food."

"That's the frigerator."

"Not everything goes in the fridge, kid. How about cans of soup?"

"I like Chicken and Stars."

"Who doesn't? Let's get it done."

Despite the endless stream of questions, he liked working with the kid, showing him how to measure, how to mark, how to hold a hammer. And he figured it showed their simpatico when Liam lasted nearly an hour before he joined Murphy on the floor with a pile of action figures.

He gave Clare credit, too. She fetched, she carried, she drove in a few nails herself—and rode herd on the kids.

He remembered his mother doing much the same when they'd added on to the house.

His father always had a project going.

After they knocked off, he found himself flattered when Liam asked to ride with him. They strapped the booster seat in the truck, strapped the kid in it.

"Where's your house?" Liam wanted to know.

"Right down the road—or through the woods if you're walking."

"Can I see it?"

"Ah. Sure, I guess."

It wasn't much of a detour. Owen made the turns, cruised up his lane.

He'd strung a few lights, had the tree centered in the front window—all on timer so they sparkled against the December dark.

"Ours is bigger," Liam announced.

"Yeah, it is. There are more of you."

"Do you live here all by yourself?"

"That's right."

"Why?"

"Because . . . it's my house."

"You don't have anybody to play with."

He hadn't thought of it quite that way. "I guess not, but Ryder lives right over that way, and when your place is finished, you guys will be right over that way."

"Can I come play at your house?"

"Sure." He hadn't thought of that either, but hell, it might be fun. "Yeah."

"Okay."

Owen turned the truck around, started toward the road. "I'm going to get a dog."

"Dogs are good." Liam nodded wisely. "You can play with them, and you have to feed them and teach them to sit. They keep bad guys away. A bad guy came in our house, but the dogs were just puppies."

Owen debated a response. He wasn't sure how much the boys knew about Sam Freemont. "You have good dogs."

"They're bigger now, but they're still puppies. But they'll keep bad guys away when they grow up. The bad guy came in and scared my mom."

"I know. But she's okay, and the bad guy's in jail."

"Beckett came and stopped him. And you and Ryder came, too."

"That's right." If Liam needed to talk about it, Owen concluded, it worried at the kid. "You don't have to worry, Liam. We've got your back."

"'Cause Beckett and Mom are getting married."

"Because of that, yeah, and just because."

"If the bad guy tries to come back, and Beckett's not there, Harry and I will fight him, and Murphy'll call nine-one-one, then Beckett. We talked about it. We practiced."

"That's smart."

"And when the dogs get big, if he tries to come back, they'll bite him." Liam slid his gaze toward Owen. "In the dumb ass."

With a laugh, Owen gave Liam a light slap on the head. "Damn right."

After dinner, while Clare hauled the boys up for a bath, Owen relayed the conversation to Beckett.

"Bite him in the dumb ass. Kid's got a way. Clare and I talked to them after it happened. Played it down, but played it straight. Still, they heard stuff at school. So Harry called a powwow, and they came to me about it."

"Keep the women out of it?"

Beckett glanced toward the stairs. "Maybe that's not politically correct, or even correct, but it feels right in this case. They need to know we're covered, and that I trust them to help take care of their mom."

"We'd've done the same."

"Yeah, we would. Speaking of, I was able to tell Clare about that situation on the way home. You pitch the radio to a certain level, your voices to another, you can actually have a conversation that doesn't carry to the backseats. Plus we used a lot of code."

"What did she say?"

"What you'd expect. Mom's entitled to a life. She's a vital woman, Willy B's a good man. Blah blah. I mean she's right, but still."

"It wasn't her mother and Willy B mostly naked in the kitchen."

On a sigh, Beckett closed his eyes. "And thank you for that fresh image to add to my growing collection."

"We could start trading them, like baseball cards."

That triggered a laughing shake of the head. "The other thing? When I talked to Clare about it, she didn't really seem surprised."

"What do you mean?" Owen lowered his after-dinner beer. "Like she already knew?"

"That or one of those woman's radar deals. With stuff like this? They're kind of like bats. Anyway, I started to ask her, but then Harry and Murphy started on each other, and that was the end of adult conversation."

The thought slapped hard into his brain. "If Clare already knew, then Avery . . . Son of a bitch."

"Coulda been that radar."

"Avery's a woman. She has radar. She's as much of a bat as any of them. Plus, it's *her* father groping our mother."

"Stop. Stop." Beckett covered his ears.

"If she knew, she should've told me." Now the thought rooted in his brain, sprouted like a weed. "I'd've told her."

"We know now. And I guess we're going to have to get used to it."

Owen started to respond, but Harry ran in, shiny from his bath in his X-Men pajamas, and announced a Wii tournament.

Roped in, Owen gave it an hour. He liked the kids, he liked Wii, but he just couldn't get the idea of Avery keeping the situation from him out of his head.

He chewed at it all the way home, sat in the truck chewing over it some more. Then he turned around, drove back to town. He went into Vesta from the back.

"Hey, Owen!" Franny stood behind the counter slicing up a large pizza. "What can we get for you?"

"Is Avery around?"

"You just missed her. She's running some deliveries. More people calling in than coming in tonight. I'm closing, so she's going to go right on up when she gets back. I can give her a call if it's important."

"No. Nothing important. I'll catch her later. How are you feeling?"

"Back to normal. Are you really opening the inn next month?"

"Yeah, we are."

"I'm spreading the word."

"Keep spreading. I'll see you later, Franny."

He went out the back and, after a quick debate, went up the stairs rather than down.

She had to come back sometime.

He considered the fact that he had keys; he was the landlord after all. But that crossed the line.

Instead, he sat on the floor outside her apartment door, took out his phone. He passed the time reading and answering emails, texts.

He checked the time, wondered where the hell her deliveries were? Portugal?

He wished he'd hit Franny up for coffee, tried to entertain himself with some Angry Birds.

He closed his eyes—just to rest them for a minute—and the restless night caught up with him. He fell asleep on the floor, his trusty phone still in his hand.

## CHAPTER SIX

❧

H AULING GROCERY BAGS, AVERY SHOVED OPEN THE
stairwell door, adjusted her load. Out of habit she
paused on the landing, checked the lock on Vesta's rear door,
then climbed up to her apartment level.

And stopped, frowning at the picture of Owen propped
against her door, eyes closed, phone in hand.

"What's the deal?" she demanded, and when he didn't
respond, realized he was dead asleep.

"For God's sake." Muttering, she stepped closer, kicked him.

"Ow! What? Damn it."

"What the hell are you doing?"

"Waiting for you." Annoyed, he rubbed his hip where
her shoe—canary yellow tonight—had hit. "Where the hell
were you?"

"I had deliveries, then I swung into the grocery store. I
ran into a friend, and we . . ." She stopped, glared. "Why
am I explaining to you? Why are you sleeping on the floor
in front of my apartment?"

"Because you weren't home. I wasn't sleeping. I was

just . . . thinking." He pushed to his feet, blinked at her. "Your hair's wet."

"It's spitting some sleet. Move, will you? These are getting heavy."

He blinked again, then reached out and took the bags. She unlocked the door, walked in ahead of him.

He crossed the living room, went straight to the kitchen, dumped the bags on the counter. Watching him, she peeled off her coat, unwound her scarf. "How long were you out there?"

"What time is it?"

Even as he checked his watch, she arched her eyebrows. "It's what-the-hell's-going-on o'clock." She tossed her coat and scarf over the back of a chair on her way to the counter.

"That's what I want to know."

"You're the one sleeping on the doorstep," she said as she began stowing groceries. Unlike her living room, which he considered messy, and she considered a *living* room, her cupboards and refrigerator were meticulously organized.

"I wasn't sleeping. I maybe nodded off for a minute, and that's beside the point."

"What point?"

"You knew. You knew what was going on, and didn't tell me."

"I don't tell you a lot of things." Eyes narrowed on him, she began plucking eggs out of the carton and laying them in the bin. "Be more specific."

"You knew your father was sleeping with my mother."

The egg slipped out of her fingers, hit the floor like a little bomb. *"What?"*

"Okay, you didn't know." Owen stuffed his hands in his pockets. "Now you know."

"I say again, *what?*"

"My mother, your father." At a loss, he pulled his hands free, rolled them in the air.

"Get out. Really? No." She laughed a little, yanked off some paper towels, dampened them to deal with the broken egg. "You must've had some dream while you were camped at my door."

"Yes, they are—and no, I didn't."

Still shaking her head, she dampened another towel, scrubbed off the tile. "Where do you get this? On a short trip to Bizarro World?"

"From me. Myself. My own freaking eyes." He forked his fingers, pointed at them. "I went over to the house this morning. I walked in on them."

Avery's jaw dropped as she slowly straightened. "You walked in on your mom and my dad? In *bed*?"

"No. Thank God. They were in the kitchen."

"Jesus!" Gaping, she took a step back. "They were having sex in the kitchen!"

"No. Shut up." Appalled, Owen slapped his hands over his eyes. "Now I really know what Beckett means about images in the head. Oh God."

"You're not making any sense. At all."

Start over, he ordered himself, because Avery had a point. "I went over, they were in the kitchen. Your father's in his boxers. My mom's wearing this, this little . . . thing. And they were . . . hands, lips, tongues."

She stared a moment, then held up one finger. Turning, she opened a cupboard, took out a bottle of Glenfiddich and two lowball glasses. Without a word she poured two fingers in each, handed one to Owen.

She knocked hers back, took a careful breath.

"One more time. Our parents are sleeping together."

"That's what I said."

"And you walked in on them, scantily dressed and groping each other in your mom's kitchen."

"I'm *telling* you." Now he downed his whiskey.

When she began laughing, he assumed hysteria, but it only took a moment to recognize genuine humor.

"You think this is funny?"

"One part is. You walking in on them?" She pressed a hand to her belly. "Oh, oh! I wish I could've been there to see your face. I bet it was like—" She mimed exaggerated shock and horror, then fell into fits of laughter again.

He had a bad feeling she'd nailed it. To compensate, he bared his teeth in a snarl. "I guess you'd have been, 'Hey, toss some more bacon on the griddle for me.'"

"She was making breakfast. That's nice."

"Nice? You think it's nice?"

"Yeah, I do. Don't you?"

"I don't know what I think."

With a nod, Avery went back to stowing groceries. "Let me ask you something. Do you think your mother should be alone for the rest of her life?"

"She's not alone."

"Owen." She turned her head, gave him a quiet look.

"I don't know. No. No. It's just that I never thought about it—her—that way."

"Now that you are, do you think she's entitled to have someone in her life?"

"I . . . yeah. I guess."

"Have you got a problem with my father?"

"You know I don't. Willy B . . . he's the best."

"He's the best," Avery agreed. "So you're not pleased your mother's with the best?"

"I . . ." He fumbled to a stop. "If you're going to be all rational and mature . . ."

"Sorry. In this case I must. They're good friends, long-time, good friends. So, they'll be good for each other." Smiling, she folded her market bags. "I tried to fix him up a couple times. It never worked out. I didn't like knowing he didn't have anyone. My mother did such a number on him."

On both of you, Owen thought.

"Mom told me they'd been . . ." He rolled his hands in the air again. "A couple years."

"A couple years?" Shaking her head again, she poured another round of whiskey. "Willy B, you're so deep. Who knew? I didn't have a clue. How could I have not had a clue?"

"None of us did. I started thinking you knew, and you hadn't told me."

"I would've told you, unless they'd asked me not to."

"I get that." He picked up the whiskey, stared into it.

"What did my father say when you dropped in?"

"That he'd better go put some pants on."

She snorted out a laugh, then tossed her head back, let a rolling one loose. Owen found himself grinning.

"It's a little easier to see the humor in it now."

"Did you make that face?" She repeated her interpretation of shock and horror. "And kind of stutter? 'Mom! What! You!'"

He tried for a cool stare as she had, indeed, nailed it. "I might have had a momentary moment."

"A momentary moment."

"At least I didn't punch your dad. Ryder wanted to when I told him and Beckett."

Avery lifted a shoulder. "That's Ry's default, but he wouldn't punch Dad. Ry's fine with punching assholes or bullies, but he loves Willy B."

"He loves me, too, but he's punched me before."

"Well, Owen, sometimes you're an asshole."

She smiled when she said it, sweetly, then tapped her glass to his. "To our parents."

"Okay." He sipped the whiskey. "Strange day," he said with a sigh. "You're not pissed at me anymore."

"I wasn't pissed at you. Very much. And now I've figured out you've got an issue with sex."

"What?" A close relative of Avery's shock-and-horror look passed over his face. "I do not. Why?"

"See." She lifted a finger off her glass to point at him. "I even say the word and you're all flustered. Issues."

"I don't have issues with sex. I believe in sex. I like sex. I like lots of sex."

"Strange. You kiss me and go into immediate brain freeze. You see our parents kissing and hit the panic button."

"No. Yes. Maybe. Damn it, that has nothing to do with issues. Any normal person would have a—"

"Momentary moment."

Smart-ass, he thought. She'd always been one. "A reaction to seeing his mother laying a hot one on a longtime family friend. And you and me? You know that wasn't expected."

"Actually, it doesn't seem that unexpected to me. But then, I don't have sexual issues."

"I don't have sexual issues."

"Hmm." She sipped, strolled over to the window. "Oh, it's snowing now. Pretty. God! I have to finish my Christmas shopping. You'd better go before it starts to stick."

"Just wait a minute."

She glanced back. "For what?"

"Damn it, Avery, you can't just say something like that then say go home."

"Just voicing an opinion." When he stepped around the counter, she took the glass from his hand. "You shouldn't have any more. I know you handle it well, but still. Whiskey, driving, and snow, not a good mix."

He repeated, with all the patience and potency he could muster, "I don't have sexual issues."

"Are we still on that? All right, my mistake. You're sexual issue–free."

"Don't placate me."

"Jesus, Owen, what do you want from me?" Her eyes fired like lasers when he gripped her elbows, hauled her to her toes. "Watch it," she warned.

"Now we're expecting it," he told her, and gave her a quick yank.

She knew where his buttons were and how to push them—and could admit she'd done so. She didn't mind irritating him into kissing her. She wanted an encore, one way or the other, to see how both of them reacted.

"Okay." Deliberately she linked her hands behind his head. "Now we're expecting it." She moved in first, before he could overthink and pull back.

Not an explosion this time, she thought, but more of a long, slow fall that picked up velocity. His hands dropped from her elbows to her hips, then molded her body inch by inch on their way up her sides. As the intensity built, he shifted her until he'd trapped her between his body and the counter.

She'd manipulated him—he knew it, but didn't much

care. The tang of whiskey on her tongue, the hint of lemon in her hair, the hot pulse of her body against his all tangled his senses into a slippery knot of need.

He skimmed the heels of his hands along the sides of her breasts, glided his fingers over them—felt her pulse kick lightly against his palms.

Felt her breath quicken as the kiss deepened.

Easing back, he struggled for equilibrium while she stared at him with drowsy blue eyes.

"Sexual issues, my ass."

Humor warmed her face an instant before she laughed. "I stand corrected."

"So . . . what now?"

On a sigh, she laid her hands on his cheeks, held them there briefly. "Owen," she murmured, then slid to the side and away.

"Owen, what?"

"What now?" She picked up her glass of scotch again. Hell, she wasn't driving anywhere. "We rip each other's clothes off and go to bed. If I'm any judge, we have really exceptional sex. But since you ask, you're already thinking what-if and what then in addition to what now—taking that rational and mature route. So you go home, and consider the what-ifs and what thens until you figure it out."

"The what-ifs and thens matter, Avery."

"You're right. You're absolutely right."

"You matter. You and me—you and all of us—matter."

"I know. The fact that you're thinking about that instead of ripping my clothes off is part of what makes you Owen, and part of the reason I'd have let you rip my clothes off."

Now he had new pictures in his brain, and found he didn't much want to hike on that rational and mature route. "You're a confusing woman, Avery."

"Not really. It's just I can appreciate you considering what matters and still be sorry you didn't wait to consider until after that exceptional sex."

"I love you."

"Oh God, I know." She turned away, as casually as pos-

sible, terrified the tears would come, terrified they'd show.
"I love you, too."

"I know what to do about that, what to think about that.
I don't know what to do about, what to think about wanting
you like this. Wanting you, a lot."

She took a careful breath, turned back, and smiled. "That
helps, a lot. It's an adjustment. You never thought about me
that way."

"I wouldn't say never."

"Really." Steadier, she studied him over the rim of her
glass. "Is that so?"

"Well, hell, Avery, of course I thought about it, occasion-
ally. You're gorgeous."

"No, I'm not. Hope's gorgeous. I've got cute, which I can
boost up to hot with time and tools. But thanks. So, what
now?" She sat on the arm of a chair, studied him. "You go
home before the snow gets too bad, and you do what you're
wired to do. You think about it. And I'll think about it."

"Okay." He crossed to her, bent down to brush his lips
over hers. "If it was anyone but you, I'd stay. And that really
didn't sound right. I meant—"

"I know what you meant, lucky for you. Go home,
Owen."

He walked to the door, glanced back as he opened it.
"See you."

"See you."

She sat, listening to his footsteps recede down the stairwell. Rising, she walked to the front window, stood, and
watched the snow fall.

And thought, for a moment through the light drift of
white, she saw a woman standing at the window of the inn,
gazing out as she was.

Waiting? she wondered. Was that what she was doing now,
too? She'd never been one for waiting, but for doing, for
acting.

And yet . . . maybe she had been, on some level, all this
time. Waiting for Owen. The idea struck her—sweet, annoying, baffling all at once.

What now? she mused again. It looked as if she had more to think about than she'd realized.

∽

IT SNOWED THROUGH the night and into the morning. Owen kept busy most of the day plowing out his lane, his mother's, his brothers'. He enjoyed the task—at least this early in the winter—the rumble of the jeep, the bump of the plow, the strategy needed to direct the snow into reasonable piles and banks.

While he worked on Ryder's lane he spotted his brother muscling his snowblower to forge a path from the door. One out the front, Owen thought, to where Ryder parked his truck, another out the back so D.A. could meander out and do his business away from the house. Each of them did their respective jobs with barely a wave of acknowledgment until Owen pulled into the cleared space beside Ryder's truck and turned off the jeep.

"That should do it."

"Good enough," Ryder agreed as he angled the snowblower under an overhang. "Want a beer?"

"Why wouldn't I?"

Together they trudged around the side, into Ryder's combination game room and home gym. They stomped off their boots, took them off on the tiled entranceway floor. Each of them peeled off layers of outerwear, hung them on pegs.

D.A. wandered over, leaned briefly on Owen's leg, then stared at Ryder. "Yeah, your way's all clear." Ryder opened the door. "That dog'll roll in the snow, run in the snow, eat the damn snow, but he won't walk through it to shit. I don't clear the path, he shits right by the door. Why is that?"

"Hence his name."

"Yeah, hence. Except I'm the one out in the cold blowing snow."

They walked upstairs into the kitchen, where Ryder pulled out two beers.

"How was the date?" Owen asked him.

"She's a lawyer, right? Smart. I like smart. Got a killer body." Ryder took a long pull of the beer. "She can even talk sports, which is a big check in the plus column. So I ask myself, why don't I want to close this deal?"

"And the answer is?"

"The giggle. I figured it out last night. She giggles. A lot. I think it's supposed to be adorable, but it's fucking annoying."

"The giggle's a deal breaker?"

"It's grating, man." Ryder shoved at his hair, as he did whenever he was overdue for a trim. "Nails-on-the-blackboard grating. And I think, what if we're heating up the sheets and she giggles?" He held up a finger, curved it down. "I know it, so why go there?"

"Earplugs?"

"Good thought, but I don't think so. I'd *feel* her giggle, or wonder if she was about to giggle. It's not worth it."

"Strict, but fair." At home, Owen dropped into a chair at Ryder's black-topped kitchen table. "Got any food?"

"I got Hot Pockets." He opened a cupboard. "I got taco chips and salsa."

"Consider all that my fee for the plowing."

"Done." Ryder rooted through the freezer. "Chicken or steak?"

"Chicken."

Once he'd stuck a few in the microwave, he tossed the chips on the table, dumped salsa in a bowl. He tore off some paper towels, pulled out some plates, and considered it done.

"You're like the male Martha Stewart," Owen commented.

"The kitchen is my temple." Ryder went over to let the dog in, then dropped down across from Owen.

"I'm thinking about having sex with Avery."

"What is it suddenly with the Montgomery-MacTavish connection?" Ry tossed D.A. a taco chip before digging one into the salsa.

"I'd rather not bring Mom and Willy B into this. I'm still scarred."

Ryder took another pull on his beer. "What's Avery think about having sex with you?"

"Unless she's changed her mind since last night, she's open to it."

"Then why aren't you having sex?"

"Because it's Avery."

After loading another chip with salsa, Ryder wagged it a little. "You want me to have sex with her first? Give her a test run?"

"That's real generous of you, Ry," Owen said dryly. "But I can handle it."

"Just trying to help a brother out." When the mic beeped, Ryder got up, tossed the Hot Pockets on the plates. "I say ride that train."

"Why?"

"Other than the obvious reasons? Because it's Avery. You've always had a little thing for her."

"I have . . . so, maybe."

"And she's always had a little thing for you—otherwise she'd have jumped me years ago." With a grin, Ryder bit into his Hot Pocket. "So get on board, find out if it's a bigger thing. Where's the downside?"

"What if it gets fucked up? What if it fucks us up?"

Ryder shook his head, gave D.A. the last quarter of his Hot Pocket, took another for himself. "It's Avery, man. Maybe it'll get fucked up. That happens more often than not. But it won't fuck the two of you up."

"Why not?"

"Because both of you are too smart for that, and like each other too much for that. Maybe it'll bring on some bumps, but you'll smooth them out. Meanwhile you'll have sex with Red Hots."

Owen scooped up some salsa. "She doesn't giggle."

"I rest my case."

"I'm going to think about it."

Ryder angled back, pulled open the fridge for two more beers. "Observe my shock."

⌒⌒

THINKING OR NOT, work had to be done. Throughout the next week, he ran trim, helped touch up paint, hung mirrors. He unboxed cartons, put together lamps, signed for deliveries, and climbed the flights of stairs at the inn more times than he cared to count.

His mother snagged him, pulled him into Elizabeth and
Darcy.

"I found the perfect little painting over at Gifts. I want
you to hang it in the bathroom."

"But we're not loading in the art until—"

"That's different. I've got everything in here to finish this
room. That mirror there." She pointed to the narrow wall
between the two porch doors. "Your grandmother's crocheting there, and that sweet little painting right here." She
stepped into the bath, tapped the wall.

"Hope's bringing up the amenities, the towels, the little
bits and bobs we've picked out. We want to see how it all
looks. We want to see one room complete."

"The Penthouse—"

"Gets art, so it's not really finished. I've got the art for this
room right here. So we'll have it finished—all the way."

She turned to the bed with its lavender brocade head- and
footboard. "You hang while I make up this bed."

"We've still got three weeks before the opening party . . ."
he began, and got the glinty-eyed stare.

"Okay, okay."

He dug out a hanger, his pencil—then went through the
"lower, higher, to the right" routine he expected to deal with
on every piece his mother wanted hung.

But he conceded she'd chosen well with the little painting,
as it struck him as charming and English, airy with its pastels.

Hope breezed in with a hamper loaded with towels, amenities, and the bits and bobs they'd settled on.

Now he had two women telling him higher or lower until
he'd satisfied them with the placement. As he hammered,
they fussed with linens.

He listened with half an ear to their talk of opening-party
plans, of reservations already booked, of additional pieces
they needed, wanted, had coming in.

"Justine, those are perfect." Hope stepped out of the bathroom to admire the framed crocheted doilies.

"They are." Justine stopped fussing with the linen shams
to nod. "And she'd be pleased to have them here, and in
J&R."

"I think it's lovely the way you're mixing in some of your family things. It makes it more personal."

"This whole building's personal." Justine reached out, rubbed Owen's arm. "You hang that mirror, then I'll cut you loose."

"Can you take a look, see if you like the arrangement in here?" Hope asked Justine.

Owen seized the opportunity to hang the mirror without two fussing opinions as his mother went into the bath with Hope.

He measured, marked, again approved his mother's choice—the mirror's frame picked up the purple tone of the occasional chair and still managed to be dainty.

With his mind on his task, and wandering toward others on his list, the waft of honeysuckle didn't register. He began to hum as he hammered, unconsciously picking up the tune that whispered on the air.

He picked up the mirror, slid the wire over the hanger. Being Owen, he reached for the mini level in his tool belt to check the position.

And saw her.

For an instant she stood in a dove gray dress, her hands folded at the waist of the bell of the skirt. Her blond hair swept back from her face, bound into some sort of net at the nape with a few wispy curls escaping to flutter at her cheeks.

She smiled at him.

He spun around, and it was Hope, dark hair clipped back, a dust rag hanging out of the pocket of her jeans, and her dark eyes wide against her pale face.

"Did you see that?" Owen demanded.

"I . . ."

But she wasn't looking at him. She stared at the doorway to the hall. At Ryder.

"When you're finished playing house with the women, I've got actual work for you," Ryder told him.

"Did you *see* that?" Owen repeated. "She was here."

"Which she? They're every damn where." He glanced toward Hope as he spoke, then he frowned. "Sit down," he ordered.

When she simply stared, he strode over, took her arm, and dumped her into the pretty little chair. "Mom! Your innkeeper's having a moment."

Justine rushed out, took one look, and dropped down at Hope's feet. "Honey, what's wrong? Ryder, get her some water."

"No. No. I'm fine. I just . . ."

"Jesus Christ, did anybody see that?" Frustrated, Owen waved his arms in the air.

"Where the hell is—" Beckett broke off as he came into the room. "What's wrong?"

"I saw her. She was right there. Did you see her?"

"Who? Hope? I'm looking at her." Then Beckett's eyes narrowed. "Elizabeth? You saw Lizzy?"

"She was standing right there."

"You saw her? Why you? That kind of pisses me off," Beckett decided.

"Did you see her?" Ignoring his brother, Owen focused on Hope. "She was right there. Then you were."

"I . . ."

Ryder yanked a water bottle from his belt, shoved it at her. "Drink."

"I'll get you a glass," Justine said when Hope stared at the bottle.

"No. I'm fine." But she lifted the bottle, drank deep. "Fine. It just startled me."

"You *did* see her."

"Yes. And no. For a second, I thought I did, but it was more feeling her. That sounds crazy." She looked directly at Ryder. "She's waiting."

"For what?"

"I . . . I'm not sure."

"She smiled at me. I was hanging the mirror, and I saw her in it. Reflected in it. Gray dress, hair thing, netty kind of thing in the back. She's blond, pretty. Young." As Hope held the bottle back out to Ryder, Owen snagged it, finished it off. "Wow."

"She was humming," Justine said. "I heard humming, and smelled honeysuckle. I stood still a moment, wondering if . . . but I didn't see her. Come on, sweetie, I'll take you downstairs."

"I'm fine," Hope repeated. "She just . . . It's an experience, but I'm not scared of her. I've felt her before. This was more intense."

"The building's nearly back. And this room?" Beckett circled around. "It basically is. Stuff on the walls, bedding on the bed, towels on the rack," he noted. "I'm thinking she likes it."

"Now that we've satisfied our ghost, maybe we can cut our way through this punch-out list."

"No romance in Ry's soul," Beckett said sadly. "Everybody okay?"

Hope nodded. "I'm—"

"Fine," Ryder finished. "How many times does she have to say it? Let's get to work." But he paused at the doorway, gave Hope one last study. "It looks good in here."

"He's right about that anyway. Take a minute if you need it," Beckett advised Owen, then walked out after Ryder.

"I saw her." Owen grinned when he said it. "Very cool. She smiled at me," he added, and strode out.

"Do you want some fresh air, some time off?"

Hope shook her head at Justine. "No, but thanks. Ryder had it right—I had a moment. I guess there'll be more of them." Hope pushed to her feet. "I'd say she likes the room."

"She'd be crazy not to." Justine continued to rub Hope's arm. "If you're up for it, we can start fussing in T&O."

"Let's."

An experience, Hope thought as she picked up the empty hamper. Owen had been right about that. And Elizabeth had smiled at him—briefly. But it had been Ryder who'd brought on that sudden burst of emotion, that bittersweet tangle of joy and grief, so strong, so *real* Hope's own legs had all but buckled under it.

Whatever it meant, she assumed she'd find out when she took up residence at the inn.

## CHAPTER SEVEN

H ER LIFE WAS CHAOS, AND SHE HAD NO ONE TO BLAME
but herself.

In Beckett's former office area, one she'd semi-transformed to her own, Avery sat surrounded by boxes, wrapping paper, tissue, ribbons, and bows.

Insanity.

She promised herself, every year, she'd do better. She'd shop earlier—and with a list—she'd keep her wrapping paper and ribbons and so on in their containers, packing them back up again after every wrapping session.

She would approach the purchase, storing, wrapping, and stacking of Christmas presents like a sensible adult.

And she meant to, absolutely.

Next year, for certain.

She knew how to organize and stay that way, but it seemed to her all her organization skills arrowed toward work and missed her life by a mile.

So, as usual, with three short days until Christmas, she dug through gift boxes, tore through piles of ribbon, panicked every time she couldn't find what she knew she put right *there* a minute ago, and generally exhausted herself.

She loved Christmas.

She loved the music—which she knew drove other people crazy by the time the big day arrived. She loved the lights, the color, the secrets, and excitement.

She loved the shopping and the wrapping, and the happy satisfaction of seeing gifts all bright and pretty in ordered stacks. So why did she *always* end up rushing through it all at the last minute?

But this year, at least, she refused to spend the last hours and minutes of Christmas Eve in a stressful, eleventh-hour whirlwind. She'd have everything wrapped, stacked, bagged, and ready tonight.

Tomorrow, latest.

She'd given up working at the counter—just too much *stuff*, so she sat on the floor, surrounded by boxes and scraps of paper, hanks of ribbons. Next year, definitely, she'd organize the counter space first, and she'd buy more containers for bows and so on. Label them, like Hope did.

Damn Hope anyway.

Thinking of Hope and her currently annoying efficiency, Avery admired the earrings she'd bought for her friend. Good shopping job, she congratulated herself. She reboxed them, selected the silver foil paper, the curly red bow, the matching tag. She head-bopped to Springsteen's "Santa Claus Is Coming to Town" as she carefully cut the paper to size, meticulously folded the raw ends.

Organization might be lacking, she admitted, but by God, her presents would be beautifully wrapped.

She reached for her tape, pulled the end—and got the sliver left on the roll.

"Damn it."

No problem, she told herself. She'd bought more tape.

She was sure of it.

After a fifteen-minute search with rising frustration, trickles of panic, and a lot of swearing, she admitted she'd *meant* to buy more tape.

So, no problem. She'd just run out and buy some.

She checked the time, cursed again.

How did it get to be nearly midnight?

She needed tape!

She spent another fifteen minutes pawing through drawers, as-yet-unpacked boxes, searching closets.

This, she decided, was a solid reason to live in New York, where a person could go out and buy anything they needed at any time of the day or night. When a person ran out of tape during a present-wrapping frenzy, she could buy more damn tape.

She took a moment, ordering herself to stop being an idiot, and surveyed the current wreckage.

The search had jumbled everything, even unearthed potential gifts she'd bought during a shop-early-shop-often phase she'd initiated the previous summer.

Bad, she admitted, but not horrible. And there was tape down in the restaurant.

She grabbed her keys, left the lights and music on, then jogged down to unlock the restaurant. After switching on the lights, she headed to the counter, searched the drawer under the register.

"Aha!" She pulled out the tape dispenser, elated. Then deflated when she saw there was only a stingy amount left on the roll.

She hunted for the refill—drawers, cubbies, the rear storage closet. When she found herself searching in coolers, she gave it up and poured herself a glass of wine.

She sat at the counter, propped her head on her hand, and wondered how all her good intentions could be upended for the lack of a roll of Scotch tape.

The knock on the front door had her jerking upright, nearly slopping the wine on the counter.

Owen stood in the security lights, peering in at her through the glass door.

New York, definitely, she thought. A woman couldn't even have a private Scotch tape crisis in Boonsboro.

She stalked over to the door, flipped the locks. "We're closed."

"Then why are you in here, sitting at the counter drinking wine?"

"I'm wrapping Christmas presents."

"Funny, it really looks like you're sitting in your empty pizza shop drinking wine."

"I ran out of tape. I thought I bought more, but I didn't, and there's not enough down here to bother with. It's too late to buy any damn tape because this isn't New York."

He studied her. Plaid flannel pants he imagined she used as pajamas, a long-sleeved tee, thick socks. Her hair held back by one of those clips that always made him think of big teeth.

"You waited to wrap everything at once again."

"So?"

"Just saying."

"Why are you here? Why aren't you home wrapping presents? Because they're all wrapped," she said bitterly. "Neatly wrapped and in shopping bags according to where they go. And I *know* you guys gave the crew their presents already because I saw the Inn BoonsBoro sweatshirts."

"Want one?"

"Yes."

"Give me a glass of that and I'll bring you one tomorrow."

"Might as well because I can't wrap presents." She went back, got the bottle and a glass. "Why are you here?"

"I saw the lights go on and you running around in here like a maniac. From across the street," he explained. "I was running my checklist. We finished."

"Finished what?"

"The inn. Well, not the loading in, but the work. It's done."

"Get out."

"Done," he repeated and toasted himself. "Final inspection's tomorrow."

"Owen!" Her mood pivoted, lighting her face. "You made it before Christmas."

"We made it. We should get the Use and Occupancy permit, no problem. Hope can move in. We'll load in the rest, polish it up. With her living there for a couple weeks, we should nail down anything that needs tweaking before the opening."

"Congratulations. Hope said you were close, but I didn't get how close."

"Lot to do yet, but it's all filling out. When the crew comes back after Christmas, it'll be on the bakery building."

She walked to the door, looked out. "It's beautiful. Every time I see it, it's a lift. Hope said you've already got reservations booked."

"We'll get more when we get all the pictures online and when word gets out. Hope's doing some interviews next week. She'll give reporters a tour, talk it up. We'll do some, too. Family business and all that. It makes good media."

"It makes good life. *Sláinte*," she added, tapping her glass to his. "I'll come over in the morning before I open. And after I go out and buy some tape."

"I have some in my truck."

She lowered the wineglass, narrowed her eyes. "You have Scotch tape in your truck?"

"In the glove box, sure. And before you make any smart remark, remember—you need it, I have it."

"I was going to say it's really smart to carry tape in your glove compartment." She smiled, sweetly.

"No, you weren't, but good catch. I'll go get it."

"I'll get it. You're parked behind the inn."

"Yeah, and it's freezing. Where's your coat, your shoes?"

"Upstairs, but it's just across the street."

No question she'd run across The Square in her pajamas and stocking feet at midnight, in December, he mused. "I'll go get it. Lock up. I'll meet you around the back."

"Thanks. Really."

He handed her his wineglass, walked out the front.

She locked back up, took the empty glasses to the kitchen. Flipping off lights, she made her way back to the stairwell, started down to unlock the back door. She heard the locks snick open.

He had a key, of course.

Landlord.

She met him halfway down, took the tape. "I'm going to Sam's Club and buying a hundred rolls of this damn stuff."

"Everything's better in bulk."

She laughed. "I bet you've got spare rolls in the truck, at home, in the shop."

Brows lifted over quiet blue eyes, Owen watched her steadily. "Is that a smart remark?"

"An observation. No, a compliment," she decided. "And I'm going to try to follow your exemplary tape-access behavior."

He stood below her so their faces stayed on level and, watching her, reached into his pocket. "Start now."

"You brought me a spare. You actually had *two* rolls of tape in your truck." Laughing, she took it.

Three, he thought, but who's counting? "I could give you a hand with the wrapping."

She arched her eyebrows. "Then you'd have many smart remarks about the state of my wrapping area—and that's after I revived you from the dead faint you'd fall into when you saw it."

"I've seen your so-called wrapping area before."

"Not up there. It's worse than it's ever been. I have more room for the chaos." She saw the move in his eyes, shifted back a little. "Owen, I've been thinking about this."

"About chaos?"

"In a way. Thinking about what we're both thinking about doing right now. At first I wondered why we hadn't thought about doing what we're thinking about doing before. Then I thought, hell yes, let's just do what we're thinking about doing. Then it occurred to me we haven't because it might mess things up. And seriously, Owen, you mean a lot to me. You mean a whole lot to me."

"Funny, I was thinking about what we're both thinking about, too. And I'd worked myself around to messing things up. Ryder says we won't mess things up."

"Ryder says?"

"I got an opinion. Don't tell me you haven't talked about this with Clare and Hope."

She backpedaled on the automatic annoyance. "Fair enough. Why does Ryder say we won't mess things up?"

"Because we mean a lot to each other, and we're not stupid."

She angled her head. "All true. Another thing, now that we're thinking . . ." She laid her hands, each holding tape dispensers, on his shoulders. "It may not give us the same buzz as before. We could check."

He put his hands on her hips. "Like a test."

"Makes sense, right? Why spend time thinking about what we're thinking about if it turns out it's not worth thinking about? Then if it is worth thinking about, we—"

"Be quiet, Avery."

He leaned in, brushed his lips lightly over hers. Like a test. Drew her in, a little more, brushed again. And watched those bold blue eyes of hers slowly close.

She made that hum in her throat as her lips parted, as her grip tightened, as all that Avery energy slammed into him.

It rocked him, that quick burst of need—his, hers. Where had it been? How had they missed it?

Tart and hot, lemons and fire—everything urgent and eager and open.

He boosted her up, and without a thought she wrapped her legs around his waist. She dived deeper into the kiss, trusting him absolutely as he staggered up the stairs to the landing, pressed her back to the wall.

She started to grab his hair—God, she loved his hair— and clunked him in the head with the tape dispensers.

Laughing, she dropped her head to his shoulder.

He said, "Ow," and made her laugh harder.

"Sorry, sorry." She hugged him, nuzzled into his throat. "Owen." She sighed, and thought—softer, warmer—*Owen* before she lifted her head to look at him. "It's definitely worth thinking about."

"Good thing you said so. Now I don't have to drop you on your head."

"Better put me down anyway."

"I can make it up. Then we can wrap presents."

"If we go up there, we won't wrap presents."

"That was code."

"Ah." Still, she eased down until she stood. "I think we should give this a few days, considering. Not to dis Ry's opinion, but if we take a few days, it won't just be impulse."

"And here I was thinking I've never given impulse a fair chance."

"I give it too many chances, so I guess we even out." If she hadn't been thinking about sleeping with him, she realized, she could ask him straight-out if he was seeing or sleeping with someone else. But to ask now felt like a demand.

Still . . .

"You probably have a date for New Year's Eve."

"Actually, I don't."

"You don't?"

"We've been pretty busy. I haven't thought about it."

She saw, clearly, he was now—and very likely along the same lines as her thoughts.

"Do you have a date?"

"Sort of. With Hope. You guys decided no work on or at the inn on New Year's Day. So we were going to hang out, watch chick flicks, and talk about how we didn't care we didn't have a date."

"We can have a date."

Sweet, she thought. Sexy. And, unfortunately, impossible. "I couldn't ditch Hope like that, not on a major date night."

"I'll have a party. My place."

Avery stared at him as if he'd just spoken in tongues. "Do you mean *this* New Year's Eve? The one in just over a week?"

"Sure."

"Owen, that's called spontaneity. You're not really familiar with the concept."

"I can be spontaneous."

"It takes you six months to plan a party. You make spreadsheets and itineraries. This kind of spontaneity? You may hurt yourself."

"Party," he said firmly, ignoring the fact that she spoke God's truth. "My place. New Year's Eve. And you'll stay over. With me."

With him. On New Year's Eve. "You're on. And if you actually pull this off, I'll not only stay, I'll make you breakfast."

"Deal." He wrapped around her again, kissed her until she went limp. "I'll lock up the back."

"'Kay." She worked on getting her breath back as he walked down the stairs. "Owen?"

He turned, smiled at her, and her heart did a long, slow roll. Was it any wonder she'd fallen for him at age five?

"Thanks for the tape."

"Anytime."

She heard the lock click as she pulled her shaky legs up the stairs. No problem with a wrapping marathon now, she thought, despite the late hour. Not only did she have plenty of tape, but she'd never be able to sleep with Owen Montgomery on the brain.

∾

OBVIOUSLY ALL THE blood had drained from his brain into his dick. Otherwise, Owen decided as he drove back from Hagerstown in the blustery afternoon, he'd never have scheduled a New Year's Eve party.

He had an inn to open, Christmas to deal with, a new project in the works. How the hell could he throw a party in a week?

He supposed he'd find out.

He braked at a light, pulled out his phone to make a few notes on food, on drink. Checked his messages. Two from Ryder, he noted, both demanding—basically—*Where the hell are you?*

As he was two minutes away from Boonsboro, he didn't bother to answer.

As he drove on, he let his mind flip from one party to another. The inn's opening bash was more involved than his impromptu holiday party. Most of the details were already in place—and his mother, aunt, and Hope had a handle on the bulk of it.

Still, he had a fat file on it in his briefcase, and a couple of spreadsheets on his computer. And, okay, an itinerary.

He considered generating one for his own party, assuring himself it wasn't obsessive. It was practical. A time and stress saver.

An obsessive time and stress saver, but so what?

He glanced over at Vesta, thought of Avery as he made the turn onto St. Paul. Why hadn't he just suggested they go out to dinner—then jump into bed? he wondered as he swung into the lot behind the inn.

Because she'd brought up New Year's Eve, and he'd had that brain drain going. It had all made sense at the time.

He got out of the truck, then just stood a moment in the cold, studying The Courtyard, the sweep of porches and pickets.

All that grace and charm, he thought, hadn't come easy. He remembered the rubble, the mud, the debris. He remembered the serious nightmare of pigeon shit—and really wished he didn't.

But they'd brought it back, and then some. If he could accomplish this, he could pull off a damn holiday party.

He headed in through The Lobby, stopped and grinned at the big, glossy table under the central chandelier, the straw-colored chairs against the exposed brick wall.

And then some, he thought again, and headed through the arch toward The Dining Room, and the voices.

He found Ryder and Beckett setting the huge, carved buffet in place under the window of exposed stone while his mother and Hope shifted the pretty wood tables around the space.

Dumbass lounged in the far corner, but lifted his head, thumped his tail when he saw Owen.

Idly Owen wondered if the dog saw him as a man-sized donut.

"Where the hell have you been?" Ryder demanded.

"I had some things. It looks great."

"It does." Justine beamed as she set a chair by the table. "We're going to put the big mirror right there. You know, the antique. And we realized we're going to need another server. It can go up there, under that window. I'll measure the space and run down to Bast, see if they have something that works."

"You have that piece you got at the fancy French place in Frederick," Ryder reminded her.

"It's warped." Instantly, Justine's face went stony. "One leg's shorter than the other three. I should never have bought anything there."

"I told you I shortened the other legs. You put enough stuff on it, you won't see the warping."

"They were rude," Hope put in. "Any business that doesn't make good on an obviously defective piece shouldn't *be* a business."

"It's paid for, I fixed it. Get over it."

"It was bought for The Lobby," Hope insisted. "We've already found another piece at Bast for that space."

"And if you hadn't had a stick up your butt, I'd've fixed it for The Lobby."

Justine aimed a hard stare. "Just whose butt are you referring to, Ryder, as I'm the one who told you to take the defective piece down to the basement?"

"Where I fixed it," he muttered. "I'm going to get it. Give me a hand," he said to Beckett.

More than willing to get out of the line of fire, Beckett aimed for the basement.

"If it doesn't work there, if you don't like it, we'll haul it out," Owen promised. "It's a good-looking piece."

"Defective, and not worth what I paid for it. I got caught up," Justine admitted, and rubbed the dog's ears when he walked over to lean on her. "Well, we'll see. Hope, that must be Carolee bringing in more kitchen things," she added when she heard the footsteps on the main stairs. "Maybe the two of you can get the chafing dishes, the coffee urn. Let's see how it all looks."

"Sure."

Owen opened his mouth, but a look from his mother cut off his offer to help. Justine held her tongue until Hope's footsteps retreated. "I wanted her out of the room for a few minutes." Then she folded her arms as Ryder and Beckett carried in the repaired server.

"Ryder Thomas Montgomery."

Owen knew that tone, that look. Though it wasn't aimed at him—this time—he felt his own balls shrink a little.

Head bowed, tail tucked, Dumbass slunk back over to his corner.

"Ma'am."

"I didn't raise you to be rude to people, to snarl at women, or to snap at employees. I expect you to be polite to Hope, whether or not you agree with her."

He set down the server. "Okay. But—"

"But?" The single syllable rang with warning and challenge.

Standing hip-shot now, Ryder put on his most agreeable expression. "Well, you said we were to treat her like family. So, do you want me to be polite to her, or treat her like family?"

Justine said nothing for a long, simmering moment. Beckett edged away from his brother as she started forward. She reached up, grabbed both Ryder's ears.

"Think you're clever?"

"Yes'm. I take after my mama."

She laughed, shook his head from side to side. "Your father's son is what you are." And poked him in the belly. "Watch your tone."

"Okay."

Nodding, Justine stepped back, fisted her hands on her hips. "That top's warped, Ry."

"Some, yeah. It's poorly made and overpriced, but it works—and it's pretty enough. Better when you put those big copper things on it."

"Maybe, yeah. Galls me. My mistake."

"Yeah, it was." Ryder shrugged. "You outfitted a nine-thousand-square-foot B&B from p-traps to four-posters, and this is your mistake? That's not shabby, Mom."

She slid him a glance. "You are clever. Maybe you do take after me."

She turned as Hope came in with a huge box, followed by Carolee with another.

"Let me take that." Ryder stepped over, took the box from Hope. "I'm being polite."

"Did it hurt?"

"Not yet. Might be sore later."

Beckett took the box from Carolee, and Owen stood back a moment, watched them. Unpacking boxes, pulling out the big coffee urn, the chafing dishes, the racks, shoving aside boxes and packing material—he'd haul it out later.

Carolee talking about washing wineglasses, his mother adjusting her hair tie. Beckett and Ryder making noises about hauling the mirror in so they could get next door and join the crew.

He waited while the three women studied the result on the piece in question.

"It doesn't show, but I'll know it's warped." Hope pushed at her hair. "That just irritates me." She shifted her gaze to Ryder. "I'll get over it."

"Good. Let's get that mirror in place and get out of here before they find something else for us to haul around."

"I need a minute first. Quick meeting," Owen announced.

"After we knock off," Ryder began.

"It's got to be now." Deliberately Owen put a sour look on his face. "It's about the U and O."

"Christ, don't tell me they're giving us a hassle with Use and Occupancy. The inspector signed off."

Owen gave Ryder a sigh, a slow shake of the head. "Yeah. I went up to Hagerstown to see if I could move this along. And . . . I got it."

Beckett pointed at him. "You got the U and O."

Grinning, Owen pointed back. "I got the U and O."

"Oh my God. Oh my *God*! Carolee." Justine grabbed her sister's hand.

Owen punched Ryder in the shoulder, then grinned at Hope. "Are you ready to move in? We can haul the rest of your stuff over. You can stay here tonight."

"I'm so ready. Owen!" Laughing she threw her arms around him, kissed him on the mouth. "I'm moving in." After the jump and squeal with his mother, with his aunt, Hope jumped at Beckett, kissed him noisily.

Then stopped short at Ryder.

"What do I get? A hearty handshake?"

She laughed again, shook her head, and gave him a very prim, very chaste peck on the cheek.

"Same thing," he complained.

But he threw an arm around Owen's shoulders, the other around Beckett's. "Son of a bitch. We did it."

Justine's eyes filled, spilled over. "My boys," she murmured. She spread her arms wide to embrace all three of her sons. She held tight there a moment, just held as Dumbass tried to nose into the hug.

"All right." Stepping back, she nodded as she brushed tears away. "Lunch, here. On me. Beckett, see if Clare can come over. Owen, call Avery, order us up some food, have her bring it over—and join us if she can. Hope, break out one—no two—of the bottles of champagne we're stocking for guests."

"Oh, you bet."

"I haven't washed all the glassware!" Carolee made a dash for the kitchen.

"Champagne?" Ryder commented. "At lunch?"

"Damn right, champagne."

"Speaking of champagne, sort of." Owen scratched his jaw. "Ry, do you have a date for New Year's Eve?"

"Yeah. The Giggler. But I'm going to bail."

"On New Year's Eve?" his mother demanded.

"Believe me, if you heard the giggle, you'd understand. Why?" he asked Owen. "You want to take me dancing?"

"I'm having a party."

"*This* New Year's?" his mother said, eyes wide.

"Yeah, yeah, this one." *Jeez!* "It's no big deal. Just a party. A holiday get-together. A thing with food and drink. You can come, right?"

Puffing out her cheeks, Justine continued to study him. "Sure."

"Ry?"

"Why not?"

"Clare's on her way up," Beckett announced as he pocketed his phone.

"New Year's Eve party, my place. Okay?"

"What year?" Beckett asked.

"Okay, that joke's old now. You in or not?"

"We were going to stay home. The boys want to watch the ball drop, but Murphy's the only one with a prayer of making it. I'll ask Clare if she wants to get a sitter."

"Good enough." Owen pulled out his notebook. "Lunch," he said, and D.A. thumped his tail in anticipation. "Give me the orders. I'll call them in."

As he started the list, he heard champagne pop from the kitchen. "That makes it official." He grinned at his family. "Welcome to Inn BoonsBoro."

# CHAPTER EIGHT

A S HOPE TRUSTED HER—AND WOULD LIKELY CHANGE
things around anyway—Avery organized her friend's
new kitchen. She liked the tidy, efficient space, and everything new, new, new.

"How much fun is this?" Still in her work jeans and Vesta
tee, Avery happily arranged flatware in Hope's drawer organizer. "Clare's missing out."

"You'll have this with kids," Hope called out from the
bath as she put away makeup.

"Yeah, you will. Ever think about having them?"

"Sure. One day. Do you?"

"Sure. Especially when I'm around Clare's boys for a
while. They're seriously addicting." She shut the drawer,
started on the next. "But having them is most traditionally
preceded by marriage—and that's the sticker."

"You've got too wide a romantic streak to really think of
marriage as a sticker."

"It's easy to be romantic for other people—it's no risk,
no fail—personally. Anyway, you're starting a whole new

adventure—and this is your first night. You're not nervous about staying here alone, are you?"

"No." Hope poked her head out. "But I thought you might like to stay. Pick a room."

"Hot damn!" Hands fisted around forks and spoons pumped jubilantly in the air. "I thought you'd never ask. Are you sure it's okay?"

"More than. Justine asked if I'd use each room over the next couple weeks. That way I can check for any glitches with plumbing, electric, even just the flow of the rooms. And I'd actually like to stay in my apartment here tonight—first night. So you can be my first guest."

"T&O. I'd be the first to sink to my ears in that big copper tub. No, wait. J&R. I'd have the fireplace *and* a copper tub. Or . . ."

Laughing, Hope came out. "It's a problem, isn't it?"

"A really good one. Maybe I should pick one out of a hat. Couldn't go wrong. Has Owen picked his room for opening night?"

"He's in Nick and Nora."

"Okay, I'll take that out of the hat since I'll probably be sleeping with him by then, and get my chance at that room opening night."

"Oh, really?"

"Yeah. We're taking a few days to make sure it's not just crazy." After closing the next drawer, she turned. "It doesn't feel crazy."

"Why would it? He's a great guy, gorgeous, smart, sweet. The two of you have a nice rhythm."

"That's part of the 'is this crazy.' We do have a nice rhythm. Sex changes the beat."

"I think both of you will adjust very well."

"I hope so, and along those lines I have to ask you for a big favor. See, last night he lent me some Scotch tape, and one thing led to another."

Now Hope fisted hands on her hips. "You've already slept with him, and you're just getting around to telling me?"

"No. Almost, but no. But while we were deciding to wait

a few days, I asked him if he had a date for New Year's Eve. Mostly I wanted to know if he was seeing—okay, sleeping—with anybody else."

"Reasonable."

"I should've just asked him, but I caged around it, and he asked me if I had one, and I told him you and I were going to hang out."

"Avery, if you want to go out with Owen on a major date night, I'm fine with it. Absolutely, one hundred percent. You should know that."

"I do, just like you should know I'd hate myself if I ditched you. You wouldn't do it to me."

"I might if Owen asked me out." Hope fluttered her eyelashes.

"Get your own Montgomery boy. There's one left."

"Maybe I could just borrow Owen. Test him out for you."

"Aw, you're such a good friend." Miming wiping a tear aside, she gave Hope a hug. "No. Anyway, Owen popped up with this idea of having a party at his place, which is very un-Owenish as he can't plan and plot it out for weeks, preferably months. So we're all going to ring in the new at Owen's."

Thoughtful, Hope opened cupboards to check Avery's kitchen organization. "Avery, I don't have a date. I don't want a date, but not having a date on New Year's at a party is just embarrassing."

"Not when you look like you do. Besides, not everybody's going to be coupled. I could practically recite Owen's most likely guest list, so I can guarantee other singles of *both* varieties. He throws a really good party when he throws one. You'll meet more people," Avery wheedled. "And that's good community relations for an innkeeper."

Hope turned the handle of a cup a fraction to the left. "Now you're digging."

"Yeah, but it's still true. Clare and Beck are getting a sitter, I checked with her. And they can bring you home. Unless you get wild and crazy and hook up."

"I won't be wild and crazy, that's a promise." Hope blew out a breath. "But I probably shouldn't decline an invitation from one of the bosses, at least this early on."

"You'll have fun. I promise." Delighted, Avery threw her arms around Hope. "Thanks."

With her arm still around Hope's shoulders, she turned, scanned the living room. "It was really nice of Ryder to bring your tree over."

"He griped about the decorations."

"But he bagged it up, brought it over, set it up here."

"Okay, it was nice of him, even though Justine probably told him to do it."

"Either way, you've got your Christmas tree in your new apartment. It already looks like you in here. It looks like Hope. Are you happy?"

"I really am, and excited. I can't wait to—"

They both jolted at the rattle of the doorknob, stared as the door opened.

"Oh, Jesus, Clare! Next time," Avery suggested, "just shoot us both."

"Sorry. Kids are asleep. Beckett handed me the key, and told me to get my butt up here for a couple hours. He knew how much I wanted to." Looking around, she pulled off her gloves. "Oh, you've already done so much! It looks—"

"Like Hope," Avery finished.

"Yes, it does. What can I do?"

"Kitchen's mine."

"I just finished in the bathroom," Hope told her. "I guess I should move to the bedrooms."

"Then . . ." Clare opened the door again, lifted the painting she'd left propped against the wall.

"My housewarming gift! Oh, I love it."

"Madeline said you could change your mind," Avery told her, "if it didn't suit once you moved in. You can exchange it at Gifts for another painting, or whatever."

"It's exactly what I want. It's gorgeous, and every day's spring when I look at those cherry blossoms. Thank you. Both of you. I know just where I want it, in the bedroom so I can wake up to spring every morning."

Taking the painting, Hope held it out at arm's length. "I'm going to hang it right now."

In the bedroom Clare made the graceful sleigh bed Hope

had chosen, fluffed pillows, smoothed the duvet while Hope—meticulous as Owen—measured and marked and leveled.

"It's perfect here. Exactly right," Hope murmured.

"So are you. It feels like you're perfect here. Exactly right here."

"I want to be."

"Kitchen's done." Avery came in, turned, smiled at the painting. "You were right about it. It says spring, even on a night like this. Welcome home, Hope."

❧

LATER, WHEN CLARE left and Avery dashed home for what she needed for the night, Hope took a solo walk through the building.

It did feel right, she thought. Like home.

As she climbed back to her apartment, she caught the drift of honeysuckle, sweet as summer.

"I'm here," she said, "and I'll be staying now. I guess neither of us has to be alone anymore."

❧

THE NEXT MORNING, Avery came downstairs to find the Montgomery family already on the job, and Hope in the kitchen making breakfast.

"We haven't organized the kitchen yet," Avery commented.

"I'm making do. I want to try out a few things, and this is a good chance."

"I'll give you a hand."

"No." To emphasize the point, Hope held up a finger. "No hand. You're a guest. Go on into The Dining Room."

"Is there coffee there?"

"There is. Avery? How was J&R?"

"Like a dream. Only missing the madwoman in the attic, which I guess would make it a nightmare anyway. Coffee first, then report."

She walked through, helped herself at the copper coffee

urn and considered. It might be the perfect time, she mused. Everyone was happy, excited. And a major project wrapped— beautifully wrapped. A few more days of work, sure, a few more details, but basically done.

Owen wandered in. "I heard you were the first guest."

"I have that distinction."

"But we're all getting breakfast. Hope texted everybody this morning." He sat across from her. "How was it?"

"Wonderful. Full report when you're all in here. You're in The Lounge?"

"Mom wants another little cabinet, for the front corner. Ry's hanging a mirror, Beck's putting some shelves in the closet in there. You look good," he added.

She eyed him over her coffee. "Is that so?"

"That's so. Rested, but revved. Are you working today?"

"Not until four. I'm closing."

"Why are you up so early?"

"Habit. And I must've sensed somebody else was cooking."

Carolee carried in a tray of thick waffles, filled the room with their scent as she put them in one of the chafing dishes. She sent her nephew and Avery a wink before she bustled out. Hope brought in a clear glass bowl of berries, a glass pitcher of juice.

"Hope, I could—"

Hope made a dismissive sound. "Guest," she said and went out again.

"I really want to try out that stove top," Avery muttered. "It's so shiny."

In came a platter of bacon, another of creamy scrambled eggs.

"We've been summoned." Beckett strolled in, sniffed. "Smells like breakfast." He lifted the lid of a chafing dish. "Looks like breakfast." And snagged a slice of bacon. "Oh yeah. Tastes like breakfast. Hey, waffles."

"Waffles?" Ryder came in, headed straight for the chafing dish. "Those fat, round ones, too."

"Help yourselves." Hope nudged Justine into the room.

"If you want anything, please ask. And honest feedback, please. It's better to know if something's not working now than to find out after we open."

She stood back, waited as plates were filled, seats taken.

Ryder took the first syrup-loaded bite of waffle. "You're not fired," he told her.

"High praise."

"It's wonderful, Hope." Justine scooped up a little egg. "And the tables look cheerful, just as we wanted. Sit down."

"I still have a few things to see to, but I'd really like to hear what Avery thought about her night in J&R."

"Like I'd won a grand prize. *The* grand prize," she corrected. "I'm really clean because I tried out the tub last night, and the shower this morning. Both are incredible. And the amenities are just delicious." She held out an arm to Owen. "Smell me."

He did. "Nice."

"Yeah, it is. The towels are soft and thick—and God, let me say the heated tile floors, the heated towel rack? Inspired. Everything about the bathroom makes you feel pampered, relaxed, indulged."

"That was the goal." Justine beamed at her. "On the nose."

"Also, I want one of the robes for my own. The fireplace is such a great feature, especially when you're in that amazing bed. And let me add it's the most comfortable bed I've had the pleasure of sleeping on. It's great having all those pillows, the different densities. I tried out the TV, the clock radio thingie, read a couple chapters of *Jane Eyre*, picked it up on the DVD.

"If I had ten thumbs, they'd all go up. It was absolutely fabulous. I really appreciate having the chance to test the room."

"That's what I wanted to hear. I'll check back in a few minutes," Hope said as she went back to the kitchen.

"No questions, complaints, suggestions?" Justine asked Avery.

"I have a suggestion. Don't change a thing in that room. There's nothing about it I didn't love."

"All right." With a satisfied nod, Justine sat back. "One down."

"While you're all here, there is something I'd like to talk to you about. Something that has to do with the inn, indirectly," Avery added.

"Talk," Ryder invited as he rose. "Want more waffles. Wait, where's Dumbass?"

"He's in Reception, by the fire. We can't have a dog in here with the food, Ryder," his mother told him.

"But—"

"You're not to feed him from the table. Hope gave him a couple of dog biscuits, and he's perfectly happy out there. Now, Avery, what's this about?"

Her heart thudded, but she told herself it was time.

"I expect when you have guests at the inn, some will come over to Vesta for lunch, for dinner, maybe a beer. Others may want something other than a family restaurant and drive over to South Mountain, or into Shepherdstown. It's too bad the restaurant on the other corner didn't work out."

"Don't get me started," Owen muttered.

"We all agree about that," Avery continued, "but the point is, we could use another restaurant in town, one a few clicks up from family Italian and pizza."

Nerves tickled along her skin. She hated being nervous, focused on keeping her voice brisk. "And people often come into my place, ask where they could get a glass of wine. Sure I serve it, but it's not the kind of place you go for a quiet drink or a romantic meal."

"We want to get the bakery project going first," Owen told her. "We're going to look for another tenant for the restaurant. We're just going to have to be more careful in the selection process this time around, find somebody with a sensible business plan, and an understanding of the location."

"I agree." Avery cleared her throat. "You bought the connecting building." To keep her hands busy, she toyed with her eggs. "I know you've considered going retail there, but it used to be one building, and if you opened it back up, there could be a lounge on one side, a restaurant on the other— connected. People could go have a drink, or come in for dinner. Or both. And there's room in the second part for a little stage. Live music's a draw. There's nothing like that in town. A good restaurant with an attached lounge or pub. Good food, nice wine and beer and cocktails, some music."

"It's a good idea," Justine began.

"Don't get *her* started," Ryder warned.

"It would add to the inn," Avery went on. "Guests would have more choices, and could walk right across St. Paul, have a bottle of wine, and not worry about driving. You could arrange for room service from there, just like we're going to do for you from Vesta. Don't want to go out? Have some pizza in The Lounge, or a nice, quiet dinner in The Dining Room. And you're doing packages. Adding a package with a dinner for two at a nice restaurant, right next door—or again, brought to them here—would be a draw."

"No question." Beckett nodded at her. "And we've tossed it around, some. The sticking point is finding someone who not only wants to run a place like that but can do it, and do it right."

"I want to." She said it fast, her hands clasped in her lap under the table. "I can do it right."

"You've got a restaurant. You've got Vesta." Ryder narrowed his eyes at her. "And Little Red, if you tell me you're thinking of packing it in over there, I'm going to be pissed off. I need my Warrior's pizza fix."

"She's not thinking of that." Concerned, Owen nudged his plate aside. "Two places, Avery? Don't you have enough to do already?"

"I'd give Franny more responsibility, use Dave in both sites on a rolling schedule. I'd need a good manager for the new place, and I've already got someone in mind. Justine, it didn't work before because it wasn't the right fit. I know exactly what to do there to make it work, to make it pop."

"I'm listening."

"Oh brother." Ryder lowered his head and focused on waffles.

"You want warm, contemporary without being showy. Maybe a couple of love seats as well as low and high tops in the pub area. One big-ass bar, and you get bartenders who know what they're doing. Relaxed, but just a touch of edge. Good wine, good drafts—maybe a mix of local stuff. Classy."

Because nobody stopped her, Avery took a breath, and plowed through.

"For lunch, you offer a wide variety of salads, sandwiches, soups, and you're open for lunch, every day—which was a problem before. You keep the prices reasonable, the service friendly and welcoming."

"Which was also a problem before," Beckett commented.

"Yeah, it was." She gave him a nod, plowed on. "For dinner, you add entrees. A good steak, fish, chicken, some interesting appetizers. As much as you can, you stay local for the produce, for the meat. You make it fun, and you don't forget you're on The Square in Boonsboro. I know the town, I know what people want."

"I bet you do," Justine murmured.

"I've written up a business plan. I've drafted out a menu, price points. I know it involves some work for you, reconnecting the two spaces, fixing up the pub area, but it'd be worth it." She took a breath. "I'd make it worth it."

"How long have you been thinking about this?" Owen asked her.

"About two years—when I could see the other place just wasn't going to work, and why. It's not impulse," she insisted, knowing that look. "I know I can be impulsive, but not when it's business. You trusted me when I came to you about opening Vesta in your building."

"We were right to." Beckett considered her. "I want to take another look at the space before we make any decisions—one way or the other."

"Sure. I'll send you the business plan, the sample menu, and so on."

"Good." Justine nodded. "I want to see what you've laid out. Still, we're going to need to talk this over, Avery, my boys and I."

"I know that. And if it's no, well . . . I'll try to convince you to change your mind. So. I'd better get going." She rose, automatically bussed her dishes. "Thanks again for letting me test the room. It was a night to remember."

"We'll talk soon," Justine promised her, then considered the coffee she'd let go cold as Avery went out. "Thoughts?"

"Running a restaurant is a lot of work," Owen began. "Running two? She'd have to manage two crews, two menus, and add this pub she's talking about, it's basically three businesses to manage."

"She's the Little Red Machine." Ryder shrugged as he got up to get more coffee for his mother. "My money's on her."

"I need to look at the space, make sure it can be done."

Justine just smiled at Beckett. "Anything can be done. The first advantage, for us, would be having someone in there we know, can trust, and who has a good, solid, innovative idea. Her concept's pretty damn perfect."

"I like the idea." Still Owen hesitated. "My concern would be having one person, having Avery, trying to do it all."

"That's concern for her. You're worried she'd run herself ragged, take on too much. A friend's concern," Justine added. "With some 'when would we have time together now that we're thinking about spending time together' mixed in."

When Owen shifted his gaze, coolly, toward Ryder, Ryder threw up his hands. "Not a word. Not from me."

"Please." Justine let out a snort, flicked a hand in the air. "Do you think I have to be told? Foolish, foolish boy. You still don't comprehend my powers?" She smiled again, smugly, when Owen only shifted in his chair. "I understand that concern. I have some of my own. But like Ry, I'd put my money on Avery to make this work—to put something on that corner that would be a boost to the town. To the inn," she added. "And the other businesses."

She sat another moment, nodded to herself. "Let's take a look at the space, then you boys can think about how it could be done, if it should be done, and what's involved. We'll look over her business plan, see what kind of menus she'd project. After that, we'll talk to Avery again. Okay?"

"Works for me," Ryder said and got a nod from Beckett.

"We'll check it out," Owen decided. "Go from there."

～

LATER, OWEN HUNTED up Avery in The Lounge. She sat on the floor, surrounded by DVDs, busily slitting open the packaging with a little tool.

"What're you doing?"

"Just basking on the beaches of Saint-Tropez."

"Are you wearing sunscreen?"

"With this skin? I use a force field."

He sat on the brown leather bench. "Isn't this your day off?"

"Yeah, which is why I'm at the beach. While I'm basking, I get to play with the movies. Hope gave me this opener thing. I didn't know they made this opener thing for DVDs. All those cumulative hours of fighting with the stupid sticky deal and the wrapping, when all I had to do was zip. I'm making up for it, opening all the inn's complimentary DVDs while Hope and Carolee have a powwow. Did you ever see this?"

She held up a DVD of *Love Actually*.

"No."

Head tilted, she gave him a wise-owl stare. "Because you think it's a chick flick."

"It is a chick flick."

"That's where you're wrong."

"Does anything blow up?"

"No, but there's nudity and adult language. It's not a chick flick, it's just a really excellent movie. I have my own DVD of this one. And this one." She held up a copy of *The Terminator*.

"That's a movie. Why are you nervous?"

"I'm not nervous. I'm basking and using my handy tool while discussing cinema."

"Avery."

Having someone who knew your moods just that well, she thought, could be an upside or a downside, depending on the situation. Anyway, it saved time.

"I'm afraid your family sent you in here to tell me no way, no how on the new restaurant idea."

"We haven't decided either way. We looked over the space, kicked some things around. It looks doable—on our end—but Beckett needs to work on it some."

"Doable—on your end." She knew him, too. "But not so much on mine."

"I didn't say that. But I'm wondering how you're going to manage your time, focus, energies. I've got a pretty good idea how much time and work you put in at Vesta."

She zipped the next DVD. "What makes you think so?"

Because I've watched you, he thought, more than I realized.

"I eat there, have meetings there. I've been working across the street from your place virtually every damn day for more than a year. I've got a picture, Avery."

"If you've got an accurate picture you'd see I know what I'm doing."

"I'm not saying otherwise. But what you're talking about means doing it in two places. It feels like you'd be taking on more than one person could handle."

Taking her time, she balled the trash, tossed it in the box beside her. "I get the feeling that your vote on this proposal's coming in on the no side."

"I didn't say that either."

"You don't have to. I've known you, Owen, as long as you've known me."

"None of us wants you to wear yourself out, or get your-self in a bind."

Just in case she'd be tempted to throw it, Avery set the DVD zipper down. Carefully.

"Do you think I don't know my capabilities and limits, and my potential? How many irons are in your fire, Owen? How many rental properties do you oversee? How many jobs have you got in various stages, how many clients on your list, people on your payroll, subcontractors to juggle?"

"There are a lot of us to handle it. There's just one Avery."

She shoved at her hair—currently the shade of glossy mahogany. "Don't give me that. I know you take the lead on the rentals. You deal with the tenants. I know, because I *am* a tenant. You're the detail man, Owen, and Montgomery Family Contractors has a hell of a lot of details. Ryder's job boss, Beckett designs the space. Your mom handles the books, helps clients with interior design, and looks at the big picture. You tie all the little pieces together. And every one of you—including your mom from time to time—builds."

"That's true, but—"

"But nothing." Temper rising, she snapped the words off. "You've worked across the street from my place for over a year. Well, right back at you. I've seen just what you've done, had to do, dealt with, figured out. You, Owen, individually as well as with the rest. If you told me you were planning to remodel the freaking White House I'd figure you could do just that. You ought to have the same faith in me."

"It's not a matter of faith," he began, but she was shoving up to her feet.

"Listen, if the answer's no, it's no. It's your property, and you've got a right to rent it to whoever you rent it to. I wouldn't hold it against you, any of you. But the answer better not be no just because you don't think I'm up for it."

"Avery—"

"No. Just no. You should've asked to see my business plan, my scheduling outline, my menu, my P&L from Vesta, and my projected budget on the new restaurant. You should've treated me with the same respect as you would any other businessperson, any other prospective tenant. I'm not a dreamer, Owen, and I never have been. I know what I can do, then I do it. If you don't get that, then you don't know me as well as both of us thought."

He knew her well enough not to follow her out when she walked away. She wasn't just mad—that he could get around. But he'd managed to hurt her as well as piss her off.

"Good job," he muttered. To give himself some time to think, he gathered up the DVDs she'd done, stacked them in the cabinet under the wall-mounted flat screen, automatically alphabetizing them as he went.

## CHAPTER NINE

H E CONSIDERED APPROACH AND TIMING, AND GAVE
a lot of weight to holiday spirit.

At five o'clock on Christmas Eve, Owen knocked on
Avery's door.

She'd dyed her hair—again—he noted, this time in a
shade he thought of as Christmas Red. She wore skinny
black pants that showed off the shape of her legs and a
crisscrossing sweater as blue as her eyes. Her feet were bare,
so he saw she'd married the Christmas Red hair with Christmas Green toenail polish.

Why was that sexy?

"Merry Christmas."

"Not yet."

"Okay. Merry Christmas Eve." Working it, he added an
easy smile. "Got a minute?"

"Not much more than. I'm going down to Clare's for a
while, then heading over to Dad's. I'm staying there tonight so—"

"You can fix him Christmas breakfast, hang out before
you both go to my mother's for her Christmas thing." He

tapped his fingers to his temple. "Everybody's holiday schedule, right here. Hope's in Philadelphia, having the eve with her family, and heading back tomorrow afternoon. Ry's swinging by Clare's, then we're both figuring on staying the night at Mom's."

"So you can get Christmas breakfast *and* dinner."

"It's a big draw."

"If you're going to Clare's, why are you here? I'll see you in a half hour."

"I wanted a few minutes. Can I come in, or are you still pissed at me?"

"I'm not pissed at you. I got over it." She stepped back to let him in.

"You started unpacking," he commented. By his gauge she'd reduced the stacks of boxes and tubs by more than half.

"Continued unpacking," she corrected. "I was pissed. I cook when I'm mad or upset. My father has a freezer loaded with lasagna, manicotti, various soups. So I had to stop and shift the energy to more unpacking. Nearly done."

"Productive."

"I hate to waste a good mad."

"I'm sorry."

She shook her head, waved it off. "I have to finish getting dressed." When she turned toward the bedroom, he followed.

He didn't wince—no point making her mad again—but she'd obviously had some trouble deciding on the sweater and pants. Other choices, rejected, were scattered over the bed. He'd always admired the antique brass bed, the turned spindles, the old-fashioned charm of it. But it was tough to appreciate it buried under heaps of clothes, pillows, and her overnight bag.

She pulled open the top drawer of her dresser—where Owen figured most people stored underwear, but saw clearly the entire drawer of earrings.

"Jesus, Avery. How many ears do you have?"

"I don't wear rings, a watch, bracelets—usually. They don't do well with pizza dough and sauces. So I compensate."

After some study, she tried on silver hoops with smaller hoops dangling within the circle. "What do you think?"

"Ah . . . nice."

"Hmm." She took them off, changed them for dangles of blue stones and silver beads.

"I came by to—"

Her gaze whipped to his in the mirror. "I have something to say first."

"Okay. You first."

She moved to the bed, added a couple more things to the overnight bag, zipped it. "I may have overreacted a little the other day. A little. Because it was you, I think, and I expected you to believe in me."

"Avery—"

"Not finished." Moving quickly, she crossed to the bathroom, brought out a hanging bag. When she laid it on the bed, he saw through the clear front it was loaded with makeup and all those tools women used.

How did she have time to use that much makeup? When did she? He'd seen her face without all the stuff. It was a really good face.

"I should have expected you'd think of practicalities first. I guess I wanted you to think of what I wanted first. Still not finished," she said when he opened his mouth.

She rolled the bag, tied it, set it in the overnight.

"Then after I'd cooked enough so that the town of Boonsboro will eat well should there be an unexpected famine, and unpacked stuff I'm not even sure why I have to begin with, I realized that while I'd be really upset if your family said no because they didn't think I could handle it, I really don't want you to say yes just because it's me, and there's a family-friendship history."

She turned now. "I want to be respected, but I won't be pandered to. Maybe that's a hard line for you, Owen, but it's my line. I'm not moving it."

"It's fair, and I'll probably slip off the line sometimes. So will you."

"Yeah, you're right, but we need to try to stay on it." She

went to the closet, got out a pair of boots. Tall black boots, he noted, with high, skinny heels.

He'd never seen her wear them. Or really anything quite like them. She sat on the bench at the foot of her bed. His mouth went dry as she pulled them on, zipped them up.

"Um. So. I wanted to say . . ." He trailed off as she rose. "Wow."

"It's the boots, right?" Considering, she looked down at them. "Hope talked me into them."

"I love Hope," he said as she pulled open the door of the closet, checked herself out in the full-length mirror on the back. "I've never seen you wear anything like that."

"It's Christmas Eve. I'm not working."

"You're working for me."

She laughed, sent him a sparkling look. "Your reaction is noted and appreciated. I rarely get a chance to wear heels. Hope's helping me fill in the wide, wide gaps in my shoe wardrobe. We'd better get going. Since you're here you can help me haul down the presents so I don't have to keep going up and down the steps in these boots."

"Sure, but I still need that minute."

"Oh, right, sorry. I thought it was about the thing, and we dealt with the thing."

"Not the whole thing." He took a brightly wrapped box out of his coat pocket. "We have this tradition in my family about getting one present on Christmas Eve."

"I remember."

"So, here's yours."

"Is this a I-better-make-up-with-her-or-she-won't-sleep-with-me-next-week present?"

"No, I saved that one for tomorrow."

She laughed again, made him grin with the quick, cheerful peal of it. "Can't wait to see that one."

She took the box, shook. Got nothing. "You padded it."

"You're a shaker. Everybody knows."

"I like to guess first, it adds to the suspense. Could be earrings," she speculated. "As you were so appalled by my earring drawer, let me say, if so, trust me, you can never have too many." She ripped away, tossing the ribbon and paper on her dresser.

She opened the box, pulled off the cotton batting he'd used to pad it. And saw two keys.

"For the building across the street," he told her. "Both sides."

She lifted her gaze to his face, said nothing.

"I looked over your business plan after you sent it to Mom. That, and your menu, the rest. It's solid. It's good. You're good."

He let out a breath when she sat on the bench again, just stared at the keys in the box.

"Full disclosure. Ryder gave you the thumbs-up from the jump. The Little Red Machine. You know he calls you that sometimes."

She nodded, didn't speak.

"Beckett came down on your side after he'd gone through the buildings again. Part of that, if you ask me, is because now he wants to design it, wants his hands in it. But the other part is because he believes in you. And Mom? You're planning to do exactly what she wants in that space, more than she thought she could get. She doesn't have any doubts.

"As for me—"

"If you'd said no, it would be no."

His brows drew together, his hands dug into his pockets. "Wait a minute. Wait. We don't work that way."

"Owen." Head down, she turned the keys over and over in the box. "They listen to you. Maybe it doesn't feel like it or seem like it to you all the time. But on something like this? On business? They know you're the go-to, and they respect that. The same as you all respect Beckett on design, and Ryder on the builds, on the hiring and firing of crew. You have no idea how much I've admired and envied your family over the years."

He couldn't think of a thing to say.

"You didn't say no."

"It wasn't a matter of not believing in you, Avery, not ever. You were right that I should've asked to see your projections and plans. But I wasn't thinking of you that way. I wasn't looking at you that way. I'm not used to thinking and looking at you, at this, at us, the way I am now. And we haven't really started."

Still staring down at the keys, she said nothing.

"You work so hard."

"I need to." She pressed her lips tight together for a moment. "I'm not going to talk about that, the whole psyche thing, the issue thing, not now. Okay?"

"Okay. Oh, man." When she lifted her eyes to his, they were brimming—gorgeous, heartbreaking, shimmering blue. "Do you have to?"

"I'm not going to cry. Goddamn it, I'm not going to ruin my makeup. I spent forever on my stupid makeup."

"You look great." He sat on the bench beside her. "You look amazing."

"I'm not going to cry. I just need a minute to pull it back." But she lost the battle on one single tear, then swiped it quickly away. "I didn't know how much I wanted this, not until I opened that box. Maybe I didn't let myself know, so I wouldn't be crushed if you said no."

Still battling tears, she took another slow breath. "I'd rather be pessimistic than disappointed, so I didn't tell anybody how much I wanted this, not even Clare. Not even my dad. I told myself it was just business, just a proposal. But it's a lot more to me. I can't explain it to you right now. I can't screw up my makeup, and I'm going to be really happy in a minute anyway."

He took her hand, considered ways to flip the tears toward that happy. "What are you naming it?"

"MacT's Restaurant and Tap Room."

"I like it."

"Me, too."

"And what does the famous MacTavish Gut Feeling say about it?"

"That I'm going to *rock* it. Oh God, it's going to be great. Oh God!" Laughing now, she threw her arms around him, then leaped up to bounce in those skinny, sexy boots. "Just you wait. I have to stop in downstairs, get a bottle of champagne. Two bottles." She leaped into his arms when he rose. "Thank you."

"It's business."

"Thanks are still appropriate."

"You're right."

"And this is personal." She pressed her lips to his, slid her fingers into his hair, swayed against him. "Thank you, so much."

"You're not going to thank my brothers like that, right?"

"Not exactly like that." She laughed, hugged him again. "Neither of them was my first boyfriend."

She broke away, grabbed for her overnight bag. "We're going to be late now. You hate being late."

"Tonight's the exception."

"Make another? Don't get that look on your face when we go over into the wrapping area to get the presents. I know it's disorganized and messy."

"I'll have no look."

He took the overnight bag while she swung on a coat, a scarf, pulled on gloves. And he manfully restrained his expression when she led him into the room full of presents, bags, wrapping, tangled ribbon.

"All this?"

"Some's for tonight, some's for Dad's, some for your mother's. I like Christmas."

"It shows." He handed her back the overnight as it would be the lightest and easiest to carry. "Go ahead, get your champagne, I'll start loading this."

"Thanks."

At least she'd stacked gifts into open cardboard boxes, he thought as he hefted the first of several. And because she'd left the room he let his eyes roll toward the ceiling.

"I heard that look!" she called out, and her laughter echoed back as she hurried down the stairwell.

❧

FROM THE TIME she'd walked into Clare's with presents for the kids, the dogs, her friends—with bottles of champagne and one of the trays of lasagna she'd made during her mad—until the time when she crawled into her childhood bed, Avery found Christmas Eve absolutely perfect.

Since Clare had come back to Boonsboro, a young widow with two little boys and a baby growing inside her, Avery had spent a few hours of the night before Christmas with Clare and her children.

But this year, the house brimmed full with Montgomerys.

This year she'd watched little Murphy climb up Beckett's leg, nimble as a monkey, while Beckett continued to talk football with Clare's father.

And Owen patiently helping Harry build some complex battleship out of what looked like half a million Legos. Ryder challenging Liam to a PlayStation tournament while Dumbass and the two puppies milled around, wrestled, and surreptitiously begged for food.

She'd enjoyed listening to Justine and Clare's mother talk about wedding plans. And she caught the twinkle in her father's eyes when he looked at Justine—how had she ever missed it? Everything in her warmed at his big belly laugh when Murphy deserted Beckett to climb up the tree trunk of Willy B's leg.

There was magic yet in the world, she'd thought, because she'd seen it in three young boys.

Still more magic, she decided now as she lay in bed watching the sun slowly tint the sky outside her window, when Owen had walked her out to her car. When he'd kissed her in the frosty air with the shimmer of lights, the smell of pine lingering.

A wonderful night. She closed her eyes to hold it to her one more moment. And a wonderful day ahead.

She slipped out of bed—quiet, quiet—pulled on thick socks, clipped her hair back. In the low light she pulled the bag out of her overnight before creeping out of the room.

She tiptoed down—right on the fourth step since it creaked in the middle—and into the living room with its big, sagging sofa, its big, brightly decorated tree, and its little brick fireplace with two stockings hung.

Hers bulged.

"How does he *do* that?" she muttered.

The stocking had been empty the night before. They'd

gone up to bed at the same time, and she'd read for an hour to decompress from the evening.

She'd *heard* him snoring in the next room.

He managed it every year. No matter when she went to bed or how early she rose. He'd fill that stocking as he had every year of her life.

Shaking her head, she filled his with the silly gifts, his favorite candy, a Turn The Page gift certificate, and the annual lottery ticket, because you never knew.

She stepped back, smiling, hugged herself.

Just two stockings, she thought, but they were full, they were close, and they mattered.

In her thick socks and flannel pajamas, she went into the kitchen, one no bigger than the one in her apartment.

She'd learned to cook here, she remembered, on the old gas stove. Out of necessity at first. Willy B could do a great many things, and do them well. Cooking wasn't on the list.

He'd tried, she remembered. So hard.

When her mother walked out, he'd tried so hard to bridge that gap, to keep his daughter level, happy, to make sure she knew how much he loved her.

He'd succeeded there, but in the kitchen? Burned pans, undercooked chicken, overcooked meat, singed vegetables— or vegetables cooked to mush.

She'd learned. And what she'd begun out of necessity became a kind of love. And maybe a little compensation, she thought now as she opened the refrigerator for eggs, milk, butter.

He'd done so much for her, been so much for her. Making a meal meant she could give something back. God knew he'd praised her early efforts to the skies.

She prepared to fix him Christmas breakfast, as she had every year since she'd been twelve.

By the time she had coffee brewed, bacon draining, the little round table in the dining room set, she heard his footsteps, and his booming *Ho, ho, ho!*

Every year, she thought with a grin. As dependable as the sunrise.

"Merry Christmas, my beautiful little girl."

"Merry Christmas, my big, handsome father." She rose to her toes to kiss him, burrowed into his bear hug.

Nobody, she thought, wallowing a little, but nobody gave hugs as wonderful as Willy B MacTavish.

He pecked a kiss on the top of her head. "I see Santa came, filled the stockings."

"I saw that. He's sneaky. Have some coffee. We've got OJ, fresh berries, bacon, and the griddle heating up for pancakes."

"Nobody cooks like my girl."

"Nobody eats like my dad."

He slapped his hand on his belly. "Big space to fill."

"That you are, Willy B. But you know, when a man has a girlfriend, he has to watch his figure."

His ears went pink. "Oh now, Avery."

Adoring him, she drilled him playfully in the belly, then sobered. "I'm happy for you, Daddy. For both of you, that you have each other. You know Tommy would be happy, too, that Justine has you, and you have her."

"We're just . . ."

"It doesn't matter. What matters is having each other. Drink your coffee."

"Yes, ma'am." He took the first sip. "Never tastes as good when I make it."

"You're kitchen challenged, Dad. It's a curse."

"It sure missed you. I like seeing you in here, baby. You were always a natural cook. And now you're going to have *two* restaurants."

"*And* a pub."

"You're a dynasty."

She laughed as she ladled batter on the hot griddle. "A tiny one, but I'm pretty excited. It'll be a while, but I need a while to finish planning it out."

"Justine's excited, too, and real pleased it's you moving in there. She sets a lot of store by you."

"As I do with her, with all of them. Wasn't it great being at Clare's last night?" Happy as Christmas morning, she flipped the pancakes. "Seeing everybody there, seeing how the kids are with Beckett, with all of them. All that noise and sweetness and . . . family."

As she looked over at her father, her smile went wistful. "You wanted a big family."

"I've got the best family any man could have, right here in the kitchen."

"Me, too. But I wanted to say, I know you wanted lots of kids, and you'd have been great with a big family—just as great as you were with just me."

"What do *you* want, baby?"

"It looks like I want two restaurants."

Willy B cleared his throat. "And Owen."

She flipped the pancakes onto a platter, glanced over her shoulder. As she suspected, her big guy blushed. "It looks like I want him, too. You're all right with that?"

"He's a good boy—man. You always had an eye for him."

"Dad, I was five. I didn't know what having an eye meant."

"I wouldn't be so sure. I just . . . you let me know if he doesn't treat you right."

"And you'll crush him like a worm."

Putting on a fierce scowl, Willy B flexed his considerable biceps. "If I have to."

"I'll keep it in mind." She turned with the platter of steaming pancakes. "Let's eat so we can go rip into those presents."

❧

IT WOULDN'T BE Christmas to Avery's mind without a crowd in the kitchen. She'd always appreciated Justine for opening her house, and the big kitchen in it, to her, to her father. And this year with the addition of Clare and the kids, Clare's parents, and Hope, crowds milled everywhere.

And kids, she mused. Clare's boys, Carolee's two grand-daughters. Squeeze in Justine's two dogs—who managed to do just that as often as possible—Ryder's D.A., and the two puppies, and Christmas was, to Avery, as perfect as it got.

She loved her one-on-one time with her father, but this— the noise, the overstimulated kids, the excited dogs, the smell of ham baking, sauces simmering, pies cooling—plucked a chord deep inside her.

She wanted this, had always wanted this, for herself. For her own.

She stopped mincing garlic long enough to take the glass of wine Owen offered her.

"You look happy."

"If you're not happy on Christmas, when?"

Curious, he peered into the mixing bowl beside her. "Smells good."

"It'll taste better when it's inside the mushroom caps and baked."

"Stuffed mushrooms, huh? Maybe you can make some of those for next week."

She took another sip of wine, set down the glass, and went back to mincing. "I could do that."

"How about those little meatballs you do sometimes?"

"Cocktail meatballs."

"Yeah, those."

"It's possible."

"I tapped Mom for a ham, thought I'd slice it up for sandwiches, maybe get a couple of party platters of cheese and dipping vegetables, like that. And—"

"Don't get platters. Just get the stuff. I'll show you how to tray it."

He'd hoped she'd say that. "Okay. If you give me a list of what you need for the other stuff, I'll pick it up." D.A. snuck up, sat delicately on her foot to get her attention. Avery gave him as solemn a look as he gave her.

"You don't want this," she assured him.

She heard wild laughter—Harry's?—roll up from the lower-level family room. "I'm number *one*! Number one, suckers!"

"Wii." Owen shook his head with mock sorrow. "Brings out the best or the worst in us."

"What are they playing?"

"Boxing when I walked up."

"I can take the kid in that. I can take him." She looked over where Clare layered a huge casserole for scalloped potatoes. "I'm taking your firstborn to the mat. It's going to be a KO. I'll show him no mercy."

"He's sneaky, and he's been practicing."

Avery flexed her biceps much as her father had that morning. "Small, but mighty."

"He hits below the belt," Ryder snarled as he came through. "You're raising a ball-puncher," he said to Clare.

"Beat you?"

"In three rounds—but he cheats." Ryder opened the fridge for a beer, frowned. "What's this fancy deal in here?"

"Trifle." Hope reached around him, took out a tray of vegetable crudités.

"A trifle of what? Looks pretty big to me."

"It's a dessert, a double chocolate trifle. Here, you can take this downstairs."

He gave it the same suspicious sneer he'd given the trifle. "Kids don't want carrots and celery and crap. They want chips—and the runt likes salsa. Hotter the better."

"They're having carrots and celery and crap," Clare told him. "And Murphy's not having hot salsa and taco chips before dinner."

"Neither are you." Justine didn't spare him a glance as she checked her ham. "Owen, grab those pot holders and take this out for me. It's heavy. Clare, the oven's yours."

"How soon do we eat actual food?" Ryder qualified.

"About an hour and a half."

"We're men. Boxing, skiing, alien-fighting, football-playing, race car–driving men. We need real food now."

"Appetizers in thirty," Avery called out and snagged his attention.

"You making some of the stuff you make?"

"I am."

"Okay." He took the tray, his beer, started back downstairs. "Why do they call it trifle when it's big?"

"I'll look that up," Hope promised.

"Do that. Come on, Dumbass. This is all we're going to get."

A little mournfully, the dog followed Ryder down where Harry's latest cheer burst out. "Still number one!"

"All right, taking five." Avery pulled off her bib apron, tossed it aside. "Somebody needs a spanking." After rolling her shoulders, she marched downstairs.

And marched back up five minutes later with Harry's catcalls ringing behind her. "He beat the crap out of me."

She paused for a moment, scanned the kitchen, the women, the movements, heard her father's big belly laugh rise up the stairs, and Justine's and Carolee's voices from the dining room.

She slipped out to the living room, still disordered from the morning. Open gifts scattered under the tree shining in the window. Justine's dog Cus sprawled on his back, feet in the air as he caught a nap in front of the simmering fire.

The ruckus from the family room rumbled under her feet like a minor earthquake.

"Something wrong?" Owen asked her, and she turned.

And she smiled as she crossed to him, slid her arms around him. Laid her head on his chest. "No. Everything's right. Everything's exactly right."

## CHAPTER TEN

❀

O N A SUPPLY RUN THE WEEK AFTER CHRISTMAS, AVERY broke down and bought her own Wii. She'd resisted—she was on her feet hours every day already; she didn't have time to play games.

And why would she play by herself anyway?

But facing a second defeat—in the rematch with Harry after Christmas dinner, then tanking in bowling so humiliatingly even Carolee's four-year-old granddaughter beat her score—changed everything.

She'd learn. She'd practice. She'd come back and take them all.

Meanwhile she juggled as fast as she could. Tossing pizzas, making sauces, firing a delivery guy—damn it—redoing the schedule to compensate until she hired a replacement.

When she could, she helped Hope put some finishing touches on the inn, and—big sacrifice—stayed a night in Westley and Buttercup for a status report.

She shoehorned in time for projections and plans for her new place, walked through it to take her own measurements, sketch out some basic ideas to pass on to Beckett.

She barely saw Owen. The brothers' focus zeroed more truly on the building next door to the inn now, and she really had no excuse—and no time—to poke her nose in there.

Yet.

Every night before bed, she took a last look out the window at the building directly across, and imagined MacT's— imagined hers. And she gave a final good night to the inn.

Once or twice she thought she saw a woman silhouetted at the rail.

Waiting for Billy.

She wondered at the devotion. Most people, to her mind, couldn't hang on to a relationship in the normal course of events, yet here was someone who held on beyond the impossible.

Maybe one day—she hoped one day—that faithfulness would be rewarded, at least with answers.

And every morning, she gazed out again, at what would be hers, and at what could be done.

Though she waited, too, she never saw that steadfast figure in the light of day.

Between those two points—the last look at night and the first look in the morning, Christmas week passed in a blur.

৵৲

AT FOUR ON New Year's Eve, she closed the restaurant, ran upstairs, ran back down to her car with the pot of meatballs she'd made the night before.

Raced back upstairs.

By five she'd showered, fussed with her hair, her face, dressed and packed an overnight bag.

A different process than the week before, she mused, seeing as she wore sexy underwear and had packed tiny black boxers and a skinny black tank to "sleep" in.

What would it be like to sleep with Owen?

Okay, she decided as she zipped the bag, she wasn't going to think about it, try to imagine it, get bogged down in speculation.

Better to let it evolve, be surprised.

She grabbed her bag, texting Hope on her way out.

Heading over now for wardrobe check.

She piled in her car, shook back hair she'd rinsed a smol-dering red, blew out a breath.

Hope's answer came back before she'd turned the key in the ignition.

I'm here to serve.

Avery drove across The Square to the inn's lot, jumped out as Hope opened the door to Reception.

"I was just organizing my office."

"You already organized your office."

"I wanted to make some changes. And while I was in there, I checked reservations. Two more in March."

"Go team. Okay, be honest." Pulling off her coat, she tossed it over the high-backed chair in front of the fire, did a quick spin.

"Slow it down, Speedy."

"Right." Avery took another breath. "I'm a little wired. I had a vicious day, which I'll tell you about later, then I couldn't decide on the earrings, and I always know which earrings, which made me realize I'm a little nervous. I'm going to have sex with Owen next year. Which is tomorrow—tonight. After the party."

"The earrings are great," Hope told her, giving a nod to the thin silver wires holding citrine drops. "Great color for you, and for the dress. Now, slow turn."

Avery complied, showing off the short, snug dress in shimmery copper. "Love it, love the shoes, the way they pick up the metallic of the dress, but subtly."

"You know I've bought more shoes since you moved here than I did in the five years prior."

"See how good I am for you? What's under the dress?"

"The Marguerite and Percy pomegranate body lotion, and the citrony-colored demi-bra and thong you talked me into."

"Exceptional choice, all around."

"Plus." Wiggling her eyebrows, Avery pointed at her chest. "The bra hoists and squeezes everything so it looks like I have more than I do."

"Which every woman is entitled to, and every man appreciates. But . . ." Considering, Hope walked a circle around Avery. "You need a little something."

"I do?"

"I've got just the thing. The bracelet my sister gave me for Christmas."

"I can't wear your new gift."

"Sure you can. My sister likes you. It's fun and comfortable—all these bronze, copper, and dull gold beads. I'll go up and get it."

"Why aren't you getting dressed?"

"Clare and Beckett aren't picking me up till about eight. I've got plenty of time. Grab a soda if you want—and there are some muffins. I'm trying out recipes."

Avery decided caffeine wasn't the best idea, and opted for a ginger ale. She was wired enough.

In a good way.

She loved a good party, and Owen tended to throw good ones. She knew the food would pass, as she'd made or would make most of it.

And she looked good. Hope would have told her if she hadn't hit the mark.

It would be fun. Lots of friends, food, drink, music, gossip. And at the end of it she'd open a new door for the new year with this new . . . connection with Owen.

"If it doesn't work, well, no harm, no foul, right?" she murmured, and took a long drink as she wandered toward The Lobby.

No flowers yet, she mused, but everything gleamed and shone. Hope would make sure it continued to gleam and shine. The air smelled of the T&O scent, Pixie Dust, subtle and sweet.

She wandered into The Dining Room, studied the building across St. Paul. In a matter of months, she thought, she'd open her new place.

She hoped she'd be ready.

She hoped she was ready for the step she intended to take tonight.

"He was my first boyfriend."

The scent of honeysuckle drifted over her, a summer breeze.

Her heart tripped into her throat, part excitement, part nerves as she turned.

"I didn't know you came down here, but I guess you can go where you want. Looks nice in here with the art hung. Actually I was thinking about saving up, buying . . ."

A still life of sunflowers tipped crooked on the wall, then straightened again.

"Ha. Yeah, that one. Wow. Nice trick. Anyway . . . Happy New Year," she added when she heard Hope—assumed she heard Hope—coming back down.

She walked to the hallway. "I didn't know your inn-mate—get it—came down to the first floor."

"Now and then. Did she?"

"Yeah. It's my first solo encounter. How are you dealing with it?"

"We're fine." Cool and casual, Hope moved toward the kitchen. "I spent the night in Elizabeth and Darcy last night."

"Seriously? Weren't you a little . . ." Instead of words, Avery gave an exaggerated shudder.

"Not really. If I can't sleep in there, we can't expect guests to pay to sleep in there. And no problem." Opening the fridge, she helped herself to a bottle of water. "It's a beautiful, comfortable room."

"And that's it? No activity from the other side?"

"Well, I was in bed, working on my laptop, and about midnight, the bedside lamps went off."

"Shit! I didn't hear you scream."

"I didn't. It gave me a moment, I can't lie, but they came back on when I turned the switch. She turned them off again a few seconds later. I finally got the picture. Lights out, get some sleep."

"What did you do?"

"I turned off my laptop." Hope laughed, took a long sip of water. "I was half asleep over it anyway. Once I settled down, the oddest thing happened."

"Odder than that?"

"I heard the door across the hall open and shut. It seemed

to me like a signal from her. She'd stay over there, and I could have some privacy. I appreciated it.

"Here, try this." Hope hooked the bracelet around Avery's wrist.

"We should try to find out who Billy is." The lights flickered on and off, on and off, then seemed to glow just a little brighter. "Ah, I think she likes that idea."

"I just haven't had time. Once we get through the opening, and I find my routine, I can do some research. I will do some."

"I'll say something about it to Owen. Between the two of you, you'll find something. Pretty." Avery wiggled her wrist. "Thanks. I should go. I told him I'd try to be there around five thirty to help him prep and set up."

"You're an excellent girlfriend."

"Not yet." But Avery laughed. "But I may be next year." Still she hesitated as Hope walked her back through Reception. "Are you sure you're okay being here alone?"

"Obviously, I'm not alone." Hope glanced back at the lights glowing behind them. "And I'm okay with it."

"Anytime you want me to stay . . ."

"You just want to wallow in luxury."

"It's a draw, but seriously, Hope. Anytime."

"I know." Hope picked up Avery's coat. "Go. Be a girlfriend."

"I'm going to give it a shot."

⁓

OWEN SCANNED THE party prep list he'd posted in his kitchen, checked off music. He had that set. Ditto for the fire, the shopping, the cleaning. He had the game area dealt with for those who aimed for it, and a couple of outdoor heaters on the deck for any who spilled outside.

Now all he had to do was put the food together, set up the bar, set up the food, haul the bags of ice he'd stockpiled in the freezer into the tubs for beer and soft drinks and . . . and, and.

What had he been thinking?

Oh yeah, he remembered. Avery. He'd been thinking of Avery.

Now he had to cook—and stir and mix and chop and slice and arrange.

Better get to it.

Gearing up, he gathered supplies, kitchen tools, bowls, trays. Even as he turned to his menu list, he heard his front door open. He heard Avery call out hello, and smiled.

His own personal cavalry, he thought, and headed out to meet her. "Jesus, Avery, let me have that."

He grabbed the enormous stainless steel pot she carried. "It weighs as much as you do."

"I make popular meatballs, so I made plenty of them. I've just got to run out and get my bag out of the car."

"I'll get it. Take off your coat," he suggested as he set the pot on the stove. "Get a glass of wine."

"Okay. Bag's in the backseat."

"Be right back."

"The place looks good," she called out. But then, it always did.

Neat and tidy, of course, but with a comfortable, open style. Quiet colors, she mused as she headed back. She might have zipped them up a few tones, but they suited him.

And she loved his kitchen. He may not do a lot of cooking—as far as she knew—but that hadn't stopped him from building an attractive and efficient space for it.

Dark cabinets and walls of pale green onion—which she'd have bumped up to green tomato, she decided, for some energy.

Dark wood trim around generous windows and the atrium doors leading to his patio. Slate gray countertops—uncluttered, naturally—and gleaming white appliances.

She read his posted lists as she took off her coat, laughed to herself. The idea of the party might've been spontaneous, but his planning for it was anything but.

Knowing better than to toss her coat and scarf onto one of his kitchen stools, she took them into the utility room, hung them on a peg beside his work jacket. Noted his utility room was tidier than her own bedroom.

She stepped back out, opened his broom closet, and took

a bib apron off a hook. With the apron over her arm, she switched the heat on under her pot, cut it down to low.

"I put your bag upstairs, so if you need . . ."

As she turned from the stove, the words—and he figured at least half of his IQ—spilled out of his brain.

"What?" Immediately she looked down at herself. "I didn't spill anything on me, did I?"

"Uh-uh. It's just . . . You look . . . You look," he managed, and her face cleared in a delighted smile.

"That's good?"

"It's . . ." Maybe more than half of his IQ. "Yeah. Oh, yeah."

"It's new—the dress. Hope's been helping me fill in my wardrobe, and thin out my bank account."

"It's worth it. I forgot about your legs."

"What?"

"Not that you had them, but that they're . . . like that."

"I think you just made my year, right at the end of it." She used the legs to walk to him, and even in the heels had to rise up to her toes a little to mate her mouth to his. "Thanks."

"Absolutely anytime."

He smelled great. Tasted great. Looked great.

As an idea formed, she stayed where she was, linked her hands behind his head. "That's quite a list you've got there, Owen."

"List? Oh, the list. Yeah, a lot of work stuff got in the way the last couple days. I didn't get as much done as I'd planned."

"Still a lot. I have this thought. We've got a couple of hours, a little more, before people start wandering in. And we've put some pressure on ourselves, you and me. Waiting until after the party, whenever that is, to ring in the new, so to speak."

His arms wrapped loosely around her waist. "I could put out signs. Party canceled."

"Extreme—and half of them would just bang on the door anyway. But what if we took advantage of the time we have now? We could go upstairs, and . . . ring out the old. No pressure at the party that way."

"It's a really good thought. I don't want to rush it—you. Us."

"I think we can work out an acceptable pace. You could even put it on your list."

He grinned at that, then dipped his head to hers. "Avery."

He eased her into the kiss, a nice, slow slide that gained a little zip as it went.

A very acceptable pace, she thought, adding some zip of her own.

The back door burst open. Dumbass trotted in just ahead of Ryder. "Got your big-ass ham. If you guys are going to roll around on the floor here, I can dump it, grab a beer, and go."

"Christ, Ry."

"Sorry." But his easy grin belied the apology. "I was under orders from Mom. Swing by, get the ham, bring it here—where she assumed you'd be busy making up for lost time, and not making time with Red Hots. Which you are, baby," he said to Avery.

"Which I am," she agreed, and grinned back at him.

"Orders included me slicing up the big-ass ham if you needed help. I figure since you're busy making up for lost groping time," he added, circling around to get the beer. "You don't need my help with that particular to-do item."

He popped the top on the opener on Owen's wall, took a good look at Avery. "Definitely Red Hots. If you're going to muss her up, dude, at least take her upstairs."

"Shit," was Owen's comment.

"I think the time has passed." Avery gave Owen's arm a pat, then put on her apron.

"Sorry," Ryder repeated. "Orders."

"Probably for the best. It's a long list," Avery added when Owen just looked at her. "And now you have another pair of hands because under the circumstances, Ryder's going to pitch in. Big-time."

"Orders. But fine." After he lowered the beer, he leaned in to Avery. "You smell good. Like exotic fruit and . . . honeysuckle."

"Pomegranate. Honeysuckle." She sniffed at her own

arm. "She must've transferred some. How can she do that? Elizabeth. I ran over to see Hope before I came, and Elizabeth popped down to say hi, or maybe Happy New Year."

"You saw her," Owen demanded.

"No, which is annoying, or a relief. I'm not sure which." She got a wooden spoon, lifted the lid on her meatballs, mixed them around a little. "Caught the scent, then when Hope and I were talking about how you and Hope should start researching for this Billy she's waiting for, she flipped the lights a few times, then boosted up the wattage. We both took that to mean she'd really like you to find Billy."

"No problem. I'll just Google Billy, Dead Elizabeth's friend, and nail that down."

"Between you and Hope, you'll figure it out." Avery lifted her eyebrows at Ryder's frown. "What?"

"How's the innkeeper handling the situation?"

"Hope doesn't rattle easily. Or almost at all. I wouldn't mind that glass of wine," she said to Owen.

"I've seen her rattled," Ryder muttered.

"The day Owen saw Elizabeth in the mirror? I'd say Hope was momentarily nonplussed. Nonplussed," she repeated, liking the term.

Ryder thought of the first time he'd seen Hope Beaumont, when his mother had brought the then-potential innkeeper upstairs where he'd been working. How she'd gone sheet pale and glassy-eyed, staring at him as if he were the ghost.

But he shrugged. "Whatever."

"She spent the night in E&D, had a brief encounter, and went, practically as she's a practical sort, to sleep. That's Hope. Okay, I've got the spinach and artichoke dip, the stuffed mushrooms, the . . . pigs in a blanket? Really?"

Owen hunched his shoulders. "People like them."

"They do. Owen you should set up the bar, and Ry, slice up that ham."

On the word *ham*, D.A.'s tail thumped.

"Why didn't he do that on spinach or mushrooms?" Avery wondered.

"The only vegetable he'll eat is french fries," Ryder told her. "He's a picky eater."

Avery only snorted, then got to work.

Probably for the best. Owen echoed Avery's words as he set up glasses, bottles, hauled ice into tubs. He'd never have gotten everything done if they'd . . . rung out the old. Much better to stick with the plan, especially since he didn't have any choice with Ryder slicing ham while D.A. sat, adoring and hopeful, at his feet.

By the time he'd finished the bar, the tubs, she had set out scrubbed vegetables, a cutting board, peeler, and knife for him.

"Peel, slice, chop," she ordered. "You've got everything, so I'm adding a pasta salad to your menu. Carbs are good since people will be drinking. Including me."

She lifted her glass to demonstrate.

The heat from the stove flushed pink in her cheeks, and amusement sparkled the blue of her eyes.

It occurred to him he'd seen her like this before, right here in his kitchen, lending a hand with a party, laughing with one or both of his brothers.

But he hadn't seen her *exactly* like this, as a woman he wanted. As a woman who wanted him.

Had that one kiss, unplanned, impulsive, really changed the tone and direction of who and what they were to each other? Or had there always been something there, just waiting for that switch to flip?

He saw her eyes change, amused sparkle to awareness as he moved to her, watched her lips curve as he drew her in and up for a kiss. Long and soft and sweet.

"You don't have to get a room," Ryder said as he washed his hands off in the sink. "You've got one upstairs."

"This happens to be my room, too. Don't you have to go pick up your date?"

"I'm stag. I told you I couldn't take the giggling."

"You canceled a New Year's Eve date?" Avery demanded.

"I'm sparing lives. If I hadn't strangled her before the night was over, someone else would have. I figured if I went for another woman, the whole date on New Year's Eve thing would add the big deal. I'm not in the mood for big deals, so I'm stag."

Avery got another knife. "Chop and slice," she told Ryder. "And don't pretend you don't know how."

She went back to the stove, but sent Owen that sparkling look over her shoulder.

He'd never before wanted a party over before it began.

❧

STILL, IT WAS a good one. Plenty of people, plenty of food, groups spread throughout the house and out on the patio.

At some point, someone turned the music up for dancing.

He mingled, checked tubs, trays, platters, replenished, took a quick spin with some friends in the game room. And kissed his mother when he found her rinsing off an empty platter in the kitchen.

"You don't have to do that."

"If I don't, you will, and it's your party. And it's a good one."

He took the platter from her, set it down. "If it's so good, why aren't you dancing with me?"

"Well." She batted her eyes, fluffed at her hair. "I was waiting to be asked."

He pulled her out of the kitchen.

Seeing them made Avery smile. She loved the way they looked together, moved together. Halfway through the dance, Ryder moved in, cut in.

"He stole your girl," Avery said to Owen when he joined her.

"That's okay. I've got a spare."

He plucked the glass out of her hand, set it down before he pulled her into the mix of dancers.

"Nice moves."

"We've danced before," he reminded her.

"You've always had nice moves on the dance floor."

"I've got a few I haven't tried out on you yet."

"Is that so?"

He brought her close. "Later."

The single word shot a rocketing thrill through her. "Later. It's almost midnight."

"Thank God."

She laughed, shook back her hair. "Are you going to open more champagne?"

"Yeah, in a minute. I want to kiss you at midnight, so stay close."

"You can count on it."

She refilled platters and bowls while he popped more corks, and the year ran down to minutes. People swarmed back in from downstairs, from outside so the noise level spiked.

He took her hands at the countdown—ten, nine, eight. She turned to him, rose up—seven, six, five. His arms came around her—four, three, two.

"Happy New Year, Avery."

His lips met hers as cheers rang out, and the New Year began to tick.

As Avery rose up, Hope slipped into the kitchen. She'd open another bottle or two, she thought, avoid the whole couples-kissing-the-New-Year-in ordeal.

She twisted off a cork as partygoers shouted out the countdown.

And Ryder walked in.

She stopped. He stopped.

"I'm just opening another bottle," she began.

"So I see."

Shouts of "Happy New Year!" burst out, rolled over them.

"Well," she said. "Happy New Year."

"Yeah. Happy New Year." He lifted his brows when she started to offer her hand. "Seriously? The hearty handshake again?" He shook his head, stepped to her. "Let's do it right."

He set his hands on her hips, cocked those eyebrows again, waited.

"Sure." With a half shrug, she laid her hands on his shoulders.

Casually, on both sides, they touched lips.

Her fingers dug into his shoulders; his arm slid around her waist. Something broke, like light, through the simple contact, and left her breathless.

He jerked away, stepped back—and so did she. For one long moment, they simply stared at each other.

"Okay," he said.

"Yes, okay."

He nodded, strode out.

She let out the breath she'd barely gotten back, picked up the open bottle with a hand that wasn't as steady as she liked.

And that, she thought, had been a very stupid way to start the New Year.

# CHAPTER ELEVEN

T HOUGH MIDNIGHT USHERED IN THE NEW YEAR, IT was nearly three in the morning before Owen ushered out the last stragglers.

He closed the door, turned to Avery. "Nobody's passed out anywhere, right? That was the last of the last?"

Signaling to wait, she peeked out the window and watched taillights blink up the lane.

"And so we say good night to the last designated driver and his haul. I think we're clear. Whew," she added as she stepped back from the window. "The earmark of a good party is people don't want to leave. It's also the downside of a good party."

"Then we can safely say, good party. Planned and executed in just over a week."

"Don't think one time makes you Mr. Spontaneity, but well done."

"You made most of the food."

"True." She reached around, patted herself on the back. "So. Do you want to have some coffee—there's some fresh left—and have the post-party analysis?"

"Yeah. Over breakfast."

She grinned at him. "My thoughts exactly."

He held out a hand, took hers so they walked through the house together, switching off lights.

"This doesn't feel weird," he decided.

"Not yet."

Hand in hand, they walked up the steps. "Anyway, I've already seen you naked."

"A naked five-year-old doesn't count."

"Actually, you were more like thirteen. Yeah, right about thirteen."

She stopped at the bedroom door. "And just how did you see me naked when I was thirteen?"

"Remember that summer we all rented that house up in Pennsylvania for a couple weeks? In the Laurel Highlands, on the lake?"

"Yeah." The summer after her mother had walked out. She remembered it very well.

"You snuck out of the house a few times, to go skinny-dipping in the middle of the night."

"I . . . did. You spied on me?"

"It's not my fault I happened to be sitting at the window, star-gazing through that little telescope I had when you did your Lady of the Lake deal.

"Telescope?"

"Yeah. I charged Ry and Beck a buck a minute to use it." Now, that was a fond memory. "I seem to recall I made about twenty-eight dollars."

"You charged them by the minute so you could all spy on me."

"*Spy*'s a hard word. Let's say *observe*."

"Enterprising."

"I've got a head for business. Plus, it was nice. The moon-light, the water. Your hair was long back then." He combed his hand through it. "What color's this?"

"Red Alert, and don't change the subject."

"It was romantic, though I didn't realize it at the time. At the time it was wow, naked girl. That's how it is with a teenage boy."

Her mind toggled back to that hot, hazy interlude on the lake. "You bought me ice cream that week. Twice."

"Maybe I was marginally guilty and felt you deserved part of my profit."

"And I thought you had a little thing for me."

"I did. I saw you naked. I was even going to ask you to the movies."

"You were not. Really?"

"Then you started talking about Jason Wexel—remember him?—and how you were going out for pizza when we got back. I clutched."

She remembered she'd had a minor crush on Jason Wexel, though she couldn't quite bring his face into focus now. "I did have pizza with Jason, and about fifteen other kids. It was somebody's birthday. I don't even remember whose. I made it sound like a date, because that's how it is with a teenage girl."

"Opportunity lost."

"Until now."

"Until now." He framed her face in his hands, laid his lips on hers.

Slow and easy, not impulsive or rushed as it might have been at any other time between them. Relaxed, she slid into the kiss, without nerves, without doubts. When his hands roamed down, over her shoulders, the sides of her breasts, the thrill gathered and beat, a strong, steady pulse.

Like a dance, they circled toward the bed.

"I really want to see you naked again."

Her lips curved against his. "It'll cost you twenty-eight dollars."

She felt the laugh rumble through him as he eased down the zipper at her back. "Worth every penny."

"Better make sure," she said and wiggled out of the dress.

She stepped out of it, scooped it up, tossed it toward a chair.

He didn't even notice the dress slip off the arm of the chair to the floor. "I think my heart just stopped. Look at you."

And he was, she thought, for just a moment looking at

her as if he'd never seen her before. Then his gaze lifted to hers again, and there was that click, that connection, the recognition before he drew her against him again.

And the feel of his hands on her skin, warm against warm, layered thrill over thrill.

She brought hers up, unbuttoning his shirt as their lips clung.

Here was Owen, tall and gorgeous. Here was his heartbeat, racing fast under her fingers, her palms. Her Owen, because on some level he'd always been her Owen, with his heart beating against her hands.

Here was the new.

He lowered to the bed with her, with Avery—compact, curvy Avery. Bright hair, bright eyes, smooth skin white as moonlight. Sensations tumbled inside him—her scent, her taste, the rustle of the sheets as she moved with him. Everything about her so familiar, and still somehow unexpected.

He linked fingers with her, pressed his face to her breast. Soft, scented, smooth.

With that hum in her throat, she arched toward him, assent and invitation. His lips brushed the curve over the lace edge, then his tongue swept under, and her fingers tightened on his.

He ranged himself over her, center to center, and again she rose to him as he kissed her, as he filled himself with the taste of her until her fingers went lax in his.

He released her hands to take his over her, over skin and silk and lace, enraptured by the surprise of her, by each new discovery.

Nuzzling at her throat, he flicked open the catch of her bra and, once again linking their fingers, he lowered his lips to her breast.

Thorough. She should have known he'd be thorough, with his lips, his hands gliding and sliding over her skin. He fired her system with that slow, focused attention to her body, with the endless patience that was so much a part of him.

Her blood swam, driving her pulse to a gallop, as he stroked her into sweet, soaking pleasure. Her breath ragged, she let herself rise, let herself open until there were no restraints, no barriers.

Just Owen.

She filled him, surrounded him with what she was, what she offered. Boundless, he thought, her energy, that quick response, that quick demand. Everything with her, so fresh, so new, yet so wonderfully familiar.

Her breath caught, released with a moan when he slid into her, when he, in turn, filled her.

Once again, it seemed his heart stopped—a stunning, breathless moment. He held here, staring down at her in a kind of wonder.

She levered up, wrapped her arms around his neck, her legs around his waist. Her head fell back, and his dropped to her shoulder.

Slow and easy was done. She moved now, sleek as a bullet, quick as lightning, driving him past that instant of wonder into pleasure and need, into greed.

She flung reason aside, reckless and eager, to clamp against him, taking as ferociously as she gave. On the desperate edge, she curled to him as sensation careened through her, and at last, at last, swept her into release.

They didn't so much lie down as fall back on the bed. There, sprawled together, they both tried to find their breath.

"Why," he managed, then concentrated on breathing again.

"Why?"

Eyes closed, he held up a finger as signal to wait another minute. "Why," he repeated, "haven't we ever done that before?"

"Damn good question. We're both really good at it."

"Praise Jesus."

With a wheezing laugh, she patted his ass. "I knew you would be. You're the detail man. And thank you very much for not missing a single one."

"You're welcome, and thank you. By the way, you have a flower tattooed on your ass."

"Not merely a flower. A thistle—a traditional Scottish symbol. That was pride of heritage," she told him. "And it's on my ass, as I knew that was one place my dad wouldn't see it and flip on me."

"Good thinking. I like it."

On a sound of contentment, she closed her eyes. "I should be exhausted."

"You're not? I didn't finish my job then."

"Oh, you finished your job. I meant it's got to be closing in on four a.m., after a really long day. I should be exhausted. Instead I feel good, relaxed and sleepy."

He shifted to snuggle her in, to pull the duvet over them. "No work tomorrow."

"No work." All but nose to nose with him, she grinned. "Let us again praise Jesus."

"Why don't we have a nap, let's say, then we can see if we missed any details the first time around?"

"I say good thinking." She wiggled her body still closer to his, opened her eyes for a moment just to look at him. "Happy New Year."

"Happy New Year."

Closing her eyes again she let herself drift away. Her last thought was her friend was now her lover. And she was happy.

❦

HE RECOGNIZED THE silence, the wrapped-in-cotton quiet that meant only one thing.

Owen opened his eyes, blinked them clear and watched the snow fall in downy drifts outside the window. Gotta break out the plow, he thought—but later. He rolled over, intending to wake up Avery in a way he hoped she'd appreciate, but found the bed empty.

Where the hell was she?

He dragged himself up, poked his head through the open bathroom door. He spotted her toothbrush on the side of his sink, considered that as he went to the dresser for a pair of flannel pants.

He smelled coffee—and, oh boy, bacon—as he came down the stairs.

A marching band high-stepped on his kitchen TV, snow

blanketed his patio outside the doors. And Avery stood at his counter chopping peppers.

She wore a white chef's apron over a blue-checked robe, her hair clipped back, her feet bare. He remembered how she'd looked the night before, in the sexy dress, then later in the even sexier underwear. But he realized he most often imagined her just like this—in an apron in the kitchen.

"What's for breakfast?"

She looked up, over, smiled. "You're awake."

"Marginally. Why are you?"

"Because it's nearly eleven, it's snowing, and I'm starving."

"Eleven?" He frowned at the clock on the stove. "I don't know the last time I slept this late. I guess it's okay." He gestured toward the snow. "No school today."

"Yippee."

Moving to her, he turned her from the counter, drew her in for a kiss. "Morning."

"Morning." She leaned against him a moment. "It's so quiet. In town, even when it's quiet there's sound. But here, with the snow, it's like the world shut off."

He turned her again so they both faced the glass doors. "Look."

Through the snow, on a ridge behind the snow-drenched trees, a trio of deer wandered silent as ghosts.

"Oh, they're so beautiful. I bet you get to see deer all the time."

"A lot."

"The boys are going to love it when they all move into the new house. You did. I remember how you and your brothers ran wild in the woods when we were kids."

"Good times." Bending, he kissed the top of her head. "So are these. What're you making here?"

"You had this and that left over from the party. We'll call them kitchen-sink omelettes."

"Sounds great. You didn't have to."

"Food, kitchen—" She spread her hands. "I'm helpless not to cook. You have most excellent tools, and I know you hardly ever use them."

"But they're here if I want to."

"True. I could toss a bunch of this in a pot—people never eat as many dipping vegetables as you figure they will. No point in having them go to waste. I can make up a soup."

"Snowy day, homemade soup?" Did that mean she planned to stay awhile? "Who's going to argue with that?" He walked over to pour himself coffee. "I need to go out and plow soon."

"I guess you do, but too bad. It's nice feeling snowed-in and cozy. Well, a man about to plow needs a manly breakfast."

While she cooked, he put away dishes, and enjoyed the easy rhythm.

"So, the delayed post-party replay," she began. "Did you get the scoop on Jim and Karyn?"

"I got that Jim's in Pittsburgh and Karyn didn't want to come without him."

"You don't talk to the right people." Avery folded the omelettes. "Jim's in Pittsburgh with his mother because Karyn kicked him out."

"What? Why?"

"Because she found out Jim's been having an affair with the mother of their oldest boy's best pal."

"Jim? Come on, that can't be right."

"No, it's very wrong, and it's been going on nearly two years according to my sources." She plated the omelettes, added bacon, toast, passed a plate to Owen.

"But . . . they seemed so solid."

"Well." Taking her own plate, she joined him at the breakfast bar. "She comes into the pizza shop with the kids, more often without him than with, and I saw her at Sam's Club right before Christmas when I was doing a supply run. She looked stressed, barely spoke to me. At the time I figured it was just mother-of-three Christmas countdown pressure, but now . . . She found the other woman's panties in her bed."

"Well, Jesus. That's not only wrong, rude, cold, but it's stupid."

"Could be the slut/lover—she's already separated from her husband—left them in there on purpose. Anyway, that was the kicker. She booted him out, and she's already got a lawyer."

"I'd say good for her, but it doesn't seem like the right phrase. It's hard to swallow it from Jim. They've been married, what, like ten years?"

"About, I guess, but for the last two of them, at least, he's been screwing around. No excuse for it. You're not happy, you fix it or you end it. Plus, since he's in Pittsburgh with his mommy, he must not be serious about the slut."

Mystified by her logic, he took the toast she buttered for him. "Why do you say that?"

"Because if he was serious, he'd have crashed at the slut's. Now he's broken his family, ruined his marriage, his rep, not to mention how much this'll hurt those little kids. All for some stranger. I hope she skins him."

"No comment?" she said after a moment of silence.

"I figure you never know what goes on between two people, or a family, but yeah, from what you've got, skinning seems appropriate. I like Jim okay. He just called me a couple weeks ago about rehabbing their master bath. I was supposed to take a look at it after the holidays."

Avery wagged a slice of bacon. "He's planning a new bathroom and screwing his slut in his wife's bed. Not serious about the slut, no respect for his wife or his family."

"No respect, agreed. But maybe the affair isn't a slut."

"Please." Avery shoveled in omelette. "She was still married when she first hooked up with Jim, and my sources say Jim isn't, or wasn't, her first cowboy."

"How do people know this stuff? Who is it anyway?"

"I don't know her. Apparently she lives in Sharpsburg, works for some insurance company. Has a weird name—no smart remark referencing Avery," she added. "Harmony, which doesn't seem to be apt."

"Oh."

"Oh?"

"I know a Harmony who works for our insurance agent. This omelette is great."

"Aha!"

"Aha?"

"Subject change, shifting in seat." Eyes keen, she wagged a finger at him. "Sure signs of guilt and/or evasion. You dated her?"

"No! She's married—or she was married. And she's not my type anyway. Let's just say I've had conversations and so on with her due to insurance. And there may have been subtext."

"Slut." With a flick of her finger in the air, Avery mimed touting up a scoreboard. "I can call 'em."

"I'll say the first lines of subtext were delivered while she was wearing a wedding ring."

"Slut! What does she look like? Tell me everything."

"I don't know, exactly. Blond."

"Bleached."

He let his gaze roam over her messy, clipped-back hair. "I'm forced to point out you have no grounds to disdain anyone for changing hair colors."

"You have a point. Still. Is she pretty?"

"I guess. Not my type," he repeated. "She's . . . obvious, is maybe the best word. She's good at her job, as far as I'm concerned. That's all I am—was—still am—interested in. When did the kick-out go down?"

"The day after Christmas. Karyn found out the week before, but let him stay so the kids would get one more family Christmas in. Why?"

"I had to drop in the agency a couple days ago, sign some stuff. She didn't seem upset. And, ah, there was additional subtext."

Those bright blue eyes darkened. "Slut—slutty slut with no conscience. She helps destroy a marriage, and now she's moving on, looking for the next sucker. That's what my mother did."

He said nothing, just laid a hand over hers.

"That's probably why I have zero tolerance for sluts and cheats." With a shrug, Avery rose to take both their mugs back to the coffeemaker. "In addition to the Karyn/Jim implosion, did you know Beth and Garrett are getting married?"

"Yeah, she was flashing the ring around last night. They both look happy."

"They are—and Beth's got an extra glow, seeing as she's about eight weeks pregnant."

"What? How did I miss this stuff?"

"By spending too much time hanging out with men who have no gossip to share. They're happy about the baby. They've been together almost two years now, and it looks like baby makes three boosted them to make it legal. I was talking to Beth about the idea of them getting married at the inn."

"At the inn."

"Clare and Beckett are getting married there next spring. This could be a kind of dry run. They want something small, and soon. They were even thinking about just doing the courthouse thing, but that made both their mothers cry," she added as she came back from getting fresh coffee for both of them. "When I suggested the inn, Beth got pretty excited. She didn't know it was an option."

"Neither did I."

"It's up to you guys, of course, but Hope's good with it. I could do the catering, no problem. Mountainside could do the flowers. They're only talking about tight friends and immediate family. Maybe twenty-five, thirty people. You've already got bookings for Valentine's Day, but the weekend after, you're clear so far."

"Next month?" He had to gulp down coffee. "That's pretty damn quick."

"As I said last night, one spontaneous—semi—party doesn't make you Mr. Spontaneity. Relax. You wouldn't have to do anything. Beth wants to get into a nice dress before she starts showing, so they don't want to wait. They'd already talked about staying there for their wedding night, and this would be like one-stop shopping."

"How much do we charge as a wedding venue?"

She smiled at him. "You and Hope will figure it out. I'd probably give them a discount, due to it's the first one and all that. Play your cards right, wedding guests will book every room the night before and the night of."

Good business, he thought. Avery knew good business.

"I'll talk to Hope tomorrow. You've got a busy brain, Avery."

"I know. Right now it's thinking we should finish this

coffee. You go out and plow the lanes while I straighten up from the party. Then to pay me back for my services, you can take me to bed."

"I can't lose."

"To my busy brain, it's more like win-win."

❦

MAYBE HE LIKED to plow, but as soon as he'd done his own lane—perhaps not with the usual finesse—Owen headed straight to Ryder's. Paths for D.A. already cleared, he noted. Good.

He parked the jeep, jumped off. He stomped his boots, then walked into the house.

"Hey, Ry."

"Down here."

"I'm covered with snow, man. You come up here."

D.A. padded upstairs, tail wagging. He licked snow off Owen's boots. Ryder followed moments later. He wore sweatpants hacked off at the knees and a sweaty T-shirt.

"What's up? I'm trying to get a damn workout in, after which my plans were to fat-ass before game time. Now it's sledding and snow wars at Mom's."

"When?"

"You forget your phone? Has the world ended?"

"I've got my phone." He dug it out. "No messages."

"Maybe you're not invited. She likes me better."

"She pretends to like you better so you don't whine like a baby. She must've called the house. Anyway, this works. I'm taking your truck. You need to finish the plowing. Get Beck's, then Mom's. We can switch back over there."

"You're Mr. Plow."

"Have you got a woman in here?"

On a windy sigh, Ryder dipped his hands in his baggy pockets. "Sadly no."

"I've got one. I'm taking your truck."

"So you can go turn on the Little Red Machine. That's said with respect and affection. For her."

"I'm taking your truck, then I'm going to have sex while you're not. You're Mr. Substitute Plow."

"Then no bitching when I don't do it your way."

"Just don't screw it up." He grabbed Ryder's truck keys off the table by the door. "What time at Mom's?"

"I don't know. We're not punching a time clock. Two or three. Whenever."

"Then I'll see you when I see you."

As Owen strode out, Ryder looked down at his dog. "One of us has to get a woman. I fucking hate plowing."

⁓

OWEN WALKED IN to the smell of soup simmering, and when he stripped out of his gear, into a clean kitchen. Though he considered it a waste of breath over the blasting music, he called Avery's name as he walked through the house.

He heard her, singing in the shower, when he reached the bedroom. She could barely carry a tune, but she made up for it with strong enthusiasm and volume.

Unable to resist, and really the only downside was a glass shower door rather than a curtain, he yanked the door open and made the high-pitched *Psycho* sounds.

Her answering scream was brilliant.

Plastered against the shower wall, eyes as big as blue moons, she gaped at him. "What's *wrong* with you?"

He had to suck in the breath laughter stole from him. "I think I broke a rib laughing, otherwise, I'm good."

"Jesus, Owen."

"I couldn't help it. It had to be done."

"Yeah? Well, so does *this*!" She grabbed the handheld sprayer, twisted the controls, and soaked him where he stood. "Now we're both twelve." Smug, she fit the sprayer back in its bracket.

"I guess I might as well come in there."

"Hmm," was her answer.

"A hot shower, a hot woman after cold work," he said as he stripped off his dripping shirt.

"I thought you'd be another hour at least."

"I switched with Ry." He yanked off his boots. "Soup smells good."

"Once I finished down there I decided to take advantage of your shower. Your bathroom rivals the inn's, and I've been getting spoiled. And your mother called."

"Sledding and snow wars, late afternoon."

"I said I'd bring the soup." She sent him a questioning look.

"Good idea."

"Clare can stop by my place, get my boots and gear."

"That'll work." He peeled off his soaked pants, tossed a couple towels on the floor to soak up the wet.

"She didn't seem surprised when I answered the phone."

"Mom has a way of knowing what she needs to know." He stepped in, closed the shower door behind him. "You know if you switch the TV to digital radio, it pipes in through those."

He gestured to the speakers in the ceiling.

"Oh."

"Just FYI." Then he just smiled at her.

"What?"

"I was just thinking when I watched you skinny-dipping all those years ago, I never figured on this." He ran his hands down her body. "You're all wet and warm."

"You're wet." She wrapped her arms around him. "But a little chilly."

"It's cold out there, doing man work."

Laughing, she tipped her head back. "You've got man work to do in here, too."

"Then I'd better get started."

He took her mouth while water rained hot and steam plumed, letting his hands roam that wet, slippery skin as she hooked her hands around his shoulders, rose up.

No, he'd never figured on this, on the ease of it, the excitement of it. Never imagined the odd discovery of someone he'd known all of his life.

Smooth and curvy, firm and agile, and so willing to touch and be touched, to take and be taken.

She smelled of his soap now, something else to make the familiar the new.

She lathered it over him, enjoying the play of muscle. She

rarely thought of his strength, as it was his mind, his kindness, his *Owenness* she thought of first. But now, running her hands over him, exploring those ridges, those ripples, reminded her he was, at the core, a man who worked with his hands, his back, his brawn as well as his brain.

And those hands, far from smooth, incited fresh needs, new wants, deeper desires.

He made her tremble, made her breath snag and tear, meeting those needs, exploiting more until her body seemed to gather into one aching pulse.

Water sluiced over her, slicking her hair back. Her eyes, brilliantly blue now, stared into his, then went opaque as she shuddered.

"I don't . . . We can't." She struggled to regain her balance, to find purchase. "You're too tall."

"You're too short," he corrected, then gripping her hips, lifted her off her feet. "So you'd better hang on."

"Owen—"

He braced her against the wet wall, and drove into her.

"Oh." Her eyes flew open, intense now, focused on his. He plunged again, ripping a cry of pleasure from her, and still her eyes remained open and on his. "Don't let go. Don't let go."

"You either," he managed an instant before she pulled his mouth to hers.

They both held on.

Later, she sprawled facedown, naked, on his bed. "I'm going to get up and get dressed in a minute."

"Take your time," he told her, admiring her thistle. "I like the view."

"What is it with guys and tattoos on girls?"

"I have no idea."

"I think it's the Xena factor. Female warrior."

"You don't have a two-piece black leather warrior suit, do you?"

"It's at the cleaners." She pillowed her head on her arms. "Maybe I should get another tattoo."

"No." Then studying her butt as he dressed, he considered. "Like what? Where? Why?"

"I don't know, have to think about it. The problem with the butt location is I hardly ever see it, and it seems like the person who goes through the process ought to be able to see the results easily. Added to it, hardly anybody else sees my butt either, so what's the point? Unless I consider it some secret ritual of teenage rebellion, which it pretty much was.

"This would be mature."

"A mature tattoo."

"Anyway." She rolled over, sat up. "I really like your shower. I really like you in your shower." On a long, lazy sigh, she reached for her blue-checked robe. "I need to check the soup."

"Stay tonight."

With the robe half on, she stopped to blink at him. "Tonight? We both work tomorrow."

"We both work tomorrow anyway. After snow wars and soup and most probably fights over football, come back with me. Stay tonight."

She wrapped the robe around her, belted it. Looked up again. "All right. I'm going to check the soup before I get dressed."

"Okay."

As she walked downstairs she wondered what to do about the flutter around her heart. She recognized it; she'd felt it before.

She'd been five.

Falling in love with Owen—again—was very likely as foolish now as it had been then. But the MacTavish Gut knew what it knew. She just wasn't so sure about the MacTavish Heart.

## CHAPTER TWELVE

※

EARLY IN THE NEW YEAR, ARMED WITH A THICK
binder, Avery did yet another walk-through of what she
firmly thought of now as MacT's. But this time she had Hope
and Clare as sounding boards.

"The bar along there. Dark wood, something that makes
a statement. I'm going to try to sweet-talk, cajole, beg, and
sex Owen into making it."

"How's that going?" Clare wondered. "The sex part."

"Look at this face." Avery pointed her thumbs at her own
face.

"Satisfied, relaxed, happy. And just a little bit smug. So
question answered."

"So far, so good. Lights there, there, there, warm tones.
And I'm thinking a leather sofa—maybe dark brown—over
there, coffee table. Some high tops in the front window, low
tops there and there. And the pass-through to the restaurant
will be right there."

"It's going to be great. But before we get into color wheels
and tables," Hope added, "one must ask why you're not brag-

ging about said sex, or offering details to the one, sad one of us who isn't having any."

"I might jinx it, and make you sadder."

"Please." Hope flicked that away. "I saw Owen earlier, and his face also looks satisfied, relaxed, and happy. I'm not sure about smug, though he may have been masking that. Are you seeing him tonight?"

"No. I've only got about an hour, then I've got to get over to the shop. I'm working. And he's—all of them—are so busy right now. Prepping for the opening in a few days, working on the other building, planning for this one. We've been together almost every night since New Year's, and I thought . . ."

"You needed a break?" Clare suggested.

"I thought I—we—should take one. You know how I can get. I always go into something like this thinking it's casual, it's fun, it's natural. You like the guy, trust the guy, you're attracted to the guy, so you go with it. Then, being me, I start wondering, is it more, should it be more, is this love— big L?"

"Are you in love with Owen?" Clare asked.

"I got the . . ." She fluttered a hand at her heart.

"The MacTavish Heart." Hope nodded.

"It can't be trusted. But the thing is, I've loved Owen forever. I love all the Montgomerys. It's in the bone. So this could be that. Kind of a false positive. If it turns into the big L, it could mess things up."

"Why," Clare demanded, "do you automatically assume he couldn't big L you back?"

"I don't know, maybe that's in the bone, too." She let her shoulders rise, then fall. "I think part of it's a mother issue, which is just depressing."

"You're nothing like your mother."

"And I don't want to be," Avery said with a nod at Clare. "She cheated and lied and used. Sex was easy for her, it was sure as hell casual for her. So I think the part of me that can't handle the thought of being anything like her takes the easy, casual sex and insists on making it more. Like a reflex. Or antidote. Then I switch it around because the big L hardly ever works. It's stupid."

"It's not," Hope insisted. "It's you."

"But now it's me and Owen. Every time I've been involved with a man I end up making it more because, you know, flutter. Then the flutter stops, and I realize no, he's not the one. He's a perfectly nice guy—mostly they have been—but he's not *the* one, if there really is a *the* one anyway."

"There is," Clare insisted.

"Maybe. Now I've got the flutter with Owen, and when it stops—"

"Why when?" Clare shook her head. "It might not stop."

"Going by history it's when, that's all. I don't want to make it more, then have to make it less again. Not with Owen. He matters more than the flutter or the mommy issue."

"I think you're underestimating yourself, and him. But—" Clare checked the time. "I can't go into depth on that as I've got to get home. But we will talk," she finished, pointing a finger.

"Fine by me. I'd better lock up. I can walk over to the inn with you, Hope, go over my part of the menu for the opening before I head to work."

"Okay."

They went out, parted ways with Clare heading across Main Street and Avery walking with Hope across St. Paul.

"She's in love," Avery said. "Love like that makes an optimist out of you, helps you see other people riding the same optimistic train."

"Why shouldn't you be optimistic?"

"I'm not overly pessimistic—I don't think. I'm more cautious."

"I'm not in love or riding the optimistic train, but I can tell you it's really nice to see the way you and Owen are together."

She unlocked the door to Reception. "And I can also see how you—anyone—might take a short, thoughtful break. Sex can be easy and casual, and it can also cloud the brain. So clear your brain for a day or two."

"That's it, exactly." God bless practical-minded Hope, Avery thought. "Brain-clearing interlude."

"I'm going to make tea while we go over the menu."

"You're making tea at the inn." Avery boosted onto a stool at the island. "And we're talking opening menu. A year ago, we weren't even close to this. You weren't even living in town."

"A year ago, I thought my future was the Wickham Hotel and Jonathan."

"Did your heart flutter?"

"No." Considering, Hope put the kettle on. "But I thought I loved him. I did trust him, admire him, enjoy him. And so, I thought I loved him. He knew that. Knew I trusted him, admired him, felt for him—and he knew I believed we were going to make a future together."

"Why wouldn't you believe?"

"Why wouldn't I?" Hope agreed, without the taste of bitterness on her tongue she'd once swallowed too often. "We all but lived together. He said he loved me, he talked about the future with me."

"I'm sorry, Hope. Does it still hurt?"

"No . . . maybe a little," she admitted as she set out cups. "More pride than heart, though, at this point. He used me, and that—that just pisses me off. I don't believe he intended to in the beginning. But in those last months, he lied to me and used me, and in the end made me feel like a fool. That hurts. Being made to feel like a fool."

"He's the fool. I don't ever want to hurt anyone like that."

"You couldn't. You don't have it in you, Avery."

She hoped not, but now and again, worrying over it kept her awake at night.

∼

IN HER QUIET, closed shop, Avery tied on her apron and began the opening process. She switched her ovens on, started coffee. She counted out her cash register, checked the level of her ice machine. Moving from open kitchen to closed and back again, she refilled her toppings trays, made a note to order more delivery boxes, opened a new tub of mozzarella.

After transferring some dough pans to her under-counter cooler, she calculated she'd make more by noon. She hauled out her big pots of sauce, set them on low. Deciding she was lower on marinara than she liked, she gathered what she needed to make more.

She paused at the knock on the door, and damn, there was that flutter when she saw Owen through the glass. He held up a key, and at her nod, used it to unlock the front.

"You look busy."

"Not too. We're low on marinara."

"Can I work here at the counter for a while? It's too noisy at the job site, and they're into the media tours at the inn."

"Sure. Want some coffee?"

"I'll get it in a minute." He set down his briefcase and a long tube, shed his coat, pulled off his ski cap. Ran his hand through his hair.

Then he walked around the counter, cupped her face in his hands, and kissed her. "Hi."

"Hi."

"Smells good."

"Best marinara in the county."

"I was talking about you, but the sauce isn't bad. Do you want coffee?"

"My hands are going to be full until I get this going. Aren't you supposed to be part of the media stuff?"

"Off and on." He walked off to get a mug, lifting his voice when she opened a huge can of crushed tomatoes. "We've got a nice slate. Hope has contacts down in D.C., up in Philadelphia, so we drew some interest beyond the local. Nice for us."

"Very."

"Mom and Carolee are handling most of it with Hope, and the rest of us will do whatever, whenever."

"Exciting stuff."

He stood, watching her stir, add her herbs.

"Don't you have to measure?"

"No," she said simply.

"I looked over the menu you've worked out for the new place. How do you know how to make all that?"

She slanted him a look Hope would've termed smug. "I have many skills."

"I figure you need to test some of those dishes on a willing subject."

She glanced over. "Do you? And you'd be willing?"

"It's the least I can do."

"Generous to a fault, that's you." But it actually wasn't a bad idea, she mused. It was like testing out each room in the inn before opening. "I'm off Monday night."

"Works for me."

"Place your order."

"Whatever you want."

"No, take another look at the proposed menu, place an order—salad, appetizer, entree. The works. When it's real I'll have a chef so I won't do all the cooking, and I'll have people working the line, but this would be a good indicator. I should try different dishes out on different people, too, make adjustments sooner rather than later."

"Speaking of adjustments. Are you about done there?"

"I am done." But she could make dough now, save time in the afternoon.

"I want to show you something."

"Has to be quick," she told him as she wiped off her hands. "I should go ahead and make dough while I have the time. And didn't you have some work?" she added as she crossed to the cooler. Deciding she wanted her caffeine cold, she pulled out a Diet Coke.

"This is part of it."

He opened the tube, took out a set of blueprints, unrolled them on the counter.

"Is that the bakery building? I never did get a chance to . . ." She trailed off, momentarily speechless as she read the name.

*MacT's Restaurant and Tap Room*

"MacT's. It says MacT's."

"That's the name you said, right? You can always change it. You can change anything right on the blueprints. This is your copy. Beckett is tied up this morning, but he'll go over them with you. For now, I can answer most questions, if you have any, explain what you don't get."

"My blueprints."

"That's right."

"Hold on a minute." She whirled away, danced around the dining room. Jumped, spun, kicked, reminding him of her cheerleading days at Boonsboro High.

When she did a handspring, he jolted, then laughed. "Jesus Christ, Avery. You can still do that?"

"Apparently." On a woo-hoo, she launched herself at him.

He caught her, staggered a little as she pumped her fists in the air.

"I was hoping you'd have more enthusiasm."

"How's this for enthusiasm?" She locked her arms around him, her legs around him, her mouth to his.

"Not bad." He turned them in a circle. "Not bad at all."

"I haven't even seen them. I have to see them!" Wiggling down, she all but fell on the plans.

"I can explain," he began, but she brushed it away.

"Do you think I can't read blueprints? I practically slept with the ones for Vesta. It's good, it's good," she muttered. "I'm going to want to move this cooler from here to here. It makes more sense for the flow, plus I'll need a table here, beside the dishwasher."

He pulled a pencil out of his briefcase. "Mark it."

She marked it, made a couple small adjustments. "The opening here, that's good. Easy pass-through from space to space for servers and customers. Sitting at the bar having a drink with a friend. Hey, why don't we have dinner? Stroll right on over."

"It's a big bar."

She gave a decisive nod. "Needs to make a statement."

"You need to tell me what you're looking for there. The wood, the finish, the style, so I can work up a design for you."

She shifted her gaze over. "Are you building it?"

"I figured on it. Why?"

"I was going to sex you into it."

"Now that I think about it, I'm pretty busy."

On a quick laugh, she turned to wrap her arms around him. The hell with head-clearing breaks. "Owen."

"Maybe not that busy."

She held tight, squeezed her eyes shut. "I'm not going to let you down."

"Nobody thinks that. Not for a minute."

She shook her head, looked up at him. It was more than a building, a business. It was Owen, and that flutter around her heart. "I'm not going to let you down."

"Okay."

Nodding, she laid her head on his chest again. Old foundations, she thought, new phases. Who knew what you could build?

"I need to make dough."

"Who doesn't?"

With a smile, she tipped up her head. "I need to make pizza dough so I can make the other kind and pay my landlord."

"While you're doing that, I'm going to make some calls in the quiet."

He gave her a last squeeze. "About these." He gestured to the blueprints. "It's going to take a while. Making the changes, getting the mechanicals, then the permits. And we're centered on the other building right now."

"It doesn't matter how long it takes." She thought of him, of them, the lifetime already shared. "It's how long it lasts."

❧

JUST AFTER OPENING, Hope dashed in the door.

Avery added pepperoni to a large. "Hey. How's it going in Hollywood?"

"It's good. Pretty smooth so far. They're doing some interviews and videos with the Montgomerys right now. I've got ten minutes."

"Have a seat." Avery slid the large in the oven.

"I thought I should run over and tell you rather than text. A lot of the crews asked about lunch, so we've been hyping Vesta."

"Your hype's appreciated. Good thing I made that extra dough."

"The thing is, a couple of them got the idea to do some video and interviews around and about. Here to start. With you."

"Me?"

"And maybe some photos."

"Of *me*? I can't do that. Look at me. I have sauce on my apron. I didn't wash my hair this morning. I have naked face."

"Sauce works, it's the job. Hair's fine. I've got nine minutes now. I can do makeup in six. Let's go."

"But orders—shit. Chad. Two large in the oven for delivery. Deal with it. Back in five."

"Six," Hope corrected.

"Six," Avery called as she ran for the door.

"Why didn't anyone tell me this could happen? I wouldn't have naked face."

"Six minutes, maybe less. The gods gifted you with gorgeous skin. We'll just pump up the eyes, give you more color, less shine."

"I'm shiny!" Desperate, Avery shoved open her apartment door, raced to the bathroom. "I'm wearing an old shirt."

"The apron covers it." Focused, Hope yanked open the drawer of the vanity.

"The saucy apron."

"I'm telling you the sauce is good. It's like a prop. Sit," she ordered. "This is simple. It's not a screen test for a major motion picture. It's a few seconds on the evening news."

"Oh God."

"Quiet. Why can't you organize your makeup into groups? Eyes, lips, cheeks?"

"Don't start on me when I'm having a nervous breakdown. Why did I use this color on my hair?"

"Why do you use any color on your hair when you have gorgeous hair to begin with?"

"It was because of the rut. It was the rut, but now it's like an addiction. Help me."

"Shut up and close your eyes."

Hope swiped on shadow, blended, drew on liner, smudged. "Didn't I tell you to buy an eyelash curler."

Wary, Avery opened one eye. "I fear them."

"Get over it. Look here." She leveled a finger, then brushed on mascara.

"Why do you always look so perfect?" Avery complained. "Why are you beautiful? I hate you."

"I can give you clown cheeks."

"Please don't."

"You have skin like porcelain. I hate you." Deft and quick, Hope feathered on blush. "And for God's sake buy an eyelash curler. And a lip liner. Relax your jaw." She chose a lipstick from the two dozen jumbled in the drawer, dusted on translucent powder, blotted.

"Done, and in four."

"My pizzas."

"Chad's got them. Take a look."

Avery rose, studied the results in the mirror over the sink. Her eyes looked bigger, bluer, her cheeks more defined, her lips rosy. "You're a genius."

"I am."

"But my hair."

"Leave it. Twenty seconds." Hope tugged here, smoothed there. Nodded. "Unstudied, casual, and just a little sexy."

"The shirt—"

"Is fine. Different earrings. Thirty seconds."

Hope made the dash, pulled open the earring drawer. A quick scan, eyes narrowed. "These. A little sparkle, a little dangle, and they're from Gifts. Symbiotic."

She did one ear while Avery did the other.

"Shouldn't I—"

"Done," Hope declared, and grabbed Avery's hand. "Switch focus. You want the reporters to mention the excellent food and fast, friendly service in a cheerful atmosphere, right?"

"Right, right. Jesus, stupid. It doesn't matter how I look. Of course it does, but I need to warn the staff. I should call Franny in."

"Wouldn't hurt. Gotta go."

"Thanks for the face. Really."

❦

BY ONE SHE was too busy to worry about her shirt, the sauce on her apron, or if she'd chewed her lipstick off. She focused on pizzas, making pie after pie, and thanked God for Franny, who'd come in at her call and dealt with pasta orders, salads.

She worked her way through it; in fact did two quick interviews while she stood at her work counter. Even tossed dough on request for a camera.

And she thought of the lovely perk of having her place on a D.C. station for even two or three seconds.

At three, with the madness over, Avery took her first break by collapsing in the empty back dining room with a bottle of Gatorade.

She waved weakly when Clare came in. "I think I used up all my electrolytes. Did they come to your place?"

Clare held up the go-cup from her bookstore. "Skinny latte with a double shot of espresso."

"That answers that."

"It was good though. Good for Turn The Page, for the inn, for the town, I think."

"I bet Hope didn't have to rush down to TTP and do your makeup."

"No, but I don't work in a hot kitchen all day."

"Good answer."

"The reporter from *Hagerstown Magazine* wants to pitch a follow-up, or a related story to her editor. You, me, Hope."

"Us? What kind of story?"

"Three women, three friends. One who runs a bookstore, one who runs a restaurant—soon two—and one who runs the B&B."

"I don't want to wear a saucy apron."

"Saucy as in sauce, or saucy as in French maid?"

"Guess." Smirking, Avery pointed at her stained apron. "We'd have more warning, right? Not have a four-minutes-from-naked-face-to-camera-face deal again."

"Much more. If it flies, we'd coordinate the day and time. It'd be good promotion for all of us. Still, I don't know how Hope does it. She walked one of the reporters down to the bookstore. She looked—"

"Perfect."

"Perfect. And relaxed. I can't wait to see how the whole thing comes out on the news tonight, then in the paper. Beckett's picking up the kids from school—or has by now. He said they needed some man time."

Everything in Avery went soft. "You struck gold there, Clare."

"A mountain of it. I was also ordered to pick up Vesta spaghetti and meatballs. Manly portions."

"We can help you with that."

"I'm going to need help with more soon. After the opening, I'll only have two months before the wedding. I know we're not doing a huge bash, but . . ."

"Everything has to be wonderful."

"Starting with the dresses. Mine, yours, and Hope's."

"We'll take a day. Name it. I'll make it work."

"Thursdays are best right now—as soon after the opening as possible. I need to check with Hope. I could shift some things and do a Wednesday if that's better."

"Either way I can make it work."

"I've talked with Carol at Mountainside about the flowers. That's pretty much set. I haven't talked to you about food."

"Why don't you leave that to me? I'll put something together, then you can adjust, change, eliminate, or add. I can give you the launch pad."

"That takes a weight off. Thanks." Leaning forward, smile brilliant, Clare took her friend's hands. "I'm getting married, Avery."

"I've heard rumors."

"Everything's moving so fast. Do you remember when they first started work on the inn? It seemed like forever. Now it's finished, about to open. I'm getting married, Beckett's finishing the house. I'm looking at tile and faucets and lighting fixtures."

"Are you nervous?"

"No, not nervous. A little overwhelmed here and there. Marriage, a new home, and if things go as we hope, a new baby on the way in a few months."

"It all looks really good on you."

"It all feels really good. Are you nervous?"

"About what?"

"You and Owen."

"No. No, not exactly nervous. But maybe, yeah, maybe a little overwhelmed here and there, too. One minute I think, sure, of course. Then the next it's, *what?* Where did this come from, and what do I do with it?"

She propped her chin on her fist. "Then it's back to *of course*. We've been friends since we were kids, and now we're looking at each other in a new way. That's a little overwhelming. But maybe that's good. Otherwise, maybe it would be too easy for that 'of course' to turn into 'so what?'"

Before she sat back again, Clare gave Avery's hand a quick squeeze. "You think you're careless with people. I don't know where that comes from. I've known you a long time, and you've never been careless with people. We were friendly in high school. We ran in different crowds even though we cocaptained the cheerleading squad."

"Go Warriors."

"Go Warriors. But when I came back home after Clint was killed, you were right there for me. Right there, Avery. I don't know what I'd have done without you. I still don't."

This time Avery took Clare's hand. "You'll never have to find out."

"The same to you. You're not the *so what* type, Avery. Not with people. I've got to get back. I'll run up for the spaghetti and manly meatballs around five."

"I'll send it down, save you a trip."

Avery sat alone for another moment. She'd had enough of a break, all around, she decided. And enough worrying about what might be later rather than enjoying what was now.

She pulled out her phone, texted Owen.

Off in an hour. Want to come over, share a bottle of wine and a large pie upstairs?

She finished off her drink, rolled her tired shoulders. Then smiled when he texted back.

Knocking off shortly, having a beer with Ry at your place. I'll walk you home.

"Yeah, you walk me home, Owen. That's what a good boyfriend does."

She got up, did a little dance in place, then went back to work.

## CHAPTER THIRTEEN

FROM THE BITTERLY COLD MORNING OF THE OPENING of Inn BoonsBoro to the teeth-chattering afternoon, Avery calculated she had run twenty miles just dashing back and forth across Main Street.

She wouldn't have missed a single yard.

Throughout the day Hope and Carolee polished and primped the inn until every inch gleamed. Each time Avery ran over, more flowers graced the tables, the mantels, even the deep windowsills in The Dining Room. Tables and chairs stood in The Courtyard and on the porches, while indoors, fires simmered in hearths.

At one point, Avery ran through with trays of food while Hope—in jeans and a sweatshirt—signed for delivery of the rental dishes and glassware.

"I'll be back," Avery told her. "One of my crew will bring the rest, then more as we need it."

"We're right on schedule. Carolee just went home to change."

"I'm going to do that, but I'll be back—an hour tops."

"Take your time," Hope assured her in her ready-steady way. "We're good."

"Why am I nervous? It's not my inn." On a dash, Avery streaked out and back across the street.

In fifty-five minutes, overnight bag in hand, feeling smug at her early readiness, she found Hope setting up a bar. And wearing a killer red dress.

"You're dressed! You look amazing. It's not fair. I hate you again."

"I timed it out. I didn't want to have to run up and finish putting myself together once the Montgomerys got here. Which is any minute."

"I was supposed to be ready first. It's annoying."

"Live with it." Eyebrows arched under spiky black bangs, Hope gestured. "I might point out you're wearing two different shoes."

"Which ones do I go with?" Testing, Avery heel-toed it, did quick pivots. "I can't decide. Plus the dress is wrong, isn't it? It's gray."

"It's not gray. It's moondust. I love the sparkle on the bodice. Where did you get those sapphire shoes? I want them."

"I bought them last year in a weak moment. I haven't worn them yet. I wasn't sure if—"

"Yes, you are. I'll tell you what's annoying. Your feet are a full size smaller than mine. Otherwise, I'd take you down for those shoes. I still might."

"Blue shoes it is. Can I put this stuff, including the rejected black pumps, in your place?"

"Go ahead."

"I'll be right down, give you a hand."

She slipped out of both shoes, ran upstairs in her bare feet. She left the bag, the shoes inside Hope's door, put the blue ones back on.

Since the door to The Penthouse stood open, she wandered into its rarified air. Flowers spread under the windows in the parlor, stood on the floating counter in the bath, with more in the bedroom. Everything shimmered and gleamed.

She couldn't imagine what the Montgomerys felt, not when she felt such pride and satisfaction, and she'd only watched it evolve. And added a little elbow grease.

She walked down, letting her hand trail on the iron banister.

Wanting more, she walked down to Nick and Nora. She'd stay here tonight, she thought, with Owen. In that beautiful bed, with the scent of flowers, the sparkle of crystal.

They'd make love here, in the crystal dark, the first ones to reach for each other in this room. She thought it a kind of magic.

She turned at the sound of footsteps, smiled at Owen.

"I was just thinking about you, and there you are. And handsome, too." So handsome in his dark suit, with a tie— that magic again—almost the same color as her dress.

"You keep surprising me, Avery."

Her smile warmed. "Tonight calls for some style, and we're definitely stylish. I was thinking how you and your family must feel. It must be amazing because I feel so proud and happy, and I didn't do anything."

"Yes, you did. You hauled, fed, cleaned. You helped us get Hope."

"You're right; I did. And I put that sparkly floor lamp together solo." She gave one of its drops a light flick. Her eyes sparkled nearly as brightly. "Pretty major."

"I think so. I have something for you."

"For me?"

"Something to thank you for everything you did to help us get here tonight."

"A present?" On a sound of surprise she stepped toward him. "I didn't do anything for presents—even considering lamp assembly—but I do love presents. So I'll take it. Hand it over."

He pulled a little box out of his pocket—then took the wrapping she ripped off, balled it up while she lifted the lid.

"Oh. Oh, God, it's beautiful."

The little platinum key hung on a thin chain fired with tiny diamonds.

"I saw it, and thought, that's it. It's symbolic. The key to Inn BoonsBoro. Anytime you want to use it."

"That's beautiful, too, the thought of that. Thank you. Thank you," she repeated, leaning in for a kiss. "I love it. My first diamonds."

"Really? They're pretty puny."

"No diamond is puny. I want to wear it now."

"I'll help you out." He moved behind her, working on the clasp. She reached a hand up to the little key, studying them both in the silver-framed cheval glass.

Then lifted a hand to the one he laid on her shoulder.

She couldn't find words, not when she saw the way they looked together, reflected in the mirror.

The flutter came again when his gaze met hers. Then something new, a slow steady beat that spread out, spread through her until she felt it even in the soles of her feet.

"Owen." Whatever she might have said, could have said, slipped away when she saw the shadow in the glass. "Owen," she repeated.

"Yeah, I see."

She swallowed. "What do you see?"

"Her. Elizabeth."

"I see a shadow. A silhouette."

"I see her. She's smiling, but she has tears in her eyes. She . . . Is she waving? That's—no, showing me her hand. Her left hand. A ring. It's red—the little stone in it."

"A ruby?"

"I don't think—it's darker, I guess."

"A garnet?"

"Maybe. Yeah, maybe. An engagement ring?"

In his head he heard it, soft as a wish. *Billy.*

"Did you hear that?"

"No. I smell the honeysuckle, I see the shape of her, I guess. Or did," Avery said when the shadow faded. "What did you hear?"

"She said his name again. Billy."

Avery turned. "A ring, an engagement ring, you said."

"That's just a guess."

"She showed you the ring, then you heard her say his name. I'm betting engagement ring. She and Billy were going to get married. We have to find him for her, Owen."

The urgency in her voice as she turned, gripped his arms, surprised him. "I'll do what I can."

"Such a long time," Avery murmured. "Such a long time to hold on."

It gave her hope, she realized. Hope that love really could matter most. Matter enough to last.

"I haven't had a lot of time to try to pin it all down, which is probably why I haven't gotten anywhere yet. I'll have more after tonight. And we've got to get downstairs. We've got the ribbon-cutting thing in about twenty minutes."

"I told Hope I'd be right down to help, and I got distracted." She laid a hand on the key again. "Thank you, again."

"Looks good with the dress." He brushed her shoulder absently. "Go ahead. I'll be right down."

He wanted a moment, just another moment, and alone walked down to Elizabeth and Darcy. "I'm sorry. I've been busy getting ready for tonight, and dealing with . . ." *Life* seemed the wrong term. "Things. But I promise I'll keep trying to find him. You should know we're going to have a lot of people here tonight, wandering around, coming into the room. It's a party, okay? And after, my mother's sleeping in here. It's my mother, so . . . I just wanted to let you know."

He caught himself, shook his head. "Beckett probably already has. So, it's a big night for my family, for the town. I've got to get to it."

He thought he felt something brush at his lapels—as a woman might brush a man's before going out. "Ah . . . thanks. I think."

He glanced back on his way out, but saw nothing. So he walked down to the lights, the voices.

AFTER CENTURIES OF change, of war and weather, of neglect and of sweaty effort, the old hotel on The Square again welcomed guests. They toured rooms that offered warmth and welcome, gathered in groups near simmering hearths, and connected with neighbors in the open kitchen.

Light filled spaces dark for so long; voices brought life to the years of silence. People walked over pretty tiles and polished wood, lounged on a sofa yellow as butter or sipped drinks under an archway. Those brave enough to face the chill wandered out to admire The Courtyard or enjoy the view from a graceful porch.

Some caught the light summery drift of honeysuckle, but thought nothing of it. More than once someone felt a brush on their shoulder, only to turn and find no one there. Twice Owen took friends through and found the doors to the porch in Elizabeth and Darcy open. He simply closed them while guests commented on the bed or the tile work, or the pretty stained-glass shade of the lamp.

"Cut it out," he said under his breath, and moved on.

Later in the evening he checked again, pleased to find them closed. Probably too busy partying, he thought, to play games with him.

As he turned to go, Franny came in. She wore black pants and a frilly blouse rather than her usual jeans and tee, and had added a fitted black jacket.

"Hi! I brought over some more trays, and I'm taking my turn at the grand tour."

"You look nice, Franny."

"Thanks. I wanted to spruce it up a bit since I'm going back and forth. Gosh, Owen." Looking everywhere at once, Franny trailed her fingers over the upholstered footboard. "It's all so beautiful. Honestly, I know how much time and work went into it, but I swear, it's like a miracle."

"Thanks. We're really proud of it."

"You should be. I've only seen the rooms on this floor, and I'm already arguing with myself over my favorite."

He'd heard variations of that sentiment all evening, and it still made him smile. "I do the same thing. Want me to show you around?"

"No, I'm fine on my own. It's like exploring," she said with a laugh, "and I'm loving it—and I'm running into people everywhere I go. I just saw Dick in Eve and Roarke."

"Dick the barber or Dick the banker?"

"Ha. You're funny. Dick the barber. And I saw Justine and Clare's parents in The Library." Moving past him, she stepped into the bath. "Oh, look at the tub. It's like something out of an English novel."

"That's the idea."

"It's a great idea. I'd live in this bathroom, which I've said about every one of them so far. Don't worry about me. Get back to the party."

"It's nice to take a quick break."

"I guess it is. Since I've got you alone for a minute, I wanted to say how good it is to see you and Avery together."

"Oh. Ah—"

"I got used to seeing you as friends—I guess everyone did—so it was a surprise. A really nice surprise."

"It was . . . a surprise for us, too. I think."

"It's good. She deserves some happy, and you might just deserve her."

"Doing my best."

"I like your best. She matters a lot to me."

"I know."

"And just so you know." She walked back, tapped him on the chest. "If you hurt her, I'll slip a hefty dose of laxatives in your calzone. You'll never know when."

She arched her brows, nodded. "And, because you matter, too, and because I'm fair, I'll do the same to her if vice versa."

Maybe, just in case, he'd stick with gyros for a while. "You're a little scary, Franny."

"Be afraid. I'm onto the next."

As she walked out, Owen caught the whisper of laughter and honeysuckle behind him. "Oh yeah, you women are a riot."

Once again he started out, and once again stopped short. This time Willy B filled the doorway. Owen supposed if highland chieftains wore suits and polka-dot ties, they'd look pretty much like Willy B MacTavish.

"Hey. I was sort of looking for Justine."

"I heard she was in The Library. Might still be. It's down the hall, to the left."

"Yeah, I remember." Willy B shuffled his feet, a sure sign

he was about to address something that embarrassed him. "Ah, since I've got you alone for a minute . . ."

"A common theme."

"Sorry?"

"Nothing. Is something up?"

"A couple things." He shuffled into the room, glanced behind him. "I thought I should tell you—you and your brothers—that Justine . . . She asked if I'd . . ." He trailed off again, looking around the room. "Here. Tonight. Stay here. You know."

"Oh." Well shit, Owen thought. He should've seen it coming. "Well," he said and stuffed his hands in his pockets.

"I understand you might feel a little . . . I feel a little . . . but. Well."

"Yeah. Should I ask if you—if this is—if you've got plans? Or something?"

"She means a lot to me, your ma. I loved your daddy."

"I know. I know you did."

"I know he'd want me to look out for her some, and I did. And . . . She's a hell of a woman, your ma. I got pure respect for her. I'd never do anything to hurt her. Cut off my hand first."

"Okay, Willy B."

"Okay." Some of the flush receded from his face. "I'll talk to Ryder and Beckett."

"I'll take care of it." Or it'll take another hour and a half of fumbling.

"If you think." Willy B nodded, cleared his throat. "Um, you and Avery are . . . My Avery."

Same boat, Owen thought, different oars. "Everything you just said about my mother? Insert Avery. She's important to me. She's always been important to me."

"I know that's the truth. She's always had a sweet-on for you."

"Oh, well." Jesus, he'd be blushing and shuffling himself in a minute. "I don't know."

"Maybe you don't, but I do. Just like I know she's still got hurt inside over her mother, how she walked away. I want you to be careful with her, Owen. She's had other boyfriends, but you're different. You've got history and connections, and she's had that sweet-on going. She's tough, my girl, but she's got places that bruise easy. It's easy to forget that, so . . . don't. I guess that's it."

On a long, *long* relieved breath, Willy B looked around. "This place sure is the cat's ass. You did yourselves proud here. Tommy's up there busting his buttons over Justine and his boys. Busting buttons. I'd better get on."

Alone, Owen sat on the side of the bed. It was a lot, he decided. A big pile of a lot. His mother and Willy B. And here, right here— The "right here" had him shooting up to his feet again with an uncomfortable glance at the bed.

Probably better, all around, not to think about that.

The door to the porch eased open.

"Now that you mention it, I could use some air."

He walked out, hissed a little at the cold. Wished he had a beer.

It looked fine, he thought. Main Street. He'd known it all his life. It changed, of course—a new business, new paint, new neighbors, kids growing up as he had himself. But it remained a constant for him.

So was Avery. A constant. A kind of touchstone.

She'd changed. They'd changed together, he supposed. Growing up, becoming, expanding their reach.

He studied Vesta, the lights, people moving behind the glass.

She'd built that. They'd provided the shell—the stone, the wood—but she'd built it into what it was. And now she'd do so again.

Yeah, she was tough and smart and willing to work hard. She'd dug in when her mother had walked out. Kept her head up, though he knew damn well some kids ragged on her about it.

He'd had a few short words with a couple of assholes over it, he recalled. He didn't think she knew, just as he didn't think she knew that once, not long after Traci MacTavish ran off, he'd walked into the kitchen back home to see Avery crying in his mother's arms.

He'd backed out again, and the next time he'd seen Avery, she'd been dry-eyed and steady.

She was rarely otherwise.

But Willy B was right. There had to be places that bruised easily, and he should be careful.

Other boyfriends. Other, which made him—by Willy B's gauge—her new boyfriend. Or current. Or . . .

He hadn't really thought about it. To joke, sure—about being her first. Now the one-two punch of Franny, then Willy B made him consider the big picture.

He'd never taken her out on a date. To the movies, a concert, to dinner.

He'd never bought her flowers.

Okay, he bought her a present, so he got some points there. If he was keeping score, which, of course, he wasn't. Exactly.

She usually ended up cooking for him. Sure, she liked to cook, but that wasn't right, was it?

If he wanted this to be a real relationship, and he did, he had to start putting more effort into it.

"I haven't put any effort into it," he admitted. "Major fail."

Fresh start, he decided, and turned to go in.

He spotted the bottle of Heineken on the table between the doors.

"How the hell did you do that?" Though a chill ran up his spine, he picked up the bottle, took a drink. "I don't know whether it's spooky or handy. But thanks."

He took another drink. "Now I'm standing here, freezing to death, drinking a beer served by a ghost and talking to myself."

Shaking his head, he went back in, secured the door. He took his beer, headed downstairs to find Avery.

He should've known she'd be doing something useful. He found her in The Lounge, passing champagne to guests.

"Where's yours?" he demanded.

"There you are. My what?"

"Champagne."

"Oh, I had some. I think I set it down in the kitchen when I was switching trays."

"You're not here to work." He took the bottle, then her hand, and drew her toward the empty flutes. "You're here to enjoy yourself." And he poured her a glass of champagne.

"I'm enjoying. Your hands are freezing."

"I was outside for a while. Let's find a place to sit. You should get off your feet."

"You need to mingle."

"I've been mingling. Now I want to sit down with you, spend some time with you." Leaning down, he laid his lips on hers.

She blinked up at him. It wasn't as if they were having a clandestine affair, but it was the first time he'd kissed her—like that—in a public setting.

New Year's, she recalled, but people traditionally kissed at midnight, so it didn't really count.

She could actually feel speculative eyes on them.

"Are you all right?"

"I'm great." He draped an arm over her shoulders to steer her out, then toward the stairs. "How are you?"

"I'm absolutely fine. I just wanted to check on the—"

"Avery, you don't have to check on anything. There's plenty of everything, and people are enjoying themselves. You get to relax."

"I don't relax at parties unless I'm doing something. My hands start itching."

"Scratch them," he suggested.

"Hey, Owen."

Charlie Reeder, old friend and town cop, crossed their path. "Could use a hand a minute."

"What's the problem?"

"Your cousin, Spence? He's getting ready to go. He was pounding them back pretty good tonight. He won't give up the car keys. I tried talking to him, but he got belligerent. I don't want to have to arrest him. Maybe you can talk him down before it comes to that."

"Yeah, sure. I'll be back."

It took him twenty minutes, much of which he spent with his cousin draped around him in drunken sentiment, or hee-hawing as he tried to walk a straight line to prove his competency.

When he fell on his ass a third time, Spence finally gave up his keys.

"I'll drive him home, Owen," Charlie told him. "We've got to get going anyway. Kids are with a sitter. Charlene'll follow me, and we'll pour him through his front door."

"Appreciate it, Charlie."

"All in a day's work." He paused a moment, hands on his skinny hips as he looked over The Courtyard, up to the porches. "She's a beauty. I booked a night for our anniversary next May. A surprise for Charlene."

"Which room?"

"She seems to favor the one with the drapes on the bed and the ginormous tub."

"Titania and Oberon. Good choice."

"Hope talked me into the package that comes with a bottle of champagne, and dinner for two and whatnot. It'll be ten years, so we ought to do something special."

"Hope will make sure it is."

"Well, I'll help you get Spence into the car."

"I've got it. Go ahead and get Charlene. Thanks for the assist."

"Not a problem."

By the time he got back inside, the crowd had thinned out. His fresh hunt for Avery was hampered by other guests preparing to leave, stopping him with thanks for the evening, compliments on the inn, and good-luck wishes.

He appreciated it, he really did, but it occurred to him they'd just had their second party as a couple where he'd spent more time without Avery than with her.

And she'd spent more time serving than being served.

He found her in The Dining Room, bussing tables.

"Don't you know how to be a guest?"

"Not really. And I promised Hope and Carolee I'd help them clean up after. It's pretty much after. It was great, Owen. Everyone had a good time, and really loved seeing the inn. Racked up some bookings, too."

"So I hear." He took the plates from her. "Where's your champagne?"

"I set it down somewhere, but I drank most of it this time. I just scooted your mom up to The Library. We're going to bring up a fruit and cheese tray, some crackers. Most of you didn't get much food." Insistent, she took the plates back from him. "Go on up. I'll be up there soon. I'll finish up with Hope, then I have to get my bag out of her apartment."

"I'll get it. Where is it?"

"Just inside the door, but her apartment's locked."

"I'll get the key."

He got her bag, put a bottle of champagne in an ice bucket, added two flutes, and pocketed the key to Nick and Nora. After setting the ice bucket in his room for the night, he found his family, including Clare's parents, sprawled in The Library and already diving into food trays.

"I didn't think I was hungry till right now." Justine grabbed some crackers. "There's my missing son."

"Spence," he said. "Car keys. It took some persuading."

"You should've found me," Justine told him. "Spence listens to me."

"It's all good." He realized he hadn't had much to eat, just as Avery had suggested, and took a handful of olives before sitting on the floor. "They came, they saw, we conquered."

"And then some," Beckett agreed, snuggled with Clare on the sofa they shared with his mother and Willy B.

"It's really done." Justine sighed. "When I think of the past two years . . ."

"Would you do it again?" Clare's mom, Rosie, asked her.

"Don't give her any ideas." Ryder cast his eyes to the ceiling.

"I wouldn't, not this. This was a once-in-a-lifetime."

"Thank you, God."

But she laughed as she booted Ryder's foot. "I have other ideas. For later. For tonight?" She lifted her glass. "Here's to my boys. Ryder, Owen, and Beckett. You made my dream come true."

Ryder reached over, laid a hand on hers.

"You dream good," he said after a moment. "Just do me a favor and sleep quiet for a while."

From the gleam in her eye as she sipped her champagne, Owen suspected she already had another dream going.

## CHAPTER FOURTEEN

GOOD NIGHTS CAME LATE AND LAZILY. AVERY CALCU-lated Justine and her father had some sort of signal to make the sleeping arrangements a bit less awkward for their children.

Or at least the male children, she thought, as she didn't feel awkward at all.

Her father lumbered out while Justine remained. A few minutes later, Justine wished them all sweet dreams.

By tacit agreement no one mentioned the fact Justine and Willy B were spending the night together just down the hall.

Maybe, if she thought about it, the fact she and Owen would be spending the night together at the other end of that same hall, awkwardness—or more likely amusement in her case—would ensue.

So she didn't think about it.

Instead, inside the Deco flair of Nick and Nora, Avery stretched her arms high. Everything felt good, she decided. Everything felt just exactly right.

To please herself, she turned in a circle to take in the room, and saw the champagne on ice.

"You copped a bottle!"

"Hey, I prefer the term *liberated*." On her grin, he walked over to pop the cork.

"This is like dreamscape—or some beautifully produced play, and I get a starring role. A beautiful and downright snazzy room after a lovely, happy party, with champagne provided by a sexy guy. I'd check my list if I had one, but I think I currently have it all."

He offered her a glass. "Now you do."

"To having it all then." She tapped her glass to his, sipped as she wandered.

"It really went well, didn't it?" she said to Owen. "Lots of happy faces, lots of happy talk."

"All of that, and you had to see and hear most of it. You seemed to be everywhere at once."

"I can't sit still at a party." She set the shoes she carried beside the dresser. "Gotta keep moving or I might miss something. You disappeared for a while."

He took off the tie he'd already loosened. "I toured some people through, then had to close the doors in E&D."

"Elizabeth was all over tonight, too. I caught her scent several times."

"I ran into your father up there. He wanted to let me know he'd be staying there—he and Mom. In E&D. Together."

"Hmm." She leaned back on the dresser, eyeing him as she drank champagne. "I suspected as much. And how did that go?"

"He fumbled around a lot, like he does, and still managed to say all the right things. Meanwhile I fought a desperate battle to keep any and all imagery out of my brain. We both did okay."

"That's good. I think—"

"Then he pinned me about you."

"He . . . What?"

No amused smirk now, Owen noted. "No fumbling there. He's a lot more on-point when it comes to his little girl."

"Well, for God's sake," she began, then tilted her head. "On second thought, it's kind of sweet. And funny. How'd that go for you?"

He pulled off his shoes, set them beside hers. "It was a little strange, a little illuminating."

"Really?" Enjoying the idea of it, she sipped more champagne. "What did he say?"

"That's between us men."

She rolled her eyes.

"You're his Avery," Owen said as he crossed to her. "The most important thing in his life. I'd say the center of his life. You're important to me, too."

She smiled. "It's nice to be important."

"You are." He set his glass down, laid his hands on her shoulders, ran them down to her elbows and back. "Maybe I haven't told you, or shown you."

He looked so serious, those blue eyes more intense than quiet, she found herself just a little off balance. "We go back. We know we're important to each other."

"We go back," he agreed, and laid his lips softly, very softly on hers. "But this is now, and this is different."

She tipped her head back a bit more. "There is that."

Not just that, he thought as he slowly deepened the kiss. He wasn't sure what, wasn't sure of the all, but it was more than heat generated and needs met.

He felt her slide into it, little by little, and knew—at that moment—he wanted exactly that. A long, slow slide.

He took the glass from her hand, set it beside his.

It always surprised him how soft she was. Lips, skin. Everything about her was so bright, so vivid, yet the soft played its part.

And her heart—a softness there, too. He'd known it, always known it, but . . . He needed to pay more attention to those soft places.

"I love how you feel," he murmured. "Your skin, your mouth. And how what you feel inside shows in your eyes."

She braced the heels of her hands on the dresser at her back. "Right now, I'm feeling dazzled."

"Good. Then I'm not alone."

He framed her face and kept the kiss soft as her skin, tender as her heart. And lifted her into his arms.

The breath caught in her throat. She'd expected fun,

maybe even foolish. Instead he swept her away, made her feel weak and trembly, and a little unsure.

"Owen."

"Your hands are so small." He laid her on the bed, then lifted one of her hands to press the palm to his. "They look delicate, but they're tireless. That's the surprise of you. Then there's your shoulders." He nudged a strap aside. "The skin's so smooth and pale, but they're strong. They'll hold a lot."

Lowering his head, he glided his lips over her shoulder, down the line of her throat.

The glitter of the room, the fragrance of flowers, and his hands on her, featherlight. Everything in her surrendered, to him, to the moment, to this new gift as unexpected as the sparkling key around her neck.

He gave her the slow, the quiet, the achingly tender. No one had ever touched her, not quite like this, or made her feel . . . precious.

He eased the dress down, gliding his lips over newly exposed flesh, making it quiver. Making her sigh. He watched the way the light played in her eyes before she closed them, the way her body moved under his hands and mouth. And felt the way her heart beat under them, thickly.

Then faster when he guided her up, as he urged her higher. She clutched at him, riding that crest. Until the wave broke, and her hands slid away to lie limp.

Like that, he thought as he undressed. Like that, open, exposed, drenched in pleasure.

He took her mouth again first, drowning her in the kiss as his hand slid down, down to cup her. To tease a moan from her.

Then slipped into her, into hot, wet silk.

Now he trembled, steeped in her, trembled in the quick, desperate wanting of her. But he gave her long, slow strokes. Torturous, glorious.

He gripped her hands, linking them as beat followed beat. The air thickened, seemed to pulse like a heartbeat. He saw her face, only her face as he said her name—or perhaps only thought it.

But her eyes opened, locked on his. Hands and bodies

joined, he lowered his lips to hers. Complete as they took that long, slow slide off the edge together.

IN THE MORNING, in the quiet, he watched her sleep. It was so rare to see her still.

He thought back to the planning stages of the inn, the debates, adjustments, countless meetings—and through the months of the long build.

He'd never imagined he'd spend his first night here with Avery sleeping beside him.

Now it was done. The inn, that first night. Another build under way, another plan. And here she was, sleeping deep, her hair a bold streak against the snowy pillow.

What happened next?

He planned, anticipated, calculated. It's what he did, in his life, in his work. But he couldn't quite formulate a plan where Avery was concerned, couldn't see his way clear to anticipate the next step, calculate the next move.

It seemed strange—they knew each other so well. Shouldn't the next step, the next move, come easily?

Maybe it would, he considered. So why worry?

He slipped out of bed, a little surprised when she didn't stir. He eased the door of the bathroom closed, studied the glass shower with pleasure.

"Let's give you a spin, baby," he murmured.

He tested out the jets, the rain head—and, sniffing at the green tea and ginger shower gel, decided, with considerable relief, it wasn't too girly.

By the time he reached for one of the fluffy bath sheets, he was awake, alert—and decided he needed coffee, pretty much now.

Shaving could definitely wait.

He pulled on jeans, tossed a flannel shirt over a thermal. He decided against the work boots—too noisy on the stairs—and settled on socks.

And still, Avery didn't stir.

He slipped out of the room, headed downstairs, and didn't

hear a sound until he turned toward the kitchen. From there he followed the scents, and the murmur of female voices.

"Good morning, sweetie." Bright-eyed and busy, his aunt offered him a welcoming smile as she set bacon to drain. "Coffee?"

"Name your price."

She puckered her lips, took his quick kiss before reaching for the pot.

"What's this?" he asked gesturing toward the white chef's coats both she and Hope wore.

"We thought it presented a clean look," Hope told him. "A little more upscale than aprons."

"I like." With the speed of experience, he snatched a slice of bacon before Carolee could slap his hand away.

She pointed at him. "No filching. Breakfast starts in a half hour."

"But there's bacon now. How'd you like The Penthouse?"

"I felt like a queen. I was so damn tired, but I just had to wander all over, sit on every chair awhile." She shook her head, laughing at herself. "I kept thinking it was like a dream. I remember when Justine and I picked out those fabrics. And there I was sitting on them."

"How'd you like your room?" Hope asked him.

"It was great. Made me wish I'd worn a fedora. I think everybody must've settled right in once we called it a night. And everybody must still be settled right in because I didn't hear anyone moving around when I came down."

"Guests are allowed to sleep in. But if you're hungry, we can fix you up pretty quick."

"I'm okay." But he grabbed another slice of bacon while his aunt had her back turned. "Maybe I'll take some coffee up to Avery."

"Aren't you sweet?" Then Carolee narrowed her eyes when he bit into the second slice of bacon. "And sneaky."

Hope poured the coffee, doctored it Avery's way. "Tell her to take her time. That's what chafing dishes are for."

He went back up, slipped back inside. She'd stirred, he noted—enough to stretch diagonally across the bed. There may not be a lot of her, he mused, but given the chance, she could fill the best part of a bed all on her own.

He sat on the corner, leaned down and kissed her cheek. When that didn't work, he brushed a hand up and down her arm. Giving up on the gentle awakening, he pinched her.

"What! Ow! Huh?"

"I wanted to be sure you were still alive."

"I was . . ." Shifting a little, she rubbed her fingers over glassy eyes. "In a Harry dream."

"A what?"

"Clare's Harry. He has these weird, vivid dreams. I had a Harry dream about green giraffes with red splotches. It sounds Christmassy and cheerful, but no. I was on one in this stampede, and dressed like Lady Gaga. I think. Is that coffee?"

"Yeah, I think you need it."

"Thanks. And the Animal Crackers monkey was on one, chasing me. He had teeth."

"Does that happen often?"

"No, thank God. But we drank all that champagne last night. After," she added with a sleepy smile. "It may have played into it. You're all dressed. What time—" Her eyes popped wide now as she scanned the clock. "Shit! It's almost eight."

"Shocking."

"I was going to be up by seven to help Hope and Carolee with breakfast."

"They've got it handled. Relax." He squeezed in beside her, bumped her over a bit more, then picked up the remote. "Watch this."

He switched on the TV. "We can kick back right here, drink coffee, and check out what's happening in the world."

"I've heard of this concept." She settled back on the pillows beside him, sipped her coffee. "I like it. It's nice."

"Yeah." He draped an arm around her so they sat hip-to-hip. "It is."

"Is everyone up?"

"No one's up."

She relaxed a little more. "Then I don't have to feel guilty. It's like a mini-vacation."

"A morning vacation?"

"It works for me."

The idea of it inspired another. "Why don't we extend it? Want to go to a movie tonight?"

"Oh." She angled her face up to his. "I'm closing tonight."

"Tomorrow then."

"Is there something you want to see?"

"We'll find something."

"No slasher flicks—or anything with monkeys."

"I can work with that. Why don't I pick you up about six? We'll get something to eat first."

"Sounds like a plan."

Yeah, he thought, it did. And as a next step, next move, not bad.

ᕫ

THINKING SPRING IN the bitter entrance of February, Avery sat in the back of Hope's car, using her phone to search for wedding dresses.

"I'm worried I left this too late." Clare fretted in the front seat. "We should've done this before the holidays."

"Plenty of time," Hope assured her. "This is a wonderful boutique. And if you don't find just what you want there, I have two more."

"Not white. My dress shouldn't be white."

"Every bride's entitled to white," Hope corrected. "But more, every bride's entitled to whatever color, whatever style, whatever wedding dress suits her. Don't go into this with limitations."

"We should've stuck with the idea of a small, family-only afternoon wedding. But—"

"Beckett hasn't done this before." While she searched and scrolled, Avery listed the reasons Clare had already laid out. "The boys are excited. You want something special and memorable for you and Beckett. You have the perfect venue with the inn. Need more?"

"No." Clare glanced over her shoulder. "Have you found anything?"

"Sorry. I keep getting distracted by the big white dresses. I mean look at this. It's art."

She offered the screen to Clare. "Gorgeous for a first wedding, and one with an unlimited budget. God, look at that train, and the beadwork on the skirt. Miles of skirt."

"I love it, but I could never pull that off." Avery shook her head. "I'd drown in a dress that big."

Hope flicked a glance in the rearview. "Is there something we should know?"

"I'm short?"

"About you and Owen—and wedding dresses."

"About— No!" Avery took the phone back, gave the dress one last look, then scrolled on. "It's knee-jerk for a woman to imagine herself in a wedding dress when in the wedding dress mode."

"But things are good." Clare shifted, angling back.

"Really good. We're both crazy busy, but we've actually managed to go out a couple times. You know, to those places where other people bring you food that yet other people have cooked? Plus, I'm trying out potential MacT's dishes on him. He's a good test subject."

"Still fluttering?" Hope asked her.

"Yeah, still fluttering. And now there's this tugging. It's good, but it's a little unnerving."

"I know," Clare said with a smile.

"It's not like you and Beckett."

"Why?"

"Because it's me and Owen, and we're . . . I don't know exactly. Anyway, today's about you."

"We have the whole day," Clare reminded her.

"Which starts now." Hope zipped into a parking spot. "That was lucky, and I'm taking it as a good omen. The boutique's right there."

"Oh, look at that dress!" Clare stared at the display window and the indulgence of the sparkling pick-up skirt, the shimmer of off-the-shoulder white silk. "It's stunning, but way too formal and first-wedding. I don't think this is the place. I don't want—"

"Trust me." Hope pulled out the ignition key.

Avery shoved open her door. "And even if you don't, I'm not missing a chance to play in there."

Before Clare could protest again, Avery jumped out of the car. She yanked open Clare's door, pulled her friend out. "It'll be fun."

It was.

The shimmer and glow of whites, ivories, creams, yards of tulle, acres of beading. In her jeans and knee boots, Avery plopped a veil on her head, struck a pose.

She looked, she decided, like she had a tulle volcano on her head.

Then she whirled on Clare.

"Get away from those."

The snap of the order had Clare snatching her fingers back. "But they're nice, elegant suits."

"You're *not* wearing a suit, elegant or not. Those are entirely mother-of-the-bride and/or groom."

"But—"

"Too sedate." Along with Avery, Hope folded her arms. "Not a chance."

"I'm not going formal or fussy. I want simple."

"Then simple you shall have." Avery nodded sagely. "The bride rules."

"Then—"

"Except with those."

"I really like the green one."

"It's lovely," Hope agreed. "If you were going to someone else's wedding, a ladies tea, a political fund-raiser." With Avery, she flanked Clare, and marched her away.

"We should pick out your dresses first," Clare suggested. "That'll give me a springboard."

"Get serious. Our dresses flow from yours, not the other way." Still wearing the veil, Avery wandered into another section.

Initial suggestions were deemed too fussy, too white, too club-night.

"Oh, not pink."

"It's not pink-pink," Avery insisted. "It's soft. It's more like a blush, and look at the hem."

"I love it." Lips pursed, Hope studied it. "The flow of that diagonal hem, should hit above the knee, go to just about midcalf."

"I don't know. I—"

"Okay, you've got to try some on. I'm making a rule. And this is one of the try-ons," Avery decreed. "We'll pick a few more, and snag a dressing room."

"You're right. You're right, and I'm being a pain in the ass. That one, that one." Clare included the one Hope held. "That one, and the green suit. I get to try on the green suit."

"Fair. Take these." Hope handed the dresses to Avery. "I'll get the suit."

Obviously noting some initial decisions had been made, a clerk set up a dressing room, hung the dresses, offered sparkling water.

Clare took the green suit first.

"Fine, get it over with." Avery shrugged, drank some fizzy water with lemon.

"It's got classic lines," Clare insisted as she changed. "It's a good color for me. And the weather's iffy in April, so a jacket's smart."

She turned to study herself in the triple mirrors. "A really pretty green—that brings out the green in my eyes. And with the right shoes . . . It's not romantic."

"No, it's not. It's a smart suit," Hope admitted. "And it looks good on you. But it's not your dress, Clare."

"I admit defeat. Let me try that blue. It's a pretty, quiet color, and it has nice lines."

Avery set down her water, rose from the plush little love seat to circle after Clare made the change. "Miles better. The color's great with your hair."

"I love the flirty hem, the little bustle in the back. I could work with this," Clare considered. "Shoes with a little spar-kle maybe."

"It didn't make you glow." Hope shook her head. "I think when you put on *the* one, it'll make you glow. But it is won-derful on you. It makes your waist look so tiny, and shows off your legs. How about we put it in Maybe."

"That works. We'll have a No and a Maybe."

She tried on another in a pale, dusty gold that immediately earned three thumbs down.

"Now the pink." Avery narrowed her eyes at Clare's expression. "We had a deal."

"All right, okay, but pink's going to be too much. Plus, it's strapless, and I don't want strapless."

"Blah, blah, blah," was Avery's opinion as she zipped Clare up.

"I'm not trying to be difficult, it's just not . . . Oh." She stared at her reflection.

And she glowed.

"Clare." Studying the bride-to-be, Hope let out a sigh. "You look amazing. The color's fabulous against your skin. And that hemline—it's flattering and it's romantic—and it's fun."

"Do the turn," Avery ordered. "Oh boy, look how it just floats, and the back, the little crisscrossing—quietly sexy. It's got just a hint of a sheen. Just enough."

"It's romantic, and it's beautiful. And it's mine. No Maybe on this one. I'm marrying Beckett Montgomery in this dress."

"You need to see it with shoes—even if they aren't the perfect shoes." Hope dashed for the door. "Wait."

"Do the turn again," Avery requested.

Clare laughed, and this time did a spin. "It *feels* wonderful on me. You were right."

"I love when that happens."

"I'll want my hair up, don't you think?" Experimenting, Clare scooped it up and back with her hands. "No headpiece. Just a clip with some sparkle."

"You look so happy."

"I am, so, so happy. I want to do this for you one day, you and Hope. I want to shop for your wedding dresses with you, and know you're as happy as I am in this moment."

"I'd like that."

At moments like this, Avery believed it could happen. She'd know that joy, have that faith, take that leap.

She turned to get her phone. "Let me take a picture of you in it. We can send it to your mom and to Justine."

"You're right. They should see."

"Front and back." Avery framed in. As she sent the pictures, Hope and the clerk came back with stacks of shoe boxes. And the happy madness began.

❧

ON THE WAY home after a long day of dresses, shoes, accessories—with some honeymoon wardrobe added in— Avery stretched out in the backseat of the car and texted Owen.

Stopped for a late dinner and a reprise of the day's haul. Your soon to be SIL is going to be a beautiful bride—and knock Beck's socks off. Her attendants aren't going to suck either. Heading home. Sorry it's later than I figured.

Clare turned at the signal from Avery's phone. "What's Owen have to say?"

"That Beck hasn't been able to keep his socks on since he first saw you—that's a knock-his-socks-off reference. And he wants to know if I want to head to his place."

"Do you?" Hope asked. "I can drop you there."

"I have to head up to Hagerstown first thing in the morning for supplies, then I have a meeting with Beckett at the new space." She texted Owen back as she spoke. "Plus I know Owen's been putting in some time trying to find Billy."

"Elizabeth's Billy?"

Avery nodded at Clare. "So far, not much luck. But then it's a tall order. I should just go home, get some sleep. It's nearly eleven already. He misses me, he said."

"Aw."

"I know, right? Flutter, flutter. I work till four tomorrow, but I can pick up some specific ingredients when I'm out in the morning, then fix another sample menu if he's up for it. And he is," she announced. "I have a date tomorrow night, with my boyfriend."

"I swear you look like you've been hit with the cute stick."

Avery just grinned at Hope. "That's how I feel. What a great day. Maybe I'll call Owen when I get settled down in bed."

"For phone sex?"

Her grin at Hope didn't diminish. "That may be a portion of the agenda. Any tips?"

"Talk low, talk slow."

"She's so wise." Avery straightened up as Hope pulled

in behind Vesta. "God, what a good, good day." She leaned forward, kissed both her friends. "I loved it. I love you guys. Pop the trunk. I know which bag is mine."

"Tell Owen . . . *hi*," Hope said, making the syllable breathy. "From us."

"I'll be too busy telling him *hi* from me. This was great, absolutely and completely great. See you tomorrow." She grabbed her bag, slammed the truck. After waving them off, she hurried into the back door.

She'd been sure she'd be back before closing—but she was not, absolutely not going in to look things over. She forced herself to continue past Vesta's rear, locked door, turned on the stairway.

And saw the woman sitting on the steps.

Avery stopped where she was, instinctively moved the keys in her hand until one jabbed between her fingers. She considered options as the woman pushed to her feet.

Avery was young, strong—and fast, if necessary.

"The restaurant's closed," she said calmly.

"I know. I've been waiting for you."

"If you're looking for work, you can come in tomorrow, during business hours. But right now—"

"Don't you know me?" She stepped down; Avery braced. "I'm your mother."

In the wash of security lights, Avery studied the face. She saw it now, of course, she saw it now. But there were so many years between her last look and this one. So much time, so much distance.

She waited for a surge of something—something, but felt numb.

"What do you want?"

"To see you. To talk to you. Can we go inside and talk?"

Saying nothing, Avery walked up the stairs, unlocked her apartment door.

She realized she did feel something after all.

She felt dread.

## CHAPTER FIFTEEN

AVERY SET HER SHOPPING BAG ASIDE, TOOK OFF HER coat, her scarf, every movement precise as she draped both over the back of a chair.

She remained silent and standing.

"This is nice." Her mother's voice piped out with nervous enthusiasm. "You've got a real nice place. I was in your restaurant earlier. It looks great, really great. It's way professional."

She needed a root job, Avery noted, and didn't care if the thought was petty and unkind. Traci MacTavish—or whatever her name was now—wore a bright red coat over tight jeans and a black sweater. Avery's impression was of a frame more bony than slim, of a narrow face too carefully made up, and short, spiky blond hair against harsh black roots.

Every thought in her head, Avery realized, struck as petty and unkind.

Well, too damn bad.

"What do you want?" she repeated.

"I wanted to see you. God, baby, you're so pretty! I love your hair. I always worried you'd go around with that Howdy

Doody red mop and those awful braces, but look at you! I just—"

"Don't." Avery stepped back as Traci started toward her. "Don't think you're getting an Oprah moment here."

Traci dropped her arms, her gaze. "I don't deserve one. I know it, honey. I do. It's just seeing you, all grown up, so pretty. I realize what I missed. Can we sit down? Can we just sit for a few minutes?"

"I don't need to sit."

"You're so mad at me." Like a courageous patriot facing a firing squad, Traci straightened her shoulders. "I don't blame you. What I did, it was stupid and selfish and wrong. I'm so sorry, Avery."

"Oh well, you're *sorry*." Letting temper rule, Avery snapped her fingers. "Bang. All better now."

"It isn't. I know being sorry doesn't make it okay. Nothing could, I guess. I did an awful thing, made a terrible mistake. I just—just wanted to see you," Traci managed as tears shimmered in her eyes. "I thought, maybe, now that you're grown up, you could understand a little."

"Understand what?"

"Why I left. I was so unhappy." She fumbled a tissue out of her purse, then dropped down in a chair and sobbed into it. "Nobody understands what I went through! Nobody *can* understand how it was for me. You can't see what's happening in someone else's marriage."

"Oh, I think a kid inside one gets a pretty good picture. You didn't just walk away from your marriage, you walked away from your daughter."

"I know. I *know*, but I couldn't stay. You were always more your daddy's girl than mine, so—"

"Be careful what you say about my father."

"I wouldn't say anything." Obviously prepared, Traci pulled out another tissue. "He's a good man. Maybe he was too good for me. I shouldn't have married him. I made a mistake."

"Mistakes seem to be a habit with you."

"I was so young, honey. Just barely nineteen. And I thought I loved him. I really did. Then I got pregnant, so getting married seemed like the best thing to do. My parents were so hard on me when I told them. You don't know how scared I was."

Whatever sympathy she might've felt for a young woman in those circumstances evaporated before it fully formed. Avery remembered her grandfather—so kind, so patient, and the sadness in his eyes to the end of his life for the daughter lost to him.

And her grandmother, strong, loving—and always a rock of support for her family.

"Did they kick you out? Threaten to?"

"They . . ."

"Careful," Avery warned.

"No, but they *blamed* me. And they said how having a baby meant I had to support it, and—"

"Imagine that. Imagine expecting you to take some responsibility."

"They were *hard* on me. They always were. I couldn't stay home with them picking at me night and day."

"So getting married was a way out."

"It's not like that. I was only nineteen. I thought I wanted to get married and have a family, my own place. And Willy B, he was just so big and handsome, and he took care of things. You know, getting us a place and all. He was real good to me when I was carrying. I tried, I *really* tried to make a nice house and cook and take care of you when you came. You were a really fussy baby, Avery."

"Shame on me."

"I don't mean it like that. I just— I wasn't even twenty when you came along, and there was so much to *do*."

"I guess my father didn't do anything."

Traci sniffled, pressed her lips together. "He did a lot. I'm not going to lie to you. He did a lot around the house and all, and he'd walk the floor with you at night, and rock with you. He was a good daddy."

"I know he was. He is."

"I did the best I could, I *swear* I did." Eyes drenched, Traci crossed her hands over her heart. "But honest to God, nothing ever got done that I wasn't doing it all over again. Then you started walking so soon, and you were into everything. I couldn't keep up. Even when I got a job and got you into day care, there was so much to do, and it was always the same. He even wanted another. Jesus Christ, he wanted more kids, and I couldn't deal with that. When I had the abortion—"

It was a sudden, sharp slap in the face. "You had an abortion."

Traci's tear-splotched face paled. "I thought he'd've told you."

"No, he didn't tell me."

"You were three, and my God, Avery, such a handful. I got pregnant again, even though I'd been real careful not to. I couldn't go through it another time. I just couldn't, so I took care of it. I wasn't going to tell him, but we were fighting about something and it came out."

"You terminated a pregnancy without telling him?"

"He'd've tried to talk me out of it, and I'd made up my mind. It was my body, my choice. You're a woman. You ought to respect that."

"I respect the right of choice. But what choice did you give him? What respect did you show him? He was your husband, the father, and you made that decision without telling him. Or was he the father?"

"Of course he was! I wasn't cheating on him."

"Then."

Traci stared down at her tattered tissue. "Well, I wasn't. And I couldn't handle another pregnancy. I was sick half the time with you, and got big as a house. I didn't want another baby. I had an abortion, and I had my tubes tied, and that was the end of it."

"For you," Avery murmured.

"He was awful mad, awful upset when he found out. And things just went from bad to worse with us. You've got to understand, he wasn't happy either. It wasn't my fault. We just weren't happy. But I went to the marriage counseling like he wanted. Nobody can say I didn't try. I just felt trapped and unhappy. But I tried."

"Did you?"

"Twelve years. That's a long time, and all that time it felt like I had to be something I wasn't."

"A wife and mother."

"I wanted more. I know that's selfish, but I wanted more than working at the mall, and coming home to this town day after day. It got so I hated this town and everything in it. That's not healthy, is it? It's not healthy to live like that. My whole life was passing me by, and I couldn't catch up."

"So you started having affairs."

"I didn't mean to. It just happened."

"I think having sex with men who aren't your husband takes some intent."

"It was only twice before Steve. I wasn't happy. I needed more. I needed something for me."

"So you cheated on your husband to get through the boredom of being a wife and mother. And when that wasn't enough, you just left."

"Can I have some water? Please?"

Avery walked into the kitchen, filled a glass from the tap. She stood a moment, eyes closed, breath even, until she felt she had her bearings.

Though she'd taken off the red coat, had it draped over her lap, Traci continued to sit, a tissue crumbled in one hand, tears on her lashes. "Thanks. I know you hate me."

"I don't know you."

"I was there until you were almost twelve, Avery. I took care of you. I did my best."

"Maybe it was your best. That's very sad for both of us. But there's been a lot of years between then and now. You never once wrote me, called me, came to see me. Not once."

"I didn't know if your father would've let me—"

"I told you to be careful. I won't warn you again."

"All right. All right." Dropping her gaze again, she smoothed at the coat. "Maybe I didn't feel like I could, or should. I just know I had to go, and I did it the wrong way. Willy B, he wanted us to go for more counseling. All that would do was string it all out even more. I didn't *love* him, Avery. You can't live your life without love. I know how he thought, I do. We should try to make it work. We had you to think of. But you were going to grow up one day, weren't you? And then where would I be? Stuck here, and older. Older and stuck here, without any chance to live my life. I didn't make Willy B any happier than he made me. What was the point?"

"You wanted out. Fine. You wanted to live your life. Fine again. There's this thing called divorce. It's hard, and I've heard it can be painful, tough on everybody. But it's how it's done in a civilized world where women don't leave their husbands, children, their homes without a fucking word."

"I just . . ." She sniffled again, set aside the glass she'd drained. "I was in *love*! When I met Steve, I felt so much. So much I'd never felt before. I couldn't think about anything else. It was wrong, I know it was wrong, but I felt alive and happy. I know I did wrong. I know I should've been honest with Willy B instead of cheating on him. He didn't deserve it, but, honey, he didn't want what I wanted. I couldn't be who he wanted me to be. And when Steve got a chance—a real business opportunity—down in Miami, he had to go. I had to go with him."

"You've been in Miami."

"At first. I was so caught up, and running away together, it seemed so romantic, so exciting. I knew your daddy would take good care of you."

"Stop it. You never gave me a thought once you walked out the door."

"That's not true! I didn't do right. I didn't think right, but I thought about you. I was real proud when I heard you'd started your own place. It's a good place, and I was real proud when I heard about it."

Little warning bells rang in Avery's mind. She hoped she heard only her own cynicism. "How'd you hear about it?"

"I looked you up on the Internet now and then. I did want to know how you were doing, honey. I can't count the times I started to email you. And I was real sorry when I heard about Tommy Montgomery. He and your daddy were like brothers. I know Justine didn't like me much, but she was always nice to me. I felt bad for her."

"That's your level of motherly interest? The occasional Google?"

"I was wrong. I don't expect your forgiveness. I guess I just hoped you'd understand a little."

"What difference does it make what I understand at this point?"

"I thought maybe you'd give me a chance, so we could get to know each other again, and—"

"What happened to Steve? The love of your life."

Traci's face crumpled. Sobbing again, she dug for more tissues. "He—he died. In November. He just died. We've been together all this time. We traveled all over, for his work, you know? He had his flaws, sure, but I loved him, and we were happy. Now he's gone, and I've got nobody."

"I'm sorry. I am. But I can't fill that gap for you. I won't. You made your choices. You have to live with them."

"I don't know how to be alone. Can't I just stay here a little while. A couple weeks?"

"Here?" Sincerely shocked, Avery gaped. "Absolutely not. You don't walk back after, what, seventeen years of *nothing* and get an open door. You'll have to figure out how to go on living your life. You're not a part of mine anymore."

"You can't be that cold."

"I can," Avery corrected. "Maybe I came by it naturally."

"Just a couple weeks, is all. I don't know what to do, where to go."

"Something else, somewhere else."

"I'm still your blood, Avery."

"You're the woman who chose to abandon me and ignore me for more than half my life. Now you're alone, so you show up. And that's why you showed up—not to get to know me, or whatever other lame excuse you have for it."

And God, the certainty of that made her tired.

"That comes under the heading of still thinking of yourself, first, last, always. I've listened to you, now I'm done. You have to go."

"I don't have anywhere to go."

"It's a big world. Take your pick."

"If I could just stay the night. One night—"

"You're broke," Avery realized.

"We had some . . . financial reversals. Things got tough, okay, and I could just use a little help getting back on my feet."

Everything, everything coalesced on that single, ugly

point. "God, who *are* you? Money? You're serious? You want money from me?"

"I'll pay you back. If you could lend me a few thousand, just to tide me over."

"If I had a few thousand to spare, I wouldn't give it to you."

"You own your own business." Traci gestured toward the shopping bag. "You can shop in fancy stores. You can spare me some, just as a loan. Don't make me beg, Avery. Please don't make me beg, 'cause I will. I'm in trouble."

Grabbing her purse, Avery yanked out her wallet, pulled the bills out without counting. "There. That's it. That's all you get, now, all you get ever. Now get out, and stay out of my life. I don't want to see you again."

"You don't know what it's like to be alone, to have nobody."

"You're right. My father saw to that." Avery went to the door, opened it. "I said get out."

Traci walked to the door, paused. "I'm sorry," she said.

Avery shut the door, locked it, leaned back against it. When the shaking started, she let herself slide down to the floor. She listened to the footsteps echo away down the stairwell before she let herself weep.

❧

SHE MADE EXCUSES to postpone her date with Owen. A change in schedule, too much to do, keeping it in a text so she didn't have to actually speak with him.

Stupid, she knew, but she didn't feel ready to put on a happy face, mask over all the misery, the doubts, and the grinding anger.

She didn't want to talk to anyone, so she avoided her friends, buried herself in work. But in small towns, friends tended to dig.

She glanced up from building a gyro as Owen walked in. She sent him a quick nod, what she hoped came off as a harried smile as he slid onto a stool at the counter.

"How's it going?"

"Busy. I've barely had time to catch my breath the last couple days."

"So you said. Maybe you've got time to catch it now, take a break."

"I'm swamped."

"Really?" Swiveling on the stool he scanned the early lunch customers, counted two tables.

"I've got to take inventory," she decided on the spot. "Glassware's taken some hits." Change the subject, she told herself. "How's it going across the street?"

"It's going. I thought you'd come over, take a look for yourself."

"I will, as soon as I can carve out a little time." She slid the gyro in, shoveled out a pizza. "What can I get you?" she asked as she sliced it.

"The gyro looked good."

"Guaranteed."

He went over, got himself a cold drink, took his seat again. "Is everything okay with you?"

"Well, I could use a break in the weather and a couple extra hours in the day. Otherwise? All good."

"Avery."

The tone forced her to look up, meet his eyes. "What? It's a busy time, Owen. You know how it goes."

"Yeah, I do know how it goes. That's why I'm asking."

"And I'm telling you I'm fine. I've got to run this place. I've got to find a new delivery guy since I caught the one I just hired smoking a joint in the basement. I'm refining my business plans for the new place, have to decide on lighting, furniture, perfect the menu, help Hope throw a bridal shower for Clare. My car needs new tires, and my rep just told me cheese is going up."

And when she unreeled it that way, she decided she had every reason in the world to be impatient and stressed.

"I just don't have time to make you dinner and play right now."

"I got that, and it's not what I'm talking about."

"Then there's nothing *to* talk about. I've got stuff to do. That's it, that's all."

She stalked over to put his gyro in, take the other out, and caught the inside of her forearm on the oven.

"Shit."

By the time she slammed the oven shut, turned, Owen was around the counter. He gripped her wrist when she tried to jerk away.

"Let me see."

"It's nothing. It happens."

"Where's your first-aid kit?"

"I just need some aloe. That's why I keep a plant in the kitchen. Let me—"

He simply pulled her into the closed kitchen where Franny worked. Before Franny could speak, Owen jerked his head to indicate she needed to go out, and kept pulling Avery to the back.

"Will you let go!" she demanded. "I know how to take care of a damn burn. I've got customers."

"Stop it, right now."

The whip-snap of his tone, so rare, stopped her protests. She said nothing as he switched on the cold water in the sink, held her arm under it.

"You weren't paying attention. That's not like you."

"You wouldn't shut up." She set her jaw when he stared down at her. "Well, you wouldn't. I can take care of this, Owen. It's just a burn."

"It's not blistering. Why weren't you paying attention?"

"Oh, for God's sake. I've got a lot on my mind, I'm busy. I messed up. It's not like I sliced a finger off."

He continued to hold her arm under the cool water while he studied her face. "I've seen you with a lot on your mind. I've seen you busy. If you don't think I know you well enough to see something else is going on, you're stupid. Is there a problem with you and me?"

"There's about to be."

"Keep the water on that," he told her, then broke off a piece of her aloe plant. "All I know is everything was fine when you were on your way home from shopping with Clare and Hope."

He cut open the fat leaf, scooped out the inside. "And the next day, you're canceling and don't have time for two words."

He pulled a spoon out of the tray, mashed the aloe into paste.

She should've known he'd be up on home remedies. Right at the moment, his patient efficiency made her want to stab him with a fork.

"Let's see that now." He switched off the water, carefully dried her arm while he examined the burn. "Not bad."

"I told you it wasn't bad."

"You also told me nothing's wrong, when it clearly is. Hold still." Gentle, thorough—in a way that made tears burn the back of her eyes—he coated the burn with aloe paste.

"So something happened between the drive home and the next day. What?"

"Maybe I just realized I had a lot on my plate, and I need to get some of it off—prioritize. Organize. We went from zero to sixty . . . Okay, more like thirty to sixty," she amended when she got another Owen look. "I need a little time to sort through everything, get my work squared away. The new restaurant needs attention now if it's going to work later. I got caught up in the sixty. I let stuff slide."

"Maybe. Maybe that's some of it, but it's not all of it. We're going to have to talk about this, Avery."

"This isn't the time. I'm at work. I—"

"No, it's not the time." He laid a dry dressing from the first-aid kit over the coated burn. "But we're going to make the time. Make sure somebody changes that dressing later." He studied her face another moment, bent down, laid his lips on hers.

"Okay." He nodded, eyes on hers again. "Okay. I'm going to take the gyro to go, get back to work myself. I'll see you later."

"Sure."

When he'd gone she leaned on the sink, had a vicious argument with herself followed by a short pity party.

"Are you okay, Avery?"

With a sigh, and a wish people would stop asking, she glanced toward the doorway and Franny. "Fine. It's just a burn, nothing major. How is it out there?"

"We're pretty slow today."

"Listen, I'm going to go upstairs, get some things done. If we pick up, just call, and I'll come back down."

"No problem."

⟿

SHE COOKED. COOKING was her teddy bear when she was upset, so she comforted herself by experimenting with a ham and potato soup and a smoked tomato bisque. She used her laptop in the kitchen to note down her tweaks.

It calmed her, soothed her, settled her enough so she sat awhile, soups simmering on the stove, worked on a layout for booths, high tops, low tops, sofa and chairs in her new space.

"Knock, knock!" Clare called out.

"In the kitchen." So much, Avery thought, for alone with her teddy bear time.

"I was going to grab a salad downstairs, and Franny said you'd burned your arm and had a fight with Owen."

"I didn't have a fight with Owen. I did burn my arm, but it's nothing."

Clare frowned at the simmering pots. "Then why are you cooking up here? What's wrong?"

"*Nothing.* And the next person who asks me that is going to get a knuckle sandwich that won't be so freaking tasty. I'm testing recipes. We're slow downstairs, as I'm sure you saw for yourself. I'm grabbing some time to refine the menu for the new place."

"I thought you were refining the menu on Owen."

"Do you see Owen?" Avery demanded. "I have time now. I'm refining now."

"You're upset. I haven't seen you for a couple days because you've been so busy, and now you're upset and fighting with Owen."

"I'm not fighting with Owen, and if I'm upset it's because everybody keeps hovering and asking me why I'm upset. Including Owen, who just won't back the hell off!"

"You *are* fighting with Owen."

"I'm not." Though she ground her teeth nearly to dust, Avery managed a calmer voice. "I've been busy. Beckett's done with the plans, and they're submitted for the demo permit. Now the mechanical plans are in the works. I've got a ton to do yet, to plan and decide on, all while I run Vesta."

"So you're nervous. I'd be nervous, too. But you know it's going to be great."

"Knowing it and making it great aren't the same." Her stomach hurt from the evasions. Lying always made her stomach hurt—and added to the side effect, she just sucked at lying, evasions, and half-truths.

"It takes a lot of time and thought," she continued, sticking with the theme. "And that doesn't leave a lot of time and thought for boyfriends. So I think we should slow it down a little until I'm back on keel. That's all."

"What did he do?"

"Nothing. Nothing. I swear." Too tired to cry, Avery just laughed at Clare's automatic assumption. "I'm just a little overwhelmed right now."

At last! she thought. The truth.

"It'll work itself out. Here, instead of a salad, try this."

Avery got out a bowl, ladled in some of the potato soup, then sprinkled a little parsley, a little grated Parmesan on top.

"I have to decide on dinnerware, too. I may just go with restaurant white, then play up the linens, the glassware. Or maybe I need something bolder."

"It's not going to matter." Clare spooned up another bite. "Nobody's going to care what this is in. It's delicious. Why were you so stingy with it?"

"Because you have to try the smoked tomato bisque, too."

Another bowl, another ladle—and a sprinkle of croutons, a basil leaf.

"Oh God, this is so good. It's smooth, a little creamy, and still has a bite."

"Excellent." To see for herself, Avery got out her tasting spoon. "Yes, excellent," she decreed. "No more changes on these. I'll give you a container of both to take home for dinner."

"You mean I have to share?" Clare slid an arm around Avery's waist. "You'll tell me when you're ready?"

Yes, she sucked at lying. Giving up, Avery leaned her head on Clare's shoulder. "Yes. Just not right now."

◦~◦

SHE'D COOKED THROUGH it, Avery decided. Or nearly. Wallowing wasn't getting her anywhere, and only drawing attention—the exact opposite of what she'd wanted.

She tubbed up the potato soup, snagged some Italian bread from downstairs. That cost her an hour, but she didn't mind. Things had picked up for dinner, and though she wasn't scheduled, she pitched in awhile.

That, too, smoothed her mood.

She needed to talk to her father, and hoped that would top off the recovery. He deserved to know, she reminded herself as she drove out of town. And he was the only person in the world from whom she never, ever kept secrets.

She'd treat him to some soup, and they'd talk it out. They could talk anything out.

But when she pulled in, spotted the bright blue Lexus with Nevada plates in his drive, her temper spiked.

He didn't know anyone in Nevada.

Moved around, Traci had said.

The MacTavish Gut told her Traci had moved around most recently to Nevada. And was here trying to dip into the next well.

She charged into the house.

Willy B pushed out of his chair when Avery stormed in. Traci stayed in her seat, eyes drenched, fingers twisting a soggy tissue.

"You've got some nerve. You bitch."

"Avery! You calm down."

"Don't tell me to calm down." She rounded on her father. "Has she got to the 'can you make me a loan' part yet, or is she still on the how fucking sorry she is?"

"Just sit down and . . . What?"

"Didn't she mention she'd paid me a visit a couple days ago?"

"No." He put an arm around Avery, as much to restrain as to unify. "She didn't."

"I was going to. I had to see Avery first, Willy B. I wasn't even sure I could face you at all, and I wanted to see Avery, to tell her I'm sorry."

"And to hit me up for money."

"I'm broke. I'm in trouble. That doesn't stop me from being sorry." Her fingers trembled as she gave up on the tissue and knuckled a tear away. "I wish I'd done things different. I wish *I'd* been different. I can't change any of it. We lost the house, right before Steve died. Everything went wrong. He had some deals in the works, and it all fell through. He didn't have time to turn things around."

"You've got a shiny new Lexus in the drive," Avery pointed out. "Sell it."

"It's leased, and I'm going to lose that, too. It's all I've got. I just need a stake until I can find a place, get some work."

"You took money from Avery?" Willy B demanded.

Color flooded Traci's face. "I just need a loan."

"How much?" When Traci shook her head and wept again, he turned to Avery. "How much?"

"I don't know exactly. Whatever was in my wallet. More than I usually carry because I was going out and wanted cash if I needed it."

Anger, so rare in her easygoing father, kindled in Willy B's voice. "You walked away from my girl, Traci. Now you come back and take her money?"

"She's got her own business. She's got a nice place. I did my best by her as long as I could."

"No, you didn't." He kissed Avery gently on the top of the head. "Have you talked to your mother, Traci?"

"I . . . She helped me out some right after Steve died. Everything was a mess. I didn't know he owed so much money. She helped me some, but she said that was all I'd get. She meant it. I went to see her before I came here, and she wouldn't help."

"How much are you looking for?"

"Daddy, don't—"

"You hush, Avery."

"But, you can't—"

"This is my business." He didn't raise his voice—he'd never had to. He simply stared Avery in the eye. "You hush. How much, Traci?"

"If I could have five thousand, to get me settled. I'll pay you back. I swear it. I'll sign papers. I know I've got no right, but I've got no one else."

"Avery, you go up, get my checkbook. You know where I keep it."

"No, I won't."

"You do what you're told, and you do it now. You want to argue with me, we'll do it later." Now he laid a hand on Avery's shoulders. "You can say your piece to me, but not now. That's our business, not hers."

He rarely drew a hard line, but once he did, it didn't budge. "All right, but it's going to be a big, ugly piece." She stomped upstairs, stomped back down.

He sat, opened the checkbook. "I'll give you the five thousand. It's not a loan."

"But I'll pay you back."

"I don't want you to pay me back. Unless Avery has a change of mind, I don't want to see or hear from you after you leave. You take the money, and go. I hope you find your way."

"I know you hate me, but—"

"I don't hate you. You gave me the light of my life, and I don't forget it. Ever. So I'll give you what you need, and we're done."

A hard line, Avery thought again, and he'd drawn it for her.

"I want you to send me your address or a phone number when you're settled," Willy B continued. "To me, Traci, not to Avery. You don't contact her again. If she wants to talk to you or see you, she can come to me and I'll give her what you send me."

"All right."

He folded the check, handed it to her.

"Thank you. I . . . You kept the place real good. You're a good man. I mean that."

"I expect you do."

"She's beautiful." Traci pressed a hand to her lips. "I'm so sorry. I'm so sorry for everything."

"I expect you are. You'd best go on now. It's dark, and there might be weather coming in later tonight."

Gathering herself, Traci stood. "I guess you were the best thing I ever did," she said to Avery. "And I did the worst thing to you. It's hard knowing that."

When Traci left, Avery walked to the window, watched her drive away. "Why did you give her that money?"

"Because she's grieving. She lost someone she loved, and now she realizes she threw away something precious. She'll never get it back, so she's grieving over that, too. And because, for us, it closes the door.

"Why didn't you tell me she'd come to see you?"

"That's why I came tonight. To tell you. I just . . . I couldn't talk about it for a while. I should've told you, then you'd have been prepared. I should've called Grandma. I just closed up. It hurt, so I closed up."

"I know." He went to her, folded her into his big arms.

"But tonight when I saw her, it just made me mad. That's better, isn't it?"

"For you? Always." Holding her close, he swayed her side to side. "We'll be all right, baby. You and me? We're going to be just fine. Don't you worry."

Soothed by his voice, his scent, the mere fact of him, she pressed her face to his chest. "You told me that then, and a lot of times between now and then. It's always been true. I love you, so much."

"I'm bigger. I love you more."

She laughed a little, squeezed hard. "I made soup. The MacTavish cook-out-the-blues potato-and-ham soup."

"Sounds just right."

"I'll go get it out of the car."

## CHAPTER SIXTEEN

OWEN OPTED TO WORK IN THE SHOP. IT GAVE HIM time to think—okay, maybe *brood* was the word, but he felt entitled.

Just as he started to take the next steps, she pulled back. What kind of sense did that make? While he makes the effort not to let things just slide, to be sure he wasn't taking her for granted, to treat their relationship like a damn relationship, she's suddenly too busy to spare ten minutes of her time.

"What kind of bullshit is that?" he demanded of Cus, and got a sympathetic tail thump as an answer.

He measured his board, marked it, and remeasured automatically before feeding it into the saw.

"She likes being busy," he continued over the scream of the blade. "She likes the freaking chaos of a crazy schedule. But out of the blue she doesn't have time, not to go out, to stay in, to have a goddamn conversation."

He switched off the saw, stacked his board, pulled down his safety goggles. "Women are a pain in the ass."

But Avery never had been, wasn't supposed to be. So it all made less sense.

Something was up with her. Didn't she *get* he could see it? Avoiding him, making excuses, closing off when she'd always been up front. She was acting like . . .

"Uh-oh."

He'd started taking her out, making plans. Christ, he'd given her jewelry. He'd changed the balance—was that it? She didn't want that next step. Everything had been fine, had been smooth until he'd started treating their thing like a *thing*.

Casual and easy, all good. Add a few shades of serious, and she pulls the plug. Just sex, fine, but try a little— romance, he supposed—and she shuts the door.

And made him look, made him feel, like an imbecile.

Couldn't she have told him if she wanted to keep things simple? Didn't he, and a lifetime of friendship, rate that?

Plus, fuck it, didn't he have a say in the whole business?

Damn right he did.

"I'm not her damn sex toy."

"Words a mother longs to hear from her beloved son."

On a wince, Owen shoved his hands in his pockets. "Hi, Mom."

"Hi, Owen." Justine closed the shop door behind her, rubbed her chilled hands together. "What's going on?"

"Just working on one of the built-ins for Beck's place."

"You're a good brother."

"Yeah, well. I had some time. I didn't see your car when I came in."

"I just got back." Both dogs wandered over to press against her, tails batting. "I was over at Willy B's. I took him some dinner, gave him a sounding board. I'm surprised you're being a good brother instead of doing the same for Avery."

"What? Why?"

"They . . . Hmm. Avery hasn't talked to you about anything?"

"That's exactly right." Annoyed, he pulled off the goggles. "She hasn't talked to me about anything. At all. Too busy, not enough time. What the hell *is* going on?"

"That's a question for her. Go ask it."

"Mom, come on."

"Baby, this is something Avery should talk to you about.

If she doesn't, then I will. But she should tell you. The fact is, from where I'm standing, she should have talked to you already."

"You're starting to freak me out. Is she sick?"

"No, no. Stubborn, I'd say, and wrongheaded." Moving to him, Justine sighed a little. "You're a practical man, Owen. God knows how that happened. I don't know whether to tell you to be practical or not when you talk to her, but I will tell you to try to be patient."

"Is she in trouble?"

"No, but she's troubled. Go, talk to her. And later, you and I, we'll have a talk, too. Go on," she said when he grabbed his coat. "I'll get the lights."

She watched him go, rubbing the heads of the dogs that leaned against either side of her. "He's in love with her. It's all over him. But he hasn't figured it out yet, and she sure as hell hasn't figured it out."

Standing in the scent of sawdust, wood oil, Justine all but felt Tommy's cheek against hers—and closed her eyes to hold on to it, for just a moment.

"It was easier for you and me, wasn't it, Tommy? We didn't do all that thinking. Ah well, come on, boys, let's close up shop."

❧

HE CHECKED THE restaurant first. Dave worked behind the counter, tossing dough.

"Is Avery in the back?" Owen asked him.

"Out on deliveries. We haven't got a delivery guy yet."

"Are you closing tonight?"

"Avery is."

"Will you close?"

Dave raised his eyebrows and a ladle of sauce. "Sure, if—"

"Good." Owen pulled out his phone, stepped away from the counter as he punched Beckett's number. "I need a favor."

When Avery came in twenty minutes later, flushed from the cold, Owen was sitting at the counter nursing a beer.

"We got some flurries coming down," she began. "Not

sticking to the roads yet, so we should be all right on deliveries for . . ."

He saw her spot him, saw her hesitate. And thought: Fuck this.

"Hey, Owen."

"I need to talk to you."

"I'm on deliveries." She gestured with the insulated bags she carried before stacking them. "Let me just—"

He rose, left his beer. "Out here," he said, and taking her hand, pulled her toward the stairway door.

"I've got to move the deliveries out."

"Beckett's filling in."

"What? No, he's not, I'm—"

"Going to have a conversation with me. Now."

"I'll have a conversation with you later. I've got deliveries, and I've got to close tonight, so—"

"Beckett's on deliveries. Dave's closing."

He knew that light of battle in her eyes, and at the moment welcomed it.

"I run this shop. You don't."

"It's running, and you can go back to it after we talk."

"This is just bullshit."

She started to push by him.

"Yeah, it is." To simplify things, he boosted her up, over his shoulder, and started up the stairs.

"Have you lost your mind?" She bucked, shoved. "I'll kick your ass."

"Keep it up and I'll end up dropping you on your head. It might be an improvement." Clamping down on her legs, he pulled out keys with his free hand, juggled out his set to her apartment.

"Owen, I'm warning you."

He shoved the door open, booted it closed.

He knew her temper all too well. She'd punch, kick, and wasn't above biting. Since he didn't want her teeth marks on him—again—and didn't want to hurt her, he considered his options.

Superior weight and reach, he decided, and hauled her into the bedroom.

"Don't you even think about—"

The rest of the words came out in a whooshing grunt as he dumped her on the bed, laid on top of her, and clamped her arms down.

"Just calm down," he suggested.

"My ass!"

She could be quick as a snake and sneaky as a shark, so he kept all his body parts out of range of her teeth. "Calm the hell down and we'll talk. I'm not letting you up until you promise not to hit or bite or kick—or throw anything."

The light of battle escalated to an explosion of full-out war. "What gives you the right? Do you think you can come into my place, give orders, tell me what to do and how to do it? In front of my crew?"

"No, I don't, and I'm sorry. But you didn't give me much choice."

"I'll give you a choice. Get the hell out, now."

"Do you think you're the only one who's pissed? I can stay like this all night, or you can pull yourself together and we'll straighten this out like normal people."

"You're hurting me."

"No, I'm not."

Her chin wobbled. "My burn . . ."

"Shit." Instinctively he loosened his hold.

It was all she needed.

Quick as a snake, sneaky as a shark. She sank teeth in the back of his hand.

He cursed, hissed in air as he wrestled her down again. "Jesus, you drew blood."

"I'll draw more in a minute."

"Fine." His hand ached like a bad tooth, infuriating him. "This is the way you want it. I'll just hold you down while I do the talking. I want to know what's wrong with you."

"What's wrong with *me*? You drag me out of my place of business, you manhandle me, shove me around—"

"I didn't shove you. Yet. And I mean what's been wrong with you, before this?"

Turning her head away, she stared daggers at the wall. "I'm not talking to you."

"Exactly, and you haven't been, essentially, for the better part of a week. If I screwed up I need to know it. If you don't want to be with me the way we've been, or move forward on it, I deserve to know that, too. I deserve a goddamn conversation with you, Avery, one way or the other."

"It's not about you, or us, or that."

But wasn't it? she realized. On some level, wasn't it—because she'd let it be.

She closed her eyes. She was sick of it. Sick of herself.

She'd hurt him. She could see that clearly enough now that she looked beyond her own bruises. And he'd done nothing to earn it.

"Something's wrong. You have to tell me."

"Let me up, Owen. I can't talk like this."

He eased back, cautious, but she only shifted, sat up. Then dropped her head in her hands.

"Is it the pizza shop?" He couldn't think of anything else. "If you've got some cash flow problems, or—"

"No. No. I'm doing all right." She rose to pull off her coat and the rest of her outdoor gear. "You know my grandmother set up that trust for me after my mother left. I guess part of it was guilt, though she didn't have anything to be guilty about. Still, I'm next in line, so . . ." She shrugged. "It meant I could open Vesta, and it means I can have the new place. I just have to make them work."

"Is your grandmother sick?"

"No. Why . . ." He asked, she realized, because she stalled telling him the reasons. "No one's sick. You didn't screw up."

"Then what?"

"My mother came to see me."

"Your mother? When?"

"She was waiting for me, on the stairs, the night I got home from shopping with Clare and Hope. It really didn't go well."

She came back, sat on the bed beside him, linked her fingers in her lap to keep them steady. "I didn't even recognize her. I didn't know who she was until she told me."

"It's been a long time."

"I don't know, maybe I'd blocked her face out of my head. Once I really looked, she hadn't changed that much. She said she wanted to see me, she was sorry. I wasn't having it. She cried a lot. It didn't touch me."

"Why should it?"

"She was pregnant when they got married. I knew that—I'd done the math. And I talked to my father about it a long time ago. They loved each other, he said, and from his side it must've been true. Maybe she thought she loved him. She pushed how young she was, just nineteen, but Dad was barely twenty-one. He was young, but he handled it."

In comfort, Owen rubbed a hand on her thigh. "Willy B's a hell of a guy."

"Yeah, okay, yeah." She swiped at a tear, hating it. "I was a fussy baby, she had too much to do, she wasn't happy. Blah, blah, fucking blah. Then she drops the bombshell of how she'd had an abortion when I was around three."

Now Owen laid a hand over hers. "That's a hard thing to hear."

"Yeah, I bet it was a lot harder for my father to hear—after the fact. She went, had an abortion, had her tubes tied, and never discussed those decisions with him. Never told him she was pregnant. Who does that?" she demanded, turning drenched eyes to him. "Who treats someone that way? She knew he wanted more kids, but she ended that possibility without telling him. It's another, horrible kind of cheating."

He said nothing, but got up, found a box of tissues in the bathroom and brought them to her.

"Thanks. Crying about it doesn't help, but I can't get a handle on it yet."

"Then maybe crying about it does help."

"According to her, what she'd done came out when they were fighting, and gee, he was upset and mad. What are the odds? She agreed to marriage counseling, but hey, she felt trapped and unhappy. So she had an affair. And another. She admitted to two, but there were more than two, Owen, before she left. Even I figured that out."

She looked at him now. "You knew. Pretty much everyone knew she was fooling around."

He considered a moment, looking into those devastated eyes. She didn't want soothing evasions. "Yeah, pretty much."

"My mother, the town slut. It was easier, really, when she left."

This time he took her hand, brought it to his lips. "It's never easy."

"Maybe not, but at least it wasn't in my father's face, in mine, anymore. She stayed with the guy she left us for. That's what she said, and it felt true. Steve. That was his name. I got all the how unhappy she'd been, how she'd needed more. How she loved this Steve guy?"

"She can justify what she did with that, to herself. You don't have to accept it. You feel what you feel."

"I felt hard. I didn't like feeling it, but I did. I got lots of sorrys, lots of how pretty I am, how proud she is of what I've done with my life. Like she had something to do with it. Then it came out this Steve died, a few months ago."

"So she's alone," Owen murmured.

"Yeah, and broke. That came out, too, when she asked if she could borrow a few thousand."

He pushed up, walked to her window, stared out at the thickening snow. He couldn't imagine, just couldn't imagine a parent using a child for gain.

But he could imagine just how deep a wound it would score, especially in someone like Avery. "What did you do?"

"I said a lot of pretty harsh things. She cried more, Jesus, and begged. She wanted to stay here, with me. A couple weeks, she said, then just for the night. It made me sick, all of it, just sick. I gave her what I had in my wallet and kicked her out."

"You did what you had to do, and that's more than a lot of people would have." He turned back. "Why didn't you tell me, Avery? Why did you push me away instead of letting me help?"

"I didn't tell anyone at first. I just couldn't."

He walked back, stood in front of her. "I'm not anyone."

"You can't understand, Owen. You can sympathize, and

I wasn't looking for sympathy. I don't think I could've handled sympathy. But you can't understand because you've never felt unwanted, not once in your life. You always knew your parents loved you, would've done anything to protect you. You don't know, you don't know how much I envied you your family, even before she left. How much I needed all of you, and you were always there. My dad and the Montgomerys. You were like my true north."

"That hasn't changed."

"No, it hasn't. But I had to make something of me, for me. No matter how bad things are, and sometimes they were bad in our house, you want your mother to be there, to love you. And when she doesn't, you feel . . . less."

Unable to think of another term, she lifted her hands, let them fall. "Just less. It didn't matter what my dad said, what your parents said, and God knows they said and did everything right, I still felt she left because of me. That I was bad or unworthy or just not enough. The truth is, I wasn't enough."

"That's not on you, Avery."

"I know that. But sometimes you know one thing and feel another. Maybe what she did is part of the reason I worked so hard, pushed so hard, and have what I have. So, good for me."

After a moment's hesitation, she plunged on. "Even with that, there's this thing—the thing that asks why I've never been able to maintain a strong, long-term relationship, why I've never felt enough to stick, or why I jump too soon, then look for a way out. So I worry that's what she gave me."

"It's not."

"I pushed you away." Steadier, she looked at him again. "You're right about that. I hit a rough patch, so my default is push away instead of pull in."

"I'm right here."

"That's you, Owen. That's because you don't give up. You just work the problem until you have an answer."

He sat. "What's the answer, Avery?"

"You're supposed to have it." But she leaned her head on his shoulder. "I'm sorry. I hurt you, and I let you think you'd done something wrong when you hadn't. I've already got issues, I guess, and seeing her just screwed me up. Not just with you—maybe mostly with you, but not just. I didn't even tell my father. Then I was going to. I'd worked through it that far."

He laid a hand over hers. "What did you cook?"

"God." She blinked back tears. "So predictable. Soup. I took a big container of soup over to Dad's, and she was there."

Shifting, he pressed his lips to the top of her head. "Harder yet."

"I don't know. It just sort of flipped a switch. I was so mad, that she'd go there, make him feel any part of what she made me feel. He looked so sad when I burst in. So sad with her sitting there crying. I couldn't *stand* it. Same tune, and the thing is, now that I've had some time, I don't think she was lying. Or not altogether. I think she is sorry, and maybe she's just sorry because she's alone now and can look back. But that's the thing. She's sad, sorry, and alone, and she knows she can't go back.

"He gave her five thousand, and told her she could have it if she never contacted me again. He told her to send him her number when she settled, and if I ever wanted to contact her, he'd pass it to me."

"That's Willy B," Owen said quietly.

"I couldn't understand why he'd give her money, and after she'd gone he told me it was because she was grieving. That's the goodness in him. And it was because it closed a door he and I needed to close. That's him thinking of me, him loving me."

"He's the best there is. But he's not the only one who thinks of you."

"I know. I'm lucky, even blessed. I couldn't tell you, or Hope or Clare or anyone who really, really matters. I just couldn't admit my mother came back after all these years because she's alone and broke. No matter how sorry she may be for what she did, she only came back because she needed something. Knowing that makes me feel less. I wanted to close everybody out until I felt me again."

He waited a moment. "I have some things to say."

"Okay."

"She's less and always will be for turning her back on you, for walking away not just from her responsibilities but from the potential of you. She'll never have a daughter who loves her absolutely, without reservation and with real joy. The way you love your dad. She's less, Avery, not you."

"Yes, but—"

"Not finished. Is your dad less?"

"God, no. He's more than most people could be."

"She left him, too. She walked out on him, without a word. Chose another man over him. She didn't even give him the respect of truth, of a clean break with a divorce, but it didn't make him less of a man, of a father, of a friend. She came back because she needed something, and she took his money."

"It's her, not him."

"That's right. It's her. Not him. Not you."

Something loosened inside her, something tight and hard and painful. "It helps to hear that."

"I'm still not done. Whether you're happy or sad or mad or glad, you're still you. If you figure I'm only around—or you decide you only want me around—when everything's solid, you're wrong, and you're stupid. It's not going to work that way for me. It's never been surface with us, and whatever else has changed, that can't. That's bottom line."

Shame wound through the lessening misery. "I screwed up."

"Yeah, you did. I'll cut you a break this time."

Relieved, she managed a smile. "I owe you a break for when you screw up."

"I'll remind you when the time comes. Next, personally I don't see the point in dragging in prior relationships, how and why they worked or didn't. This is you and me. If you decide it's not working, you better damn sure not look for an out. You tell me, to my face. I'm not some loser you need to shake off."

"I never thought—"

"You tried shaking me off."

Excuses, rationalizations trembled on her tongue. Weak,

she realized. Weak and wrong. "I don't know if I tried because I thought I could or I knew I couldn't. I just don't know the answer to that. Either way, it was wrong because yeah, this is you and me."

She laid a hand on his cheek. "Solemn promises, here and now. I'll tell you to your face when I'm done with you."

That got a smile. "Same goes."

When she shifted toward him, he put her on his lap. She curled in, held on. "I'm glad you acted like a bully and dragged me up here. I've missed talking to you, being with you."

"I had to be a bully because you were a moron."

"Calling me names isn't cutting me a break." She eased back. "And you've got Beckett out there making deliveries."

"He's got three kids now. He can use the tips."

She laughed, reached for his hand, released it when he yelped. "Oh God." She lifted it again, carefully. "I really nailed you."

"Tell me about it."

"It's your own fault for falling for the 'oooh, you're hurting me' ploy."

"Won't happen again."

"Let me clean it up."

"Later." He pulled her back in, just sat while the world rode smooth again. "You wouldn't have any of that soup left?"

"I have smoked tomato bisque in the freezer. I can heat it up."

"Sounds good. Later." He tipped her head back, found her mouth with his.

"Definitely later."

Feeling sentimental, she roamed his face with kisses as she unbuttoned his shirt. He smelled of sawdust, even along the column of his throat.

"I've missed this, too," she murmured. "Missed touching you."

Only a few days, really, she thought, but the distance had spanned so wide, so deep, it felt like weeks. And here he was, smelling of sawdust, his chest warm and solid under the rough thermal shirt, and his hard-palmed hands confident and easy as he drew her sweater up and away.

Her true north, she thought. Constant and steady.

He ached for her. Not just physically, but in his heart for the hurt she'd endured. For the fact she'd felt obliged to endure it alone.

She said he couldn't understand, but she was wrong. He'd never believed you had to experience pain to understand it.

He'd thought he knew her, every facet, but there he'd been wrong. The parts of her that questioned her worth, her courage, her heart, those were new to him, added complexities and vulnerabilities.

To those hurts he offered a gentle touch, an easy glide, pleasing himself with the curves of her, the pulse beats, the sigh of breath warm against his skin.

When she caught his face in her hands, when he saw her smile up at him before their lips met again, he thought: There. There was Avery. All of her.

She stroked her hands down his back, over his hips, back again as if measuring the length of him. Wanting to give, just give and give, she shifted to wrap around him, heard him curse when her shoulder pressed against his sore hand.

"Oops." It choked a laugh out of her, and everything just fell away. All the guilt and grief, the apologies and worries.

You and me, she thought again. It's you and me. So she wrapped around him and nipped her teeth at his shoulder.

"I've got a taste for you now." She rolled him over, nipped again.

"Want to play rough?"

"You already did. Hauling me up here, throwing me down on the bed. Let's see how you like it." Mindful of his hand, she clamped his wrists, ranged over him.

"I like it fine."

"Because now we're naked."

"It's a factor."

She lowered her head, stopped a breath from his lips, pulled back, lowered again. Pulled back.

"You're asking for trouble."

"Oh, I can handle you."

She leaned in again, then slid down to glide her tongue over his chest.

Okay, he thought as his blood surged, she could handle him.

She owned his body, every inch, teasing, inciting, seducing, exciting. Quick and rough one moment, slow and tender the next, leaving him off balance, off rhythm, and totally possessed.

"Owen, Owen, Owen." She whispered it again and again as she rose over him, drunk with power and lust.

She took him in, deep, deep, clamped her hands on his shoulders as triumph and surrender catapulted through her system. He took her breasts, pressed his hand against her galloping heart.

She lowered again, and this time let her lips take his in a long, trembling kiss.

And she rose again, let her head fall back, let everything that was the two of them fill her.

Then she rode them both empty.

⁓

LATER, SHE DOCTORED his hand, kissed the little wound. In her blue-checked robe she heated soup in the kitchen while he poured them each a glass of wine.

On impulse she lit candles for the table. Not quite a midnight supper, she thought with a glance at the time. But pretty close.

"It's snowing hard now. You should stay."

"Yeah, I should."

Content, she ladled soup into thick white bowls while the snow fell on the rest of the world.

# CHAPTER SEVENTEEN

FOR AS LONG AS HE COULD REMEMBER, OWEN LIKED TO figure things out, find the answers, wiggle out details. His innate propensity for schedules, agendas, bottom lines, and solutions made him a natural as coordinator of Montgomery Family Contractors. He'd never imagined, not seriously, doing anything else, and couldn't imagine anything else giving him the same level of satisfaction or pride.

Working with his brothers suited him. They could and did disagree, piss each other off, bitch and complain. But they always came around. He understood their rhythms as well as he understood his own. He knew the weak spots in each, which could be handy if he *was* pissed off and wanted to needle.

Solving problems in a way that presented the facts, offered possible compromises and the occasional ultimatum was his thing.

He approached the situation with Elizabeth as a problem.

They had a ghost at the inn. Weird fact, yes, but fact. To date she'd proved mostly amenable, somewhat temperamental, and she'd put them all in her debt by warning Beckett when that asshole Sam Freemont assaulted Clare.

She'd only asked one thing. For Billy.

The problem was, who the hell was Billy? *When* the hell was Billy? What connection did he have to the woman they'd dubbed Elizabeth?

The ring indicated a relationship, possibly an engagement. But that, in Owen's world, wasn't fact.

Their resident ghost wasn't saying either way.

It seemed to Owen the best place to start would be to identify Elizabeth, and to pin down when she'd died.

Where, though it wasn't verified fact but logical supposition, was the inn.

"Makes the most sense, right?" He'd set up his laptop in The Dining Room on the theory Elizabeth might give him more direction if he worked the problem on location.

"That's how it strikes me," Hope agreed, and set coffee at his elbow. "Why else would she be here?"

"I've been poking around paranormal activity sites. You pick up all kinds of wild stuff, and a lot of it has to be crap—but what I've pulled out is most people who haven't, you know, passed over, tend to stick around where they died, or go back to a place that was important or significant to them. If she died here, she could've been a guest, could've worked here, could've been related or connected to the owners."

"Death records would be a starting point, but where to start?"

"That's part of it, yeah?"

"Well, the way you described what she wore, it makes me think after the start of the Civil War, and before 1870. Not the wide, wide hoopskirt, but still a wide skirt."

"Yeah. Kind of . . ." He held his arms out. "It was a pretty quick look."

"If she'd let me get a look at her, I'd have a better idea." And why wouldn't she? Hope wondered. After all they were—as Avery said—inn-mates. "How about the sleeves?"

"The sleeves?"

"Of the dress, Owen. Long, short, snug, poofy?"

"Oh. Um . . . long. Kind of big, I think."

"Gloves? Did she wear gloves?"

"I don't know that I . . . you know, I think so, but without fingers on them. Kind of lacy, or like my grandmother's crocheting. And now that I think about it, one of those wrap things."

"A shawl—and you said a snood."

He could only stare. "I did?"

"You said she had her hair up in a net in the back. That's a snood."

"If you say so."

"I do. I've got a minute or two. Can I?" she asked, gesturing at his keyboard.

"Help yourself."

He turned it toward her as she sat, and waited, enjoying his coffee as she typed.

"I'm pretty sure if you put those elements together, you're talking early to mid-1860s."

He let her work in silence for a few minutes. Peaceful here, he thought, in the middle of the day. He should get back next door before too much longer, give Ryder a hand. And maybe slip over to Vesta later, see if he could talk Avery into going out—or staying in.

"How about this?" Hope turned the screen toward him. "What do you think?"

Curious, he studied the illustration of a small group of women in a kind of drawing room. "I think I wonder why women wanted to wear something that looks that uncomfortable."

"Fashion hurts, Owen. We live with it."

"I guess. This is pretty close, in type, I mean. The skirt was pretty much like this one, and the sleeves, and it had a high neck like this one. Maybe some lace or something on it."

"This is fashion from 1862. So you could start there. And I doubt you're looking for a maid or servant," Hope added as she studied the illustration. "It's too fashionable. Not impossible, as it could've been a dress passed to her by an employer or relative, but going with the odds, she dressed like a woman of some means."

"We'll play the odds to start. Thanks."

"You're welcome, and it's interesting. I'll be in the office if you need me."

He intended to give it a half hour, then strap on his tool belt. But he got caught up, poking through old records, old newspaper articles, genealogy sites.

At some point, Hope walked back in, freshened his coffee, added a plate of warm cookies.

He finally sat back, frowned at his screen.

"What the hell is this?" Ryder demanded. "You're sitting here eating cookies while I'm up to my ass next door?"

"Huh?"

"It's two-fucking-thirty."

"Oh. Sorry. I think I found her."

"Found who?" Ryder snatched the last cookie, and his scowl eased off after he bit in.

"You know." Owen pointed toward the ceiling. "Her."

"For Christ's sake, Owen, we've got work. Play ghost-hunter on your own time."

"Eliza Ford, of the New York Fords."

"I'm glad we cleared that up."

"Seriously, Ry, I think it fits. She died here, from some kind of fever, in mid-September 1862. She's buried in New York. She was eighteen. Eliza, Elizabeth, Lizzy. That's kind of cool, isn't it?"

"I'm riveted. She's been here for about a hundred and fifty years. I think she can wait until we finish the goddamn work next door." He picked up the mug, took a drink. "Coffee's cold."

"I'm going to go up, try to talk to her. I'll make up the time after. Avery's working until six anyway."

"Really glad this petty business of the job fits in with your social schedule."

Because Ryder's tone put his back up, Owen matched it with his own. "I said I'd make up the time, and goddamn it, we owe her. She warned us about Sam Freemont. He might've—damn well would have—done worse to Clare if Beck hadn't gotten there in time."

"Shit." Ryder dragged off his gimme cap, raked his hand

through his hair. "All right, go talk to your dead friend, then get next door. Are there any more of those cookies?"

"I don't know. Ask Hope."

On a grunt, Ryder headed out.

Owen shut down, but left his laptop on the table as he climbed the stairs. He'd found several women between the ages of eighteen and thirty who'd died in town during the right time frame. And there'd be more yet if he went with the theory that a ghost could pick his or her own age.

But Eliza Ford *felt* right.

He got all the way up before he remembered standard operating procedure had Hope or Carolee locking all the guest room doors when they weren't occupied. By the living anyway.

He started to turn, go back down. And the door to Elizabeth and Darcy opened.

"Okay. I'll take that as a come on in."

It felt strange, stepping into the room that smelled of its signature English lavender scent and Elizabeth's—or Eliza's—honeysuckle.

"So."

The door eased closed, with a quick click, behind him, and had a little chill running along his spine.

"So," he repeated. "We've been open over a month now. Things are going pretty good. We had a little wedding last weekend. I guess you know about that. It went fine, from what Hope reported. So anyway, I've got to get to work in the next building, but I've been doing some research downstairs. On you. It'd help us help you if we knew who you are. Eliza?"

The lights flickered on and off, made his fingers tingle.

"Are you Eliza Ford?"

The shape came first, blurred and soft, then sharpened into the figure of a woman. She smiled at him, and curtsied.

"I *knew* it! Eliza."

She laid a hand on her heart, and he swore he heard the whisper inside his own head. *Lizzy.*

"They called you Lizzy, a nickname."

*Billy.*

"Billy called you Lizzy. Billy who?"

She crossed her other hand over the one at her heart, closed her eyes.

"You loved him. I got that. Did he live here, in Boonsboro, near here, what? Did you come to visit him? Was he with you when you died? Or maybe he died first."

Her eyes flew open. He recognized shock, cursed himself. Maybe she didn't know she was dead—or that Billy had to be dead. He'd read up on that, too. "I mean, did you meet him here. At the hotel, at the inn?"

She faded. A moment later the porch door swung wide, then slammed shut.

"Okay. I guess you've got some thinking to do. I'll talk to you later. Nice going, Owen," he muttered to himself as he went downstairs. "Really tactful. So, Lizzy, how does being dead feel? Shit."

He carted his laptop out to his truck, got his tools. Then he went through the gate and into the building next door to do penance with his nail gun.

๛

"THAT'S SO SAD." Avery poured the marinade she'd made that morning over the tuna steaks. "Only eighteen. I know people didn't live as long, and women usually got married and had kids a lot sooner. But still. Eighteen. A fever?"

"I couldn't find much—I'll look more now that I have this name to go on. It was really just a few lines."

"Eliza. That's so close to what Beckett started calling her—and the Lizzy nickname, too."

"It makes it all feel kind of ordained, I guess. Mom picked the name and location of the room, Beckett started calling her Elizabeth because of that. Then Lizzy."

"I don't know about ordained, but it's spooky—a good spooky. And I think you're great—I'll even give you brilliant—for finding her, but how's that going to help you find this Billy?"

"I needed something solid. I have her name, where she lived, where and how she died—even if she didn't know that—so I can try to follow those dots to him. Was she meeting him here? Was he a local? Another traveler?"

As she washed field greens, she glanced back at him. "September 1862. That could be the answer."

"Why?"

"Owen." She let the greens drain, stepped toward him. "How long have you lived in southern Washington County?"

"All my— Oh, shit. I didn't think of it. I was so focused on finding her, and when I hit that name . . . the Battle of Antietam."

"Or Sharpsburg, depending which side you were on. September 17, 1862. Bloodiest single day in the Civil War."

"He could've been a soldier. Maybe, maybe," he mused. "She could've come here to try to see him, make some contact. People even went out and watched battles, right? Made frickin' picnics out of it."

"People have always been screwy. Anyway, she died the day of the battle. You said she came from New York, so it seems logical she stayed at the inn. If she had friends or relatives in the area, it feels like she would've stayed with them. Could be Billy's from New York, too, and she followed him down here for some reason."

"Or he's from the area, and she came to be with him. Or he, like most men his age—if we figure he's close to hers— was fighting in the war."

"That seems most likely. Taste this."

He took the piece of thin, crispy bread. "Good. Really good. What is it?"

"An experiment. Pizza dough, rolled almost paper thin, herbed, baked. I'm thinking of serving it in the new place. So, it feels like if she'd come to see him, and they'd hooked up, she wouldn't need to find him now. She died, but if he was here, wouldn't he have been with her? So he, following that train, wasn't here when she got sick."

"Or he just let her down. Didn't come. Could've been married, not interested."

She snatched the plate of bread away before he could grab another piece. "That's not romantic. Stick with romantic, or no more for you."

"I'm just considering possibilities." When she continued to hold the bread out of reach, he rolled his eyes. "Okay, they were the Civil War version of Romeo and Juliet. Star-crossed lovers."

"I don't like teenage suicide. Think of another."

"I'm too hungry to think."

Relenting, she set the plate back down. "Either way, or any way, it doesn't seem like it helps find Billy."

"I'm going to see what else I can find out about Lizzy. Stage one." He broke the bread in two, offered her half. "You could call it Crack Bread. For the sound when you break it, and because it's addicting."

"Ha-ha. Maybe Snap Bread. I'm thinking of putting it and breadsticks in a kind of glass tube on each table."

"We should be able to start the demo next week."

"Next week? Really? Seriously?"

He loved watching her light right up. "Just the demo, but yeah. I checked on the permit status. I should be able to pick it up tomorrow afternoon."

"Oh boy!" She swung around the counter, jumped in his lap. "Oh boy, oh boy!"

When his mouth was free again, he grinned. "Can't wait to see what you do when I get the building permit."

"It may include costumes. Oh boy."

"What kind of costumes?"

"Owen." On a sigh, she nuzzled in. "It's probably going to be crazy for a while. The planning, the prep, the execution. I'm probably going to be crazy for a while."

"And that's different from usual how?"

She got a pinch in before she slid off his lap. "I just want you to know it won't be because I'm avoiding you or pulling back."

"Okay." Since she'd opened the door a little, he stepped through. "Did your mother send any contact information to your dad?"

"No." She lifted her shoulders, let them fall. But she couldn't shrug it off when he took her hands, held her gaze, just waited her out.

"Okay, I'm not holding my breath, but maybe she's not

settled yet. Or, face up, maybe she's never going to send anything. He gave her money, and it's possible that was the bottom line. I don't know how I feel about it, or her, exactly," Avery continued. "It's like thinking Billy wasn't with Lizzy, on purpose. It's harsh. There's enough harsh in the world. I'm going to try a little optimism for a change."

"Then we'll go with he'd have been with her if he could."

"I like that better. If Traci never sends anything, I'm going to have to be okay with it. I don't know, honestly, why I'd contact her anyway. She's not a part of my life, and that was her choice."

"I hate that it hurts you."

"So do I. It's hard knowing anyone has that kind of power over my feelings. So, I'm going to get over it. Enough about her."

Avery waved her hands in the air as if erasing. "Welcome to MacT's Testing Kitchen. I'm going to be your server, your chef, and your sommelier this evening."

"All that?"

"And more, after—if you're lucky."

"I'm feeling lucky."

"Tonight we're presenting seared, pepper-crusted tuna over a bed of field greens and julienne vegetables, finished with a champagne vinaigrette."

"Luckier and luckier."

"To start, our hopefully soon-to-be-famous Crab and Artichoke Heart appetizer. All served with our recommendation of a crisp sauvignon blanc."

"Sign me up."

"Honest feedback," she said.

"You can count on me."

She got out a pan for the tuna, smiled. "I do."

∽

TO MAKE UP the time spent on his search for Billy and his evenings with Avery, Owen put himself at Ryder's disposal. At the rate they were going, he calculated they'd have the bakery ready by June, and the apartments above it ready for tenants.

He'd gathered a little more information on Eliza Ford, but wanted to let it settle in his mind awhile.

As promised, demo began on the pub side of Avery's new restaurant, and the two projects moved forward as February raced toward March.

As the April wedding drew closer, the brothers—and some of the crew—devoted weekends to Beckett's house.

On a Sunday afternoon, the sudden rise in temperatures melted the snow cover, and turned the ground into a muddy mess. But inside the house, the floors gleamed around the trails of muddy cardboard as the three brothers stood scanning the nearly finished kitchen.

"It looks good," Beckett pronounced. "Damn good. Counter guys are coming in tomorrow to start the install, here and in the bathrooms. We may just make it."

"You'll make it." Owen had the schedule, and refused to be daunted.

"If you hadn't let it sit here, half finished—less," Ryder pointed out, "we wouldn't be busting ass now."

"Live and learn. Anyway, this way Clare gets to put her own stamp on it. It's ours instead of mine."

"So speaks the man already prepared to be whipped."

"So speaks the man marrying the love of his life." Beckett turned. "Good light, good space. It'll be great to spread out again. There's not an inch of room left at Clare's place. I'm always stepping over a kid or a dog."

"And you think that's going to change?" Owen asked.

"No." Beckett thought about it, and laughed. "I'm okay with that, and looking forward to stepping over kids and dogs right here. Barely a month to go till the wedding."

"It's cool they're using the inn for the bridal shower thing," Owen commented. "It may be another area of revenue down the road."

"More important. Bachelor party." Ryder hooked his thumbs in his tool belt. "We've gotta send you off to the great unknown right."

"I'm working on it," Owen reminded him.

"Yeah, yeah. Why all the work and fuss? Why can't we just go to a titty bar? It's a classic for a reason."

"Poker, cigars, and whiskey—groom's choice."

"No strippers," Beckett confirmed. "It's just too weird."

"Man, you're breaking my heart."

"When it's your turn, we'll have strippers."

"I'll be too old to appreciate them. No plans to walk into the great unknown until I'm eligible for Social Security. On second thought, a man's never too old to appreciate naked women. Make a note."

Justine, arms full, used her elbow to tap on the glass atrium door.

Owen opened it, took the big insulated bag, the enormous thermos.

"Oh, look at this! Beckett, it's wonderful."

"He didn't do it alone," Ryder reminded her.

"All for one," she murmured. "You're going to have a beautiful home. You've all done so much since I was here a few weeks ago."

"I'll give you the full tour."

"I'll take it. First, I brought lunch. Minestrone, grilled ham and cheese sandwiches, apple crisp."

"Best mom ever." Ryder opened the insulated bag.

"I'll stick with the soup." Owen laid a hand on his stomach. "I've been eating more since Avery's using me as a tester, and working out less with Beck's place on the schedule."

"Interesting you should mention working out." Justine took paper plates, bowls, spoons out of her enormous purse. "That's something I want to talk to you all about."

She set everything out on the plywood currently covering the base cabinets. "I've got cold drinks out in the car."

"We got you covered." Beckett opened a cooler.

"Any diet in there?"

"Why would there be?" Ryder wondered.

"Oh well, give me the straight shot," Justine decided. "I'll work it off soon enough. Especially in, oh, say nine months to a year, when I can put in an hour or so in Fit In Boonsboro."

Ryder paused on his way to taking a huge bite of grilled ham and cheese. "Mom."

Placidly, Justine poured soup into a bowl, offered it to Owen. "It's come to my attention the building behind the inn, one we currently share a parking lot with, is for sale."

Beckett sighed. "Mom."

"And it occurred to me there's no fitness center in town, even close to town. People have to get in the car, drive, go to the gym, get back in the car. And Hope's already reported a number of guests at the inn have asked about workout facilities."

Owen stared down at his soup. "Mom."

Cheerfully, Justine plowed on. "Currently it's not a particularly attractive building, not one that affords our guests a nice view from The Courtyard or the back porches. But it could be. We'd also gain parking."

"We haven't finished the bakery," Owen pointed out. "We've barely started on the new restaurant."

"And of all my sons, you're the one who understands best the value of advance planning. I'm in negotiations. I haven't bought it yet, and wouldn't without discussing it with you first. Negotiations take time, settlement takes time. If it goes well, Beckett could start working on drawings when he's back from his honeymoon."

"Mom," Beckett began, "have you been in that place lately?"

"As a matter of fact, I have. It needs work." She offered him soup. "A lot of work. Aren't we lucky we know how? And it's not nearly as complicated as the inn was."

"Ought to buy it just to level it," Ryder muttered.

"And you know better. Gut it, yes, level it, no."

"You already know what you want in there."

She smiled at Owen. "I have ideas. We'd be on the small side, of course, compared to big, chain fitness centers. But we'd offer everything we could in that setting. A twenty-first-century fitness center with a small-town appeal—a large and varied menu of classes."

"Even if we could turn that place into what you're talking about, you'd have to staff it, find trainers, instructors."

"Leave that end to me," she told Ryder. "A large classroom on the second floor, and a small child-care area, maybe a treatment room for massages. Fitness area with cardio equipment, circuit training, weights on the main level, a small classroom, and locker rooms—each with a steam room and a sauna. Very spa-like in there, I'd think. We'll figure it out." She gave Beckett a pat on the cheek. "Won't we?"

"I guess we will. If you get it."

Her smile widened. "Leave that to me, too. Now, how about that tour?"

"Sure. We'll start upstairs, work our way down."

Frowning, Ryder watched them go. "Damn it. Damn it, it's a good idea."

"She mostly has them. Even if she got it quick, it would be mid-spring earliest, more like early summer before we had the plans and permits. That's mostly on Beck."

"Thank Christ. Wouldn't mind gutting that place," he considered. "I like me some serious demo. But we ought to get the bakery settled first. We have to get somebody in there, unless Mom thinks we're going to start baking cupcakes."

"I might have a line on that. Somebody Avery knows a little. She's moved up here from D.C., where she worked as a pastry chef. She's looking for a space for her own bakery."

"Another city girl?" Ryder shrugged. "What does she look like?"

"Married."

"Just as well. You figure that part out, Beck'll figure out what we're doing on the gym. And I'll keep the crew going."

"It's what we do," Owen said.

"And she has to run out of old buildings eventually."

With a laugh, Owen took a sandwich after all. "Don't count on it, son."

❧

"A GYM?" HOPE said.

"That's the plan. If they get the property." Avery sat with Hope in The Dining Room, finalizing the plans for Clare's shower. "Owen says his mom's all over it."

"And they'd paint it, right? They wouldn't leave it that fugly green it is now?"

"I think you can count on that. Owen said Beck's made noises about raising the roof, getting rid of the flat job, doing a pitched one."

"It'd be nice for guests. And for me. Just walk across the parking lot to a shiny new gym? Happy days. I've been limited to DVDs since I moved here. I'd love an honest-to-God yoga class."

"I've always wanted to take one. Enough stretching, maybe I'd get taller. So, if this is the last of it, I can pick all this up at the end of the week when I do my next supply run."

"Perfect. It's going to be lovely. Flowers, pretty food, champagne, a fussy cake—a few silly games with classy prizes. It'll be Clare."

"And before we turn around again, we'll be watching her marry Beckett."

"Which leads me to ask if you and Owen are thinking about the same."

"No. No," Avery said with a half laugh. "We're in a good place right now. Smooth, which is nice. And you know I've never been sold on marriage—for me. Maybe we'll move toward living in sin one of these days."

"I hear the words, but I don't feel convinced. You love him."

"I love him, and I've maybe slipped right along to in love with him." It was easier to say it, to feel it, than she'd ever imagined. "I'm trying to get used to that, see if it sticks. Like I said, we're in a good place right now. And we're both crazy busy. It sounds like that's not going to end anytime soon. The crazy busy."

"Avery, I've never known you—or him, since I've gotten to know him—wanted anything but busy. It's who you are. Both of you."

"It's a plus."

"I'm not pushing, but I want to say every time I see the two of you, I think, perfect. Avery's found her perfect match."

Shifting, Avery rubbed her hands on her thighs. "I think you're scaring me a little."

"Toughen up. Take your time, sure, but if he's not every bit as in love with you as you are with him, I don't know how to organize an office."

"Keep it up, I'll start pairing you up with Ryder."

"Talk about scary. My lips, from now on, are sealed. Tight."

## CHAPTER EIGHTEEN

❦

AVERY GAVE HERSELF AN EXTRA HOUR IN OWEN'S BED. He'd been up, dressed, and gone by six forty-five to make a seven o'clock meeting on the job site.

Her job site this time, she thought as she snuggled in to let herself drift in and out. She'd considered going in with him, just to see the next stage, but she didn't have to be told she'd be in the way, bog things down. She'd just stop in later in the morning, after she'd made her supply run, finished her list of errands. By then, the demo should be well under way.

More fun, she thought lazily, to be surprised by progress.

Lots of progress in lots of areas, she mused. Her best friend would be married in less than a month, and she'd be a part of it. She'd be a part of watching two good friends make promises to each other, make a family, celebrate a kind of miracle.

Love seemed a kind of miracle to her, one she'd never been absolutely sure existed. But she'd seen it for herself with Clare and Beckett, seen them come together, find that miracle—and have the faith and courage to trust it.

Part of her errands that morning included picking up the

last of the party supplies for the shower—from the exacting and detailed list Hope had printed out for her.

She loved knowing Clare and Beckett would take a week for themselves after the wedding with an island honeymoon on St. Kitts.

One day, Avery thought, she'd have to take a vacation in some tropical paradise.

One day she'd have to take a damn vacation, she thought, opening one eye to look at the gloomy sky outside the bedroom window.

She would. She'd get her new place up and running, get the routine smooth—then reward herself with a few days of sun, white beaches, and blue water.

Someplace she'd never been—someplace where no one knew her.

Maybe Owen would go with her. Wouldn't it be interesting to see how they dealt with nothing to do, with being strangers in a strange land—together.

And she loved that later in the summer, after school let out, the newlyweds planned a week's vacation with the kids. A familymoon, she'd heard little Murphy call it.

What could be better, she decided, than a familymoon?

Meanwhile Owen—and Hope—dug deeper into the mystery of Eliza Ford when one or the other could squeeze out the time. Were Lizzy and Billy a kind of miracle? she wondered. Had love brought them together before tragedy crept in? Or was the answer less romantic—and probably more realistic—as Owen had suggested?

A young girl dreaming of love, and a young man going his own way.

She'd dreamed of love once. But she'd been a child, and for a child, magic and miracles were always possible, and happy-ever-after simple and real.

Over time, she'd learned it was best to believe in the miracles and happy-ever-afters she could achieve herself, with hard work, determination, and long hours.

Plenty of satisfaction in that, she told herself. And she'd better get started on the day's miracle and get the hell out of bed.

She sat up, then just hugged her knees in and smiled at the fire he'd left simmering. He was sweet that way, she mused. Sweet to stir up the fire, add a log so she'd wake up to its warmth and light on a gloomy March morning.

She was lucky to have him in her life—had always known that. But now she was lucky to have this new, fascinating connection with him, luckier still he was as content to take things one day at a time. No pressure, no scary talk about futures.

She'd barely rolled out of bed when her phone signaled an incoming text.

She rolled back, hoping it was Owen suggesting she come in and have a look at the initial demo after all.

But she read the quick message from Clare asking her to stop by the bookstore before she headed into Hagerstown for supplies.

A little puzzled, she answered, changed her plans to include a stop by the store—and hell, since she'd be right there, take a quick peek in at the demo.

She grabbed a shower, pulled on jeans, added a sweater over a short-sleeve shirt to accommodate the fickle March weather. Lips pursed, she considered her hair. The latest rinse had faded some, so she added a mental note to check out the range of colors, see what she was in the mood to be.

Downstairs, she discovered he'd made coffee, set a travel mug for her beside the pot. Another reason to smile, she thought. You could always count on Owen. She couldn't think of another man, other than her father, who was so consistently *solid*.

On impulse, she went to his kitchen board, drew a heart with their initials in the center.

Fueled with coffee and a quick yogurt, she pulled on boots, wrapped on a scarf, and shrugged into her coat before she saw the note by the door.

*Take this,* it read.

She rolled her eyes and grabbed the folding umbrella.

She'd take it, but he'd be lucky if she didn't lose it somewhere along her morning run.

Halfway to Boonsboro, the first drops of rain splatted

her windshield. She could only cast her eyes skyward and think how annoying it was that Owen was always right.

Minutes later, going over her morning plans, she forgot the umbrella and dashed through the rain to the bookstore's covered porch.

She tapped on the glass, then used the key Clare had given her after the trouble with Sam Freemont the previous fall. As she stepped in, shaking rain from her hair, Clare walked down the stairs.

"Coffee's fresh," Clare announced.

"I just had some, but . . . who can say no to a latte?"

"I'll fix you up. Thanks for coming by."

"No problem. It's just the excuse I needed to nose into the new place. They're starting the demo this morning."

"I know. Exciting." She steamed milk while Avery glanced at the bestsellers on the front display.

"I need an afternoon off, a rainy afternoon like this one will probably be, so I can catch up on my reading. I couldn't get through the book club book this time. Why do I want to read about someone else's misery? Is it supposed to make me feel better about my life? Smug? Or just depressed? Because it was bringing me down."

"I hated it, too. I choked it down the way I used to choke down the brussels sprouts my mother insisted were good for me. It was a brussels sprout book, and I'm not convinced they're good for me."

"Exactly." Idly, Avery pulled down a thriller, skimmed the copy. "Plus, if I sit down to read, I want crème brûlée, or a good meaty steak, maybe pepperoni pizza, possibly a hot fudge sundae. And now I'm hungry."

She turned back, smiling as she reached for the coffee. "Thanks. Hey, you look a little ragged-out."

"Feeling a little draggy, a little off this morning."

"You can't catch anything." Avery pointed a decisive finger. "You're getting married in less than a month. You're not allowed to catch anything. Here. You look like you need this more than I do."

Clare shook her head at the offered latte. "I haven't caught anything the way you mean, and I'm off coffee for now. I'm not sick." Clare drew in a deep breath. "I'm pregnant."

"What? Now? Pregnant as in baby-on-board?"

"Yes, now. Pregnant as in." On a laugh, Clare pressed her hands to her belly. And Avery wondered how pale could go to glow so fast.

"Oh, Clare. You're pregnant, and you're happy." Setting the coffee down, Avery rushed around the counter, folded Clare into a hug. "I'm so happy for you. When did you find out? How far along are you? What did Beckett say?"

"I don't think I could be happier. This morning, though I suspected yesterday. Probably about two weeks. And I haven't said anything to Beckett yet."

"Why?"

"I need you to do me a favor first. You're going into Hagerstown, aren't you?"

"Yeah, I'll be heading that way."

"Could you pick me up a home pregnancy test?"

"You haven't taken one already? You said you found out this morning."

"Morning sickness, the second day running. I know the signs—this would be the fourth time. I'm wifty and tired, and sick in the mornings, and my body feels . . . It's hard to explain." Again she touched her belly, then her breasts. "My body feels pregnant. But I want to confirm before I tell Beckett just in case I'm wrong. I just don't want to pop in the pharmacy here or in Sharpsburg to buy the kit."

"Word spreads fast."

"You got it, and since you're going into Hagerstown anyway, you could get one for me, in anonymity."

"Happy to. Wow. Wedding, honeymoon, familymoon, baby! Beckett'll be good with it, right?"

"Very good." Reaching down, she chose a ginger ale for herself from the under-counter cooler. "We wanted a baby, though we thought we'd wait a few months. We weren't trying, but obviously, we weren't *not* trying. If I've calculated right, we'll be a family of six next January, right about the time the inn has its first anniversary."

"Can I tell Hope? I'm going to see her later, but I'll swear the vow of silence if you want."

"I'll let you know once I've taken the test. You can tell her right after I tell Beckett."

"Vow of silence until. This is such good news. Good, happy news," she added with another huge hug for Clare. "I'm not going to stop by to see the demo before I go. I don't want to risk it. I talk to no one. I'll be back in a couple hours. Oh boy!"

"Think, oh girl." Clare laughed. "I know it's silly, but God, I'd love to have a girl this time."

"Thinking pink." She gave Clare a last hug. "I'll be back as soon as I can."

"Thanks. Wait, it's pouring. Let me get you an umbrella."

"It's okay. I've got one in the car." She ran out, was soaked through before she got behind the wheel.

But she grinned all the way out of town.

&

OWEN LEFT THE crew to the demo, did a quick pass through the bakery project. Mostly on schedule, he noted, and with Ry at one helm, Beckett at the other, he was free to drive into Hagerstown for materials, knock off some personal errands—and the ones his brothers had added to his list.

He didn't much mind the multiple stops—more materials meant more progress. He didn't much mind driving in the rain. It could've been the snow currently hammering the northern part of the county and up into Pennsylvania.

He'd had enough of snow, enough of winter, so he'd take the rain.

He hoped Avery hadn't ignored the umbrella, as he knew she'd be doing just what he was doing. Multiple stops, multiple parking lots and dashes into stores, crossing off chores.

Too bad they couldn't have gone together, but the stops didn't match up well enough to make it practical. If the weather guys were right, they were in for a full day of rain, a full night of it. He remembered Avery had scheduled herself to work, and to close. He could grab dinner at Vesta after work, use her apartment to finish up paperwork while she was downstairs.

Stay at her place.

He had to remind himself not to assume, but damn it, he'd reached the point he *wanted* to assume. He wanted her to do the same.

Why shouldn't they? Why wouldn't they? But he couldn't shake the certainty that she'd braked on that particular step and wasn't quite willing to take the next.

Then again, he had to admit the step they'd stopped on was pretty comfortable.

He swung off for hardware, put an order in for lumber, picked up paint, then carpet samples for the over-the-bakery apartments.

He streamed through his list, making a circuit, making his last stop the drugstore. He clicked through his own items, added Ryder's shaving cream, Beckett's Motrin, tossed in a couple of fresh sets of playing cards—to supplement the naked women cards he'd already bought for Beck's poker night bachelor party.

He started to turn down the next aisle, and spotted Avery.

It gave his heart a quick lift, to see her like this, unexpectedly—and made him shake his head when he noticed her damp hair.

She hadn't used the umbrella after all.

He thought he'd ease down to her, come up behind—grab her. Imagined her reaction—the jolt, the squeak, the surprise, then the laugh.

She was concentrating so hard, he thought, amused, trying to figure out which . . . pregnancy test to buy.

Jesus Christ.

It was his last clear thought as he watched her take one off the shelf, give it another long study, front and back, then add it to her basket.

He stood exactly where he was, rooted to the floor as she strolled away down the aisle, turned the next corner.

A home pregnancy test? But she took . . . He used . . . How could . . . ?

Avery pregnant? How could she be pregnant? Well, he knew *how*, but she'd never said anything. Never gave the slightest hint she thought maybe.

She just picked up the am-I-or-aren't-I kit and added it in with her shower gel and shampoo and mouthwash.

Just another item on the list?

He wanted to go after her, ask her what the hell.

Not the time or place, he told himself. Not the right frame of mind since he couldn't decide what his frame of mind was, exactly.

He stared down at the things in his own basket, couldn't think what to do, couldn't think at all. Numb, a little shaky in the knees, he set the basket aside, and left without buying a thing.

⟡

HE WENT BACK to the new job site, put his back into the demolition. It was hard to beat tearing out walls as a tension reliever. He hauled out hunks of drywall, lengths of splintered framing, personally busted up an old counter.

And still felt shaky, frustrated, and tense as a wire about to snap.

Avery. Pregnant.

How long did one of those tests take? How accurate were they?

He wished he'd taken the time to look up the answers, give himself at least that much solid ground.

First, if she'd bought a pregnancy test, she had reason to think she might be pregnant. Women didn't buy that kind of thing on a whim.

Did they? Why would they?

People bought Band-Aids before they cut themselves, but didn't buy pregnancy test kits before they thought they were pregnant.

So since she had reason to think she was, why hadn't she mentioned it? Just say: Owen, there's a possibility I could be pregnant, so I'm going to buy a pregnancy test and find out.

She had to be freaked out. Except she hadn't looked freaked-out.

She'd looked calm, he remembered. She'd even smiled a little as she'd added it to her basket.

Did she *want* to be pregnant?

Thought she might be, liked the idea. She'd decided not to say anything until she knew one way or the other. If she wasn't, he supposed she'd planned not to mention it at all. And that didn't seem right, no, that didn't sit well with him.

If she was pregnant, he imagined she'd let him know whenever she wanted to let him know. Not telling him the maybe left him in the dark—or would have without that mutual trip to the CVS—so she got to choose if and when. That didn't sit well, not one bit.

When you factored in what her mother had done, shouldn't she, of all people, know the father (Jesus, maybe he was going to be a father) had a right to know? There were two people involved in this, not just Avery. They weren't casual sex pals or an impulsive one- two- or three-night stand.

They were . . .

He wasn't absolutely sure now that he considered it, but they were in more than a casual, get-laid-now-and-again relationship.

Whatever they were, trust and honesty had to be key elements.

She hadn't trusted him enough to tell him about her mother's visit until he'd put her back to the wall, he remembered. Instead, she'd holed up, walled off, shut him out.

If she thought she could pull that on something like this, she was in for a major attitude adjustment.

"Son of a bitch!" He heaved broken plywood into the Dumpster.

"Okay." Beckett came up behind him. "You haven't worked off whatever it is, so spill it."

"You want me to spill it?" In a rare show of temper, Owen kicked the Dumpster. "I'll spill it. Avery's pregnant."

"Holy shit." Glancing around as one of the crew came out, Beckett waved the man off before taking Owen by the arm and pulling him under the overhang and out of the rain. "When did you find out?"

"Today. This morning. And you know how I found out? You know how because she doesn't fucking tell me? I found out because I walked into the goddamn CVS, and there she is, picking up one of those pregnancy tests."

"Christ, Owen. It was positive?"

"I don't know." Temper rising, rising, he marched up and down the concrete walk. "She's not telling me any damn thing. She's sneaking off buying one of those pee sticks instead of talking to me. I've had it."

"Okay, take it down a notch." To halt his brother's angry pacing, Beckett moved into the path, held up both hands. "You don't know if she's pregnant."

"I'd say, the way she handles things, I'll be the last to know." Along with the sudden hot rage ran a cold stream of hurt. "I've had it."

"What did she say when you asked her about it?"

"Nothing. I didn't."

After a moment staring at Owen's angry face, Beckett rubbed his hands over his own. "You didn't ask her why she was buying the kit?"

"No. I froze, okay? Jesus. She's tossing it in her basket like it's a bag of candy—with a little smile—and I froze. What the hell would you do?"

"It's not the same for Clare and me." Beckett stared out at the rain, steady and slow, from under the pitch of the roof. "We've talked about having a baby. We want to have another kid. I take it the two of you haven't discussed what you'd do on the if."

"No. I never thought of the if. She should've told me, Beck, that's bottom line. She should've told me she needed a test. Why does she think she has to deal with everything by herself? I can't work that way, and I don't want to live that way."

"No, you can't." Not Owen, Beckett thought. His brother was a born team player, an innate believer in partnership and shared loads. For Owen, secrets were for Christmas and birthdays, not for day-to-day living. "You need to talk to her, but Christ, not now. She's in the middle of her lunch rush. And you need to cool off some anyway."

"I don't think cooling off's going to happen. The more I think about it, the more pissed off I am."

"Then think about this. If she is pregnant, what do you want to do?"

"If she's pregnant, we should get married."

"I didn't ask should, I asked want."

"I . . ." He waited for his mind to make that subtle and vital switch. "If we're making a baby, I'd want to get married."

"Okay, so take an hour to figure it out. You always figure it out, Owen. By that time, her place will have cleared out some. Go over and tell her you need to talk to her in private. And find out, for Christ's sake, if you're going to be a daddy before you freak out any more than you are. Then handle it."

"You're right. Jesus, I feel a little . . ."

"Sick?"

"Not exactly. Off. I never figured on anything like this. It's out of . . ."

"Owen's Order of Events. Adjust," he suggested, giving Owen a light punch on the shoulder.

"Adjust. Yeah, I can adjust." His face darkened, his eyes glinted. "But I'm not the only one who's going to."

He waited an hour, decided he'd calmed down, steadied up. He walked over to Vesta in the unrelenting rain, and into the warm, into the scents of sauce and spice.

Behind the cash register, Avery rang up a customer, sent Owen a sassy wink.

A wink, he thought, heating up again. This wasn't the time for cute little winks.

"Good timing," she told him. "Things've just slowed down. I was going to run over and see what you guys have demolished so far."

"I need to talk to you."

"Sure, have a seat. I'm going to get Franny to take over. Do you want a slice?"

"No. And I need to talk to you upstairs. In private."

"Oh. Crap. Is something wrong in the new place?"

"It's got nothing to do with that."

"Then what—"

"Avery." His tone flattened, had her eyebrows drawing together. "Upstairs, now. In private."

"Fine. Fine, but you're screwing with my really good mood." She stalked to the doorway between the kitchens. "Franny? I need to run out." She pulled off her apron as she spoke, tagged it on a peg. "I really want to see the new place," she began.

"You can go after if that's what you want."

"What are you pissed about?" she asked as they went through the side door. "I haven't done anything."

"Maybe not doing is the problem."

"Really screwing with my mood," she repeated and shoved open her apartment door. "Now, what the hell is the problem?"

His carefully planned, thoroughly reasonable approach fizzled away. "Why the hell didn't you tell me you were pregnant?"

"What? *What?*"

"Don't give me that shock-and-awe crap, Avery. I saw you at the drugstore. I saw you buy the pregnancy test."

"You . . ." Her hands fisted on her hips. "You were *spying* on me."

"Don't be stupid. I was out running errands, and went into the CVS. And there you were pulling one of those tests off the shelf and tossing it in your basket. Goddamn it, what's wrong with you that you don't tell me? That you don't trust me, or respect what we are to each other enough to tell me you're pregnant."

"Maybe because I'm not."

"Not?"

"I'm not pregnant, you moron."

Something odd worked inside him, but he couldn't identify the sensation. "The test was negative."

"No, the test was positive." She yanked out her phone.

Now his heart jumped several beats and landed hard in his throat. "If it was positive, then you're pregnant. Who's the moron?"

"You." She turned the phone around to show him the

picture of the test stick, and the PREGNANT. "Because this is Clare's pregnancy test. The pregnancy test I picked up for her this morning when she asked me to."

"I saw Beckett ten minutes ago. Clare's not pregnant or he'd have told me."

"She hasn't told *him*. She wants to tell him when they're alone, wants to make it a special moment—which you'd also get if you weren't the moron. And she asked me not to tell anyone, and now I've broken my promise. And that pisses me off."

"I won't say anything to him, for Christ's sake. I won't spoil it for them." Unsteady, unsure, a little light-headed, he shoved both hands through hair just damp enough to stand out in tufts. "But, Jesus, what was I supposed to think when I saw you buying the thing?"

"I don't know, Owen. Maybe the solution might've been to walk the hell up to me, say, hey, Avery, fancy meeting you here, and why are you buying that pregnancy test?"

"I have to sit down." He did. "I'm going to remind you, you owe me a break." He breathed for a minute. "I couldn't think. And then you were just walking off. You were so damn casual about it, and I just couldn't think."

She said nothing as she studied him. He looked so perplexed, so confused, as Owen rarely did. "You wigged."

"In a manner of speaking. Maybe."

"And you jumped to conclusions."

"I . . . Okay."

"You never jump."

"I've never seen you buy a pregnancy test before— especially when I'm the only one having sex with you."

She considered. "That's actually sort of understandable. Sort of." When a grin tugged at the corners of her mouth, she let it come. "You totally freaked."

"I semi-freaked," he corrected. "I was more pissed, and . . ." Might as well admit it, he decided. "And hurt when I thought you weren't telling me. We've never talked about if."

She blew out a breath. "That's a conversation. I don't know, and it's not something we can talk out in ten minutes,

I guess. We're fine now, right, because I'm not, and Clare is. And she's so happy. Beckett's going to be happy."

"Yeah, he is. He really is."

"So let's just be happy for them, and let me have the pleasure of knowing you were a moron. We'll talk about ifs sometime, but I really want to see the demo. Then I told Clare I'd get the kids from school and bring them to the shop so she can tell Beckett. She doesn't want to tell the kids until she's further along. Probably not until after the wedding anyway. It's for her and Beckett now, and I guess you and me and Hope and Ryder and your parents and hers. Which is already a lot."

"All right." Steadier, he rose. "But we'd both better think about it, and talk it out, in case."

"You worry about 'in case' more than I do, but we'll do that. It's a really good day, Owen."

"You're right." He settled a bit more when she reached up, smoothed at his hair. "It's a really good day."

"For right now, let's just be happy for Clare and Beckett. They're getting married, making a family, expanding one. It's all exactly what they both want."

"All right," he said again, and reached for her, drew her in. "We'll be happy for them. Sorry I was pissed at you."

"I'm not, because I get to say *moron*." On a laugh, she tipped back her head, kissed him. "Let's go over to the new place. Can I knock something down?"

"I'll find something for you to demo. It's the least I can do."

## CHAPTER NINETEEN

H OPE SHIFTED THE CLEAR VASE OF WHITE ROSES AN
inch to the left.

"There."

Though Avery didn't see the difference, she nodded approval.

They'd transformed the long table borrowed from Turn The Page with a draping of white linen. With Hope's focused eye, clear, square vases of newly opened white roses and tiny white tea lights in silver holders graced what would serve as the dessert and champagne bar.

Clare may have opted against a white wedding, but her wedding shower was going full-out.

"Gifts there, food there, desserts and champagne here." Hands on hips, Hope turned a circle in The Dining Room. "You did a great job on her chair."

"I amazed myself."

They'd positioned one of the high-backed chairs to face the room. An enormous bow of white tulle crowned the top, its tails flowing to the floor. Garlands of white and pale, pale pink twined around the rungs, the arms, the legs.

"I forget how much I like girly stuff until I have a chance to do some."

Gorgeous red heels clicking on hardwood, Hope walked over to shift candles minutely. "I'm going to put some wine, some nibbles in The Lounge so people can wander around, settle down wherever they like."

"You know a lot of people coming haven't seen the place yet. You're going to get hit up for tours."

"Already figured on it. It's just too bad it's really not warm enough so we can spread out into The Courtyard. Anyway, the place looks great, and we look . . ." She turned, hooked an arm through Avery's so they reflected together in the gold-framed mirror. "Fabulous."

"Agreed."

"So . . . Pre-party champagne?"

"Twist my arm."

They went into the kitchen where Hope poured two flutes. She clinked hers against Avery's. "To maids of honor and godmothers."

"That would be us."

"And in about eight months, we'll be hosting a baby shower."

"Four kids. Whew." Avery took a drink, then hoisted her glass again. "More power to them."

"They've got it. Love runs the engine."

"You think?"

"I do." Hope slid onto a stool. "How long do you think they can keep this a secret? The two of them are absolutely radiant."

"Most people will think that's about the wedding, and part of it is. If they can keep it quiet until after the honeymoon—that's Clare's goal anyway—it gives them a little breathing room."

"I can't believe you kept it from me for an entire day."

"I was *dying* to tell you." In her spring green dress, Avery hopped onto her own stool, tugged down the narrow skirt. "And I would've come over and filled you in after work, but the whole Owen thing was so weird."

"What are the chances?" Because it still amused her,

Hope leaned back and laughed. "Seriously, he turns the corner in the drugstore just as you're buying the test kit."

"Fate's twisted little joke on him."

"Poor guy. Imagine what was going through his mind."

"That's just it. I can't, or not clearly—and I usually get Owen's mind. But he was so serious. I can't figure out if he was mad, scared, what."

"A combo of both, I imagine."

"Even after I explained?" It continued to nag at her, just a little. "We both brushed it aside, but really, I can't be sure. Mad and scared because maybe I was, or maybe I was and hadn't said anything."

"I'd guess he had to process the okay, it's Clare, but what if it had been? Didn't you?"

"Maybe. A little. But only because I had to think what if we'd gone down that road after his reaction. You know Owen by now. He's a planner. Everything in its time, in its place. He's the guy who actually checks the expiration date on the milk carton before he buys it."

"So do I."

"Which is why you get him. An unplanned pregnancy?" Avery rolled her eyes. "That would shake the very foundation of his life plan."

"What's his life plan?"

"I don't know, but you can bet he's got one."

"I think you're wrong." Hope topped off their flutes. "I say that because I share a lot of sensibilities and traits with him. Yes, he probably has a basic plan, which includes goals, achievements, events, steps. But he's also capable of adjusting the plan." She lifted a hand, gesturing around her. "I did."

"Sure, he can adjust." Organized and efficient wasn't rigid, she told herself. It was just . . . a little stiff by her personal gauge.

"Okay, since we're playing what-if? If I'd been buying that kit for myself, and if the results had been positive, he'd adjust, and plan out from there. The first step of the plan would be marriage."

"That annoys you?"

"No. No. He'd see that as doing the right thing, the

necessary thing. I wouldn't want to get married because it's the right thing."

"Better that than the wrong thing," Hope pointed out.

"You know what I mean. I'd want to get married because I *want* to get married, I'm ready, in love, excited about the idea of spending my life with someone."

Because they were there, Hope took one of the little pastel mints from a bowl on the island. "You'd say no."

"I don't know."

"I do. You'd say no because you'd feel obligated to prove a point, and to let him off the hook—both of those in equal measure." Recrossing her legs, Hope studied Avery over her next sip of champagne. "I can take care of myself, and you're not obligated to marry me. Share responsibility for the child, yes, be a vital and integral part of the child's life, yes. But under no obligation to you, individually."

"That sounds hard-line."

"I don't think so. It sounds like you—pride, caution, heart, tangled up with parental issues."

"Would they have gotten married if she hadn't been pregnant with me?" A bit grimly, Avery took a gulp of champagne. "I don't think so."

"If they hadn't, you wouldn't be sitting here wondering about it. They made a choice; you're the result."

Avery lifted a shoulder. "The Hope Beaumont Practical School of Logic."

"It generally works. Listen, I wouldn't be sitting here with you if Jonathan hadn't made his choice—which led to mine. I've thought about that, a lot, in the past months. I'm happy here, happier than I was when I was with Jonathan, when I thought my life was proceeding according to my very solid, very Practical School of Logic plans."

Avery considered a moment. "I get your point, but, Hope, Jonathan was an asshole."

On a laugh, Hope lifted her glass. "Yes, but I thought he was *my* asshole." She checked her watch. "We should start putting the rest of the food out."

They'd barely begun when Clare tapped on The Lobby door.

"I know I'm a little early," she began when Avery answered. "I dropped the kids off at the new house—which is really almost entirely a house. Beckett and his brothers are going to put the kids to work. God help them all. Oh wow. Just wow, look at those flowers!"

"Wait till you see The Dining Room. Give me your coat first. We've got a rack for coats in the laundry. How are you feeling—it's just me and Hope. Nobody else is here yet."

"Good." Laughing a little, she tossed her sunny blond hair off her shoulders. "When I threw up this morning, all I could think was, I'm having a baby. Beckett and I are having a baby. So I'm good."

"It shows. I don't mean the baby," Avery said with a snicker when Clare laid hands on her belly. "Come see."

When she dragged Clare into The Dining Room, Hope stepped back from the buffet.

"What do you think?"

"It's beautiful. Oh, it's so beautiful. All the flowers, and candles. You made me a chair!" Clare blinked at the tears swirling in her eyes. "I'm watering up again. I don't know if it's happiness or hormones, probably a mix of both. I got teary when Beckett did the breakfast dishes this morning."

"A bride's allowed to get teary at her shower," Hope told her.

"I hope so, because I have a feeling . . . Thank you, so much, for everything. For all this. For being mine."

"Keep it up," Avery warned, "we'll all be crying. I'm going to go hang this up."

She hurried out, hung Clare's coat next to her own jacket. As she started back again, something drew her across The Lobby, and down to the base of the stairs. Had she heard something? It was more *felt* something, Avery thought. She walked quietly up, away from Clare's and Hope's voices.

The door to Elizabeth and Darcy stood open. But then all the rooms stood open, as Hope wanted to allow the guests to wander, to enjoy the rooms if they were busy playing hostess.

In E&D, the porch door stood open as well. A touch of

honeysuckle hung on the cool March air blowing gently into the room.

She didn't hear, or see, but again felt. And what she felt was sorrow.

"Please come in," she murmured. "Please come inside. I know you're sad. It must be so hard, so hard to accept. Owen's looking for Billy. If anyone can find things out, figure things out, it's Owen. But meanwhile, you're not alone here. I know how it feels, because I've felt alone."

She took another step toward the door, waited. "But I was wrong to feel that way. I always had someone who cared about me, even when everything seemed so hard, so sad. You do, too. We care about you."

She hesitated, then chose impulse. The majority of the time, Lizzy seemed happy, even playful. Romantic, Avery thought. A young woman with a cheerful nature.

"I have a secret. I think I could tell you because I bet you know how to keep a secret. Especially a happy secret like this one. Please come inside."

The door to the porch slowly closed.

Taking the presence on faith, Avery sat on the side of the bed. "We're having a party downstairs today. A bridal shower for Clare." She wasn't sure if they'd had the tradition of bridal showers in Eliza Ford's time. "It's something we do. Women, I mean. We have a party to celebrate our friend's upcoming wedding. We have food, games, we bring her gifts. It's happy. Only a few people who'll be here know the secret, but I know Clare wouldn't mind if I tell you. You care about Beckett, and Clare, and the boys. They're making such a nice family. And in a few months, they'll be a bigger family. Clare's pregnant. She and Beckett are going to have a baby next winter."

The scent bloomed, strong and sweet as summer, and the air warmed with it.

"I know. Isn't it great? You watched them fall in love. I think it really started here, in the inn. Now they'll be married here, in just a couple weeks. Everything about them is so strong and sure and right. That's rare, don't you think? To be that strong and sure and right? To find the person who fits and fills in, links up. I don't even know the words."

She glanced down, saw she was clutching the little key Owen had given her. And there were tears, her own tears, on the back of her hand.

"Clare's hormones must be contagious. I'm not sad. I'm not."

She felt something stroke her hair, and she closed her eyes in wonder that she could be comforted by the touch.

"I'm not sad," she repeated. "I'm just not as strong and sure as I wish I could be. How do people risk it? You must have risked so much for Billy. How do you do that?"

As she watched, a light fog covered the glass of the porch door. And the outline of a pretty heart shone against it.

"It seems so simple," Avery murmured. "Why isn't it?"

The sound of voices, of laughter, drifted up the stairs. "Party's starting. I've got to get down."

She pushed to her feet, moved to the little mirror to make sure her eyes showed no sign of tears. "You should come. I'm issuing an official invitation. You don't have to be alone," she added, and went down to be with her friends, knowing she spoke as much to herself as her ghost.

She dived into the party. Yes, she did enjoy the girly when she had time. Pretty dresses, pretty food, talk of weddings and men and fashion and morsels of gossip.

Even better to remember she had a very juicy morsel herself, known only to a handful of the women—and one ghost—in attendance.

She drank champagne and served it, ate fancy finger sandwiches and carried dishes to the kitchen. While Hope efficiently kept a log of gifts and givers for Clare, she bagged the torn wrapping. Carolee artfully fashioned a paper-plate bouquet out of discarded ribbons and bows.

Silly things and female things. The scents, the sounds against the backdrop of bride white and flickering candles. The bride-to-be and expectant mama drinking ginger ale disguised in a champagne flute and laughing at the whistles and cheers when she opened a nearly transparent black nightie.

"You girls did good." Over the boisterous competition in another game, Justine gave Avery a squeeze. "Couldn't have done better."

"We loved every minute."

"It shows. Clare's smart and lucky in her friends."

"I feel the same about myself."

"That shows, too. I think we could use another bottle of champagne. Give me a hand?"

"Sure."

"I really just wanted a minute with you," Justine said as they went into the kitchen.

"Okay."

Justine took the bottle Avery got out of the fridge, set it on the counter. "I'm a really good mom."

"I don't know better."

"And you won't." She grinned back at Avery, then her face softened as she stroked a hand over Avery's hair. "I've thought of you as mine even before Traci left."

"Oh, Justine."

"I always figured you knew, but I never said it to you. Maybe I should have."

Touched, so touched, Avery could only shake her head. "I always knew I could count on you, could go to you."

"I hope so, and I hope you always will. Avery, you're one of the brightest lights I know, certainly one of my brightest. I'm sorry to see some of that bright dim off and on the last few weeks."

"I'm working on it."

"You don't have to. You feel what you feel."

Owen had said exactly the same, Avery remembered. Like a stroke on her hair, it comforted.

"I'm going to take a chance now and say something I've wanted to say for a lot of years. Traci was, and is, a flighty, selfish woman who always wanted more than she had, and always blamed someone else if she didn't get it. If she did get it, it was never really right, never really enough—and *that* was always someone else's fault. You're nothing like her. I've watched you grow up, and I know who you are, what you are."

"Do you think she ever loved me?"

"Yes." With no hesitation, Justine gave Avery's hand a squeeze. "Yes, she loved you, and I think she loves you now. Just not enough."

"Not enough might be worse than not at all," Avery murmured.

"Maybe, but that's not on you, honey. It's nothing about you, and all about Traci. I want to think you know that, deep down. Maybe you haven't gotten there yet. Meanwhile, you're smart and lucky in your friends, and you can count on them. But sometimes a girl needs a mom. You have me."

Avery went into her arms, held hard. "I knew. I always knew, but it helps hearing you say it. I don't want you to worry about me."

"Part of the job, but I don't worry much when it comes to you." She lifted Avery's face, smiled. "Bright light. You've always found your way."

༂

AFTER THE GUESTS, after the cleanup—and with Carolee handling the two party guests who'd booked rooms for the night—Avery talked Hope into coming to her apartment for a break.

"Feet up." Avery plopped down, put hers on the coffee table. "Congratulations, co-hostess."

"Back at you. Jesus, I'm exhausted."

"Half of that's adrenaline drain. You get hyped."

"I do—but that was one kick-ass shower."

"And onto one kick-ass wedding." Self-satisfied Avery stretched her arms up, rolled her shoulders. "I'm going to make us some tea in a minute, then we can talk about Janice and what she was thinking when she put on those pants. They made her butt look like an enormous beefsteak."

Laying her head back, Hope closed her eyes, chuckled. "God, they really did. On the other hand, Laurie looked so pretty, and so excited about her own wedding. It's too bad they'd already booked the venue before we were finished with the inn."

"You're a glutton for punishment."

"Maybe. Charlene did pull me aside. She and the other bookstore girls want to give Laurie a shower. And now they want to talk about having it at the inn. I need to talk to Justine, figure out a venue fee for an event like that."

"I thought I was a workhorse." She pushed herself up, kicking off her shoes on the way to the kitchen—then detoured at the knock on the door. "Please don't be a problem downstairs, please don't be a problem downstairs," she muttered. "Owen."

"Saw the light. I thought we could— Hi, Hope."

"Hi. I was just leaving."

"No, she wasn't. She was about to have some well-deserved tea. Carolee's in charge at the inn for a couple hours. You want some tea?" she asked him. "Or I've got some beer."

"I'll take the beer. We put in a long one, too. I can take it to go if you—"

"Jeez, sit." She pushed him toward a chair. "All this politeness is making my teeth hurt. And my feet already do."

"She's always so welcoming." But he bypassed the chair, sat on the couch. "I had some time last night and early this morning," he told Hope, "for a little research."

"As soon as the wedding's done, I swear I'll put in more time on that, help you out."

"No problem. I couldn't give it much today because we're really pushing on Beck's place."

"How's it coming?" Avery called out.

"We're nearly there. A lot of painting, punch-out, details."

"Sounds familiar," Hope said with a smile.

"I'm working out the time line—"

"Also familiar," Avery said from the kitchen.

"It's going to be close, but we can just about knock it out by the wedding, get the final inspections. I was thinking we could load them in while they're on their honeymoon. We couldn't have everything in where they're going to want it— you know, like hanging pictures or the fussy stuff—but we could get the furniture in there, stock the kitchen. That kind of thing."

Avery came out with a tray and mugs of tea and a bottle of beer. She set it down, leaned over and kissed him. "That's you. That's you who'd think of that."

"It'd be nice for them to get back and basically move right in."

"It's a great idea. I'll help all I can," Hope promised. "I do know where she plans to put a lot of things. We've talked about it."

"Hope's got a memory like an elephant."

"But not an ass like an enormous tomato."

Owen just lifted his brows when Avery snorted in her tea. "Girl joke," she told him.

"Okay. Anyway, we'll plan for it. How'd it all go today?"

"It was perfect." Hope curled up her legs. "And we had one unexpected guest. I caught her scent off and on all through the party—and I really think she helped herself to some champagne, if that's possible. I found an empty glass up in E&D, *after* I'd already done the check through and all the others had gone."

"I invited her." Avery sipped her tea. "I went up there before, and I don't know, I just got the feeling she was down. Sad. I told her about the baby, and the shower. It seemed to cheer her up."

"That's you," Owen murmured. "That's you who'd think of that. I might have more on her. I've been looking into her family. She had two older brothers and a younger sister. One brother died in the war. The other came back, got married, had four kids, so I've got those threads if we need them. The sister married a couple years after the war. Five kids, but one died as a baby. From what I've found, the sister lived way into her nineties. They moved to Philadelphia a couple years after the marriage. That might be something for you to look into, Hope, as that's where your family's from."

"Can do."

"Do you know anything about Liberty House School?"

Surprise flooding her face, Hope looked up from her tea. "As a matter of fact I do. Why?"

"I haven't pulled all the details yet, but I ended up going off on a tangent—you know how it happens—and I came on the Liberty House School for Girls—founded in 1878. It has the sister as one of the founders—and a big influence on providing education to girls at a time when it wasn't a big thing. It's coed now, but still a respected private school up there."

"It is. I went there."

"Seriously?" Surprised, Owen leaned forward, forearms on thighs. "Small world."

"Yes." Frowning, Hope set down her tea. "What was the sister's name?"

"Ah, Catherine."

"Her married name?"

"Darby. Catherine Darby. I read that the library in the school's named for her."

"It is, and it is a really, spookily small world. The Catherine Darby who helped found the Liberty House School for Girls in 1878 was my great-times-three-grandmother."

"Holy shit." Avery gaped. "And again, holy shit! Hope, if all this is right, you're related to Lizzy. You're her great-times-three-niece."

"You're sure about this, Hope?"

Hope merely glanced at Owen. "I went to Liberty House from kindergarten through middle school. Just like my mother and uncle did—and my maternal grandmother, like my brother did, like my sister did. It's a family tradition. And before you ask, I don't know much about the family history—not that far back. I imagined Catherine Darby as the old woman—old to a kid—in the painting in the library at school. I've never heard about her having a sister who died. I didn't even know her maiden name."

"Do you think anyone in your family would know more—the more personal stuff that might not show up in research?"

"Honestly, I don't know, but I can find out. This is . . . so strange." So strange she felt a tickle at the back of her throat. "I need to let it settle in. I can't think straight on this yet. I'm going to go."

"Do you want me to go with you? To stay with you tonight?"

"No, no, I'm not afraid. I'm not upset. I just need to process."

"Why don't I walk you across?"

"Stop it," Hope insisted with a little laugh before Owen

could stand. "I think I can make it across The Square. I just need to clear my head, then think. This is just really strange."

Avery popped up, went with Hope to the door. "You call me if you can't settle. Promise."

"All right. Processing." She tapped her temple. "You know I need to."

"Yeah, otherwise, I wouldn't let you go without me. But Hope?"

"Hmm."

"Wow."

"Yeah, you can say that again."

When Hope went out, Avery turned back to Owen, and did. "Wow."

"The sister," he murmured. "I don't know why I followed that path, really. I just wanted the information. The-more-you-know kind of thing. But I didn't see how it could help find the Billy Lizzy wants. And now . . . I know coincidences happen, but this? This is really stretching it."

"So what? Fate?"

"What else?" He pushed up to pace. "You're born and raised in Boonsboro, and Hope's born and raised in Phila-delphia. You end up being college roommates, and friends. Solid friends. So solid, she visits here, makes solid friends with Clare. The same Clare my brother's about to marry. My mother falls in love with the old hotel, manages to buy it, we put blood, sweat, and tears into rehabbing it. The person we're hiring as innkeeper gets pregnant, has to bow out, and you and Clare come up with Hope."

"Who's looking to relocate because she's been screwed over by her asshole and his family."

"She's tailor-made for the job," Owen continued. "Hotel manager, knows all the ropes—some we hadn't even thought of. Overqualified, and not really looking to relocate here. And my mom hires her on the spot—barely talked to her, and boom, she's hired. Hope accepts the same way—boom."

"Well, when you add it all up that way . . ."

"That's how it adds up." He stopped his restless pacing to face her. "One twist, then another, one choice, then another, all leading to the same place. The inn, Lizzy, Hope—and maybe, if it keeps adding—to this Billy."

"Do you think she knows—Eliza, I mean?"

"I don't know. It seems if she did, she'd have made more effort to connect with Hope. When you think about it, it's been more with us—Beckett, me, Ry—though Ry doesn't talk about it much. My mother. Even you."

"And Murphy. He's the first one who saw her, that we know of."

"Kids." Owen shrugged. "They haven't learned not to believe the impossible. This is . . ."

"Is what?"

He looked at her, lit up with a grin. "So fucking cool. And . . . wait a minute. I was distracted, caught up. I just noticed."

"Noticed what."

"Your hair. It's back." He crossed to her, ran his fingers through the bright golden red. "It's Avery's hair again."

"I decided to try being me for a while, see how it goes."

"The way I like you best," he told her.

"Really?" Intrigued, she studied him. "Why didn't you say anything?"

"It's your hair, but this is *your* hair." Bending down, he sniffed at it. "Smells like it, feels like it, and now it looks like it. I'm crazy about your hair."

"Come on."

"Always have been. I've never made love with you and your real hair."

She laughed, then laughed again when he boosted her up. Obliging, she hooked her legs around his waist.

"I think I should," he continued, "just to see. Get a comparison study."

"You do like your research."

"And some more than others," he agreed as he carted her into the bedroom.

# CHAPTER TWENTY

❧❦

DECKED WITH FLOWERS AND SPARKLING LIGHTS, THE inn shimmered like a wish. Of all it had seen, all it had held in its long life, this celebration of love, faith, and endurance shone bright.

The air bloomed with the scent of roses, hints of honeysuckle, a sweet drift of lilies. Overhead, the sky cupped blue and clear.

Inside the fairy bower of Titania and Oberon, Clare stepped into her wedding dress. She took a breath, smiled at her mother as Hope fussed the dress into place. "No crying, Mom."

"My girl's so beautiful." Rosie blinked at the tears, stepped forward to take Clare's hand. "And so happy."

"Perfect." Hope stepped back to stand with Avery.

"That's how everything feels, right this moment." Clare took another breath as she turned to the mirror. "Perfect."

"And right on schedule, too. Out on the porch for some photos," Hope ordered, "so we stay that way."

"Are you sure Beckett's not around? I don't want him to see me before the ceremony. I know it's silly, but—"

"It's not," Avery corrected. "I'll go back to J&R and make sure the men stay on that side."

"We need you for pictures," Hope reminded her.

"I'll be back. Just let me round up the boys and Justine. And report on progress from the groom's world. Get started, and give me five," she said and dashed out.

She noted the door to Elizabeth and Darcy stood open. "Can't visit right now. Timetable. But I'll be back."

Clicking along in her wedding shoes, enjoying the way her dress—the color of frothy champagne—flowed around her legs, she hurried toward the back, through the door, across the porch.

She heard the voices before she knocked—the boys' excited tones, a low, rumbling laugh. "Everybody decent?" she called out as she eased the door open.

"Define decent," Ryder said.

Amused, she stepped through the door.

Justine, hair tumbling down her back, stood cheek-to-cheek with Beckett. Another one of those perfect moments, Avery thought, while Ryder and the boys—all in their dark suits—sat on the bed with cards spread out in what appeared to be a marathon game of War.

"It's time!" Liam started to scramble off the bed, causing a stampede.

"Not yet. We're taking some pictures first, then the photographer will come down here, take some of you guys. Where's Owen?"

"Liquid refreshment detail," Ryder told her.

"You look great. God, everybody looks great. I need to steal Justine and the boys for the pictures, then I'll ship them back. The rest of the groom's team stays rear of the inn. No sneaking around the front."

"How about a pizza delivery?" Ryder asked, and as with the stampede, incited a small riot among the younger set.

"After." Justine turned, gave the boys the eye Avery imagined had quelled riots for decades. "Let's go, troops. See you soon," she murmured, kissing Beckett's cheek.

"But I'm pretty thirsty." Murphy sent Justine an imploring look laced with a hopeful smile.

"I'll take care of that. I'll be right behind you," Avery promised Justine.

"I win by default."

Harry spun around on Ryder's smug grin. "Nuh-uh!"

"Uh-huh. The war's over for you, loser."

"Moratorium," Justine declared. "A pause in the battle," Justine explained to Harry as she herded them out. And she sent Ryder that same quelling eye before she shut the door.

"You really do look great," Avery said with her hand on the knob. "But wait until you see Clare."

"Just tell me I don't have to wait much longer."

"Nearly there," she promised Beckett, and scurried out.

Avery glanced down at The Courtyard as she started down. The tents, wedding-gown-white under the softening blue sky, more flowers, more lights.

Hope would say perfect, she thought. And she'd be right.

Owen stepped out, a tray of drinks in his hands. Their eyes met, she on the steps, he below. The moment held—romantic, fanciful—and her heart gave that quick flutter.

He couldn't take his eyes off her. "You look amazing."

"Wait till you see the bride."

Owen only shook his head, watching the sun play on her highland queen hair. "Amazing."

"It's all so beautiful." She continued down. "Think of this a year ago. It's hard to believe the changes, what can happen, what can, well, become I guess."

His eyes stayed steady on hers. "I was thinking the same thing."

"Justine took the boys to the bride's side for pictures. I'll deliver their liquid refreshment."

He glanced at the tray he carried. Odd, for a minute he'd forgotten it, forgotten the wedding, forgotten the world. "Yeah. Sprite, which Liam claims is the same deal as champagne. The real deal for Mom."

"And beer for you and your brothers. We'll be about fifteen minutes more—according to Hope's scary timetable. Then the photographer will be over to deal with you guys."

"We'll be ready. I've got the schedule."

"Of course you do."

He carried the tray up to the porch, made the beverage transfer. "Seriously amazing," he added, making her laugh as she hurried away.

He opened the door, stepped inside.

"You know how if Avery had been pregnant I said I'd want to marry her?"

"Jesus, Avery's pregnant?" Quickly, Ryder grabbed a beer from the tray.

"No." But now he understood what that odd feeling had been when he'd learned the test kit had been Clare's. Just a touch of disappointment.

"The thing is, I realized a minute ago—I didn't realize, and now I do."

"Spit it out," Ryder advised, "or you'll screw your own timetable."

"I just want to marry her." A little stunned, he looked from Ryder to Beckett and back again. "I want to marry Avery MacTavish."

"Well. Let's drink to that." Beckett took his own beer, then Owen's, set the tray aside. "Here you go."

Owen frowned at the beer. "Aren't you even a little surprised?"

"No. Not even a little."

"Wait. Wait." Ryder edged back, eyes narrowed. "You said marry—as in *marry*? First Beck, now you?" He gave his beer a suspicious stare. "Is there something in the beer? Some sort of get-married drug? That's going to piss me off."

"It's not in the beer, you dick." Beckett grinned at Owen. "You should ask her tonight. Asking her at a wedding feels like good luck."

"I've got to work on it." Owen blew out a breath. "I've got to work on the how and when and all that."

"He's going to work on it." Ryder took a pull of his beer. "This'll be fun."

❧

ONCE THEIR PART of prewedding photos was done, Rosie gave Clare another embrace. "I'm going to help with the boys, then I'll bring your father up."

"About twenty minutes." Hope held up her phone. "Owen and I are texting, so I'll know when the photos are finished. Then we'll know when Beckett and his party go out to The Courtyard."

"I'll check with Owen, don't worry."

"You're texting?" Avery said when Rosie went out. "Remember how this was going to be informal?"

"Informal doesn't mean sloppy. Guests are already arriving, by the way."

"Countdown." Avery picked up the champagne. "Anybody else?"

"Not for me," Clare began, then frowned. "No, a swallow. I think I should have a swallow for luck."

"A swallow for the bride, and a full glass for the attendants."

Hope picked up her glass. "To the bride."

Clare shook her head. "No, to marriage. To the promises, the compromises, the endurance. That's what I'd like to drink to."

"To marriage then," Hope agreed as they touched glasses.

"And to family," Clare added after a minute sip. "It's not just marriage, children when you have them, the parents you came from. It's this, too. It's the people who make your life whole and rich and steady. You both do that for me."

"You're determined to make us cry," Avery managed.

"I thought I would." Clare took another tiny sip, then set her glass down. "But I'm feeling very clear-eyed. I thought about Clint last night. A lot about Clint. And I know, absolutely, he'd be glad I found Beckett. That I have Beckett, and the boys have him. Knowing that makes me happy. And all I want to do now is walk out to The Courtyard, walk to Beckett and the boys, carrying this one," she said, pressing a hand to her belly. "And make those promises.

"Then I'm going to dance with my husband and our sons."

"After I touch up your lipstick," Hope declared.

While Hope fussed, Avery wandered onto the porch. A minute alone, she thought. Just a minute.

But she heard the porch door open, glanced down toward

Elizabeth and Darcy. She had company after all. And, she decided, that was fine.

"I can't figure it out. I'm not sad, but I don't know if happy's the word. For Clare, yes. Ecstatic for Clare. But otherwise, I'm somewhere between. I just wonder how it works, you know? I look at her, and I see she's so sure, not at all nervous, no questions or doubts. What's it like to feel that way? How do you get to that point?"

She looked over to Vesta, then down Main Street to Turn The Page. That she understood—that commitment, that endurance. But what flipped the switch inside to let someone take those steps for and with another person?

"Doesn't matter. It's not about me. It's a happy day. It's Clare's day."

She turned to go in, saw something on the table between the doors. Frowning, she walked over, picked up a small stone. It was smooth as a cobble, shaped like a heart. It sat in the cup of her hand as she stared at the initials carved in its center.

*L. F.*
*B. R.*

"Lizzy Ford. 'B' for Billy? It must be." Heart drumming, she looked over. The door remained open, that summer scent fragile as petals.

"Did he give this to you? Billy? He must have. And it . . . endured. But how? How am I holding it right here, right now? How can—"

"Avery!" Hope called out. "Countdown."

"It's Clare's day," she repeated as she closed the little stone in her hand. "I can't show them now, but I'll get it to Owen. I promise." She laid the hand holding the stone on her heart. "I promise," she said again.

"Avery!"

"One second!" She hurried in, went straight to her purse. "Lipstick." She tucked the stone safely inside, wondered if it would be there when she came back.

❧

AS THE SUN slid toward the western hills, she watched her friends marry, heard their promises to each other, to the children that formed their family, saw the rings they exchanged glint—another promise—in the soft sparkle of light.

Joy, simple and huge, just flowed from them, she realized, in a slow, warm river. She felt it rise in her as well, something lovely and real, steady and strong.

The tears that swam into her eyes were of that joy when they moved together in their first kiss as husband and wife.

Then there were hugs, applause, music. Owen took her hand, led her down the aisle formed by chairs to The Lobby door. More hugs, a few tears, then laughter as Murphy announced, loudly, firmly, he had to pee, right *now*.

"Pee first, then pictures," Hope announced. "Bride, groom, wedding party and family. Then Clare, Beckett, and the boys, then Clare and Beckett." She glanced at the photographer. "Forty-five minutes. That would keep us on the mark."

"Have you got a stopwatch on you?" Ryder asked.

"In here." Avery tapped her forehead.

"Clare and Beckett need to be able to dance, eat, have fun," Hope began.

"I don't think they're worried about it," Ryder pointed out as the bride and groom shared another long kiss. "Relax, Commander."

"You relax," Hope muttered, and did her best to herd the group.

Avery considered pulling Owen aside, but the timing didn't work, the circumstances weighed against it.

It could wait, she told herself, and fell into the moment.

After the pictures, the return of the bride and groom, the first dance, a few toasts, she managed to pull him back inside.

"I want to dance with you."

"I'm all about that," she agreed, "but I have to show you something first. Upstairs."

"There's also food—it looks good."

"We'll get food, drink, dance. We'll get it all." She kept his hand clutched in hers as she hurried upstairs. "Backstory. I was standing out on the porch right before we came down. I was feeling . . . pensive maybe. Big day. And she came out. Or anyway, the door to the porch opened. I was thinking about Clare and Beckett, getting married, taking vows—that sort of thing. Wondering, really, how people get up the spine or whatever it takes to move on that."

"It's not spine," he began.

"Whatever." She unlocked T&O, drew him in. "Hope called me in, and when I turned around, this was on that table between the doors."

She closed her eyes a moment, reached into her bag, let out a sigh of relief when her fingers closed over the stone.

"A rock. God, that's earth-shattering."

"Shut up. Look at it, Owen."

He took it when she shoved it at him, turned it over. His expression shifted from amusement to puzzlement, then wonder.

"She gave this to you."

"She left it on the table. It wasn't there when I went out. I'm sure it wasn't. Then it was. I wouldn't say she gave it to me, but she wanted me to see it. Don't you think?"

"I'm still trying to get on board with how she could have this, or make it materialize. Or . . . I don't know what."

"I decided not to think too hard about that or my brain might explode. He must've given it to her. The shape, the initials."

"Why would he give her a rock? When you think about it—"

"It's a heart, with their initials inside. Sentimental, right?"

"I guess so. *B* for Billy works. William. *R*. It might help some having the first initial of his last name."

"You and Hope are the ones looking into it, so I wanted to get it to you as soon as I could. Hope's helping run the show here, so you're elected. But we should get it to her after the reception."

"She gave it to you."

"Lizzy? No, she just left it where I'd find it."

"Not much difference."

"She'd want Hope to have it. Hope's her descendent."

"She didn't leave it where Hope would find it." He handed it back to Avery. "You need to keep it."

"It doesn't feel right."

"I figure there's a reason she left it for you. Maybe holding on to it awhile will help you find the reason. And meanwhile I'll look for William R. We'll fill Hope in after the wedding."

"All right, but I feel weird about it." She traced the initials before she tucked it back in her purse. "And if she takes it back, she takes it back."

"Did I tell you, you look amazing?"

Her eyes twinkled at him. "You might have mentioned it in passing."

"You do. And I . . ." No, he thought, not on impulse, not on his brother's day, even if it was lucky. "We need to get back down. My brother doesn't get married every day."

"You're right."

"What did you mean about spine?" he asked her as they headed down.

"What?"

"About needing spine to get married. You need spine to, I don't know, go to war or take on the IRS or skydive."

"I just meant people have to gear up to take that step into until-death-or-divorce-do-us-part."

It struck him wrong, just wrong. "Were you always this cynical?"

"I'm not cynical." Even the word annoyed her. "Just realistic—and curious. I'm a curious realist."

"Take a look at that," he suggested when they'd walked back out where couples danced—Clare and Beckett, his mother, her father, Clare's parents and more. "That's real."

Real, he thought again, and what he wanted. What he wanted with Avery.

"And it's nice. Really nice. A moment. An important moment. But there are thousands of moments after the party. And speaking of that, why aren't you dancing with me?"

"Good idea."

He did his best to keep it light, but something had shifted between them with her words. And he understood she felt it, too.

∽

SHE DIDN'T HAVE time to brood about it, even to think about it. They only had a week to finish the last details on the house, to load in furniture, stock the kitchen.

It reminded Avery of the final push on the inn, but this time with Beckett and Clare off on their honeymoon, they were short two pairs of hands.

Still, that sense of déjà vu trailed through as she and Hope loaded dishes, glassware, flatware, pots, pans, platters into cupboards.

"She's not going to be disappointed she didn't do all this herself, right?"

Hope shook her head. "I thought about that, second-guessed, third-guessed. Then I thought about her coming back from a week off—the work facing her at the store, the kids, the new routine, *and* being pregnant. I really think she'll be relieved not to face hauling boxes, unpacking, and the rest."

"I think so, too—but sometimes I fourth-guess. It's great the boys are spending a few days down with Clint's parents. It's good for all of them, but I have to admit I miss them. And being able to use those tireless legs to run little errands."

"We're nearly there. With Justine and Rose handling the clothes, the linens, Owen and Ryder muscling in the big stuff, we'll have it perfect for their homecoming."

Hope paused, fingers reaching for her phone. "I should check, make sure Carolee ordered the flowers."

"You know she did. Relax, Commander."

"If he calls me that again, I may kick him in the balls."

Hope paused, rolled her shoulders. "It's a beautiful house—the wood, the details, the sense of space."

"The Montgomerys do good work."

"They do. Speaking of the Montgomerys, what's going on with you and Owen?"

"Nothing."

Hope glanced toward the stairs. "Justine and Rose are up on the second floor. Owen and Ryder are getting another load. It's just you and me."

"I don't know exactly. Things have been a little off since the wedding. My fault, I guess—sort of. When I showed him the heart stone, I made some comment about marriage. I do till death or divorce, something like that. He thinks I'm cynical."

"I wonder why?"

"I'm not."

"No, you're not. But you put your mother's baggage in your own closet. Eventually, you're just going to have to pitch it out."

"I don't. Maybe I do," she admitted, annoyed with herself. "But I really think I've got it down to an overnight bag. Now it feels weird between us, and that's the last thing I want. We've been friends forever. In fact—"

She glanced around, making absolutely sure they were alone. "The other night I dug this out of my keepsake box."

Avery opened her purse, unzipped a pocket. And pulled out a plastic ring in the shape of a pink heart. "He actually gave me this when I was about six, and crushing on him."

"Oh, Avery, it's so cute. So sweet."

"It was, it is. Gum-ball-machine ring. He was just playing along with me, but it put me on top of the world. He does that kind of thing. The sweet thing."

"You kept it, all this time."

"Of course. My first engagement ring." To amuse them both, she slipped it on, wiggled her fingers. But oddly seeing it there made her feel a little sad. "And now something's off between us," she continued as she pulled it off again. "I think he must want to take a step back and—"

She broke off when she heard the door open, and mimed zipping her lips as she tucked the ring back in her purse.

෴

WHILE D.A. LAY on the kitchen floor, obviously exhausted, she helped arrange tables, lamps, pillows. When duty called Hope back to the inn, Avery unpacked towels, set out soaps, moving from master to kids' bath, to guest bath, to half bath, to lower-level bath.

It was full dark when she came upstairs again, and stopped to grin at the great room. Homey, she thought, comfortable, and pretty.

She heard the sound of hammering, moved through to the playroom. Owen, tool belt slung at his hips, hung a framed X-Men poster.

"You put the cubbies together."

He glanced back at her. "Ryder did it before he took off."

"He's gone?"

"We're about done. Mom said to tell you she and Rosie will be back tomorrow, after a grocery store trip for fresh produce."

"Great. I guess you're right. I can't think of much else to do. I wasn't sure we'd make it, and we're a full day ahead."

"We had a lot of hands."

"And you and Hope with your checklists. This is a great room. Fun. happy. The house feels that way, too."

"Yeah, it does."

"Do you want a good-job beer?"

"I wouldn't mind it."

She went out, opened two. They were so freaking polite, she thought. So matter-of-fact. So damn weird.

Enough, she decided as she set them on the kitchen counter. She waited until he'd unstrapped his tool belt. "Are you mad at me?"

"No." He gave her a steady look out of quiet blue eyes. "Why would I be?"

"I don't know. But we—you—something hasn't seemed all the way right since the wedding."

He considered her as he took a pull on the beer. "Maybe you're right."

"If this isn't working for you, I wish—"

"Why do you go there? Why do you automatically go to it not working, it not lasting, it not sticking?"

"I don't mean it like that. I—" When he waved that away, walked to the far window, she set her jaw. "You are mad at me."

"I'm getting there." He took another pull on the beer, then crossed back to set it on the counter. And looked her dead in the eye. "How would you feel if I said it wasn't working for me? No bullshit, Avery, straight truth. How would you feel if I said I was done with it?"

The jaw she'd set wanted to tremble. And everything inside her trembled with it. "You'd break my heart. Is that what you need to hear? You need to know you could do that?"

"Yeah." He closed his eyes, let out a breath. "Yeah. That's exactly what I needed to hear, and what I needed to know."

"Why would you want to hurt me that way? You're not a hard person. You're not cold. Why would you hurt me that way? If you want to step back, you could do it without being cruel."

"Stop it." A world of patience sounded in his voice. "I'm not stepping back. I don't want to step *back*. That's just it. But you don't believe in me, in yourself. In us."

"I do. Why would you think I didn't?" Even as the words came out of her mouth, she knew. "I say stupid things sometimes. I think stupid things sometimes. You should know me well enough to get that."

"I do know you, Avery. I know you're loyal and generous, you're tough and ambitious."

Since Beckett's wedding, Owen had looked for the answer, worked the problem. He thought he had it.

"Avery, you question yourself too much, you worry too much you're something and someone you're not. Because you're nothing like her. Nothing, and you never have been. It pisses me off you don't see that."

"I'm working on it."

"Okay." He started to pick up his beer again, stopped. "No, it's not okay. We'll end up just circling around and getting nowhere. It's not okay because I'm in love with you."

"Oh my God."

"I probably always have been. It's taken a long time for it to sink in, so I figured you needed time to do the same. But it's enough now. Do you see this place?"

"Yes. Owen—"

"It's not just a damn house—a damn good house. It's a place to build, to come back to, to depend on." Everything he felt for her filled him. Everything he wanted surrounded him.

The hell with working it out, thinking it through.

"I've got a damn good house, too. You should be in it with me. Build in it with me, and come back to it with me, depend on it—and on me."

"You want me to move in with you?"

He'd been working on it, he thought, and this wasn't the direction he'd planned on. Screw it, he decided. All or nothing.

"I want you to marry me."

"Oh, Jesus." After a couple hitching breaths, she looked down. "I can't feel my feet."

"Trust you to have the most frustrating reaction."

"I'm sorry. Just give me a minute."

"No, Damn it. No. It's not about spine. It's about love and faith, and hope, I guess. I watched my brother marry Clare, and I knew I wanted that. I've always wanted it, but I thought, sure, eventually. Eventually I'd settle in, settle down, make a family. It's eventually, Avery, because the other thing I know is eventually never came until you. It's always been you. My first girlfriend."

"I need to sit down a minute."

She did, right on the floor. She clutched the key around her neck. Locks, she thought, had to be opened. And he was wrong; it did take spine. But she was no wimp.

"What would you feel if I said no, I didn't want any of that?"

He crouched down, looked her dead in the eye again. "You'd break my heart."

"I'd never do that."

"You'll marry me to spare my feelings?"

"I love you enough to do just that. You make my heart flutter, Owen. You always did. I got used to it—and maybe getting used to it I didn't value it enough. When we started to be with each other, it was more than a flutter. Something more, and I didn't know what to do with it. No one else ever made me feel the way you did—do. I thought something was missing in me because I couldn't *feel* enough. But the only thing missing was none of them were you."

He sat down across from her. "Now nothing's missing, for either of us. Say yes."

"Just wait. What I feel . . ." It lit inside her, all at once. "God, it's like the stone heart. Was she trying to show me? It's so strong, so solid, so enduring. I never thought you'd feel it for me, so I just couldn't open that place and let it come out. And it does take spine." She dashed a tear away. "I just had to find mine."

He took her hand. "I'm in love with you, Avery. Say yes."

"I'll probably suck at marriage."

"That'll be my problem, won't it?"

She looked at his face, so familiar, so precious to her. No, she thought, nothing was missing for either of them. "I need my purse."

"Now?"

"I really do."

"Jesus, break the moment much?" Griping, he pushed up, grabbed it off the counter, dropped it in her lap.

And stared when she pulled out the pink plastic ring.

She offered it to him. "I want to be your problem, Owen, for the rest of my life."

"You kept it," he murmured. Grinning, he started to slide the ring on her finger, but she closed her hand. "Don't mess with me, Avery. Say yes."

"Just wait. I don't have Clare's—what's the word?— equanimity, or Hope's efficiency."

"Am I asking either of them to marry me?"

"No, and you'd better not. I don't have your patience, and thank God you've got it. I'll try it a lot—but you already know that."

"I already do. Say yes."

"I love you. You're my friend, my lover, my match." She smiled now, kissed his cheek. "My first boyfriend is going to be my last boyfriend. Yes." She held out her hand for the ring. "Absolutely, definitely yes."

He slid it on. "It fits. Mostly."

"It was way too big the first time. Looks like it works now." She climbed into his lap.

"Took you long enough."

"From where I'm sitting, it took exactly long enough." She held out her hand, wiggled her fingers. Not sad now. Just happy.

"I'll get you a real one." He took her hand, kissed her finger above the pink plastic heart. "You know, a diamond or whatever you want."

"This is a real one—but I'll take the diamond. I'll take you, Owen, and thank God you'll take me."

He wrapped her tight and hard. "Avery." Emotion swamped him as he took her lips. His eventually, he thought, right here in his arms. "Here we are."

"You and me," she murmured. "I know what Clare meant now."

"About what?"

"How she felt right before the wedding. She said she didn't feel nervous. She felt clear-eyed." She drew back, framed his face. "So do I. Steady and sure. You're my eventually, too. Let's go home, and get started on building."

He helped her up, and together they switched off lights, locked doors, and walked out hand in hand.

She thought of the key around her neck, and the heart stone she still carried in her bag. And the sweet, silly gumball ring on her finger.

Symbols, all of them—of unlocked places, and lasting love.

KEEP READING FOR AN EXCERPT FROM
THE THIRD BOOK IN THE INN BOONSBORO TRILOGY
BY NORA ROBERTS

*The Perfect Hope*

NOW AVAILABLE FROM BERKLEY BOOKS.

WITH A FEW GROANS AND SIGHS, THE OLD BUILDING settled down for the night. Under the star-washed sky its stone walls glowed, rising up over Boonsboro's Square as they had for more than two centuries. Even the crossroads held quiet now, stretching out in pools of shadows and light. All the windows and storefronts along Main Street seemed to sleep, content to doze away in the balm of the summer night.

She should do the same, Hope thought. Settle down, stretch out. Sleep.

That would be the sensible thing to do, and she considered herself a sensible woman. But the long day had left her restless and, she reminded herself, Carolee would arrive bright and early to start breakfast.

The innkeeper could sleep in.

In any case, it was barely midnight. When she'd lived and worked in Georgetown, she'd rarely managed to settle in for the night this early. Of course, then she'd been managing The Wickham, and if she hadn't been dealing with some small crisis or handling a guest request, she'd been enjoying the nightlife.

The town of Boonsboro, tucked into the foothills of Maryland's Blue Ridge Mountains, might have a rich and storied history, and it certainly had its charms—among which she counted the revitalized inn she now managed—but it wasn't famed for its nightlife.

That would change a bit when her friend Avery opened her restaurant and tap house. And wouldn't it be fun to see what the energetic Avery MacTavish did with her new enterprise right next door—and just across The Square from Avery's pizzeria.

Before summer ended, Avery would juggle the running of two restaurants, Hope thought.

And people called Hope an overachiever.

She looked around the kitchen—clean, shiny, warm and welcoming. She'd already sliced fruit, checked the supplies, restocked the refrigerator. So everything sat ready for Carolee to prepare breakfast for the guests currently tucked in their rooms.

She'd finished her paperwork, checked all the doors, and made her rounds checking for dishes—or anything else—out of place. Duties done, she told herself, and still she wasn't ready to tuck her own self in her third-floor apartment.

Instead she poured an indulgent glass of wine and did a last circle through The Lobby, switching off the chandelier over the central table with its showy summer flowers.

She moved through the arch, gave the front door one last check before she turned toward the stairs. Her fingers trailed lightly over the iron banister.

She'd already checked The Library, but she checked again. It wasn't anal, she told herself. A guest might have slipped in for a glass of Irish or a book. But the room was quiet, settled like the rest.

She glanced back. She had guests on this floor. Mr. and Mrs. Vargas—Donna and Max—married twenty-seven years. The night at the inn, in Nick and Nora, had been a birthday gift for Donna from their daughter. And wasn't that sweet?

Her other guests, a floor up in Westley and Buttercup, chose the inn for their wedding night. She liked to think the newlyweds, April and Troy, would take lovely, lasting memories with them.

She checked the door to the second-level porch, then on impulse unlocked it and stepped out into the night.

With her wine, she crossed the wide wood deck, leaned on the rail. Across The Square, the apartment above Vesta sat dark—and empty now that Avery had moved in with Owen Montgomery. Hope could admit—to herself anyway—that she missed looking over and knowing her friend was right there, just across Main.

But Avery was exactly where she belonged, Hope decided, with Owen, her first and, as it turned out, her last boyfriend.

Talk about sweet.

And she'd help plan a wedding—May bride, May flowers—right there in The Courtyard, just as Clare's had been this past spring.

Thinking of it, Hope looked down Main toward the bookstore. Clare's Turn The Page had been a risk for a young widow with two children and another on the way. But she'd made it work. Clare had a knack for making things work. Now she was Clare Montgomery, Beckett's wife. And when winter came, they'd welcome a new baby to the mix.

Odd, wasn't it, that her two friends had lived right in Boonsboro for so long, and she'd relocated only the year—not even a full year yet—before. The new kid in town.

Now, of the three of them, she was the only one still right here, right in the heart of town.

Silly to miss them when she saw them nearly every day, but on restless nights she could wish, just a little, they were still close.

So much had changed, for all of them, in this past year.

She'd been perfectly content in Georgetown, with her home, her work, her routine. With Jonathan, the cheating bastard.

She'd had good, solid plans, no rush, no hurry, but solid plans. The Wickham had been her place. She'd known its rhythm, its tones, its needs. And she'd done a hell of a job for the Wickhams and their cheating bastard son, Jonathan.

She'd planned to marry him. No, there'd been no formal engagement, no concrete promises, but marriage and future had been on the table.

She wasn't a moron.

And all the time—or at least in the last several months—they'd been together, with him sharing her bed, or her sharing his, he'd been seeing someone else. Someone from his more elevated social strata, you could say, Hope mused with lingering bitterness. Someone who wouldn't work ten- and twelve-hour days—and often more—to manage the exclusive hotel, but who'd stay there—in its most elaborate suite, of course.

No, she wasn't a moron, but she'd been far too trusting and humiliatingly shocked when Jonathan told her he would be announcing his engagement—to someone else—the next day.

Humiliatingly shocked, she thought again, particularly as they'd been naked and in her bed at the time.

Then again, he'd been shocked, too, when she'd ordered him to get the hell out. He genuinely hadn't understood why anything between them should change.

That single moment ushered in a lot of change.

Now she was Inn BoonsBoro's innkeeper, living in a small town in Western Maryland, a good clip from the bright lights of the big city.

She didn't spend what free time she had planning clever little dinner parties, or shopping in the boutiques for the perfect shoes for the perfect dress for the next event.

Did she miss all that? Her go-to boutique, her favorite lunch spot, the lovely high ceilings and flower-framed little patio of her own town house? Or the pressure and excitement of preparing the hotel for visits from dignitaries, celebrities, business moguls?

Sometimes, she admitted. But not as often as she'd expected to, and not as much as she'd assumed she would.

Because she had been content in her personal life,

challenged in her professional one, and the Wickham had been her place. But she'd discovered something in the last few months. Here, she wasn't just content, but happy. The inn wasn't just her place, it was *home*.

She had her friends to thank for that, and the Montgomery brothers along with their mother. Justine Montgomery had hired her, on the spot. At the time Hope hadn't known Justine well enough to be surprised by her quick offer. But she did know herself, and continued to be surprised at her own fast, impulsive acceptance.

Zero to sixty? More like zero to ninety and still going.

She didn't regret the impulse, the decision, the move.

Fresh starts hadn't been in the plan, but she was good at adjusting plans. Thanks to the Montgomerys, the lovingly—and effortlessly—restored inn was now her home and her career.

She wandered the porch, checking the hanging planters, adjusting—minutely—the angle of a bistro chair.

"And I love every square inch of it," she murmured.

One of the porch doors leading out from Elizabeth and Darcy opened. The scent of honeysuckle drifted on the night air.

Someone else was restless, Hope thought. Then again, she didn't know if ghosts slept. She doubted if the spirit Beckett had named Elizabeth for the room she favored would tell her if she asked. Thus far Lizzy hadn't deigned to speak to her inn-mate.

Hope smiled at the term, sipped her wine.

"Lovely night. I was just thinking how different my life is now, and all things considered, how glad I am it is." She spoke in an easy, friendly way. After all, the research she and Owen had done so far on their permanent guest had proven Lizzy—or Eliza Ford, when she'd been alive—was one of Hope's ancestors.

Family, to Hope's mind, ought to be easy and friendly.

"We have newlyweds in W&B. They look so happy, so fresh and new somehow. The couple in N&N are here celebrating her fifty-eighth birthday. They don't look new, but they do look happy, and so nice and comfortable. I like giving them a special place to stay, a special experience. It's what I'm good at."

Silence held, but Hope could *feel* the presence. Companionable, she realized. Oddly companionable. Just a couple of women up late, looking out at the night.

"Carolee will be here early. She's doing breakfast tomorrow, and I have the morning off. So." She lifted her glass. "Some wine, some introspection, some feeling sorry for myself circling around to realizing I have nothing to feel sorry for myself about." With a smile, Hope sipped again. "So, a good glass of wine.

"Now that I've accomplished all that, I should get to bed."

Still she lingered a little longer in the quiet summer night, with the scent of honeysuckle drifting around her.

◈

WHEN HOPE CAME down in the morning, the scent was fresh coffee, grilled bacon, and, if her nose didn't deceive her, Carolee's apple cinnamon pancakes. She heard easy conversation in The Dining Room. Donna and Max, talking about poking around town before driving home.

Hope went down the hall, circled to the kitchen to see if Carolee needed a hand. Justine's sister had her bright blond hair clipped short for summer, with the addition of flirty bangs over her cheerful hazel eyes. They beamed at Hope even as she wagged a finger.

"What are you doing down here, young lady?"

"It's nearly ten."

"And your morning off."

"Which I spent—so far—sleeping until eight, doing yoga, and putzing." She helped herself to a mug of coffee, closed her own deep brown eyes as she sipped. "My first cup of the day. Why is it always the best?"

"I wish I knew. I'm still trying to switch to tea. My Darla's on a health kick and doing her best to drag me along." Carolee spoke of her daughter with affection laced with exasperation. "I really like our Titania and Oberon blend. But . . . it's not coffee."

"Nothing is except coffee."

"You said it. She can't wait for the new gym to open. She says if I don't sign up for yoga classes, she's signing me up and carting me over there."

"You'll love yoga." Hope laughed at the doubt—and anxiety—on Carolee's face. "Honest."

"Hmmm." Carolee lifted the dishcloth again, went back to polishing the granite countertop. "The Vargases loved the room, and as usual the bathroom—starring the magic toilet—got raves. I haven't heard a peep out of the newly-weds yet."

"I'd be disappointed in them if you had." Hope brushed at her hair. Unlike Carolee, she was experimenting with letting it grow out of the short, sharp wedge she'd sported the last two years. The dark, glossy ends hit her jaw now, just in between enough to be annoying.

"I'm going to go check on Donna and Max, see if they want anything."

"Let me do it," Hope said. "I want to say good morning anyway, and I think I'll run down to TTP, say hi to Clare while it's still my morning off."

"I saw her last night at book club. She's got the cutest baby bump. Oh, I've got plenty of batter if the newlyweds want more pancakes."

"I'll let them know."

She slipped into The Dining Room, chatted with the guests while she subtly checked to be sure there were still plenty of fresh summer berries, coffee, juice.

Once she'd satisfied herself that her guests were happy, she started back upstairs to grab her purse—and ran into the newlyweds as they entered from the rear porch.

"Good morning."

"Oh, good morning." The new bride carried the afterglow of a honeymoon morning well spent. "That's the most beautiful room. I love everything about it. I felt like a princess bride."

"As you wish," Hope said and made them both laugh.

"It's so clever the way each room is named and decorated for romantic couples."

"Couples with happy endings," Troy reminded her, and got a slow, dreamy smile from his bride.

"Like us. We want to thank you, so much, for making our wedding night so special. It was everything I wanted. Just perfect."

"That's what we do here."

"But . . . we wondered. We know we're supposed to check out soon . . ."

"If you'd like a later check-out, I can arrange it," Hope began.

"Well, actually . . ."

"We're hoping we can stay another night." Troy slid his arm around April's shoulders, drew her close. "We really love it here. We were going to drive down into Virginia, just pick our spots as we went, but . . . We really like it right here. We'll take any room that's available, if there is one."

"We'd love to have you, and your room's open tonight."

"Really?" April bounced on her toes. "Oh, this is better than perfect. Thank you."

"It's our pleasure. I'm glad you're enjoying your stay."

Happy guests made for happy innkeepers, Hope thought as she dashed upstairs for her bag. She dashed back down again, into her office to change the reservation, and, with the scents and voices behind her, hurried out the back through Reception.

She skirted the side of the building, glancing across the street at Vesta. She knew Avery's and Clare's schedules nearly as well as her own. Avery would be prepping for opening this morning, and Clare should be back from her early doctor's appointment.

The sonogram. With luck, they'd know by now if Clare was carrying the girl she hoped for.

As she waited for the walk signal at the corner, she looked down Main Street. Ryder Montgomery stood in front of the building Montgomery Family Contractors was currently rehabbing. Nearly done, she thought, and soon the town would have a bakery again.

He wore jeans torn at the left knee and splattered with drips of paint or drywall compound or whatever else splattered on job sites. His tool belt hung low, like an old-time sheriff's gunbelt—at least to her eye. Dark hair curled shaggily from under his ball cap. Sunglasses covered eyes she knew to be a gold-flecked green.

He consulted with a couple of his crew, pointed up, circling a finger, shaking his head, all while he stood in that hip-shot way of his.

Since a dull wash of primer currently covered the front of the building, she assumed they were discussing the finish colors.

One of the crew let out a bray of laughter, and Ryder responded with a flash of grin and a shrug.

The shrug, like the stance, was another habit of his, she mused.

The Montgomery brothers were an attractive breed, but in her opinion her two friends had plucked the pick of the crop. She found Ryder a little surly, marginally unsociable.

And, okay, sexy—in a primitive, rough-edged sort of way.

Not her type; not remotely.

As she started across the street a long, exaggerated wolf whistle shrilled out. Knowing it was a joke, she tipped her face back toward the bakery, added a smoldering smile, then sent a wave to Jake, one of the painters. He and the laborer beside him waved back.

But not Ryder Montgomery, of course. He simply hooked his thumb in his pocket, watched her. Unsociable, she thought again. He couldn't even stir himself for a casual wave.

She accepted the slow kindling in her belly as the natural reaction of a healthy woman to a long, shaded stare delivered by a sexy—if surly—man.

Particularly a woman who hadn't had any serious male contact in—God—a year. A little more than a year. But who's counting?

Her own fault, her own choice, so why think about it?

She reached the other side of Main Street, turned right toward the bookstore just as Clare stepped out onto its pretty covered porch.

She waved again as Clare stood a moment, one hand on the baby bump under her breezy summer dress. Clare had her long, sunny hair pulled back in a tail, with blue-framed sunglasses softening the glare of the bold morning sun.

"I was just coming over to check on you," Hope called out.

Clare held up her phone. "I was just texting you." She slipped the phone back in her pocket, left her hand there a moment as she came down the steps to the sidewalk.

"Well?" Hope scanned her friend's face. "Everything good?"

"Yeah. Good. We got back just a few minutes ago. Beckett . . ." She glanced over her shoulder. "He's driving around to the back of the bakery. He's got his tools."

"Okay." Mildly concerned, Hope laid a hand on Clare's arm. "Honey, you had the sonogram, right?"

"Yeah."

"And?"

"Oh. Let's walk up to Vesta. I'll tell you and Avery at the same time. Beckett's going to call his mother, tell his brothers. I need to call my parents."

"The baby's all right?"

"Absolutely." She patted her purse as they walked. "I have pictures."

"I have to see!"

"I'll be showing them off for days. Weeks. It's amazing."

Avery popped out the front door of the restaurant, a white bib apron covering capris and a T-shirt. She bounced on purple Crocs. The sun speared into her Scot's warrior queen hair, sent the short ends to glimmering.

"Are we thinking pink?"

"Are you opening alone?" Clare countered.

"Yeah, it's just me. Fran's not due in for twenty. Are you okay? Is everything okay?"

"Everything's absolutely perfectly wonderfully okay. But I want to sit down."

With her friends exchanging looks behind her back, Clare walked in and straight to the counter, dropped onto a stool. Sighed. "It's the first time I've been pregnant with three boys fresh out of school for the summer. It's challenging."

"You're a little pale," Avery commented.

"Just tired."

"Want something cold?"

"With my entire being."

As Avery went to the cooler, Hope sat down, narrowed her eyes at Clare's face. "You're stalling. If nothing's wrong—"

"Nothing's wrong, and maybe I'm stalling a little. It's a big announcement." She laughed to herself, took the chilled ginger ale Avery offered.

"So here I am, with my two closest friends, in Avery's pretty restaurant that already smells of pizza sauce."

"You'll have this in a pizzeria." Avery passed Hope a bottle of water. Then she crossed her arms, scanned Clare's face. "It's a girl. Ballet shoes and hair ribbons!"

Clare shook her head. "I appear to specialize in boys. Make that baseball gloves and action figures."

"A boy?" Hope leaned over, touched Avery's hand. "Are you disappointed?"

"Not even the tiniest bit." She opened her purse. "Want to see?"

"Are you kidding?" Avery made a grab, but Clare snatched the envelope out of reach. "Does he look like you? Like Beck? Like a fish? No offense, but they always look like fish to me."

"Which one?"

"Which one what?"

"There are two."

"Two?" Hope nearly bobbled the water. "Twins? You're having twins?"

"Two?" Avery echoed. "You have two fish?"

"Two boys. Look at my beautiful boys." Clare pulled out the sonogram printout, then burst into tears. "Good tears," she managed. "Hormones, but good ones. Oh God. Look at my babies!"

"They're gorgeous!"

Clare swiped at tears as she grinned at Avery. "You don't see them."

"No, but they're gorgeous. Twins. That's five. You did the math, right? You're going to have five boys."

"We did the math, but it's still sinking in. We didn't expect— We never thought— Maybe I should have. I'm bigger than I've ever been this early. But when the doctor told us . . . Beckett went white."

She laughed, even as tears poured. "Sheet white. I thought he was going to pass out. Then we just stared at each other. And then we started to laugh. We laughed like lunatics. I think maybe we were both a little hysterical. Five. Oh, sweet Jesus. *Five* boys."

"You'll be great. All of you," Hope told her.

"We will. I know it. I'm so dazzled, so happy, so stunned. I don't know how Beckett drove home. I couldn't tell you if we drove back from Hagerstown or from California. I was in some sort of shock, I think. Twins."

She laid her hands on her belly. "Do you know how there are moments in your life when you think, this is it. I'll never be happier or more excited. I'll never *feel* more than I do right now. Just exactly now. This is one of those moments for me."

Hope folded her into a hug, and Avery folded them both.

"I'm so happy for you," Hope murmured. "Happy, dazzled, and excited right along with you."

"The kids are going to get such a kick out of this." Avery drew back. "Right?"

"Yeah. And since Liam already made it clear if I had a girl he wouldn't stoop so low as to play with her, I think he'll be especially pleased."

"What about your due date?" Hope asked. "Earlier with twins?"

"A little. They told me November twenty-first. So, Thanksgiving babies instead of Christmas/New Year's."

"Gobble, gobble," Avery said, and made Clare laugh again.

"You have to let us help set up the nursery," Hope began. Planning was in her blood.

"I'm counting on it. I don't have a thing. I gave away all

the baby things after Murphy. I never thought I'd fall in love again, or marry again, or have more children."

"Can we say baby shower? A double-the-fun theme," Hope decided. "Or what comes in pairs, sets of two. Something like that. I'll work on it. We should schedule it in early October, just to be safe."

"Baby shower." Clare sighed. "More and more real. I need to call my parents, and I need to tell the girls," she added, referring to her bookstore staff. She levered herself up. "November babies," she said again. "I should be able to shed the baby weight by May and the wedding."

"Oh yeah, I'm getting married." Avery held out her hand, admired the diamond that had replaced the bubble gum ring Owen had put on her finger. Twice.

"Getting married *and* opening a second restaurant, and helping plan a baby shower, and redecorating the current single guy's master suite into a couple's master suite." Hope poked Avery in the arm. "We have a lot of planning to do."

"I can take some time tomorrow."

"Good." Hope took a moment to flip through her mental list, rearrange tasks, gauge the timing. "One o'clock. I can clear the time. Can you make that?" she asked Clare. "I can fix us a little lunch and we can get some of the planning worked out before I have check-ins."

"One o'clock tomorrow." Clare patted her belly. "We'll be there."

"I'll be over," Avery promised. "If I'm a little later, we had a good lunch rush. But I'll get over."

Hope walked out with Clare, grabbed another hug before separating. And imagined Clare telling her parents the happy news. Imagined, too, Avery texting Owen. And Beckett slipping off to check on Clare during the day, or just stealing a few minutes to bask with her.

For a moment she wished she had someone to call or text or slip away to, someone to share the lovely news with.

Instead she went around the back of the inn, up the outside stairs. She let herself in on the third floor, listening as she walked down to her apartment.

Yes, she thought, she could just hear Carolee's voice, and the excitement in it. No doubt Justine Montgomery had already called her sister to share the news about the twins.

Hope closed herself into her apartment. She'd spend a couple hours in the quiet, she decided, researching their resident ghost, and the man named Billy she waited for.

## ABOUT THE AUTHOR

Nora Roberts is the #1 *New York Times* bestselling author of more than 200 novels. She is also the author of the best-selling In Death series written under the pen name J. D. Robb. There are more than 400 million copies of her books in print. Visit her website at NoraRoberts.com, and visit her on Facebook at Facebook.com/NoraRoberts.

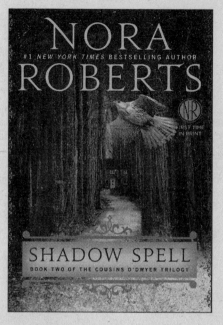